UNDER THE LIGHT

The Sandes Chronicles ~ Book One

Copyright © 2019 by Louise Crouch

ISBN: - 978-0-6484878-2-1

For more from Louise Crouch please visit http://loucrouch.wordpress.com

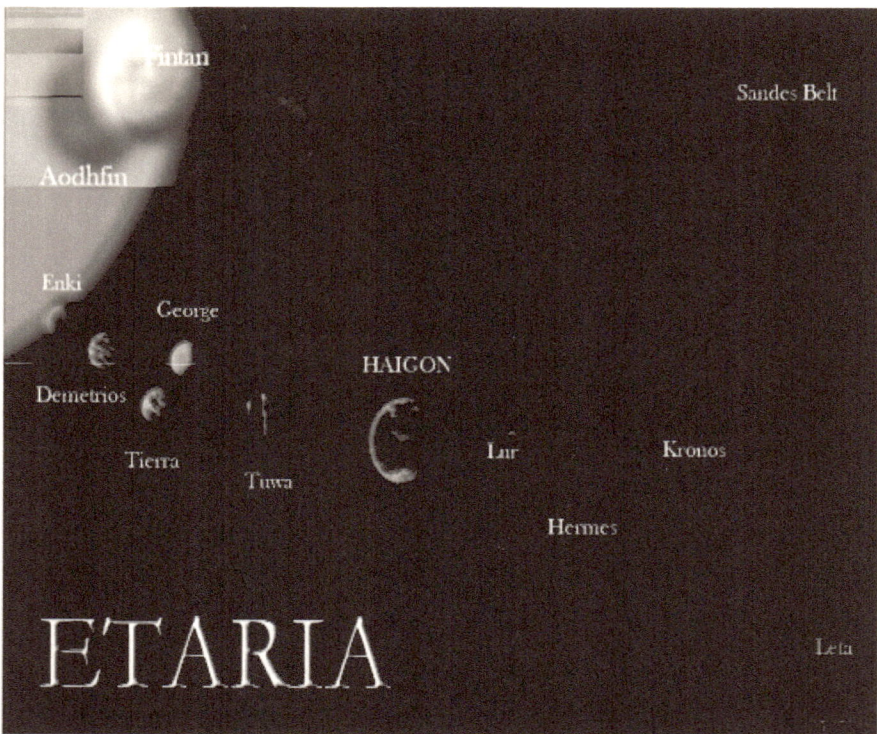

Fintan

Sandes Belt

Aodhfin

Enki

George

Demetrios

HAIGON

Tierra

Tuwa

Lur

Kronos

Hermes

ETARIA

Leta

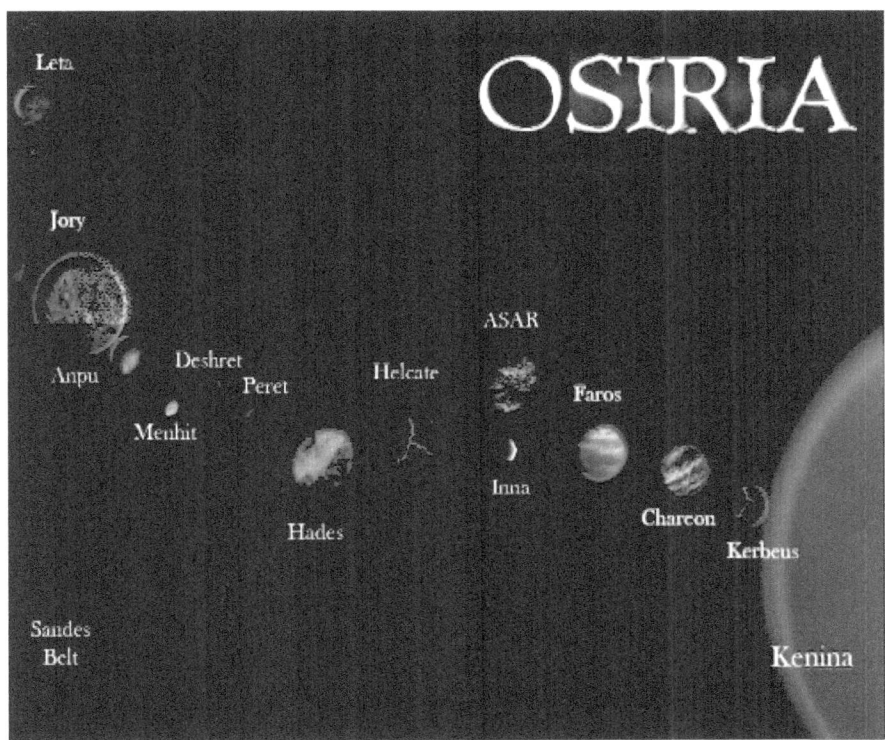

TABLE OF CONTENTS

In the Shadow
Special Thanks

DEDICATION

To my family for their love and support

To my children for their patience

To my husband for saying yes

THANK YOU

Thank you to those that have assisted in this journey of bringing Under the Light into the light, namely:

Robert, Brendan, Lyndal, Ben, Laura, Peta and Robyn.

"The Light, who provides life, controls the source, and master of the known is Ea, all that is visible under the light belongs to him,

The Shadow, where souls find rest, controls the dark and the master of the hidden is Erebus, all that find sanctuary in the night belong to her,

In the sliver between Light and Shadow where madness and mayhem reign you will find Chaos; no-one and nothing belongs to Chaos, the influence of anarchy touches all.

Fear neither life nor death, as even Ea and Erebus fear Chaos, the nothing, the unknown, the catastrophic undoing."

Gaian Galaxy Proverb

CHAPTER 1

Aedan *shifted* her brown braid into a bob, the strands shortening and darkening to a glossy sable, as she pushed the choppy fringe over her eyes. A flush of heat signaled the *change* and Aedan blinked her silver eyes into yellow. It would be "Kegan", her male alter-ego that would set foot on Jory's single moon, Anpu. Aedan bet her reputation, moreover Kegan's reputation, that the fugitive Chigslin Skeeter had made a break through the Sandes Asteroid Belt and into the Osirian Solar System. Capturing the Etarian fugitive, Skeeter would add another name to Kegan's total.

Aedan's ship, the *Venator* gained on the shuttle until it entered the orbit of Anpu. The oyster-colored surface drew Osirian and Etarian thugs, murderers and thieves alike to its densely populated slums. It was an escape for some, but to her, the World was as perfect a hunting ground as any. A steady stream of transports landed in the piecemeal and jury rigged docks; the arrival of her *Venator* went barely noticed by the less than officious authority. She landed on a suspect gantry, secured her ship's resources and controls then set to work preparing herself for the hunt. It would prove nothing if she ended up dead, or Skeeter for that matter. Someone had to pay for the fuel cells.

Aedan buckled a utility belt and concealed knives, cuffs and a pair of magnetic bracelets, which she slid into her back pocket. In moments she'd filled her pants' pockets, boots and thermal jacket. Aedan attached the Arc gun on her usually feminine hip then thickened her waist and bulked her shoulders to complete the transformation to Kegan. While shapeshifting wasn't troublesome, getting caught out could be. She had to be Kegan now, no distractions and no slips up. Shapeshifting the body from female to male was simple, changing the mind? Well, so long as he remained Kegan the male mindset would have to be maintained. He clenched his trembling fingers into a fist, sighed and settled into the persona many fugitives had come to fear.

The cargo ramp squeaked into motion, and the busy docks and the stink of foul air embraced him. Osirians, or as Kegan and the rest of Etarians called them, "Oddworlders", hawked and begged, between ribbons of polluted gangways. On this side of the Sandes Asteroid Belt, Kegan should feel somewhat at ease with their rudimentary weapons and even cruder technology, yet despite their limitations, Oddworlders lacked civility and that made them just a little more dangerous, a little more savage. Kegan stepped into the throng knowing where to look, even if he didn't really want to go there. The lilac and orange gaseous bulb of Jory, hung pendulum-like over the city, brightly visible through the murky Anpu atmosphere. He inhaled again, adjusting to the air that had been recycled a thousand times, the scents of sour desperation added to the grim scene before him. He waited for the *Venator* ramp to click into place before moving into the bustle of beggars.

Kegan. Kegan. Kegan. He kept up the mantra as he advanced. He tossed his mercenary tags across the littered security desk, earning a wave of acknowledgement from the lumpy headed oafs that ran the border control. Kegan tugged his hood over his hair. Even with the façade, it took a while to realize the people saw the male camouflage and not the woman underneath. He watched hopelessness stain the already fear-twisted features of the beggars. A local thug reclined against the cornice of a barricaded mercantile. The man ran his eyes over Kegan's masculine frame, starting at the width of his shoulders, then darting to his utility belt, next his arc gun, he even seemed to watch the cadence at which Kegan walked through the crowd. Inside the camouflage, Aedan wrestled with the urge to cower under the thugs' acquisitive eye. Kegan straightened his shoulders and lengthened his strides; he raised his chin an inch and narrowed his gaze. The thug gave Kegan a second assessment, and slumped back against the barrier, too risky for today. Kegan continued his pace, double checking the blades tucked against his forearms. The boardwalk narrowed as it neared the settlements epicenter, the sides of the timber walkway lined with huddled shapes, bent double on their knees, with a bowl in front. Some clothed in threadbare laborers' jackets, the high-vis strips torn from the fabric, and since on-sold. Others were wrapped in swathes of once bright colored fabric, now discolored by age and filth. Each beggar had strips of material plated throughout their matted hair, an Anpu local custom, those who could afford it, had beads of silver or copper tied into their strands.

One traveler stumbled from side to side of the boardwalk, his comrade held him upright as a cloud of fire-whiskey stung Kegan's nostrils. His friend fumbled with the burden, the man's belt unclipped, Ketos tumbled across the timber. A scuffle broke out as the beggars and drunks both tried to claim the currency chips. Boot's stomped down on fingers, knees met skulls before Kegan slipped between the combatants. In his fingers, his blade sparkled in the tangerine sunset.

"Let me," Kegan said, his knife point directed at the drunks' saliva stained shirt. The man sneered, but retreated all the same. In one move, Kegan drove the dagger down to the boardwalk and retrieved the Ketos pouch. He handed it back to the drunkard. He and his mate tugged down their shirts and wandered on, not before mumbling a few curse words about Mercs minding their own business. Kegan dug into his jacket and donated all but a few of his remaining Ketos chips. Kegan had what he needed to survive. There were no second chances in Osiria. You took whatever means necessary to ensure your survival. Always. Kegan knew it. Inside the charade, Aedan knew it too; it was etched deep on her bones and seared across her soul.

Kegan slipped between bodies, the sleeves on his bulky black jacket barely touching passer-by as he crossed the dock in search of Skeeter, the rapist. Kegan avoided eye contact; he searched through the crowd surging away from the main dock, a place where Skeeter's shuttle had landed. He stepped in a puddle it splashed up his multi-buckled boots. His grey pants were saturated by the stinking mulch, but at least the glimmering platinum of the boot buckles that climbed up over his knees kept their authoritative zeal.

Leaving the docks and moving further into the slum regions, he caught sight of Skeeter's stocky frame ducking into a Tank. The broken neon out front said Dusty's. A joke on a dry moon that made living hard and survival harder. Sulphur light splashed across the grey and weary crowd as the doorway opened and he stepped inside after the man. The patrons ignored him, which was good, it also meant no trouble. Kegan's gaze studied the room. His reflexes were honed, his ribs tensed, waiting for a slice of crimson or ebony. It didn't matter who they were, Etarian or Oddworlder, a person's true emotions were never hidden from him. A glint in an eye here, the narrow stare or the casual glance would give a person's true self away eventually. He could see it and wonder if anyone could see the true self in him.

An image of grey flecked irises coated in fear swirled in Kegan's mind, Aedan would be an easy mark on any planet. But Kegan, with his tanned skin, masculine physique and hooded yellow eyes could slip through a crowd of raiders, Rebels or rejects without so much as a snort. Sometime last year, he'd added a tattoo to Kegan's façade and decided to keep it. It wasn't just being male, it was being a bounty hunter, a Mercenary and even amongst criminals that meant something.

Two feminine forms danced naked on stands; rusted collars preventing their movement too far or too close to the swarm of customers that edged the stage. Noise erupted from one side of the bar as a miner, judging by the cut of his woolen coat and smudged face, mauled one dancer. The miner's fingernail shredded the delicate skin and three red streams burst forth through the layer of grime. A Myrmidon, a fletch-infected Oddworlder, struck the miners hand with a bully-bar, an immediate blue welt visible as the dancer spun away. The grey tones of fear, only visible to Kegan, brimmed from the dancers' eyes as she awkwardly clutched her wound, the collar clinking in its recess. The bar-guard and miner exchanged shoves and shouts, heated slashes of red, anger, crossed both gazes before the miner shook his head and shelled out a single payment chip of Ketos. Striding over to a separate curtained area, the miner paid another silver currency chip to the Myrmidon. After the bouncer pocketed the chip, he pulled aside the curtain and Kegan glimpsed the premium merchandise.

Skeeter would already be out back sampling the wares, slaking his appetite before moving on. Kegan shifted through the crowd, zig-zagging to the curtain. His legs shook, dumping adrenaline into his system. He drew a knife from his sleeve. As he narrowed in on the bouncer's right side, he slashed. Ketos chips clattered to the scuffed tiles, and a rush of Oddworlders sent the bouncer sprawling to the floor. A second Myrmidon, broad nosed and red eyed launched into the crowd and into the midst of the crush. Kegan slipped through the curtain. A wash of overwhelming pity swept through him as each girl begged for attention.

Kegan narrowed his gaze.

The corridor's darkness enveloped the bounty hunter as he moved unnoticed through the gallery of second hand commodities. Halfway down, Kegan faced a fork, both alternatives lined with small rooms; thin mesh curtains afforded the barest of privacy for the occupants. The smell of sex and despair assaulted Kegan's nose from where he stood at the divergence. Far down the left, he caught a flash of movement; the netted curtains chimed and bristled. A slender hand escaped only to be snatched back. A bone mashing thump made it to Kegan's ears and he focused on that alcove. Skeeter! The muscles in Kegan's thighs twitched and his ankles felt feather light. All moisture evaporated from his mouth as he drew back the mesh. Kegan couldn't recall when he'd reached for the Arc gun, but as he drove it in Skeeter's bare back, a haze lifted from his mind. Skeeter fell forward and the girl squirmed out of the way. Scratches and welts lined her ruddy complexion as the silver-rust colors of her eyes gave way to the light cherry tones of amusement. The girl bowed, as Kegan slipped metallic rings over Skeeter's ankles and wrists. Kegan threw an arm across the girl's waist, Skeeter groaned, his boots scuffed the chipped ceramic. Kegan sliced the sweat laden shirt from Skeeter's waist, and shoved half in his mouth, tightening the other half behind his neck. His fawn colored irises flashed inky-black. Oh good, hatred the most reliable emotion of all.

The girl snatched at her customers' boots. Kegan tugged Skeeter's Iridone stained fingers, three gold rings dripped into the girls' palm. As Kegan's fingertips made contact with the girls, the image of a bright constellation blazed behind Kegan's eyes, born on Asar, Kegan registered. The girl slipped past the curtain as Skeeter wriggled in his magnetic bonds, arms trapped to his hips, ankle to ankle.

"Chigslin Skeeter, you are worth a pretty penny." Kegan said as he holstered the Arc gun and slung a Merc ID tag around the fugitive's neck in preparation of the frog-march to the *Venator*.

The mesh curtain chimed as a Myrmidon Bouncer entered.

"You can't be here…" A flash of platinum, reached his eyes. He fumbled the Merc ID, and let it fall back against his customer's chest, "Bounty hunter!" He spat onto the ground, narrowly missing Kegan's extravagant footwear.

"Yes." Kegan snatched at his belt, and drove the Arc gun muzzle into the wrinkled prickly folds under the guard's chin. Lumpy was the best word he could think of to describe the Bouncer. His shaven head bitten by mites and a gravely shadow around his chin concealed the worst of his pock-marked scars. His red eyes flashed over in sunset panic. Kegan's favorite of all the emotional colors. When Kegan saw orange on its own, he knew he had the upper hand. Mixed with the red tones of anger and it was a different story, similarly red blending with the true black of hatred in someone's irises meant it was time to move! "But, if you help me get him to my ship, you can have whatever's in his pockets." Kegan jingled Skeeter's trousers, as the magnetic cuffs forced him to his feet.

The Myrmidon dragged his fingers across his chin and eyed Kegan, "Deal," He rumbled and pulled back the mesh.

Together they marched along the crowded boardwalk to the docks; a few Oddworlders took the time to note their passing. Once they saw the silver Merc ID, they nodded in amused satisfaction at the folly of the target.

"What's your name Merc?"

"Kegan Capare."

"Capare? Shit, even I've heard of you." The Myrmidon responded, his boil covered neck swiveled to take stock. Between them Skeeter rolled his eyes.

"And you are?"

"Rold, first names are not important." He rotated his arm like a paddle, through the thick and desperate crowd.

Ahead a pair of Rebel Brawlers sauntered through the mass. Their charcoal colored armor sat broad across their chests, Arc guns, and bully-bars swung from their waist, a troubling large sword strapped to one, a cross bow on the other. Where were the Rebels when Kegan had dealt with the drunks? As the grunts strolled, the mass of people broke around them like a wave and Kegan and Rold, together with Skeeter tried to do the same. One Rebel was eating something, and when his eyes caught sight of the fugitive, he pegged the object their direction, the fruit ruptured against Skeeter's bare chest. Kegan kept his eyes ahead and walked on. The circle of civilians surrounding Kegan threw themselves to the boardwalk, savoring any part of the fruit remnants they could find. Kegan tucked his head low as the two tormenters passed.

The Rebels laughed and shouted obscenities to Kegan's occupation and his quarry. Kegan gulped down his anger, the quicker they moved past these enforcers, the better. Maybe Kegan had been lucky they weren't on the boardwalk earlier. So much for Osirian governance, the protectors were as corrupt as the criminals. When they reached the *Venator*, Rold took no time in emptying Skeeter's pockets, silver Ketos chips spilled into his hands.

"Thanks Merc."

"Thanks Rold. If I'm ever near here again, can I count on your help?"

"Damn right." He smirked, the lumps on his scalp, mirroring the lopsided smile.

Kegan tossed the Myrmidon a small transmitter, no bigger than a Ketos chip, "I promise I'll call."

"That's what they always say," He said and pocketed the bronze tube, while Kegan tucked Skeeter into one of the two *Venator*'s cells.

After closing the ramp, Kegan climbed the faded white ladder, rust flakes spiraling under his boots. Once in the cockpit, Kegan signaled to the Atmos-Tower and dusted off from Anpu.

As the last tendril of Anpu's gravity snapped free from the ship, the Kegan façade evaporated and Aedan stretched. She set the coordinates for the Etarian Solar System and reclined into her pilots' chair. The ships computer could handle the trajectory mapping up until she reached the Sandes Belt. Then Aedan would have to fly manually through the asteroids, to avoid colliding with the rocks or the abandoned mangamines. Aedan yawned; throwing off her adrenaline rush shivers and waited.

It took over an hour to navigate the *Venator* through the asteroid field, but Aedan sighed as her ship finally reached Etarian controlled space. Aedan reset the computer for Kronos just as she approached the Etarian Jump Gateway, Nero Station. Dual beacons flashed in warning, as a spiral of silver revolved between them. Ripples spread across the surface as a ship approached. Aedan focused on the impotent technology of the *Venator*'s Jump Drive. The casing edges dusty and seized, the tech limiting her to Jump Stations located in Osirian territory, a grand total of two, AK and PK station. How efficient could Kegan Capare be, if he could use the Etarian controlled interstellar gravitational highway? Jumping from Etaria to Osiria would halve transport time and save on fuel cells. If only Etarian's hadn't closed out the Jump gateways to everyone but themselves after the Borders War.

An Etarian Expedition Freighter shimmered into sight between the Nero Jump Station beacons. The freighter's burners sparked to life as the ship disappeared into the inky dark, the beacons silenced. What were the chances the Etarian Government would trust Kegan Capare with a Jump Code? Aedan has plenty of time to consider those odds, as the *Venator* continued its labored journey to Kronos.

Aedan reduced thrusters as the Etarian prison planet, slowly enlarged through the windshield. Aedan rose from the pilot's chair. The blunt black fringe and hooded yellow eyes of Kegan settled like cello wrap over a cadaver as he entered the bulk hold of the ship.

After 25 days on the run, Chigslin Skeeter, eyed Kegan through darkened eyes. Waves of ebony swept across each iris. Skeeter's hatred overwhelmed the frantic orange shards, and eventually simmered to a healthy fearful slate. Back on the Etarian's capital planet, Haigon, Skeeter had stalked his prey to their homes after work, attacking in the twilight hours before the dual sunrise. He'd been tried and sentenced without issue, fleeing the Etarian's system as his Prison warrant rolled across the dual systems' Newscaster channels. He would be most certainly getting his just desserts, and Kegan wondered what color, if any, would show in Skeeter's eyes after he faced down four life sentences. What color was defeat? If that last of his four victim's succumbed to her injuries, Skeeter would face a death sentence.

Kegan cleared his throat and activated the prisoner pod, "Better buckle up."

Skeeter stood at Kegan's magnetic command, the cuffs on both ankles and wrists preventing him from doing much else.

Another button released a reverse seat from the rear panel

and he strapped Skeeter down. As Kegan's fist struck the release, the *Venator* fell with dizzying nausea towards Kronos. Skeeter's groans reverberated around the cabin and Kegan tried to ignore the rolling of his own stomach. The shuttle rocketed towards the monolithic metal structure in the habitable northern hemisphere of the prison planet.

The red and yellow surface of Kronos churned, the planetary winds swirling the gaseous contents into beautiful whirlpools of copper, peaches and cream. Kronos lingered as the last planet in the Etarian Solar System, closest to the Sandes Belt. The wide strip of asteroids had been the final barrier through countless wars which separated the peaceful Etarians from the rabid soulless Oddworlders.

Upon Kegan's approach, the guard post radioed for identification and disclosure of cargo.

"This is Kegan Capare, Merc ID 426, cashing in on Bounty 5461 Zeta."

A throaty chuckle crackled across the speaker, "Welcome back Kegan and is it really Chigslin Skeeter about to grace our presence?" Kegan recognized the rasped voice of Vance, the Senior Guard at maximum security. Kegan watched the tangerine laser lines of the Facial Recognition software scan Skeeter for confirmation.

"He will be gracing your presence when payment is received, Vance." Kegan said. The laser lines flicked to lime green upon acceptance.

Kegan regarded Vance as a friendly father figure, with sparse white hair that softened the well-lined face of a man who had fought and survived both the Border War and the Great War. If Aedan lived as Kegan permanently, he might sit and enjoy a drink with Vance at some Tank on some shady planet, talk about life, Fireball and the shortage of women. Kegan tapped the comm display and a holographic representation appeared on the dashboard.

"That was too quick Kegan, 25 days hasn't allowed for much bounty to be added. A little longer and Skeeter's bounty might have reached 25 thousand Ketos."

Kegan shook his head "I'll settle for the 15 thousand now and be back with another one soon enough."

"Bay 12 please." The aging Sentry chuckled.

In all his dealings with Vance, he had seen nothing but a pink tinge, Kegan thought as curiosity or amusement mixed with a healthy dose of grey cross his irises. If Aedan could live as herself in Etarian Territory, she'd probably still be able to count Vance as a friend.

The *Venator* touched down on the icy steel gangplank like a ballerina's pirouette. Already waiting at the rear ramp, the prisoner pod hovered. Skeeter rocked silently back and forth as much as his transport pod would allow, fearful grey filling his lids to the brink.

Kegan closed the Perspex lid and clambered onto the runway as the piercing wind cut at his skin and snatched at his jacket. With the soup consistency hindering visibility and grinding his joints, Kegan followed the yellow halo lights along each side until he heard Vance's booming voice over the howling blizzard.

"25 days, Kegan, you may have set a record."

Kegan shook Vance's forearm in greeting, crooked fingers struggling to curl around Kegan's arm. He gave Vance's shoulder a quick but solid pat, choosing to comment on the fugitive, rather than Vance's condition.

"Well he wasn't happy to see me on Anpu." Kegan said, gesturing to the transport cell hovering behind.

The gale buffeted the edges of Skeeter's cell, until it seemed the prisoner might be blown right off the gangway and swallowed by the peach-soup abyss. The bay door slammed behind them, the echoing trills hinting at the true expanse of the Northern Quadrant prison cells.

With "Kronos Mist" briefly silenced, Vance continued, "I didn't think he was clever enough to get through that Belt. If you hadn't caught him, the filthy Oddworlders would have eaten him alive soon enough"

Kegan doubted that. Skeeter seemed to be doing just fine in Oddworld. Together Vance and Kegan marched Skeeter into the North Tower reception area, an eclectic mix of Etarian's old and bitter, young and jovial greeted them.

"You left these behind too." Vance flicked Kegan a matching set of magnetic cuffs and he clumsily caught them before they hit the ground.

Vance harrumphed to himself amazed that such an awkward fellow could wade waist deep in Erebus's offal to deliver the Dual Systems most dangerous prisoners, yet struggled to catch an object thrown three feet away. As if anticipating the change in thought, the bounty hunter stepped backwards.

"I'll take my payment and leave you to it before that squall gets any worse." Kegan said and offered his last payment chip. Vance smiled and tucked it into the register. A few buzzes and clicks later and Kegan had earned 15 thousand Ketos.

"You wanna stay and watch the game with us?" Vance offered, gesturing gnarled fingers to a muted projection on the wall. Kegan appreciated the offer, but turned him down.

"It'll be a good one, its Haigon versus Tuwa. 100 Ketos on Haigon."

Kegan watched the monitor as the Haigon team, all dressed in pale blue, entered the brimming Haigon stadium, to the adulation of the crowd. The spectators sat in ordered lines, dressed in their Sun-day best, the pale, rubbery skinned Etarian's crammed into the stands, children waved their teams' flags. A rolling light display advertised products and refinement processes to improve a person's visual appeal, sales of residential high rises, droids, cruise ship holidays and the latest in fertility solutions.

"A win'd do me nice, that EHIR 2 solution is expensive," commented one guard.

"You could save some money and adopt an Osirian; they breed like roaches over there." Another added.

A jovial argument broke out over the possibility of finding a pleasant Osirian. Kegan ignored the banter and answered

Vance instead.

"No thanks, Haigon will win for sure; I'm not taking that bet."

"Oh come on, fifty mini-Keto's says Orec scores the first points."

The multi-generational, mixed Tuwa team entered in lime green with white stripes across their chest, the crowd half-heartedly booing the opposition. The referee tossed the blazing ball in the air and blew the whistle.

"Another time." Kegan pocketed the payment chip as the guards removed Skeeter's magnetic bindings.

"You filthy fucking Merc!" The prisoner spat.

Kegan took back his magnetic cuffs from the guard, "Did you know, Skeeter, there are 996 days in a Kronos year?" Kegan began counting on his fingers, "Enjoy those next 40, you son-of-a-bitch."

Not until Kegan had the *Venator* clear of the ochreous cloud mass did he relax and the façade of Kegan vanished. Aedan rolled her narrow shoulders and took off her bulky jacket. Holding onto the male camouflage drew on her energy and it felt good to release the alter-ego. Aedan turned the heat up to max, warming her pearl colored skin and sore cartilage. She hit the burners and the *Venator* purred under her ministrations, setting a course for Leta.

CHAPTER 2

The Sisters of Leta didn't acknowledge the *Venator*'s' plotted course via radio, they didn't even ask for identification. The *Venator* was one of a handful of ships fitted with a tracking chip that allowed the pilot to find Leta and land on the tiny island surface that maintained the planet's population. Steep marble cliffs surrounded Leta's only inhabitable land mass, if the island had been named, it was now lost in the Buried Histories. The island lay off the southern coast from one of the planet's rocky continents, the altitude of all other areas too great for the residents' survival.

Aedan recalled fond memories of safety and security, academic lessons by the Sisters between flight training from the retired guests. Aedan sighed, wishing the peace she once found here, could be replicated somewhere in the dual systems. The *Venator* descended through the foggy atmosphere to the mossy and moist surface. Although Leta lay technically in the border of the Oddworlders' System, no record book, chart, map or database held any details of the hidden planet and not one visitor told a tale.

Aedan didn't bother pulling on "Kegan" or his jacket and exited the *Venator* as herself. Blue singlet, grey cargos and gaudy boots stepped into the humid and minty flavored air. Aedan strolled towards the Stone Colosseum, remembering her years of protection on this secret sanctuary. The arena's ruins stood on the outskirts of the primary city, beyond which lay three circles of settlements hidden amongst the undergrowth of the giant Boak Trees. As she entered, her cushioned footfalls muted by the Hundred Silent Sisters that worshipped as they wandered in prayer circles. The Sisters voluntarily took vows of solace and isolation to care for, protect and nourish the most vulnerable in the Galaxy. Both Etarian and Oddworlders found asylum here. Aedan never spoke about it and although she had occasionally spied other visitors attending and paying tribute, she had never approached them. It seemed natural that the only visitors, welcome on Leta, were female.

One Sister greeted Aedan with a rushed kiss on each cheek, her husky voice low, "You have returned to us little Sister." The pearl edged lavender woolen shawl pulled back from her silver hair and rested on her thin shoulders. Aedan had known Sister Marg for as long as she could remember.

"Not to stay, Elder Sister, just visiting for now. I have brought tribute for you." Aedan whispered back, as she handed over her newly minted payment chip from Kronos.

"So soon again, Aedan? You are a prosperous and busy little Sister aren't you?" Sister Marg cooed as she looped her arm through Aedan's and walked her further into the Colosseum. Her round toed slippers muffled against the stone, "Sister Yulna will want to thank you."

Sister Yulna, a short fuzzy hair Oddworlder with an unhealthy yellow tinge to her skin, greeted Aedan just as warmly, "Aedan you grow bigger and stronger every day." Both Sisters' irises were ringed with pink and yellow, "Where from this time?" Sister Yulna's hushed words combined with her hands habitually tugging Aedan's auburn pony tail stirred warm memories.

"And how much?" Sister Marg added careful not to disturb the fellow worshipers.

"15 thousand Ketos for Chigslin Skeeter."

"Skeeter." Sister Marg raised an eyebrow as she smoothed out her lilac shawl. Neither Sister queried Aedan's ability to morph into her alter-ego. Silence kept the best sins.

"We're still waiting for a reply from his victims if they will choose to seek refuge here." Sister Yulna nudged Aedan to the back of the arena towards the hidden gates of the city that existed beyond. "Did you need to rest, would you like a room?"

Aedan stepped out from the stone monolith, the dappled light dancing off the lush foliage. Somewhere deep in the underbrush, a Hummer-bird sung to its mate, the din of Rushes Rapids bubbled away. Aedan paused, she had taken refuge here for a short time, but Leta wasn't her home. Any time taken to rest now, would delay repayment of the debt she owed the Sisters.

"Aedan, your money will be well spent and you must rest sometime. Let us feed you, take an hour if you need."

Aedan inhaled, "No," a silent Sister, near the entrance raised her head and Aedan lowered her voice, "Thank you, but I must go."

Sister Yulna and Marg nodded in unison.

"Take what you need from the stockpiles." Sister Yulna handed Aedan a wrought iron key from one of the many folds in her linen shift. "I got this for you as well, only three this time to add to your collection."

Aedan regarded the tiny data device and smiled, "Thanks, I might need some extra diodes."

"Of course." Sister Yulna said.

Aedan nodded, "I'll swap out some fuel cells and then leave."

"Not for long dear," Sister Marg cuddled Aedan's slim shoulders and squeezed, leaving her to raid the store rooms alone.

"Not for long," Aedan repeated as she embraced Sister Yulna. There are always more mouths to feed. Aedan thought. New refuges, from both the Etarian and the Osirian System arrived weekly. The Dual systems needed the Sisters of Leta and Leta needed Ketos.

As the *Venator* snapped clear of Leta's orbiting protections, Aedan's overhead monitor squeaked another fugitive's warning.

"Hunter Dios, Haigon. 21 E-years old."

A single headshot of a young attractive male revolved on the screen. Aedan pushed the 3D imager as the monosyllabic rhetoric continued. A one sixteenth 3-dimensional image of

Dios leapt onto the dashboard.

"Height 189 centimeters, 90 kilograms, solid build, blonde hair, blue eyes. Student. Stolen transporter Icarus III, left Haigon Jump station at 22:30 hours heading outbound. Offences of multiple Homicides..." now came the interesting bit, *"Reward offered for capture, alive or dead, 5 T."*

Aedan blew out a long low whistle. Five trillion Ketos! That could buy a lot of supplies for Leta. It could buy Aedan a plot of land somewhere, a place to settle down. With five trillion Ketos she could afford to buy land on Tuwa, maybe a Cube in the lower hemisphere of Haigon if she was thrifty. She could settle as "Kegan". Hell, she could even live as Aedan! In Etaria. Forever. With five trillion Ketos she could buy herself a fleet of ships. Imagine how much Ketos a fleet of ships would earn Leta. Aedan schooled her stomach to calm, "Multiple Homicide?" She hesitated. Yet, if Aedan could find him. She activated the ships thrusters, and jetted off to the edge of Sandes.

Leta stayed hidden for so long due to the shelter of the Sandes asteroids, pregnant with magna-mines. From a distance and on the long range scanner, Leta popped up as just another large piece of asteroid junk. Like a silk ribbon pulling through freshly washed hair, Aedan spun the *Venator* around and through the asteroid field. She glanced at the 3D rotating image of Dios. The same age as Aedan was, if she counted in Etarian Years, yet his smooth skin and high cheek bones, portrayed him younger somehow. The expression on the headshot displayed blue eyes, peeping out of dark furrowed brows. His full lips pulled an awkward grimace or perhaps he had too many teeth in that square jaw. How could this striking young male become a mass murderer? Aedan shrugged her shoulders; something beautiful could be evil all the same.

Aedan concentrated on the facts. He had stolen a transport vehicle, the *Icarus III*. Although not inherently fast, they were renowned for their reliability and strength. He had used a Jump Station so he could be anywhere in the Gaian Galaxy by now. Aedan turned on her signal array and waited until the beeps descended to regular blips. Dios had taken off at 22:30 hours. Aedan pulled out her time gauge, the tiny bronze dials spinning into place. Aedan rolled the next silver dial, until the *Venator*'s clock aligned with Haigon. The Etarian system revolved around Haigon Time. Oddwolders ran on Chaos.

If Aedan calculated correctly, Dios's escape would have been right in the middle of the Haigon v Tuwa Grand Final of Fireball. An opportune time to make a break for sure. 5T was a preposterously large reward; Hunter Dios was obviously very dangerous or had killed the wrong people. Given that the reward stated Dead or Alive, Aedan surmised the later of the two. Aedan could taste the extra helpings of personal revenge that had been smoothed onto this one. Student. Not a hardened criminal, low chance of multiple criminal contacts. Maybe he wasn't so dangerous after all.

Multiple Homicides.

Facts, Aedan reminded herself. The *Icarus III* was heading outbound, away from Haigon. Skeeter, had needed more victims and lots of alcohol, so Aedan had to track him from bar to dirty bar. Hunter however, would be seeking sanctuary. Maybe he had family off-planet. Maybe he was just running for his life at this point. He'd Jumped so he'd have access to at least seven other Jump sites in Etarian Territory, unless he used a Galaxy Code. The only two codes the *Venator* had been programmed with gave Aedan access to the Osirian Jump Stations. Intra-system travel only. She'd used them frequently to jump from AK or Ante Kenina to PK or Post Kenina, save crossing multiple orbits and eye-watering billions of years of space.

If Hunter had used a Galaxy Code, he could use the Jump gateways to jump to any point in the Gaian Galaxy. There had been rumors of Universe Codes, enabling the traveler to jump *outside* the Gaian Galaxy. Aedan regarded the flecks of light that shone in the dark, she spun Sister Yulna's data device in her fingers. She shook her head, Etarians weren't that adventurous. Well, Aedan didn't even know any Etarian Codes, let alone a Galaxy Code, so she was stuck with the AK and PK

Jump stations.

Something told Aedan, Hunter would "Go to Surface" somewhere and hide it out. Aedan knew where the best hiding spots were in this Galatian game of hide and seek and she'd just left there. With Hunters large price tag, Mercs from all around the dual systems would be onto his trail. All Oddworlders were the same, shut out from the jump gateways. Even if their ships had the required tech, it mattered for naught without the proper keys.

Luckily Aedan hadn't recalled her sensors yet. She sat in prime position to scoop him up. With the sensor array active, any squeal would alert Aedan to gravitational waves being manipulated, a Jump Station suddenly awakening. Aedan had to remain confident, the young student wouldn't run some where he could be easily followed, and he'd have to cross the Sandes Belt first.

There were rumors the Sandes Belt used to be a planet, a large body of rock and ice that stood as an outpost between the Dual Systems, the prosperous Etaria and Oddworld Osiria.

Sometime before the Great War, the apocalyptic actions of one government or another detonated a hydrogen bomb in the planets' core causing total destruction. Leta might well have been just a moon of Sandes before then. Others say the Sandes was a natural barrier put there by Ea himself to sep- arate the civilized Etarians and the savage Oddworlders. Al- though religious bullshit aside, it was hard to believe a hydro- gen bomb would be let loose by the Etarians. And Ea knew, the Oddworlders didn't have the technology.

Aedan spent the next few hours wisely, her muted signal array confirming her suspicions. First she showered, a treat since refueling at Leta. She needed to catch a few hours, to rest and recoup, the adrenaline in her system had worn off since collaring Skeeter and now weariness crept in. She lay face down on her thin mattress and closed her eyes but the nar- row confines of her quarters, pressed inwards. The *Venator*'s heating element thickened the air, as the netted strings of her cupboard threw disjointed shadows across her eyelids. The reels of images, long suppressed began to turn in her mind and Aedan turned on her back. The memories halted for a second, before they started again. The familiar echo of bare feet on concrete, the smell of sweat and rotting food, the pressure of the wire against her back invaded her thoughts. She yielded to the futility of it all and returned to the main cabin. She made herself a Flat Teeta and loaded it with the tastiest protein paste she had and washed it all down with a large jar of Buzz. The home-made contraband, consisting of caffeine with a hint of ethanol, sent her nerves into overdrive and Aedan focused on the blanket of blackness ahead, dotted intermittently with flecks of light. She knew her signal booster would burn some power, but five trillion Ketos was worth it.

She reclined in her pilots chair, grabbed her mini-driver and opened up her Star-Scape, the holographic display of the constellations splintered around the cockpit. It had been a broken toy when she picked it up at a Faros Junking station. After she amplified the hard-drive and replaced the holographic crystals, she replaced the diodes on the lower hemisphere. She tested the new widened display, a near complete real-time night sky projected onto the *Venator*'s Bulkheads. She switched it off and added Sister Yulna's data device, while she chewed over Hunter Dios's hiding spots. She could see the red glow emanating from the curved edge of Kronos, highlighted by the twin suns of the Etarian System. Dueling balls of fire, Aodhfin and Fintan sent light and heat throughout the system. With the aid of two suns and nuclear terraforming, the Etarians could support life in one form or another on most of their nine planets.

On the other side of the Sandes Belt, the Osirian's that Aedan and the rest of Etaria called Oddworlders, survived with one sun, the blue bulb Kenina who maintained their eleven planets. Only a few planets managed to support life naturally on its surface. Only Ea, the holy entity of the Light, knew how Leta sustained life, the muggy atmosphere trapping whatever heat it could for the survival of its occupants.

After Kronos, Aedan could spot a tiny black dot cross-ing the surface of Aodhfin, the largest and brightest of the two. That would be the planet Lur perhaps, spinning with its golden rings of dust, quite a small planet, pleasant, civilized, with mountain ranges that led to fresh water gullies, one large ocean and another smaller salt water oasis landlocked by the largest continent, Lur-Kia. She had been to several of the Etar-ian plants, Lur included. Hermes, George, Tierra to name a few, each planet a little piece of white gold heaven, clean and healthy. Citizens who needn't live in fear, because the law was upheld. They had infrastructure, Government officials, health care, Universities. Etarians had set in place the *Etarian Charter*, protecting the rights of its citizens and governing their every-day lives. Every citizen had the right to earn a decent honest living, trade was encouraged. The Etarian Militia was the elite of the elite upholding the *Etarian Charter* and protecting their way of life. Five Trillion Ketos could buy her a slice of that life. She could feed herself and Leta for centuries.

Aedan glanced behind her, to the small window afforded by the Gatling laser she had mounted there. Osiria stretched out behind, Leta to her immediate left and overhead, and Kenina a soft blue haze. She could only just make out the dark outline of an arc folded back against the stars, the gaseous mass of Jory, behind that Anpu spun in the darkness. Chigslin had chosen well. Anpu was just one of the many hellish, pits of lawless civilizations that existed in Oddworld. Anpu and the other planets and moons, Hades, Helcate, and the capital planet Asar were all the same. Lawless, vicious, malicious mis-creants, Rebels and rejects built up the Osirian population. No infrastructure, no organization, and a sad little Admin-istration, a pseudo-government that constantly wrestled for power with the Rebels.

As well as the encounter on Anpu she had seen Rebels kill two men for shoulder jarring them in the street. No one had lifted a finger to stop them. A time when she had stopped in on a bar on Helcate to find a fugitive and had watched children being sold in cages, for what she didn't know, slavery, food? It chilled her to walk away, helpless. "Kegan" couldn't have lifted a finger either. What good were the Administrators if they couldn't protect their own? Aedan had heard the Rebel leader, Zern to be a ruthless vicious man who wielded a metaphorical axe in one hand while he reaped from the populace with the other. How could the Administration stand up to his vice grip of corruption?

Aedan screwed the last pin into the plastic and pressed the "project" button. The 3D holographic image spiraled into place, the tiny diamonds glistened on every surface. With her fingers across the sensor, Aedan rotated the view, the mass of constellations nebulae and satellites sparkled across the *Venator*'s bulkhead. She sat there, letting the time drip by as she studied Sister Yulna's newest additions; the Queen, Ph'erseus, and the Bull. Aedan manipulated the sensor again, her eyes studying each cluster and label. Her lids grew heavy, her bones weary, her head lolled to one side.

The Sandes' sensors squealed. She turned off the star-scape and keyed in the sensor details. The constellations now replaced by the lime colored illumination of the geo-map of that quadrant.

A ship had made it through alright. Aedan increased the thrusters until she had the *Venator* clear of the danger then boosted the power to full. Her quarry made it past Jory and Anpu before her sensors bleeped again, she closed the distance as the fugitive encroached on Hades. As she closed in, her ID confirmed the transport *Icarus III*. The dual engine freighter pulled laboriously into a highway of mining rigs returning to the smoky jade atmosphere of Hades. The bright yellow safety labels on the mining ships helped to camouflage the *Icarus III* and its dirty lemon coloring. The *Venator* needed a new paint job, yet her silver and grey markings stood out in this crowd. No sooner had the thought crossed Aedan's mind the radio jumped to life.

"Merc ship identify?"

"Merc ID 426, needing supplies. Two hours max required."

"Merc ID 426 you say...."

Two hours should give her enough time to find the errant Hunter Dios and take him down. Aedan watched Hades scarred surface rush to greet the *Venator*. Empty quarries littered the outlying areas, a rusted Mega-excavator slid from an ashen mountain top into a pit of slurry, the resulting wave of oil spread over the Hub's central structure, carbon tainted windows that protected the largest life bearing city of Quinil. The city survived as the central hub between two discarded craters, a warren of foot bridges and tunnels lead to the sister city Karnol. Aedan had been to Quinil enough times to recall, the poverty stricken docks that clogged every newcomer, the cavernous walls of the city, where the occupants carved their houses into the rock. If Aedan was quick, she might have half a chance. The Visitors region lay on the lower hemisphere border, the mining Port to the north and in the middle Tristown. The Hadeans often joked about shit flowing down hill and today Aedan hope they were right. That's if Hunter doesn't have allies to hide him in the caves.

"2 hours max!"

Aedan's revere was broken by the guttural voice of the guard, who returned an affirmative answer and directed her to the visitors' area to sign in. Aedan shuffled into Kegan, and flushed the tattoo onto his forearm before exiting into a throng of refugees. They begged Kegan and a handful of other visitors who made their way along the gangplank to the Administration tower. Kegan dug into his pockets, fumbling the few Keto's chips he had left, when a visitor in front tossed his purse and mass hysteria erupted blocking the path. Kegan pushed ahead, inhaling as little of the pitchy air as possible, and made a mental note to donate whatever Hunter Dios had in his pockets, on the return. A Myrmidon sentry raised his meaty fist as Kegan reached the head of the line.

"Name!"

"Kegan Capare, merc ID…"

"Capare!"

Kegan sighed, as the Myrmidon squinted one ruby eye over his frame. Seated at a desk and behind the murkiest panel of Perspex Kegan had ever seen, the thick skulled guard leaned forward.

"Who you chasing this time?"

Kegan regarded the digital time piece behind the guard's pimpled shoulder, each hand spun to a different planetary time. To Kegan's surprise the central marker ran on Asar time and not Haigon or Etarian time. Kegan shook his head, Hades seemed the last Rebel free port, maybe the Administration was making headway, but if they ran to Asarian time constraints, then Zern's Rebel's had some control.

"Chasing a hot meal and supplies… " Kegan said.

The Myrmidon had already turned to his counterpart in the neighboring docking booth.

"Hey, look who I've got here, Kegan fucking Capare."

Kegan gritted his teeth, hopefully Hunter was likewise delayed in the mining ports. Did he have a mining Tag, did he have allies this side of the Sandes?

"No shit! Capare – who you hunting?"

"Do you want my fucking autograph?" Kegan bit back, palm out waiting for the Tech pass.

"Cool your jets, Capare, time is Ketos,"

The Asarian dial clicked over, the second Myrmidon rose from his chair, Kegan spied the muted communication hub, each screen whirling through the Osirian Newscaster channels, not one Etarian face to be seen. News of Hunter hadn't reached Hades. Yet.

"Yeah don't I know it," Kegan dug out a Keto's chip, the silver currency spinning wildly on the countertop.

The first guard winked, before he logged the *Venator* onto the visitors' manifest and handed Kegan a tech-pass.

"Two hours, Kegan, then you'll be removed, got it!" A vision of being pushed out the airlock doors sprung to mind.

The chartreuse pollution soured Kegan's tongue as he strolled into Tristown. Hades had once been nutrient rich and mining camps had sprouted like boils across the planet's surface. The Etarians had mined successfully for centuries until a riot exploded one day and the Oddworlders took over. Now everything had turned south for the worst. The security on Hades seemed a joke. Visitors couldn't stay a night and spend their money in the economy, perhaps improving the World. Although the nutrients had dried up, they hoarded the machinery needed to process the Dual Systems minerals and ore mined from off-planet. The process left the air outside the hubs inhabitable and the air inside, recycled and tart. Yet the locals had to live here, had to work the mines at any chance to get rich - fast. One person could strike it lucky in an abandoned mine, past the Quinlan city limits, or you could get work on a freighter. Each employee had to work the math of surviving the toxic chemicals and possible explosions against a reasonable pay check.

More importantly, how would Hunter use Quinlan to his advantage? Kegan wondered as he made his way to Tristown. Another throng of pungent misfortunates begged at this gate waiting for any successful and empathetic miner to walk through. Kegan tried to avoid eye contact. Orange and grey flashed at every glance. He spied another set of Administration Myrmidons logging miners. Kegan spent another Keto's chip on reading the list of docked ships. So far, the *Icarus III* had just landed. Kegan regarded the narrow strip of food outlets and dimly lit Tanks that bordered the security gates. A bustle of hawkers called their wares over the crowd, kicking any beggars that crept close enough to snatch a morsel. Kegan perched on a barstool and ordered a skewer of miscellaneous meat and a jar of Buzz. The bartender shook his head, the contraband brew had already sold out. Kegan watched the crowd, deciphering and cataloguing each passer-by, from the rugged clothes and oily scents of miners, to militant boots of Rebels in disguise, until a sweet scent of something fruity and almost feminine drifted to Kegan's nose. He turned only to be met by a Hawker offering a tray of dried protein snacks, gnats buzzed between the samples. Kegan waived the merchant away, and rose to order another skewer. The comms screens above the bartender now flicked between Osirian and Etarian newscasters, a rolling information bar heralded the latest man hunt. An argument erupted between the fruit hawker and a beggar and Kegan stepped into the crowd, another Keto's chip twirling between his finger and thumb. He approached the Guard, only to halt in his tracks, as a rainbow of colors erupted from a dirt faced youth who stalked Kegan's direction.

Hunter Dios' shoulders hunched into a caramel colored jacket, a hood pulled low over a knitted cap that covered his hair, filth hastily rubbed onto his skin. Only Kegan could see the spectral illumination of his target. He'd never seen anything like it. Hunter Dios glowed, sparkled, beamed, all colors of the rainbow from his eyes. It seemed like a prism of light had shattered into a thousand glass pieces and each piece found a ray of sunlight. How could one being be so emotive? Kegan turned his gaze in an attempt to fade into the background. It didn't work, the quarry approached him.

"Are you the Eagle?"

Little cogs spun in Kegan's brain. He'd spoken soft enough that only Kegan could hear him. His irises lit up with tangerine, grey and white. Hope? So the Eagle, whoever that was, was aiding and abetting an Etarian fugitive.

"Yes."

Hunter's eyes continued to flicker between orange, yellow and white like a sunset on fast forward. His head tilted forward and Kegan's chest filled with pity. So trusting and so naïve, he wouldn't have made it on his own for more than a day.

"You better come with me." Kegan resisted the urge to handcuff his brawny frame, he would come willingly.

"Now? I just got here, my stuff is in -"

"They'll be here soon, we need to leave now." Kegan turned

on his heels and Dios fell in behind as Kegan retraced to the visitors' gate.

"They?" His voice sounded deeper when he didn't whisper.

"Mercenaries. Quick. Keep up." Luck had fallen into Kegan's hands. Although, looking back at the fresh faced murderer behind, maybe Hunter had been the lucky one. Another Merc might have killed him on the spot. What if he had run into a Rebel? Kegan had listened to the whispers at the Tank, Rebels were seizing transports now.

"Did you have trouble with the Administration guards?"

"Yeah the pass you sent, the code had expired, but a few Ketos chips did the trick, and they relented."

"Good…" Kegan mumbled. So the Eagle was resourceful, whoever he was. Surely the Eagle wouldn't be the Dual Systems second best bounty hunter, Calder Vien! That man and his explosive HMX crystals were the walking embodiment of Chaos.

As Kegan passed the Administration Tower, the sentry who had signed him in, approached from the right.

"Hey, did ya find what you're looking for?" the guard called.

"No luck, but thanks" Kegan shouted as he flicked the tech-pass and closed the ramp before the guard could say anymore. Kegan focused on a footprint trail left on the cargo ramp.

"We don't need the tags?" Hunter said.

Tags? What tags? "Not anymore."

"How long will it take to get to INNA?" So that's where Dios was heading, he must have family in the Oddworld system after all.

"Not long, we just have to make one stop first." Turning, Kegan saw one of the *Venator*'s cell doors had been opened.

"I hope the girls can hold out that long."

Kegan faced Hunter Dios and paused, the orange and white glow held tight across both eyes. Something about his physic, the broad shoulders buried in a skinned coat, the tanned complexion under blonde wisps, or the scent of pine and something animalistic tickled Kegan's nose. He couldn't put a finger on it, but Hunter seemed more *present* or more grounded. It peeked Kegan's curiosity.

A shadowy figure materialized in the far corner, a deep resonating timbre cut the air, "Leaving so soon Merc?"

Kegan turned with shaking legs towards the voice, all Kegan's effort concentrated in shifting his right foot back and bending his knees, calm and controlled to face the threat.

"Merc? You're a Mercenary" The soft planes of Dios's cheeks fell across his perfect square jaw. His eyes shone blood red.

Kegan couldn't see any details of the man in the shadows except his size, the syrupy venom of his voice indicated who was the more dangerous of the two. He moved into the light, taller than Kegan, a hand taller than Dios and with thicker shoulders coated in black. Immediately Kegan realized he'd never seen him before and even though he dressed like a Merc; black cargos, military boots, and a silver chain ID around his neck, he moved like water gliding over ice. Kegan's jaw cinched. The stranger's dark brown eyes emitted no light or tint. Not even black.

"Who are you?"

"I've been waiting for you Capare." His black long sleeved shirt exposed the build of a fighter. The light revealed burnt sienna colored skin, and rough black hair that framed a battle hardened face.

"Capare. Kegan Capare?" Dios asked. Even Hunter Dios had heard of Kegan.

"Yeah, kid. Capare's cashing you in." The man's words slid down Kegan's spine.

Rubber squeaked across steel. Kegan's leg retracted. Fast and high, his heel landed square in the stranger's chest. A spear of pain climbed Kegan's ankle up to his knee. The stranger stepped back, but not far enough. Kegan snatched at his belt, his shoulder rising until the Arc-gun was level. His fingers stung, as the stranger backhanded the weapon from his grip. The stranger advanced and Kegan rolled, his knee landing on the steel floor. Kegan curled his knuckles and brought his fist upright, but the stranger twisted to one side and brought Kegan with him. His grip tightened on Kegan's forearm. Something wasn't right. The strangers' strength outmatched Kegan which wasn't unusual, but the magnitude and speed took Kegan by surprise. This man wasn't just a thug, or a fugitive. His movements reeked of training, power with efficiency, ferocity without losing accuracy.

Kegan stomped down, his elbow flew backwards, Kegan tried to roll again but the stranger's power took them the opposite direction. The stranger's fingers closed around Kegan's neck, lifting the bounty hunter upwards until his toes scrapped the wall. The man advanced, ramming Kegan backwards, the cell door forcing the air from Kegan's lungs. He clawed at the warrior's fingers to no avail. Kegan blinked to clear away the stars that exploded in front of Kegan's eyes. He gasped a shallow breath as fear invaded his senses. He lost sight of Dios. Kegan snatched for the knives in his pockets. He had to be quick. Real quick. He gripped the hilt and slashed at the man's ribs.

As the knife's blade made contact with fabric, it split like an overripe melon, but where the blade should have dug into skin, it glanced off as if the metal had scraped metal. Kegan's eyes widened as the blade failed over and over again. The stranger's shirt now a mass of tendrils on his rib cage, the burnished copper gleamed undamaged between the cuts. Kegan regarded the stranger's reaction and caught a tiny rippling on the surface of his skin, the cells knitted together to form a hard impenetrable layer.

"What are you?" Kegan croaked.

"Not like you, Etarian traitor scum." He spat. With his right hand firmly around Kegan's neck, he used his other to tear the jacket from Kegan's shoulders, shaking it and all its weaponry contents onto the floor and out of his grasp. Kegan brought his knees up, his boots kicking at the man's hips. It didn't work, the man was as immovable as a Helcate volcano. Panic slithered under Kegan's skin.

Kegan's breaths became ragged as his heart assaulted his ribs. The memories fogged his brain, like a poisonous gas sapping strength and dissolving courage. The stranger's hand tightened, fingers dug in. Kegan tried to inhale, his windpipe closed. The facade began to slip. The scene in front of Kegan grew long shadows until a single spot of light was all he could see. As Kegan's consciousness waned, Aedan's control slipped.

And then Kegan vanished.

"What are you?" The stranger gasped, his fingers released as Aedan involuntarily shifted into feminine form. Her spine slid against the wall as she landed on the floor in a heap. As focus returned, Aedan could see Dios standing a foot behind her attacker, his mouth agape. Fuck, both had witnessed her shift.

Aedan gathered her breath and kicked at the stranger's feet, landing one on his ankle and another on his inner thigh. He went backwards and hard, the adrenaline squirmed through Aedan's system. She grabbed her jacket. If she could get one cuff on the stranger, then she would deal with Dios. Internally she acknowledged that neither of the men could live. She considered abandoning Kegan's façade as some of her energy peaked.

Hunter froze, too stunned to react. Aedan couldn't resist, and effortlessly pulled Kegan back into place. The magnetic bracelets jangled in Kegan's hand, the arc of steel closed over one of the warrior's wrist. He twisted to his feet, and with the other hand tugged at the magna-cuff. The metal fracturing into shards and scattering to the floor. Kegan gasped and backed away, his throat scoured like steel wool. Like a predator gaining on prey the stranger stalked out to reach Kegan, his brown eyes pits of nothingness. Kegan dug into his boots and threw two knives dead center. Both bounced off the stranger's chest in opposite directions. He didn't miss a step.

"You can't hurt me." The stranger sneered.

Kegan's heel collected the soldier's jaw; his head snapped

back, a deep throaty laugh roared from within. The stranger threw himself forward, low and crouched, his hands clawed at Kegan's thighs and they went down together. His inflexible weight compressed Kegan's smaller frame, pinning arms and legs underneath. Kegan's nails clawed frantically across metal, knees collided with immovable bulk as Kegan's primeval cry reduced to a whimper. The stranger closed his grasp, Kegan's throat compressed.

"I don't want Kegan anymore, girl." He barked.

The heat of his breath licked at Kegan's slanted lids and the light waivered. As his fingers ratcheted closed, Kegan winked out of existence. Aedan saw Hunter above the tangle, an iron bar in his hand. He swung low and fast, the stranger's bulk shuddered. He rolled to one side, clutching the back of his skull, and Aedan squirmed to freedom.

"I'm sorry," Hunter snapped, before he swung the bar again.

The air rushed out of Aedan's lungs as the bar sunk into her gut, the rear wall of her own cell stopped her fall. Aedan dashed for the exit, her palms struck the Perspex, just as Hunter hit the lock panel. Hunter pulled on the ramp lever and dashed out into the throng. The stranger moaned and rolled over, the muscles in his back bunched and heaved as he eventually found his feet. Aedan could still see Hunter as he dashed through the Hades' crowd, throwing Ketos chips behind him. Aedan marveled at Hunter's resourcefulness, as the crowd reacted. The soldier wouldn't make it through that throng in a hurry.

Aedan's whole body trembled and she blinked back the liquid that pooled in her lids, her ribs ached, her palms swollen, knuckles bruised. She rested her hands on her knees and sucked down chafed breaths and pondered her new predicament. She looked at the door, why had she never engineered a fail-safe for the cell locking system? Before self-pity totally overwhelmed her, the stranger bounded back into the *Venator*. He slammed the ramp shut and scaled the vertical ladder to the cockpit. The engines whined to full thrust, and as Aedan grasped for a hand grip, her ship leapt to life. She kicked at the Perspex to no avail, as the *Venator* climbed into the atmosphere. *Shit.*

CHAPTER 3

Hell. Deuc hadn't forgotten about the beauty in the cargo hold, he had just forgotten to lock his cruiser. That damn Hunter Dios had taken his ship, the *Arion* to Ea-only-knew-where. Now he had to fly this foreign hunk of junk and hopefully catch him before he made it into the Sandes Belt and back to the Etarian system. *Damn!* What was she? He had thought waiting for Kegan Capare, the Dual systems most successful bounty hunter to catch the prey was better than doing any work himself. When he'd heard Kegan's ID tag over the Hades Atmos-Tower, he heeded the call. Kegan Capare had always been accurate, unrelenting and swift. He never failed a mark. She. *She had never missed a mark.* Deuc mused over what he had seen. Each time he had caused Kegan to lose conscious-ness, Deuc had seen the image shimmer and melt, his hand warmed, the edges fuzzed, before *she* appeared. Sweet vanilla, glistening pearl skin, dark russet hair and eyes the color of li-quid silver. Her splendor didn't change her allegiance though. Etarian-traitor scum.

It took Deuc two hours to completely loose his own ship, the *Arion*. All black, sleek, armed to the teeth. Fast. Really, really fast. He sat in the outdated cockpit, boots on the clunky dash, and decimated Kegan's Teetas and protein paste. He even enjoyed a glass of Buzz. It took him another hour before he finally admitted defeat. He reduced thrusters, and hit auto-pilot, and headed down to the cells. He had the best tracker in the dual-systems right in front of him and if she'd found Hunter once, she could find him again.

With arms crossed over his slashed shirt, Deuc eyed the infamous bounty hunter caged in her own two by two. Black shiny hair and yellow eyes, which lifted slightly at the outer corners glared at him from under the bright halogens. What was the tattoo for? Did Kegan truly exist and she was just the mimic. No, the enchanting feminine scents told another story, the male façade a necessary survival instinct. In both systems lawlessness, terra-forming and war had turned women into a highly valuable commodity and their safety and freedom had been greatly reduced as a result. However, this one had floored him, thrown knives at his heart, and possibly had the ability to morph into anyone. She was quick; very fucking quick, with reflexes that superseded even his. She had managed to survive all the foulness, mayhem, and brutality that had taken her kind and destroyed them. He would have to be careful, very careful with this one.

"I know this," Deuc gestured up and down, "is supposed to be Kegan Capare, but what's your real name?" Deuc asked.

No answer.

"Listen traitor, every minute you waste is another minute Hunter gets away from you."

No answer.

Why had someone with these talents become a turncoat for the dog Etarians? "I have a proposition for you."

Kegan's voice came to him muffled through the Perspex and magnetic locks of the pristine cage. "No."

"No. How can you say no, in your position?"

"Exactly, I'm not negotiating from in here." Yellow eyes tracked the compact space before they returned to glare at Deuc.

"Fine." Deuc tapped the lock, as he simultaneously solidified his upper epidermis layer. He caught the barest of warning, in the slick movement of Kegan's knees, before the bounty hunter had landed a kick at Deuc's solar plexus, he covered the space in two steps. He clasped down on limbs to avoid another volley, his fingers closed in on the carotid artery, while his forearm rested against Kegan's sternum, the Merc's back flat against the wall. Vanilla and jasmine hovered outside his shield.

"No more Kegan."

The yellow eyes flared, yet Deuc's hands remained cold and calm.

"Listen, *Laelaps*, I'm not beyond bargaining, you can have your freedom, but there are rules. Understand?"

"Or?" Kegan said, his bottom lip thinned, teeth gritted.

"Or, I might take my time, checking how anatomically correct, you made this fraud." He raised an eyebrow and added a smirk for emphasis. Kegan took a sharp intake of breath and Deuc waited.

Kegan's tanned skin heated beneath his touch and the shimmering beauty appeared. Molten mercury with a jaw clenched around a petulant mouth. Deuc's desire stirred, and he pushed away. As Deuc's fingers retracted, they slid down her pale throat and hovered over a tight jagged scar that stretched from collar bone to the hollow in her neck.

"What happened here?"

When she didn't answer, Deuc licked his lips, the air heated.

"A man. I stabbed him."

"Oh really, what for?"

She swallowed hard, a slight sheen glassed over her pupils.

Deuc winced at his previous quip. He didn't doubt she had stabbed the bastard, probably numerous times. He had witnessed her speed first hand. Deuc sighed and stepped back, "Rules. No more Kegan. You stay in your original form until I say otherwise."

She clicked her tongue, "What does it matter to you?"

"I like to differentiate between friend and foe, most of the time." He didn't know just where this shapeshifter sat right now.

"Second, I'm calling a truce, you've seen how effective bladed weapons are against me, same as Arc guns. You probably want to keep this ship in one piece so don't risk it. Besides, the clock is already ticking."

The dazzling creature eventually nodded.

"You find Hunter, and then we'll part ways. Understand." On impulse, his gaze wandered over her feminine form, a full head shorter than himself, athletic with a slender waist in a singlet that accentuated her perfectly adequate chest. Deuc cleared his throat and stepped clear of the cell door.

"I have my rules, Oddworlder." She said, chin lifted, eyes alight.

Deuc tossed her his most charming smirk, silver eyes trapped in his gaze, "I promise to keep you safe until then."

The heat flared up her neck, pearlescent cheeks flushed with peach and rose, she clenched her jaw, "I don't need any more of your clumsy interference." She drove a finger into his chest, "Since you lost him, I will find Hunter and I will be keeping 80 percent of the reward."

"65 percent."

"70."

"Fine."

"Right," The bounty hunter paused at his sudden agreeance, "On my ship, you follow my rules." She said and squared her shoulders.

"On-planet you follow my lead."

"On-planet, I can use Kegan to keep - "

"I said I will keep you safe, without Kegan."

The woman snorted, "I need you to stay out of my way, more than I need your protection." She crossed her arms and leaned back.

Deuc pulled the shreds of fabric on either side of his abdomen, "Trust me."

"I can use Kegan." She persisted.

Deuc's eyes narrowed, "On-planet, if it's not a risk to our mission."

"Agreed, you tell no-one, of Kegan, of this?"

He nodded although this condition didn't matter. Hunter had already taken off with that golden nugget of knowledge, "Sure, whatever."

"Deal? On your word?"

"Yeah sure, Deal. On my word so help me Ea." He rolled his eyes and pushed his hand forward.

Aedan took the stranger's hand, a bright constellation revolved into view, three stars, two very large and bright, closer together and another nearby but smaller orbited by five small planets. She recognized the system and failed to censor herself, "Alpha-Centurion."

"What?" He barked and dropped her hand like a hot coal. Aedan didn't know what to say, if she could only read his eyes.

"What are you?" Aedan asked as she climbed to the cockpit, the stranger's boots echoed off the steel rungs.

"Osirian. And my name is Deuc, and it's the Osirian system. Oddworld is the name those Etarian assholes gave to keep the down trodden, down."

"Well, you can stop calling me Etarian Traitor Scum too, my name is Aedan."

"Well Aedan, what are you?"

Aedan waited at the top while he pulled his frame from the narrow internal ladder. Deuc stood over her, his head a good foot above hers, half his black hair braided back from his forehead while the remainder touched the collar of his torn shirt. At this distance, the difference between Osirian's and Etarians became glaringly obvious, the Osirian's denser muscle tone, sharpened features, thicker builds compared to the waif like Etarians and their waxy complexion, slender limbs and plumper facial structures. Aedan thought of Hunter's grounded aura, the explosion that coated his irises. Aedan released her train of thought and shrugged her shoulders.

"You need another shirt."

"Surely, Kegan has spares?" He sneered.

"Down the corridor, first on your left." Aedan said. She had a dozen shirts that Deuc could use. Aedan had perfected the ruse of Kegan to plump up and thin down, depending on the occasion. Granted the Myrmidons on Hades had practically swooned over Kegan, perhaps he needed another revision.

Aedan mentally catalogued the locations of her hidden weapons, in case her new ally had alterative motives. He could ditch her mid voyage, sabotage her ship, after all he was Osirian. She'd have to have counter measures in place, if he did.

Deuc followed Aedan's instructions and paused at the threshold. Kegan Capare's sleeping quarters took him by surprise. The bed was a narrow bunk, the sheets tucked in at the corners seemingly undisturbed. The coverlet had several imprints of a slender frame wrinkled across the fabric, no doubt Aedan. Was this a temporary ship? Surely Kegan's rewards allowed her to travel in comfort. He regarded the narrow space. A bevy of tools and weapons, including knives, more magna cuffs, a spanner set, had been strapped to one wall, an Arc gun partially disassembled rested on a fold down bench, smears of Inox and grease collided with gentle feminine scents.

Deuc stepped over the threshold, a netted clothes rack caught his attention, only a handful of shirts and even less pants were stacked in it. Another smaller net held her small clothes, socks and a spare belt. Deuc pulled out one shirt, the fabric thin, the collar stretched and loose. He picked up a pair of cargo pants. The dye faded, creases of a lifetime of use, set around the hips, knees and ankles. To the left of the bunk, he found compact shelves with fingerprint security, yet the set was unlocked. He stepped closer to two drawers that burst at the seam; a wad of paper protruded from one and he pulled it out, the drawer widening. Deuc couldn't resist as he opened it further, curious as to the treasure of the infamous Kegan Capare. Deuc paused. The contents were as strange as they were common. A ticket to an Etarian cinema, a collection of buttons, data devices coated in rust, books with the pages thumbed back with over use, a bangle with the clasp broken, ribbons, a single mechanical key. He closed the drawer and opened the second one, only to be met with more regular items. Broken circuit boards, data cards, spare shoelaces, dried flowers pressed into a mold, three feathers, pliers with leather handles, a mirror in a silver case. He closed the drawer, surprised to realize he still held the paper in his hands. He unfolded it and read an application for residency in Etaria. The first line had been attempted, the letter A crossed out and replaced by the letter K, only to be crossed out again. Deuc returned the paper and stepped back. He eyed the room again with fresh eyes. The bundled socks had holes in the toes, the waist belt was imitation, the black plastic peeling where it regularly met buckle, the strap thin, the holes wide. Deuc's legs felt heavy. He recognized this scant life, the sad connections to ordinary items, when someone had nothing, they held on to everything.

Aedan listened as Deuc's footsteps brought him back to the main cabin. Within seconds, Deuc had shucked the shredded remnant and for a moment stood bare chested in Aedan's full sight. Muscles bunched and rolled as Deuc moved and Aedan couldn't deny the strength she witnessed under his shining copper skin. Aedan focused on the dash, the *Venator*'s trajectory that Deuc had coded, the speed he'd been burning her fuel cells at, even the flat Teeta debris that littered the pilots chair.

Deuc's oval eyes caught hers and held them. Aedan cleared her throat, and reclaimed First Chair in the cockpit. "Now where in Ea's name have you got us?" Aedan clicked the radar and found Deuc had tracked within half a click of the Sandes Belt and then commenced a bizarre zig zag sweep of this quadrant. A flippant comment about his gender formed on her lips, she left it unsaid. "Did you not listen to Hunter when we walked in?"

"Pardon?" Deuc rested his boots back on the dash and helped himself to another cup of Buzz.

"Never mind," Aedan sighed and plotted a course to INNA.

CHAPTER 4

"For a famous bounty hunter, I expected more." Deuc rumbled around his seventh helping of Teetas.

The Interplanetary Entity Allocation Centre, or INNA, orbited Asar, the primary planet of Osiria. The giant metallic structure was responsible for all distribution, supply and payment of resources, yet Aedan couldn't fathom Hunter's next move. Thanks to Deuc she had a few hours to ponder it. The normal electric hum of the *Venator* became a blizzard of sub audible irritancies as the silence stretched out.

"You said you were Osirian?"

"Yep."

"What's your Merc ID number?" She glanced at the silver chain around his neck.

"I'm not a Merc." He spat.

"What are you then?"

"I think the better question is what are you?"

"A filthy Merc like you said."

Aedan turned on the broadcaster and watched the latest headlines roll on, scanning for any information about Hunter or the *Arion*. A dull summary of the previous events scrolled up the screen. *Skeeter captured. Etarian surveyors attacked. Haigon wins Fireball Grand Final.* Then a pretty blond newscaster sprung to life. A Synth, perfect right down to her last nanotransistor. *"While burials for Hunter Dios' victims are arranged, the fugitive appears still at large."* Aedan breathed a sigh of relief.

Deuc chuckled, "You're obviously an 'Oddworlder' as you call it."

Aedan chose to ignore him and instead hacked into the Etarian communication cables via Shadow comms, the standard non-official hacker platform.

"Why work for those despots?"

"They pay the bills." She ran through a few cables listening and reading a few choice words here and there but nothing of her quarry.

"Does your ship have a location beacon?"

"Yes,"

"Then why – "

"I disabled it."

"Trying to hide from someone, or something?"

"No"

Aedan pondered what he meant, "Are you sure?"

Deuc didn't answer instead, he said, "Well, is that all it takes, a few Ketos and you're bought?" Deuc chuckled, he seemed to enjoy the bursts of anger that flourished her cheeks.

"What about you? You say you aren't a Merc, you wear a silver ID tag and you're chasing fugitives." Aedan turned the cables down to a low hum, trusting her ability to pick Hunter's voice or name from the din.

"I'm an Osirian ... Administrator."

"Never heard of them," Aedan tried to joke.

"That doesn't surprise me, *Laelaps*." That was the second time he'd used that name and judging by his tone, it was meant to sting.

"Well you're doing a fantastic job." Aedan levelled a flat stare in his direction. His dark eyes never moved, yet he chuckled in response. She guessed his eyes would reflect the "black" of hatred, if she could see them, but why had he laughed? If he was lying, his irises would cover over in an oil slick sepia color. She swiveled her seat back to facing the dash and listened to the Osirian news channels, a small contingent of Rebels had overtaken the Hades port. She'd caught Hunter just in time.

"It's more like procurement. It's my job to find things, Etarian things that could be useful for the Osirians."

"Things? People?"

"Sometimes."

"Why?"

"Well despite what most *Etarians* think, there is no peace-treaty."

Aedan pondered the truth of his statement. Almost two centuries ago, the peace treaty had been signed, declaring Oddworld no longer a Colony of Etaria. Conditions for Odd-world's independence had been set. After 30 years of peace, the Borders War had ignited over a claim by Oddworlders the original treaty was unjust. The Administrators at the time had been under duress and fumbled the conditions. Others like Zern said the Administrators didn't speak for all Osirians and had yielded like cowards. At the conclusion of the Borders War, after 110 million souls had been wiped from existence, the new Skyolios Treaty was signed.

"And you want to collect those people or things that'd be most useful to your cause?"

He nodded and now his expression changed, eyelids lowered, "So we both trade bodies for Ketos." he spoke slower causing Aedan to shiver.

"What about Chigslin Skeeter then?"

"Oh he can rot on Kronos for all we care."

Aedan turned back to the communications cables, yet something didn't seem quite right. "Why don't you ask for assistance now, you're an Administrator call for government recourses?"

Deuc snorted but didn't answer.

"His bounty is for you, not the Administration." Aedan shook her head, "Osirian corruption at every turn." Aedan let her gaze wander to the stars, before snagging on another thought, "How can we both claim Hunter's reward? I'm delivering him to Kronos when I catch him."

"He has something I need, after that, do as you please." Deuc stopped inspecting his fingernails.

"What do you want from Hunter? He is just a murderer?"

"Tell me Aedan, you didn't think it strange, that for a murderer they've offered a five trillion Ketos reward? His victims weren't even named." When Deuc leaned in, the communication cables nattering away in the background, Aedan's brain simply froze. What had the pretty little Synthetic said? Had she actually named them? Aedan didn't get a chance to ask more as the *Venator*'s proximity alarm squealed in high definition. Deuc twitched more than Aedan, and at any other time she might have laughed. She hit the scanner and a holographic image of a strange freighter appeared in flashing red. Aedan reached for her boosters just as an arc of blue light surged across the dashboard frying all her electrics.

"Seize-machine." Deuc snarled, holding onto the arm of his chair preventing him from floating any closer to the bulkheads.

"What?" Aedan's skin prickled as the climate control failed and the icy snap of space crept into the cockpit. She threw her hands out sideways, desperately trying to find purchase amongst the wires and cables.

"You'd better get -, " he frowned when his brown eyes found her yellow, "Kegan."

"What are they?" Kegan said.

"*Lestas.*"

The *Venator* hung motionless, as the windows frosted, blotting out the weak blue hues of Kenina. Rusty metallic jaws scraped closed around the ship, the *Venator* suddenly pitted into darkness. A second later gravity returned, and hurled them face first into the floor. Deuc was first on his feet, his skin, tight and rigid. Kegan stood and thickened his form, eyes rapidly scanned the secret holds, for the closest weapons.

"You said *Lestas?*" Kegan wiped a bloody smear from his hair line.

"Pirates. Oddworlders. Raiders and slavers."

Kegan dashed to the heating element and yanked, a shelf appeared containing a set of knives, and a snub nosed arc gun.

"Bad idea. Have you got any Francium to bargain with?"

"Francium? Who carries Francium?" Kegan snapped and pushed the shelf back empty handed. He tucked the Merc tag into his collar and swallowed hard. Kegan had never faced a Lestas before and braced himself as scratches and thumps echoed through the steel.

The ramp lowered sending forward sepia rays of light and an odor of unwashed bodies. Five Raiders lumbered forward, clicking as they moved. They looked like all other Oddworlders', grimy villains with red and black that danced across their irises, except the red was a little more pink, and something about their shapes look malformed. Each carried a weapon of some kind, a mace, a blue-bar, an organic scanner and a set of magna cuffs, one even held a single shot plasma rifle.

"Two active, Sinta," The tallest one spoke over a crowd of bald heads. Kegan glimpsed pointed teeth behind a beak like mouth.

"Any women?" a call came from the back.

Every hair on Kegan's skin stood to attention. Deuc's jaw began to move but he just yawned.

"Nope," the one in front answered, his meaty hands twisted around the handle of the organic scanner.

"Keep them till we strip the ship."

As their captors lead them across the cargo bay to a dark corridor, Kegan registered each surface was caked in dirt, exhaust fumes and rust. The familiar metallic smell of dried blood confirmed the plentiful splatters that decorated the walls and floor.

Deuc whistled behind gritted teeth, "That's a beauty."

Kegan gasped as he saw a sleek black cruiser with twin nacelles that must be Deuc's *Arion*, strapped down and being pulled apart by three scaly Lestas. Kegan admired the dual purpose space craft; able to traverse atmospheric environments and not; an expensive piece of equipment for an Oddworlder. Kegan clenched his fists and drew a deep breath. Where the fuck was Hunter?

"Did I ask you something? I don't remember asking you anything," the tall and scaly, Lestas said as he smacked the blue-bar across Deuc's shoulders. He flinched but Kegan knew no bruise would be left in its wake.

"No need to get rough, we can bargain."

"We don't bargain. We already have your ship." He snarled. He shook the foot long blue-bar close to Deuc's face and clicked his tongue.

"That you do."

Deuc continued to stroll beside Kegan while he concentrated on taking one step after the other. Nervous energy bled into Kegan's limbs as he counted Lestas and multiple hatches that lead off from the cargo bay. When they reached one gloomy corridor, a Lestas kicked open a hatch and shoved them through. Kegan's boot clipped the lower edge and he stumbled inwards. Deuc caught Kegan's arm and kept him upright.

"No more Buzz for you, I think."

"Buzz? You have Buzz?" the tall Lestas lowered his face to Kegan's, and grinned, his hot rancid breath rolled over his slanted cheeks and choked his senses.

"There is," Kegan caught Deuc nodding his head, "In the galley. Top shelf. There's a full still."

The tall one elbowed Kegan forwards into the next room. A chair trapped in a wire cage dominated the room, encrusted hooks and chains hung from the ceiling and on the far wall a clear resin cell peeked from underneath long shadows. Both empty.

"Inside." The tall one barked and Kegan entered the holding cell.

The bounty hunter leaned back and let the shadows fall across his yellow eyes, where he could size up the creatures. He thought the soft clicking noise, had come from the olive shaded plate armor they wore, however now he noticed it came from their feet. A strand of webbing bridged between their four sausage thick toes and again on their fingers. Hazarding a guess, they had suckers or the like on the soles of their feet. Deuc ducked as he entered and Kegan heard his boots splash into puddles when he walked.

"Hosed them out first watch, nice and fresh for you,"

Kegan immediately thought of Hunter. Five trillion Ketos might just have been washed down the drain.

"Thanks," Deuc said.

All three hijackers turned, with snorts and cackles they hurried out the room.

"Great plan this is, how can we fight from in here?" Kegan whispered.

Deuc tapped the Perspex as if testing its strength, the three primary walls had been laced with steel reinforcements, "First we wait."

"Wait?" Kegan tried to lower his tone. Would Deuc bargain his life for Kegan's?

"Yes, we wait. Do you have anything valuable on that ship?"

The breath froze in his lungs. Only, the transponder to Leta! "No."

Deuc rose from his squat position and walked towards Kegan, "No?"

"Do you think they've killed Hunter?"

"I don't think so. They may be stupid, but not that stupid." Deuc stared down a nose that would be too straight on any other face and tilted his head to one side.

"So, we wait until they destroy my ship?"

"They'll be three skins deep before they start that. Question is, what have they done with him?"

"Thanks to you he had a decent head start."

Deuc ignored the comment and continued, "Hunter is here so we stay. I reckon we use this time to sleep."

"Sleep?"

"Yeah, when was the last time you slept?"

Kegan thought back to Leta. No. It had been longer. Before Anpu, before Skeeter?

"A while."

"Same," Deuc stifled a yawn, "Too long, my shield is… it won't take them long to work out who they've caught."

"Do Administrators have any sway over them?"

Deuc paused at her word, "Administrators, ah no. Look, whatever happens after they've stripped your ship involves one of us in that cage. I like to be rested before I have to start snapping necks. Don't you?" He arched his eyebrows and grinned.

Kegan resumed her pacing, "There was at least twenty-five in the cargo bay, I saw six hatches on the starboard side."

"I've dealt with *Lestas* before, this ship would be crawling with at least seven thousand, maybe more. I can take at least five hundred, how about you?" Deuc cracked a yawn. "We need the *Arion*, I need sleep. Although I doubt it, there is every chance Hunter has Jumped to safety and my bird is vacant. If not he'll soon be in here with us, worst case we'll have to search the ship. Either way, we have a better chance at success if we wait."

"Sure. Whatever." Kegan hated to admit Deuc might be right. Twenty-five drunken Lestas was better than seven thousand angry. What did Deuc mean about his shield? A weakness Kegan might have to exploit later. He felt a measure of relief that the Oddworlder would be fighting if it came to that. And it made sense to protect him, after all Kegan was Deuc's money ticket, if Hunter was still alive.

"There's just one problem, you."

Kegan stopped. "What do you mean by that?"

"Well, what happens when you sleep? What happens to this?" He took his time gesturing up and down the facade. "Did you see those monitors we passed outside?"

Kegan hadn't, "Yeah, so?"

Deuc exhaled slowly.

Kegan rolled his eyes, "How long do you plan on taking a nap? I can wait." The Perspex walls slanted inwards, the sweet tang of Deuc's skin forced Kegan backwards.

Deuc laughed a rich thick sound that taunted.

"I can do it." Kegan snapped, crossing his arms across his chest.

"Sure be my guest, but doesn't this drain your energy. My shield.... I have to sleep..." Deuc trailed off. "I don't care what you look like, but you at full capacity is better than Kegan running tired."

"What then?" Kegan clenched fists tight under his arms, if he didn't need Deuc as an ally he would put his boot in his face again.

"Just pick a spot, a nice dark spot." His brown eyes sparkled and Kegan wished on every star that he could read his irises there and then. Nothing changed.

"Fine." He searched the two dark corners against the wall to find the driest and cleanest and curled into a ball.

"You'll have to lie down, facing the wall."

Instead of protesting like every sinew in his body wanted to do, Kegan sunk down onto the metallic floor, tucking his arm under his head. He heard Deuc's movements as he slid down behind Kegan. The darkness became total and Kegan's heart thundered in his own ears. He tried to swallow and reduce the rapid breaths. The metallic acid smells, the sound of chains clinking and Deuc's heat weaved in through the façade. Kegan almost slipped.

"What are they, the *Lestas*?" Kegan croaked.

"Raiders and slavers. Hijacking ships before or soon after they Jump. Reaping their supplies and tech and jettisoning the rest."

"I gathered that, I meant, what *are* they?" He added. A citrus taint invaded the space and Kegan twitched his nose. Weariness crept into sore limbs and in the darkness, Kegan waivered.

"They are Osirians or whatever you call them. Like us."

Then what are we? Kegan thought before saying, "They're not like anything I've seen."

"You have, you just don't realize it. Have you ever seen the Hermes Crocodilians, or the Black Dart Adder from Chareon?"

"Reptiles?"

"Exactly."

"And what about you?"

"Me. I'm special." He scoffed.

"Yeah right." Kegan sniggered back. The Kegan alter-ego became unmanageable during sleep, so did Deuc's skin become penetrable?

"I am special. Besides," Deuc's voice suddenly became serious, "In all my time as … an Administrator, I've seen a lot of different Osirians but I've never seen one like you."

"Nor have I." Aedan tried not to sound melancholy, "Or at least I wouldn't know it if I had."

"Where are you from?"

"I don't know. I remember living on Asar when I was younger." The darkness began to form around the edges again and Kegan changed the topic, "What about you?"

Deuc sighed, "I know Asar."

He had felt Kegan stiffen beside him and decided to end the inquisition. Kegan, moreover, the woman underneath the façade had survived Asar, one of the most predatory, impoverished and insidious places in the Dual Systems. More often than not, Deuc had been on the wrong side of that world. Then he had been corrected, tutored and finally protected from most of that harshness. Now he was in a position to rectify some of it. He's previous exploits on Hades had left him fatigued. He'd eaten most of the bounty hunter's supplies but to be fully rejuvenated he needed sleep. He could handle more than a few Lestas on his own. And this time he had Kegan. Well Aedan and her speed on his side.

Deuc rested on his side and mirrored his companion, blocking out most of the monitors view. It would catch the edge of boots and legs but that didn't worry him. However the bounty hunter had managed it, Aedan had created a handy ruse. Kegan's subterfuge was at times, subtly boring. Boring enough that Deuc would overlook Kegan in a crowd, despite his fame. Capare seemed so unremarkable that Deuc's eyes wanted to move past the blurred edges of his image and find something, anything more appealing. A splash of warm energy caressed his front, signaling the shift in Aedan back to her true form. He listened as the Bounty hunter's breathing evened out and then closed his eyes.

Deuc woke to the sensation of warm fingertips brushing the hollow in his neck. He almost cast up his guard until he realized it was Aedan. She lay hidden in the dark, yet instinct told him her actions were deliberate. He ignored his body's natural response and willed himself to absolute stillness as her fingers traced the location of his arteries. She tentatively ran fingers over his neck and down the join near his shoulder before finally resting over his heart. She had found his weakness, so similar to her own.

The hatch flew open and in stumbled a few Lestas. Deuc threw his guard up and placed a cautious arm across Aedan's waist. She froze underneath his grip.

"Is Kegan ready?" He sensed her nodding in affirmation. "Follow my lead, trust me."

More nodding.

"Get up, you bastards!" someone slurred and Deuc resisted the urge to react instantly. Had they finally recognized his ship?

"What time is it?" Deuc stretched his arms up and backwards.

"He said get up" This time a sober voiced measured out each syllable and Deuc's ears pricked. Perhaps they had. Now they would drag him from the cell and try to take him apart piece by piece. Deuc almost laughed.

"I said what time is it?" He rolled over and watched as Sinta, the tallest and broadest of the Lestas stood at the door to their cell tapping an electro-plasma whip against his thigh.

He could take care of the Electro-plasma whip, easy, and there were only two of them, one skull-thumping drunk. Their chances might not get any better than this.

"Where is the human?" Sinta barked.

"Human?" Kegan whispered. The bounty hunter had

stretched out against the back wall, yellow eyes glaring from the shadows. If Kegan hadn't spoken, Deuc may have overlooked him.

"That's him, that's Kegan." The drunken bandit pointed, holding onto the caged chair for support.

Kegan? No! Deuc didn't think he could get any tenser, but it must have showed because Sinta stared him up and down and then back at Kegan.

"What are you? His star-wife or something?" Sinta scoffed.

"Why, you interested?" Deuc winked at him to draw some attention. It failed.

"If you're Kegan, you know where Hunter Dios is."

"Do I?"

Deuc gave Kegan credit, he didn't flinch.

"All the cables are chattering away. Your ship was the last to be seen with his on Hades."

"That's my ship, not his." Deuc snarled. Here it comes, he thought. The chains clinked as the Lestas crossed the distance.

"You're going to tell us where he is, and you're going to do it now." Three more Lestas entered through the hatch, one carrying an Arc gun, another clutching a replica xR6, expired tech from the Borders War. Nothing Deuc's shield couldn't handle. One Lestas approached the edge of the cell, his webbed fingers splayed across the steel struts.

Deuc heard mechanisms winding somewhere out of sight. The gate opened, the same time a panel of Perspex slid down from the ceiling, separating Deuc from the bounty hunter. He hammered his palms against the barrier to no effect. The Lestas snatched Kegan from the cell, his struggles and grunts echoed off the alloy surfaces, before Sinta levelled one punch to Kegan's cheek. For a moment, his yellow eyes flashed silver as his consciousness ebbed.

"Kegan!" Deuc shouted and golden eyes focused on him. Kegan stopped struggling as the Lestas strapped him into the chair.

CHAPTER 5

Hunter uncurled from his hiding spot amongst the waste valves. The last place a Raider would look for fortune is in another man's excrement tank. For some reason the filthy creatures had left, which allowed Hunter to peak into the cargo bay. They had done a half-assed job on stripping the *Arion*. Hunter knew jack shit about flying except, go, stop, and go Jump, yet he knew they had disabled the Jump drive first. Now he worked his way towards the vital tech where it sat in the middle of the dock and he would take a few calculated guesses on how to rewire it. As he crept forward, he spotted a dusty white transporter with grey decals. The *Venator*! Kegan Capare was here! Vaguely proud of his efforts to attract the greatest bounty hunter to chase his reward, he smiled. Was Kegan or whoever she was in league with these creatures? Either way, he had to leave, the girls depended on him.

Sinta pulled Kegan's shirt over his head and tossed it, the jangle of his Merc ID slid over the rusted floor. A sigh escaped Deuc's lips as he eyed the solid pectoral and biceps of the bounty hunter. Sinta paced out of view and Deuc heard the electro-plasma tendrils slither in an invisible wind of energy.

"Where is Hunter Dios?"

"You tell me," Kegan barked.

Sinta brought the weapon down across Kegan's shoulders, and he gasped. Deuc glimpsed the briefest flash of silver across yellow irises. Deuc's gaze darted top to bottom of the barrier, the reinforced Perspex would shatter but stay in place if he smashed it. A thick sense of dread sunk into his bones. With the next recoil of the whip, Deuc found his muscles winding tighter like a snare ready when the door would open. His nerves pumping acid as soon as they strapped the bounty hunter into the chair. On the third stroke, Sinta paused. The

Buzz had affected their aim and rather than neat stripes, the welts had crisscrossed, leaving a spider-web of blood adorning Kegan's skin. Inside his cell, the scent swamped Deuc, the metallic taste burned his throat. Kegan glared at Deuc through the wired cage and he held his eyes. He had failed to keep his word and now Kegan would pay for it. Deuc wedged his fingers between the joins in the Perspex, the material flexing but not breaking.

The moments dragged by and every time he watched Kegan's eyes color over in silver, he thought it would be the last. His breathing had become ragged and heavy and Deuc had to think fast. Soon that tanned skin would shine pearl, the black bob would blossom into chocolate silk and pectorals would revert to breasts. Hunter wasn't worth this? What was keeping Kegan going?

"We're running out of room." One Lestas chuckled.

"Pull him forward," Sinta said and the other reached for Kegan's belt loops.

"If you give me my ship back I'll tell you where he is," he said, his pitch higher than before.

Deuc blinked. How was that going to work?

"We don't bargain." Sinta nodded and the other tugged at the belt buckle.

"I don't know where he is but -" Kegan croaked. Deuc seized the moment.

"Kegan, don't. I won't tell them -" He said putting his back against the wall. That got their attention.

"So the Star-wife keeps the secrets!" Sinta's teeth chattered in his smile as he clicked over to the cell.

"Let him go." Deuc bit down on his fingernails and edged closer to the separating panel, the door still ajar.

Sinta wandered closer, his narrow eyes sizing up his new target. Sinta released the panel.

Deuc's fingers crashed around the tormentor's scaly throat, yanking forward, and the arteries and tendons came free with a sucking tear. Deuc let the body sag behind him.

Two steps took him to the chains, his skin a metallic shield against the electro-plasma tentacles that danced across his chest. He snatched the whip and slammed his hand on the opponent's shoulder, the bones cracked and snapped under the blow. He tightened his fingers and more blood and screams ensued. He released the Lestas and tugged loose the chains holding the bounty hunter. Kegan rolled to the ground, his feet collected the closest Raider, drunk and surprised by his speed, the Lestas had no defense to Kegan's punch to his throat.

Even Deuc paused as the marauder rolled on the ground choking under his crushed windpipe. Kegan regained his footing as Deuc advanced on the fourth Lestas who tried to make a break for it through the hatch. He let the whip slither through the air, coiling around the neck in a sizzle of crackling skin. Deuc ran his hand down the length of the vibrating blue strands and the Raider's head came off with a "pop".

Kegan had the last one down and subdued with the Arc gun. Deuc hammered the gun's hilt and sent the electric charged prongs into the Lestas' chest. Deuc stepped over the stiffening body and reached out to Kegan. Even with Deuc's epidermis singing like a struck gong he could feel Kegan's tension building and energy waning so he retracted his hand from his shoulder.

"Ready?" He grabbed at a blue-bar while Kegan hastily threw on his shirt. Kegan unraveled the electro whip and followed Deuc into the cargo bay.

Hunter had the Jump drive in and had gone back for the ion stabilizers, when the hatch door opened at the far end of the dock. His boots slid across the grimy surface. He turned and ran for the *Arion*, he stumbled and had to use his hands to keep momentum. Hunter scrambled up the rear ramp as boot steps shadowed his desperate escape.

"Wait Deuc – " Kegan said.

Hunter heard the shout behind him and glanced over his shoulder to see the bounty hunter in male form being dragged towards the black ship, by his other pursuer, the bronzed soldier.

"If the Lestas don't have him, he's probably transferred at INNA, we should back track."

"I agree, now get in!"

"My ship!" Kegan shouted.

"The *Arion* is faster!" The soldier hollered and began tossing parts into the rear. Hunter had to dodge the missiles as they clanged around him, "And in less pieces."

Kegan stumbled to a halt and took in the two ships that filled the Lestas cargo bay. Hunter tried to sink between the excrement tanks again, but curiosity got the better of him and he crept forward to watch the exchange. The bounty hunter was right. The Lestas had taken the *Arion*'s Jump drive, and the smaller electrical components, but the Etarian bird had drawn their eye faster. Etarian tech was naturally superior, or was there some other reason, that the black bird stayed reasonably untouched.

"Get the fuel cell boosters!"

"But -" The bounty hunter snatched at the numerous pieces that the Lestas had stripped from the Etarian ship.

"Leave it." Said the soldier, Kegan had called Deuc. Now the tall copper skinned man, sprinted to the numerous hatches. Hunter's jaw gaped as the Oddworlder twisted the steel handle into the jam. He moved onto the next as a thunder of noise brewed behind the sealed entrances. Hunter regarded the metal shelving struts, and turned one over in his palms as Lestas battled the now closed hatches.

The bounty hunter scooped up an odd-shaped box with wires and cables dangling from one end, "You have Shadow comms?"

"Faster!" The Osirian barked, his shoulder hooked under Kegan's arm and the two shuffled towards the *Arion*.

"Why my fucking ship!"

"Don't worry about it. Besides by the looks of it, you can buy a new one."

Hunter's stomach cemented into his toes, as Deuc's cold brown eyes held his. The bounty hunter clung to the taller man's shoulder, Kegan's yellow gaze tracked up the *Arion*'s ramp to where Hunter froze. He had nowhere to go.

Both pursuers, turned as a hatchway opened across the corridor and two raiders entered.

"Hey!" One raider squeaked, Deuc shoved Kegan forward and closed the distance, cutting the Lestas cry short with the blue-bar. The soldier stomped down and Hunter heard a crunch turn into a squish under the black boots. The second raider dashed through the hatchway from where he'd come. Deuc spun the handle to the locked position and snapped it off.

"Get it started!" He yelled at Hunter. The Osirian warrior attacked a control panel, the blue bar severed the wires and switches. Could Hunter run? The *Venator* sat across the cargo hold. In pieces! Another unbarred hatch opened and more Lestas poured into the cargo bay.

Hunter turned back to the *Arion*'s control panel and flicked every switch he could find. He'd take his chances with the Oddworlders than the Lizards. The bounty hunter limped into the cockpit alongside him. It had all been running when he'd procured it last time.

"Fuck! They've hardly touched this. Where's your weapon's Deuc?"

Hunter gaped at the blood red smears that soaked the dark fabric of her shirt. Kegan's shirt? No, hers.

"Far left panel, second from the bottom. I can't hear her purring!" Deuc shouted from somewhere behind, more parts clanged into the ramp, more bones crushed under foot.

"What's the damage?"

"Ah," Hunter twitched into action, "The systems look mostly intact just disabled, defense mechanism maybe?" Hunter said. A pair of yellow eyes bored into his skull.

"Shit!" Kegan plonked down in front of the weapons array, "Think of something, Hunter and make it quick!"

Hunter stared at the multitude of circuits and bulbs that intermittently flashed red, green and white. He scanned the symbols as fast as he could and discovered the shield system and transmitter system blinked steady. Hunter activated the shields, they'd probably need that soon. Then Hunter located the central patch transponder, now he had hacker-access to the Lestas outer door.

Aedan watched in awe as Deuc fought the Lestas hand to hand, well more like fist to throat combat, as she waited for the lasers to warm up. She hadn't registered her shift, only the spike in energy she gained added clarity. She accessed the ships targeting grid, the laser cannons that clung to each wing finally answered her ministrations on the joy sticks. The display illuminated in iridescent 3D shapes, as the software came on line.

Deuc caught a blade on his forearm, the edge found no purchase on his shielded skin, it glanced off and caught another Lestas cheek bone. Blood splashed across them both and Deuc collected the weapon from the dead. With speed and power he swung at the next, the Lestas sliced in half, until the third Raider fired an Arc gun into Deuc's face. His head snapped back with the force, but remained unharmed.

A mass of Lestas entered the far corridor and swarmed towards Deuc, just as the Laser jumped to life under Aedan's hands. She squeezed the trigger and the effect was devastating. The laser blasts cut through the Lestas as each round found chest or head. Limbs separated from torsos, the odor of reeking reptile, offal and blood reached her nostrils through the open cargo ramp. Aedan closed her mouth. Bile rose to the back of her throat and she closed her eyes against the massacre. When she opened them again, she saw Deuc a mess of blood and sweat as he rushed into the *Arion*.

Hunter heard the scrape of metal that signaled the outer door had responded to his hacker-commands. The *Arion*'s ramp sealed behind the soldier, who plonked into Second Chair.

"What's working?" The stench of his gore covered clothes made Hunter dry reach, he'd smelt that meaty piss and blood odor before. The soldier looked the part too, all the Lestas' insides where on the soldier's outside.

"The shields, environmental systems, oxygen, gravitational stabilizers."

"Good, now the bad?"

"Both drives, atmospheric engines, lasers -"

"Manual override only," Aedan added.

"Thrusters, ion stabilizers, trajectory mapping; the list goes on."

"Fuck. Jump drive?"

"Only just" Hunter answered as the vacuum of space pulled the *Arion* forward.

Aedan felt the ship slide underneath her, across the cargo bay, the *Venator* mirrored the movement, the sound of metal scraping against metal, pierced Aedan's ears. The parts that lay on the cargo bay floor rocketed towards the *Arion* like missiles without a target. As the outer doors opened wider, the *Venator* would soon be beyond Aedan's grasp. She stared at the dusty silver and white space craft that limped towards freedom, her home for the past five years. It contained everything she owned, despite the knick-knack memorabilia of a transient life, it also held all her clothes, weapons, her star-scape she'd spent so long on, all her Ketos and most importantly the transponder to Leta.

Nightmare images of the Lestas finding the Dual Systems Sanctuary scrolled through her mind. She had to protect Leta. As the tug of space intensified, Aedan trained the *Arion*'s lasers onto her home. Her forearms vibrated as the lasers pulsed, until the rounds penetrated the disabled shields. Metal shattered and splinted until finally her fuel cells ignited.

The explosion of the *Venator* sent a heat wave towards Aedan, eyes already watering, she blinked furiously at the sight. The flames forced the *Arion* backwards to the outer doors and space took over. Aedan clung to the narrow fold-away seat, until the *Arion* reached maximum velocity and the gravitational system equalized.

Aedan wiped her eyes with the back of her hands before she drew breath. Deuc regarded her condition and then Hunter's. Numb exhaustion crept into Aedan's spine as adrenaline vacated her muscles. She turned away from the rainbow luminesce of Hunter's eyes. Aedan rose from the weapons display and sunk into a bunk that doubled as an eatery behind the pilot and Second chair.

"I thought you said there was nothing valuable, Aedan? So you just sacrificed your ship for us?" Deuc bit down on wires and twisted others together. He flicked the thruster switches and redirected power from the muted sensors to gain some control over the disabled craft.

"You blew up your ship?" Hunter said. His eyes spun panicked orange and fearful grey into a whirlwind, with a tinge of blue. Aedan didn't know what sentiment blue represented. And she didn't have the energy to sift through any more emotions that wanted to play out in Hunters irises. She concentrated on the bridge of his nose, the aura muted.

"You better be worth it." Aedan said and threw her brown braid over her shoulder, the hairs snagged in open cuts.

As Deuc wired in another component, Aedan looked about at disjointed cabin, parts lay in disarray, the contents of Deuc's compartments emptied on the floor.

"Lestas' anti-theft system, it'll take a bit but we can get her back online."

She didn't get a chance to offer any assistance as a laser round flew past the ship's nose.

"You only slowed them down." Deuc jumped to the controls.

"What can we do? Your lasers aren't going to do anything to that seize-machine." Aedan returned to the jack-seat, the weapon joysticks back in hand.

"I know, Aedan." Deuc flicked the thrusters again, the *Arion* tilted heavily to the right.

Hunter swallowed hard, his eyes flicked between Aedan and Deuc and back to the weapons array, "I ah, I put the Jump drive back in." He tugged down the straps of his belt.

"You want to Jump back to Etaria?" Deuc stared at Hunter, brown eyes bored into rainbow and Aedan chewed her bottom lip. Did Hunter know a Jump Code? Of course he did, he Jumped the *Icarus III* from Haigon. But that was within the dual systems. Did he know a Galaxy Code? The Human shook his head.

"Not Etaria?" Aedan whispered.

"The trajectory mapping is still offline," Hunter said.

Deuc glanced down at the floor and then to Aedan. If Hunter input a Galaxy code, were they near enough to the AK Jump field that the interference would be minimalized? The surrounding radiation or magnetic energy wouldn't send them off course or into a black hole? Jumping only worked when you could plot your next Jump point, if they couldn't map the AK Jump field to a specific Galaxy Jump field, would only Ea himself be able to find them?

Another shot slid across their bow.

Would the Osirian tech even accept a Galaxy Code? After all, the AK Jump station lay within the Oddworlder border? As if he read her mind, Deuc spoke, "That Jump Drive was built in Osiria – "

"I can bypass the security protocols and input a code manually." Hunter said, "The Drive acts as a beacon when the gateways open – "

"Just jump!" Aedan snapped.

Hunter nodded. His hand grabbed the largest dial on the Jump Drive panel and pulled upwards, a low whine of expensive technology increased in pitch. Hunter thumbed the silver cogs into an unknown sequence; he struck the digits on the keypad. Aedan twisted in her chair to watch the magnificent tech restart and idle red lights suddenly switched to green.

Tiny strokes of light revolved around the dial until they were all illuminated. Deuc punched it down and the *Arion* filled with so much hot white radiance that Aedan's skin felt heated from within. The g-force slammed her into the back of the seat and her ears popped. The brightness faded to uncompromising darkness. Aedan lost all directional sense and her tongue choked her throat. If there was a way for a person to feel inside-out without dying, Aedan had felt it then. Suddenly the front windshield cleared to a shade of grey as light caught up to them, and the crescent hemisphere of a planet came into view.

"Is everyone alright?" Deuc's mouth worked out of sync as the *Arion* returned to normal speed.

"Your proximity alarms would probably be sounding, if they worked." Hunter said an icy blue giant pulled them in.

CHAPTER 6

"Yeah, she wants us." Deuc laughed as he pulled two levers from the arm rests of his chair and extend them to joysticks, "What's our speed?"

"Speed?" Hunter said, as he stared at the dials that moved in different directions.

"Move over," Aedan ordered. Her head spun but at least she could read the console. She shoved Hunter from the chair and pointed him to the seat at the weapon's display. Aedan managed to strap on the harness as the *Arion*'s nose dipped into the clouded atmosphere of the frozen planet.

Hunter's belt clicked closed. "You've got no power remember!"

"I can land her, it's just math, right?" Deuc said as he winked at Aedan.

"Land, can't you just orbit?" Hunter said.

"Too late, we're already falling. Speed?"

"We're at 3.2 clicks a second." Aedan answered Deuc.

"Too fast." Deuc kicked a pedal under the console, activating the air brakes.

The acrid air tore around the cabin, Aedan's harness buckle heated against her clenched abdomen, as the *Arion*'s slick nose cone glowed amber against the white atmosphere.

"Now hold on." Deuc said, another lever released the flaps.

He shifted each joystick and pitched the ship left and right. Aedan paled, gripping the arms rests till her knuckles burned. Hunter moaned behind them, and the sound of his stomach in turmoil took Aedan to her breaking point. Instead of the rolling horizon, Aedan tried to focus on the floor until the panels started shaking. Then she spotted Deuc's boots until she noticed they were covered in caking slime. She moved her gaze upwards and locked on to Deuc's forearms, tanned and tense.

The serpent like tendons recoiled under the skin ready to strike.

Through clenched jaws he asked, "Speed?"

"2.8" Aedan read.

"Angle?"

"Umm..."A black compass rolled and bobbed like Aedan's stomach, "17 degrees, sort of."

"Looking good then," Deuc released the controls and let the *Arion* level out.

As the ship broke through white clouds, Aedan took her first look at the foreign planet. Three dark bands crossed the surface, pale blue ice covered the top half of the hemisphere before it passed through a thin strip of mottled green on its way to a dark grey ocean.

"Are those towers?" Aedan asked.

"Ah Reactors," Hunter said.

Aedan's eyes followed his arm to the left.

"Try to land close but not too close. If there's food it will be where the air is sweet," Hunter said, he took his eyes off the scenery and scanned the others. Aedan didn't respond. Deuc just nodded.

The *Arion* swam through the atmosphere banking left and right shaving off speed as it went. Like a crack that tore the hemisphere in half, two rows of reactors had been spaced along the pale ice. Ice caps receded against one side of the reactors and greenery peeked out from under the other. From this height, the flora extended for a narrow strip before it struck the ocean. As they descended, the *Arion* glided over the green belt and followed it east along the continent. A boiling cloud of gas erupted on the horizon as they approached.

Aedan signaled to the others, "What's that?"

"A Landscaper," Hunter answered.

"Landscaper?" Deuc banked to the right to avoid the mountainous cloud of gas, and ice.

"Yeah," his voice grew in confidence, "they're mega-machines, completely automated landscape perfectors. They cut and chop the land to create variations to support life."

"You mean Etarian life?" Deuc snarled.

"Exclusively," Hunter's voice heated as he spoke. A brief flash of red sparkled in his eyes. The Osirian warrior registered Hunter's tone and gave him a curt nod. Aedan turned back to the scenery taking in the flat grey ocean.

"There's no waves?" She leaned over as the *Arion* hit a bump of turbulence.

"There's unlikely to be trees yet either, probably phase 2 of the terraforming. I'd land on the snow if you can." Hunter said, "That greenery is probably just algae floating on the ocean's surface or near to it."

"Well we don't want to get her wet, do we?" Deuc scoffed and steered further to the left.

Another bump of turbulence and the seat belts cut into Aedan's skin. The sensation of the chair rubbing still open wounds, reminded Aedan of the Lestas' cage. She gritted her teeth and shifted forward. The turbulence bounced the *Arion* again and this time didn't stop.

Deuc yanked on the joysticks and lowered another set of flaps, "Hold on."

The white snow obscured the distance to the surface and the clouds thickened as they descended. In the next break in the clouds, the ground rushed forward. Deuc swore as the *Arion* struck the ice and the force slammed Aedan back and down into her chair. She managed a single breath before the belly scraped the surface. The white clouds spun in front of the windshield. Aedan's groans were swallowed by the crackling and screeching of metal, as the ship slid across the surface. Mountains of white covered the windshield and a metallic squeal erupted in Aedan's ears as the hull collided with ice and rock. The steel plated floor and plastic molded walls shuddered, items fell from their holdings.

The *Arion*'s nose, peaked upwards slightly and Aedan braced herself for the pending fall. It never came. Aedan blinked at the debris, the interior panels that hung loose, lights that blinked. Thank Ea or Erebus or even Chaos that they were alive. The environmental systems appeared in working orders as the oxygen generator clunked into action. Aedan inhaled slowly and reached for her buckle. Deuc's belt clicked loose, his hands snatched at Hunter and the fugitive stood upwards, with sharp winces and huffs. A rib or two the likely culprit of Hunter's discomfort.

Aedan's fingers clawed at her clasp, "It said, dead or alive, and I mean to keep him alive," She screeched. Her hand slapped on Deuc's upper arm, the bronzed giant paused.

Deuc clenched his jaw, and his fingers released, "He's no good to me dead either. Are you hurt Dios?"

Hunter shuffled to a healthy distance from both of them, feet stumbled over debris, "I'm alright I think."

"Good." Aedan took a step backwards.

"*Laelaps*, it's my ship."

"Yeah, sorry about that." Hunter chirped as his breathing steadied.

"Don't mention it." For a moment Aedan thought he said it in jest, but Deuc's eyes never moved, "So it's my ship, my rules." Deuc took a step forward. Hunter's back straightened.

Aedan swallowed hard and tried to shake out her tired muscles. Was Deuc going to challenge her for the bounty? She bent her knees and sunk her hips, her hand inched closer to her boot.

"Yeah. Get the knife." Deuc said as he lifted his chin and arched one eyebrow.

Aedan froze. Her back began to sting and then burn. Adrenaline rushed out of her system and her legs quaked. Hunter turned towards Aedan. When had she released Kegan? Here she stood in her natural form before these two men, one tiny knife the sum total of her arsenal.

"Wait," Hunter snapped.

"What?" Deuc snarled.

"You're not going to fight here and now are you?" Hunter turned himself in front of Deuc, his back towards Aedan.

Deuc smirked and crossed his arms, "Do you think you could stop me?"

"I don't have to stop you, just slow you down." Hunter spread his arms wide and planted his feet.

Masculine flavors thickened at the back of Aedan's throat, the scent of her own blood stung her nostrils. Why was her mark defending her?

"Nice move. But you're both wrong." Deuc hung his arms by his sides, "Give me the knife."

"No. Not ever." Aedan laughed, her eyesight fuzzed at the edges and her feet tingled. She regarded the confines of the cabin.

"You're bleeding all over my ship."

"No."

"You're getting worse. Hunter help her." Deuc ordered.

The captive caught Aedan as she stumbled. The weight of her fall and Hunter's injury sent them both to the deck. Deuc's image doubled and swam as the soldier stood above them.

Hunter snatched the knife from Aedan's hands, "Stand back."

Deuc's forearm pushed forward, the blade bit, the blood trickled down his copper skin and splashed onto the metal gangway. As the red liquid flowed, it ebbed and then abruptly stopped. The surface of Deuc's arm constricted and the wound closed.

Deuc smirked, "Like I said, you're both wrong. Want me to fix your back Aedan?"

Aedan sat on a circular bunk in the only bedroom at the back of the ship. Her legs folded, on unwashed beige linen as she let Deuc peel away what was left of her shirt. She held the knife, as agreed, while he skimmed two fingertips across the blade. Deuc's blood burst forth from the slash and Aedan presented her back to his ministrations. The fuzziness in Aedan's brain helped keep the darkness from closing in as Deuc's fingers made contact. Slick heat spread forth as he traced each stroke the electro-plasma whip had laid across her skin. At each slippery caress the edges of her wounds began to pull together, leaving an echo of warmth in its wake.

"They did a good job."

Aedan's eyes closed. She could hear Hunter's pacing under the sill of the poly-spec door.

"So did you," Deuc whispered.

A tingling sensation swept down her back and into her abdomen.

"And you." Aedan smiled, as the warmth spread through her chest. The man had carved through Lestas with unimaginable strength and speed.

Aedan felt Deuc's weight lean forward on the bunk and her eyes slammed open. Deuc sliced his fingers on the knife again and returned to healing her injuries. The fog cleared from Aedan's mind as Deuc began to trail down to the lower cuts and skimmed her hips. She took a long slow breath and clenched the knife.

"Almost done and then we can bargain."

"I heard that!" Hunter shouted.

Deuc rifled through a pile of clothes at one end of the room and retrieved a clean black singlet and shirt. Aedan pressed the blood soaked shirt into her chest, elbows tucked, chin defiant. She hadn't the strength to call on Kegan.

"Here." Deuc tossed the fresh clothing to Aedan and opened the door. "See, she's alive," Deuc pushed Hunter's shoulder and closed the door leaving Aedan to dress.

Aedan glanced around the room. Each corner was filled with something. Clothes, dirty and clean by the looks of it, clustered in one. Another held an impressive pulse long arm, locked in a display casing, the trigger locked with a fingerprint barricade. In the third corner a small chest had tumbled open, the contents strewn across the deck. Aedan pulled on her shirt, surprised at the ease of her movement and wandered to the chest. Her boot struck metal. She picked up a tiny Digi-frame, her finger automatically powered the screen.

She scrolled through the images, the first a holographic medal. She touched it again and the medal illuminated with the words, "Valor". The next medal image shone with the inscription "313 TCK" and then flashed "in less than 5 minutes". She scrolled again. An image of 5 people sitting on a set of stairs, arms around each other emerged. Positioned in the center back was Deuc, a dark haired girl on his left and a tall ruddy skinned guy to the right. He had the same size as Deuc, but older. In the front row a red haired girl smiled back at Deuc and another guy with spiky blue hair grasped the girl's knee. They all looked in their late teens and wore black military clothing.

Didn't Deuc say he lived on Asar? Nothing about this image told Aedan that it represented life on Asar. For starters both girls were smiling and without chains. They appeared happy and free. The stairs behind seemed polished timber and the bannister had gold lining. The males even had a carefree look about their disposition. Aedan didn't have time to scroll further as footfalls approached the doorway. She tapped the Digi-frame off and tossed it onto the bunk.

The door zipped open to Hunter's worried look. He'd taken off his fawn colored jacket and the remaining plain blue shirt and denim jeans accentuated his civilian status.

"He said if I didn't believe him to check on you."

Aedan focused on the grey and lilac swirls in his gaze. Not one bit of oil slick could be seen, so she knew Hunter's concern was legitimate. Was it chivalry or something else that influenced his concern? After all he was supposed to be her captive.

"Yeah I'm fine. Thanks." She pondered her predicament as she returned to the bridge of the *Arion*. She was trapped on this icy giant with her bounty and an Oddworlder. Negotiations would need to occur to ensure she made it out alive. She paused as she entered the cabin, some cupboards had snapped from the bulkheads depositing their contents across the deck, the windshield obscured with a sheet of white, and clustered wires hung torn from their casings.

"I told him to trust me," Deuc snorted, his boots and arms

crossed as he reclined in a chair.

"Yeah right," Aedan sneered.

"I could have left you with the lizards."

"So could have I."

Deuc spread his arms out palm upwards, "And yet here we are."

Aedan leaned against a narrow bench, supposedly used as the galley, a tiny cooker buried in its surface. She cocked her head to one side, hoping for any color change in Deuc's deep umber eyes. Zero.

"Here we all are." Hunter added and leaned back, one foot rested against the wall.

Standard Etarian fashion shoes for a male, canvas fabric, white rubber sole, nothing about Hunter screamed military. Then why the five trillion Ketos reward? Aedan regarded Hunter's eyes and caught a flash of peach and white revolving into gusts of violet and blue. When Hunter turned his attention to Deuc, a storm of greys and oranges brewed with cyan and green. Green appeared to indicate envy and Aedan's memory kicked in.

"What's the green?" Aedan asked.

"Pardon?" Hunter straightened his back.

"What was the green, algae or something - where are we?" Aedan covered.

"If you're talking about this planet, I think Hunter's the man to tell you." Deuc said.

"We Jumped to the Theia solar system which is outside of the Gaia Galaxy."

"What?" Aedan's knees moved to the narrow bunk that rested behind the pilot chairs. Her stomach quivered as she gripped the threadbare fabric between her knuckles. The cabin air suddenly chilled her bones and it had nothing to do with the falling snow. She thought back to her star-scape, what constellation held the Theia solar system?

"Yeah, keep going Hunter."

"You may get a bit of Jump-lag soon too, if you've never

Jumped before. The further you go the worse it is and the longer you take to recover. This is a low gravity world so we should bounce back in as little as an hour or so. Trick is; you never know when it's going to hit."

"You used a Universe Jump code?" Aedan finally spoke.

"Question is what are the Etarian's doing terraforming here?" Deuc hit the nail dead center.

Hunter swallowed hard before answering, "They harvest from lots of....I mean...I'm not sure."

"So we have low gravity, what about oxygen?" Aedan said

Deuc tapped his keyboard, "No sensor's yet."

"Judging by the algae, there might be some, but not a lot." Hunter walked forward to the snow covered windshield.

"Food?" Aedan asked.

"Maybe, in the ocean." Hunter said.

"I have emergency supplies that could keep us going for five maybe six days, unless the Lestas got them?" Deuc turned to Hunter.

"No, they didn't get that far. Caught the *Venator* and then started getting drunk."

Aedan tensed. With impenetrable skin and self-rejuvenation, Aedan pondered how safely Deuc had meant to land his ship. Surely he would have survived the crash regardless. "Will anyone know we've landed here?" she asked.

"I don't think so. The landscapers and reactors are automated. Unless one of them stops, there's no reason for anyone to come here." Hunter said.

"How do you know all this?" Aedan asked.

"It was part of my training." A flash of red spiked in his eyes with the slightest covering of oil. So Hunter was keeping secrets.

"You're angry at them?" Aedan clucked her tongue when she heard her words out loud, but it was too late.

Hunter glared at her in shocked surprise. The cabin air suddenly felt stuffy with heated bodies. Aedan's cheeks colored. Deuc uncrossed his arms.

"What do we do now?" Hunter changed the subject.

"And that is where we come to an impasse." Deuc turned his chair to the others. Aedan saw his skin flinch and tighten.

"You want to bargain?" Aedan said, stacking the vertebrae in her spine.

"Not like an Etarian Bargain, *Laelaps*." Deuc said.

Hunter retreated to neutral space until his back struck the cooktop, loose cables swung about his head, "Neither of you want me dead."

"I want my five trillion Ketos reward first." Aedan levelled.

"It was 65/35 split, but now I'm thinking 50/50."

"65 was the deal."

"Fine, I'll take my 35 percent and the Jump codes." Deuc turned to Hunter and added, "All of them, System, Galaxia, Universal. Every one you know."

In Hunter's eyes, Aedan saw a burst of white shine forth from an ocean of orange. Wait. Those tangerine swirls meant to represent panic and yet he had hope?

A wry grin pealed back over Hunter's perfectly even teeth, "Deal."

"Deal?" They exclaimed together.

"Deal."

CHAPTER 7

"You know he's an Oddworlder – you know what he'll do with those codes?"

"Oh, is that how it is?" Deuc said, he covered the distance to Aedan in three strides, "To you, the Etarians are entitled to whatever they like, and get fat and rich in the process while us Osirians get the scraps from their tables? You're nothing to them, what do you care?"

"I can just imagine these Worlds in a decade or two, Oddworlders exhausting all resources, infectious corruption multiplying," Aedan countered, "Look how well you take care of the ones you've got." She stood in the middle of the deck, fists by her thighs.

"The Osirian's inherited that shit from your god-like Etarians. You're so fucking naïve, Aedan!"

Aedan drew in a sharp breath, "Naïve? I know that you're a shining example of the kind of filth that breeds in those worlds." She measured her voice as her cheeks heated.

Hunter coughed harshly in the corner.

"Perfect, cause you're Osirian too, remember."

"I'm…"

"Yeah?" Deuc taunted, "- and this despicable Oddworlder just saved you."

The air raced out of her chest as the weight of her words slammed into her. The fluffy snow behind the bronzed soldier contrasted his disposition and Aedan let her eyes wander over the sharp planes of his cheeks and the dark brows framing his eyes. A bitter taste crept up the back of Aedan's throat and she fought the urge to swallow.

"How does that taste, *Laelaps*?" Deuc snorted and returned to his seat, "I want the jump codes and I'm not letting you cash him in until I have them". Even at recline the Oddworlder dominated the room.

"I'll give them to you," Hunter said as he placed a hand gently on Aedan's arm, "I'll give you all the ones I know."

Deuc's lips curled and inflicted dimples in his cheeks.

"And what about me?" Aedan began, "What about that reward? You're just going to let me take you back, I suppose." Aedan's throat began to constrict. A strange smell entered her nostrils, thick and slimy it trickled down into her stomach.

"I'll walk myself to the gates of Kronos if you like." Hunter tilted his head, a strand the color of wet sand fell across his narrow nose. Sculptured arms crossed over his abdomen, and instead Aedan focused on his blue eyes. Not one hint of oil, and definitely no fear.

"Multiple homicide, you're facing an injection of Francium," Deuc added.

"I know," Hunter said.

"Why?" Aedan whispered. She blinked twice, her eyelids scratching like sandpaper.

"Because I want something and you're both going to help me get it," Hunter said.

"Bullshit, no offence man, but I don't believe you." Deuc chuckled.

"No, he's not lying – " Aedan paused and looked away, a shimmer of images cascaded across her vision.

"Why should I believe you?" Deuc's deep voice strummed the words into a challenge. His cheeks all harsh angles and jaw clenched.

Whatever situation Aedan found herself in, she'd have to work all the possible angles. Deuc demanded her trust, but so far he hadn't earned it. He'd healed her injured back, when he could have let her suffer. But he doubted her and with good reason. With Hunter's immense price tag cashing him in would prove difficult. Deuc's abilities would more than likely come in handy, and she'd still be left with a hefty purse of Ketos. She could buy a small fleet of ships. A steady stream of income for Leta and put Calder Vien out of business once and for all.

"You said you wanted to bargain Deuc, go on Hunter, what do you want?" Why did her fingers hurt? Aedan felt the inside of her cheeks plump up and her words rushed out in a garbled mess, "What's happening?"

Instantly Deuc and Hunter caught her elbows, as Aedan lifted her swollen hands to her stinging face.

"Jump-lag," Hunter whispered.

"No!" Aedan wailed. Not now!

Deuc shook his head, and rapped knuckles on his temples, "Shit!" he pressed his palms into his eyes and spat on the floor, Deuc slipped out of sight. Aedan heard metal bouncing off metal.

"You both need to rest, lie down if you can."

"Help me carry her to the bed."

Aedan heard the thick words snag in Deuc's throat, and Hunter started to object as Aedan's knees gave way. She peeled back grizzly lids and stared at the steel floor now pressed to her cheek. A slab of panic punched her in the gut. Deuc moaned somewhere behind her. If only he could stay as incapacitated as long as she would be, how long did Hunter say, an hour?

Thin blades of steel dug into Aedan's hip, a blanket tickled her nose, splashes of white snowflakes blossomed into scaly Lestas and Aedan opened her eyes. She had to blink several times before the room stopped spinning and she turned slowly onto her back, easing the throb her belt buckle impressed upon her abdomen. Aedan's heart thundered, she tensed assessing her body for any lingering injures. None. A familiar scent surrounded Aedan and as she stretched into the chilly air, warmth leached from her limbs. She retracted back under the blanket and snuggled deep, pressing her face into the pillow, a mix of sweet sylvan, cinnamon and citrus teased her senses. Aedan caught sight of the small Digi-frame, a pile of dirty clothes, and the secured pulse rifle. Deuc's bed. A spike of irritation rushed into her blood. As if he'd heard her thoughts, the door opened and he sauntered inside, beads of moisture sparkled on polished amber.

"You'll feel better after a shower." He tossed a towel on the end of the bed and readjusted the one around his waist.

Aedan closed her eyes as he shucked on a fresh pair of pants. Soft murmurs of clothing reached her ears and she dared take a peek. Bare chested he watched Aedan stir from her Jump-lag coma, her eyes darted around the small cabin.

He zipped up his fly, "Time to bargain." Deuc added as he scooped up a singlet.

Aedan dragged her lead laden legs to the shower and relished the warm clean water that drenched and refreshed. After dressing, Aedan entered the main cabin. Hunger exploded in her stomach and her limbs shivered with energy depletion that recovery had stolen. How long had she been left to sleep? What in the name of Erebus had she gotten herself into and how could she get out?

"Sleep, water, food, fixes any lasting effects." Hunter greeted her in the main cabin with Teetas. The dusty carbohydrate staple totally devoid of toppings.

Curses formed on her parched lips and she pushed them aside as the captive handed her a water filled jug.

Deuc pushed a jar of brown gloop into her hands, "Saved you some."

Protein paste, "Thanks," she said.

Mentally Aedan chided herself for her ungrateful attitude, despite both men's attentiveness, one was an iniquitous brutish corrupt individual, and the other a homicidal fugitive. She regarded Hunter's emotive aural display, did he really slaughter seven people? Could there be one Oddworlder with a shred of decency? Deuc devoured another Teeta, the crumbs tumbled down the black fabric that stretched tight across his chest. He winked. No. Did Hunter make a pact?

"How long was I out for?" She asked.

"Two hours. A big jump for you." The fugitive replied.

"And him?" Aedan gestured with her chin to Deuc.

"Just over an hour, *Laelaps*."

"Am I supposed to know what that means?"

"Don't you know any Osirian culture?"

"I know enough Deuc," Aedan said. What she did know was how considerably behind she was in the negotiating stakes. Wires and components spread across the metallic floor, tools haphazardly jumbled in the mess, "And you?"

"Twenty-five. I went down for an hour last time, I woke up and that seize-machine was pulling me in. Don't feel too bad, you were injured. You had a lot to recover from." Hunter said. Clearly the air had affected the captive too, as he'd redressed in his fawn colored jacket. The preserved animalistic odor permeated the cabin.

"You could have run?"

Hunter gestured with his lunch to the whitewashed windshield, "Where to?"

"He still hasn't put the oxygen sensors in yet." Deuc kicked a square plastic tub with his boot, now free from the thick coating of Lestas' innards.

Aedan pushed the thoughts from her mind as she spread the protein paste along her thin crust of puffed carbs, the brown gritty staple reeked of fish, "You're getting along like two Pie-eaters in a Tank."

Deuc gulped down a glass of yellow additive-riddled water, "Language Aedan. Don't worry, Hunter wouldn't deal until you could bring something to the table."

"Why?"

"I'll need your help. Both of you."

Aedan rested back against the bunk, took a bite of her breakfast and turned her full attention to Hunter's eyes. It seemed another rainbow exploded across his features before he started to speak.

"When I left Haigon, I was trying to escape."

"Yeah, I get that." Deuc sighed.

"I was trying to escape with two others. I want to go back for them."

"You'd better just give me the codes and let her kill you."

"Why?" Aedan asked, "Who are they?"

His eyes hinted at bursts of white through azure. "They're friends of my sisters."

"Not enough information for me to change my mind, Dios." Deuc said.

"They're humans, like me, and they'll die in the hands of Etarians."

"Are you going to sell them?"

"Ea no!" Hunter barked at Deuc.

"Wait, what?" Aedan said, remembering something the Lestas had said. They had asked where Dios was, they knew he was human, Aedan thought. Her gaze stripped over his frame, the jacket was real leather. A slice of pain cut through the fog. "The Lestas, they knew, wait, I have a headache."

"It'll pass," Deuc handed her a jug of his mineral laden water, "That explains the high price tag. I thought the Lestas were going to torture you for the Jump codes, imagine the damage they could do if they got through the gates," Deuc paused to glare at Aedan, "But they knew you were human, that's a different story all together."

"What's....?"

"A human?" Hunter answered Aedan, "They're genetic building blocks of the universe. The Etarians are getting ready to test the others, for genetic deficiencies. If they fail, they'll be killed, like my sister, Juliette."

"And if they pass?" Deuc queried.

"They'll be used up and eventually destroyed. There is no alternative," Hunter said.

Aedan searched for a hint of oil, and saw nothing but red and white crashing into each other, crimson waves of anger blended with hope. Aedan noted the difference, Hunter's skin flushed warm unlike the washed out rubbery Etarian natives. His natural physic more substantial and grounded compared to the slender and ethereal Etarian race or the hard lines of Osirians. Was it a behavioral trait of his species that made him behave so strangely, chivalrous and trusting, hesitant yet flippant. What did these others look like?

"And that's why you were meeting, someone, the Eagle, they were supposed to help you?" Aedan said and earned another scoff from Deuc.

"Good choice."

Aedan sighed, "What now, Deuc?"

The Administrator put his hands behind his neck, "The Eagle is a Rebel."

"A Rebel? I didn't know, I never met them, they just promised to get us out."

As the men talked, Aedan felt her gut clench. The Rebels almost had a hold on Hunter. Deuc as an Administrator now had his hooks in. The five Trillion Ketos price tag had already been whittled down to a percentage. Her future life in Etaria, a life that would be safe and beyond the long reach of the shadows that plagued her mind, was now slipping away. Aedan felt the cool steel of her knife against her inner calf. Her body tensed, and suddenly Deuc's cheeks flattened. His brows dipped. Aedan's fingers itched to retrieve her weapon but against Deuc it was useless. She regarded Hunter's throat that bobbed as he spoke. Within seconds she could have her knife on the precipice. Liquid heat revolved inside her, the Human was hers and she'd be damned if this Oddworlder would steal her chance at freedom. Deuc shifted in his seat, one boot heel raised, the other slightly forward. His eyes glued to Aedan's. Aedan brought her knee up, her boot flat against the wall, her blade within easy reach. Deuc's fingers spread, his palms slid across his knees. Aedan dug her thumbs into the top of her boot and tugged the multi buckled footwear upwards as if adjusting for comfort.

"He's my bounty, so you better start explaining. The codes die with him."

"Aedan," Hunter stuttered, "Relax. Like it or not," his breathes deep and slow, "We're stuck here, for now. I need you. I need him. You both need me."

"We go from one trust exercise to the next with you don't we? We're just talking." Deuc's brown eyes targeted hers, voice feather-soft like the dark lashes that brushed his cheeks.

Aedan's thumb stroked the top of her hilt. With one move she could take Deuc's jump codes out from under him. Hunter's eyes spied Aedan's movements, perspiration broke out across his forehead and he tugged down his blonde fringe.

He put his palms up to Aedan, "I'll explain what I mean but just don't -" He ruffled his jacket sleeves up to his elbows.

Aedan glared at Deuc, his hands rested loosely in his lap, one militant boot flat, the other heel raised. What would her trust cost? Deuc had saved her hide. He didn't have to. He could have let her strength wane, jettison her from the cargo hold. Hunter the same, he could have already made a pact with the Oddworlder and leave her marooned in the Theia system. Aedan closed her eyes for a second, "He's my bounty."

Deuc moved like a feline reclaiming it's kill, his fist closed tightly on her wrist. Aedan met his gaze, but refused to release her grip.

Hunter's eyes flew wide as he took in the twisted pair, "Fucking instinctive Osirians. Give me time to explain."

Deuc's grip gently increased in pressure, but Aedan re-sisted. They moved as one, extracting her hand from her boot. A deep rumble erupted from Deuc, "Slick," He said as he relaxed his grip but didn't let go of her forearm. "We need to set down some new rules. Aedan and I have already set down the terms of our arrangement but not you Dios." Deuc's other hand lay palm up until he brought Aedan's knife out of her boot. Hunter gasped in unison with Aedan, as Deuc tucked the weapon into her belt.

"Rules," Aedan barked, tugging backwards, accidentally drawing the Oddworlder closer.

"Hunters right, we're in this together until we get the *Arion* back into space." Deuc dipped his lips to her ear, "Aedan relax and trust me," Goosebumps multiplied as Deuc's warm breath licked her cheek, he released her arm and cleared his throat.

"No one benefits if we're trying to slice and dice each other."

"I'm being honest, Aedan," Hunter said, "I need your help." Waves of slate, snow and teal tinted his iris, his blonde fringe flicked across his nose.

Aedan rolled her neck from side to side until something cracked, "Fine, go on."

"Everyone keeps their hands to themselves. We can listen to the rest of your terms Hunter while we're fixing my bird."

Before Hunter could continue, the *Arion* trembled under their boots.

"What was that?"

Hunter pointed behind Aedan to the shuddering windshield. A sheet of white powder cracked and bounced away revealing a storm of steam and snow, "Landscaper."

The gigantic structure masticated the surface in front of their eyes, simultaneously creating a mountain range and valley system in one swift churn. Brackets of steam wafted skyward, chunks of wayward rock hurtled their direction. The mega-machine was on a collision course with the *Arion*.

"How long?" Deuc asked.

Hunter's cheeks paled, "Ten maybe twelve minutes."

CHAPTER 8

Deuc looked from the sensor calibrator on the floor, to the thruster wires that dangled from the dash, "Twelve minutes?"

"Ten even, what do you think?" The Human scooped up the sensor.

Deuc regarded his emergency supplies. The Lestas had helped themselves to the air regulators.

"Do it! I'll try the thrusters." Deuc pointed to the bounty hunter, "You get the power sorted."

Boots stampeded down to the belly of the *Arion*, brown braid swinging above the belt line of narrow hips. Deuc's teeth dragged across plastic, and he twisted frantically on each copper thread of conduit. The cold steel floor vibrated against his back, the components above shook violently in the console. Lucky the Lestas knew what they were looking at when they seized the *Arion* otherwise his black bird would be in more pieces. Hunter cursed, the sensor bounced from the rear wall panel to the bunk, rolling to strike Deuc's boot.

"Get it together Dios."

"Fix the thrusters and I won't have to!" Hunter wiped a sweaty palm down his thigh. Deuc snorted. So the Human had a backbone.

Aedan shouted in a small but clear voice, "Power coils?"

Deuc smacked his head on the console, the pain ignorable as the ceiling panels fluttered in the tremors, "They're there!" A long breath escaped through Deuc's teeth, a screwdriver slipped through his fingers and clattered away before he retrieved it.

"Five." Hunter shouted.

The escalating roar inside the *Arion*'s shaking cabin told Deuc enough, "No time!"

"We don't know if we'll survive out there!"

Deuc wriggled free from the console, "We take our chances out there or be juiced in here."

Hunter's eyes darted around the cabin, "If only we could increase our chances."

"I don't want to leave her but we've got no choice."

"Aedan?"

"The *Arion*!" Deuc snapped just as the bounty hunter dashed up the stairs two at a time.

She held a blue cell in one hand, "Give me that!" She tore the sensor from Hunter.

The Landscaper's bellow drowned out the quaking floor, its blade slicing through acres of land at a time, shunting the residue to one side, an instant mountain range. Deuc's heart assaulted his rib cage.

Aedan jammed one cord into the cell and snatched Deuc's screwdriver, burying the tip into the top panel, "Open the door."

Deuc obeyed and Aedan threw a switch. Glacial gusts blustered into the cabin as Aedan tossed the blinking electronic into the snow; it bounced twice before it settled.

"How do we know – "

"Blue we're good." Deuc's eyes burned into his skull.

"And if it's not – "

Visions of fish beached along the banks of the River Gauntlet popped into Deuc's head, "Just run Hunter."

The *Arion* fell into shadow. Aedan bounced to Deuc's side and Hunter held onto the bulkhead. Deuc threw up his shield.

Blink. Blink. Blue.

The funnel of snow enveloped Deuc; the wind buffeted him backwards as ice crunched underfoot. The low gravity allowed more and more ground to fly underfoot and increased Deuc's distance from the encroaching destroyer. In his peripherals Hunter sprinted to his left, each stride ate away at the distance. Hunter's tan jacket turned russet with the blizzard. Where was Aedan? A scream rent the air.

Aedan's hands touched the solid silver floor of her prison cell. An icy haze fell upon her shoulders, eyes swollen. She'd already had Jump-lag! A strong acrid odor of chemicals and curing meat stirred in her nostrils. The chill of the structure tore up her forearms, strength faded along with Aedan's comprehension. The blue electro-plasma bars sizzled in the atmosphere, as a hailstorm of boots approached.

"There she is." The disembodied words drifted through the bars and stung her heart. Throat tight, legs jelly, Aedan raised her eyes.

Beyond the violent blue, shimmered silhouettes of men, tall, uniformed, hungry.

"No!" The sound crisp to Aedan's ears but filtered through snow.

"Aedan?"

"Who's first?" One man asked, his grey glove reached for the release panel.

"Aedan!"

Bile rose and fell, fingers clawed at her ankles. The knife where was it? They took it of course, Aedan's back struck steel.

Flat Teetas and protein paste surged forward and splashed onto snow not steel.

"Aedan!"

An oil slick of images sped past Aedan's eyes, perforated by bursts of Deuc. The molten vision became transparent and faded all together as the Landscaper pounded to a halt. The sleet parted to reveal Hunter who paced with his head in his hands.

Hunter's boots waded through the thick smear of blood, the two girls' lifeless bodies, arms crisscrossed, lay on the specimen tables. The height of the room lost in darkness as a spotlight illuminated the horror. Decanters and swabs littered the benches, the stench of the innards too much. Hunter retched onto the snow. An icy gust turned tears to ice crystals that pierced his cheeks. The dimly lit room ebbed, the vision pock marked by windows to a blizzard.

"Aedan," the deep timbre, instantly identified as the warrior's voice.

Hunter's eyes widened to find the Landscaper stationery, a plume of steam rising from the top. His knees wobbled as he stood, the machine's shadow eclipsed their position and stretched towards a blanket of floating emerald; the ocean?

Deuc watched both parties come to their senses, and his curiosity peaked. He let his guard slip for a moment.

Like a glass slate had been pulled across his eyes, Deuc stood on a mountain of ash, bleached white skulls submerged in the cinders. He held something soft. The horizon ablaze, city structures crumbling and the sky blackened with atomic poison.

Deuc solidified his skin and the image vanished.

"Are you alright Hunter?" The quiver in Aedan's voice tugged gently on something inside Deuc. He could guess what vision she had faced, yet her voice dripped with concern for the Human.

"I was too late."

Aedan gasped, her hand paused on Hunter's shoulder.

Deuc watched the duo's chests rise and fall while he'd hardly cracked a sweat. At least they were alive. "It's not real. It's the air making you hallucinate."

"What is it?" Aedan said.

"The gases in the air maybe, some kind of compound. Without the sensors it's guesswork." Deuc tore his gaze away deciding to stare at the rippling surface of the ocean, rather than the pair in close proximity.

The bounty hunter came to rest beside Deuc as she rubbed her upper arms, "Look!"

All three regarded the air around them that suddenly cleared. The Landscaper's output had created a barrier of breathable air. Half a click across the shimmering water, the fog thickened, the view distorted as the noxious gases swirled beyond their oxygen buffer.

Hunter coughed, "The Landscaper is a Cryo-distiller making breathable atmosphere as it goes. See the steam."

They pivoted to take in the massive structure that dominated the scenery. The domed peak barely visible in the fluffy clouds above, heavy track laden cogs moved it forward and giant solar panels for power. The drab taupe shielding emblazoned with three cyan stripes enclosed in a circle, the Etarian System logo. Paused mid-cycle the blade was buried in the earth while the black *Arion* rested at its base, a tiny blot against the snow.

"Why did it stop?"

"I don't know – unless..."

"Unless what?" The wind pushed Deuc's cuff against his ankle and he shook his boot.

"I guess, the Landscaper is designed to recognize life," Hunter said.

Aedan grabbed Hunter's elbow, "What are you talking about?"

"Can it do that?" Deuc said, shaking his boot again. Heat infused into his ankle.

"It would make sense, the Etarians always have countermeasures. They must have factored in an emergency protocol; they wouldn't want their repairers stuck out here with no assistance." Hunter continued.

"So it's transmitting information? An emergency signal!"

"Oh hell! You're right Aedan; it'll be transmitting our location to the Etarians!" Hunter spat.

"How long will it take for them to get here?" Irritated at the building sting, Deuc pulled his leg forward, and found a pressure wrapped around his ankle, "Hey!" Suddenly he ate snow, Deuc's fingers splayed grasping at nothing to slow his descent to what lay behind him.

"Deuc!" Aedan shouted.

His speed increased and chunks of freezing powder filled his ears and eyes. He spun on his back as a forest of wet emerald tangled in his limbs. He sucked a sharp breath expecting to be dragged under, yet the muddy loam lay flat as a Teeta. Deuc clawed at his legs, pulling himself upright to catch sight of his would be assassin. A clear jelly like substance, thin as obituk noodles had spun a web around his right ankle, it convulsed in tiny waves dragging itself upwards, intensifying the bite that penetrated his shield.

Aedan retracted her shoulder, "Deuc, my knife!"

He snatched it out of the air and hacked at the gelatinous mass, black ink spewing forth and coating his hands, soothing the thorny flames. Floral blooms of algae licked at Deuc's clothes as he fumbled at his salvation, the jelly thief harder than he first thought to overcome. He hacked at another tendril just as the organism tugged forward; he toppled back, tasting leafy brine.

"Deuc!" Aedan called her voice another octave higher.

Deuc laughed out loud, one minute she wanted to slice and dice him, the next her voice wailed in despair, "Almost there."

Rising from the water, he flicked the carcass loose. Deuc stared at his wounds, splashing the black goo over his ankle and hands before he reached the shoreline.

"What in Ea's name was that?"

"A Ctenophore or a Skyphosian, but to be honest, Hunter I don't really care." Deuc ran his hands down his thighs, and winced. Aedan's eyes raked down his legs. Deuc pointed to the Landscaper, "You said that thing is transmitting to the Etarians?"

"I'm assuming it's a T540 operating system, primitive tech and we're in the Theia system so maybe 36, 48 hours if we're lucky."

"Will it start up again?" Aedan said retrieving her knife from Deuc's sticky fingers. He released it willingly.

"No. The powers switched to idle, look at the steam."

Hunter was right, instead of blowing a single plume of white from the top; it now puffed individual pillows from the shaft, which delicately descended to its base.

"It's on life-support mode," Aedan sighed.

Inside the *Arion*, Deuc set about sorting through the junk, his skin had healed completely from the jelly-assassin. Whatever poison it held in its membranes was powerful enough to infiltrate his defenses. He should trap a specimen but Aedan's suspicions were already running high. With the Jump codes he could come back another time. Deuc's ears pricked at their conversation, Osirian and Human, as they worked side by side. Aedan as wild as Osirians get, highly skilled, fast, vicious, beautiful. Pity her loyalty lay with the damn Etarians. Hunter joked and scoffed at Aedan's probing questions.

Deuc mused over the Human who had stood between Deuc's menacing tactics and Aedan's ill placed rage and not relented. He had honor, courage, and intellect. If he could keep them both alive…. Deuc thought he'd found a win win situation, buy his freedom with Hunter and improve Osiria with the Jump Codes, but Aedan seemed a lose-lose equation. Osiria would surely benefit from having her skills on their side instead of Etaria. Would she even consider it? If she accepted would he be trading her freedom for his?

He thought of Aedan tied with the same strings that bound him. It was tempting, to consider that their entanglement would continue beyond Hunter's bounty, but would he be satisfied knowing he'd landed her in the same trap he was in? Would she forgive him? On the other hand could Osiria succeed without her skills or his? Did either of them deserve freedom when their home Worlds suffered so terribly? Deuc's neck heated. He turned his attention back to the pair, as they rapidly started reinstalling the console to its former glory, the tools flowing as freely as the conversation.

"What will they do with them after they –"

"They'll use their DNA for variation of the species."

"I don't understand."

"You'll have to start at the beginning with her; she's not likely to believe anything I tell her." Deuc scoffed.

"Go on, Hunter," Aedan said.

So much for her earlier concern, Deuc thought. He picked up a rotary manifold and realized it must have come from the *Venator*. He put it to the side.

"Like I said before, humans are the building blocks of the universe; their DNA is malleable, dynamic and resilient. The Etarians need us to combine with their species for their benefit."

"I've seen the adverts for EHIR 2 serum, that's Human based?" Aedan asked.

Deuc couldn't resist, "The Etarians have supreme intelligence, prosperity and immense longevity. But what good is all that if you can't breed. While your enemies grow stronger and more numerous, your species beings to decline and eventually through invasion or otherwise, your future generations are facing extinction. Domination of the dual systems has always been a numbers game."

Hunter picked up the train, "So they found something, a species that takes the least amount of time for females to mature reproductively albeit with a limited timeframe. Yet the males are successful reproducers until they die." Hunter continued, "So they spliced the Etarian reproductive cells with a Human and Etarian hybrid. Instead of breeding once every 400 years, the EHIR 2 Solution hybrid can produce multiple cycles of reproduction."

Aedan recalled the Kronos guard who hedged his bets on the fireball game, "And is it working?"

"There's more to it, but now, after selection refinement yes the cycles are narrowing, the multiple live births more frequent."

"Does the Etarian public know about using Human DNA?" Aedan asked.

"There's a lot of propaganda, government bonuses, medical and tax deductions, but as far as Humans are concerned only a few at the facility know the truth." Hunter's eyes clouded over in anger.

"I don't understand, at some point, wouldn't a generation

emerge that no longer required Human DNA?" Aedan asked.

"Etarians have been gene splicing for thousands of generations, unsuccessfully." Hunter started.

Deuc snorted, "Is that what you call it."

Hunter cleared his throat, "The Buried Histories talk of failed live trials over millennia. The various hybrid mixes were increasingly unstable, the process of genetic engineering suffered major setbacks with the wrong, for want of a better word, recipe. Another drawback of EHIR 2 is there is only one cycle before the hybrid needs to be spliced with Human DNA again, otherwise the natural interspecies defense kicks in, and they start producing genetic mutations, congenital defects and sterile offspring."

"Besides do you honestly think Etarians would allow another species to prosper?" Deuc said.

Aedan ignored him, "And what of the Oddworlders, what are they?"

Deuc concentrated on the tone of her voice rather than the words, he couldn't resist, "The wrong hybrid."

"Seriously, Deuc." Aedan said. She regarded Hunter, his eyes downcast. "He's right?"

Deuc stopped sorting and looked at her bleak wide eyes, "From what I understand, the live trial failed spectacularly, those genetic mutations, and those congenial defects found a home across the Sandes."

Aedan didn't reply.

Deuc turned his back and resumed his work, "Told you Dios."

"And how do you know all this Deuc?"

"Because," Deuc picked up his multi-tool, she almost sounded as if she trusted him. He had to tread carefully, "We have, the Administration that is, has its own version of the Buried Histories."

"Alright tell me what you're going to do with those codes." Aedan said returning to the floor.

He watched as her hips rolled from one side to the other

against the steel as she tucked the wiring into its clips. "Help us." He let his last word hang there and set the timer to 34.

"Oh no, you don't get to throw that in my face. You want my help, sell it to me." She crawled out and opened another hatch. On her knees, scuffed cheeks flushed, eyes intent on the problem at hand.

"Look around you Aedan. The Etarians are terraforming outside the Dual Systems, outside of the Gaia Galaxy. What other resource rich worlds do they have at their disposal? The Osirians are choking on their own filth. Give us the jump codes and see how we'd prosper. You want safety..."

She sat back on her haunches and glared at him.

"Security? Civility?"

"Humanity" Hunter added, earning himself a raised eyebrow from Aedan.

Deuc continued, "Give us the necessities so we don't have to squabble –"

"Is that what you call it?" Her eyes narrowed.

"Give us the ability to prosper, induce pride and watch Osiria flourish."

"The darkest malice thrives in the most prosperous of places, Deuc. Nothing will change."

Aedan shifted through the next set of spare screws until she found the one she needed and then laid back down to wind it home. "Osirian corruption is like Helcate Lantana, intrusive and evergreen. Those Jump Codes won't change that, if anything you will make it worse."

Deuc shook his head, "Give them a chance."

For a moment, Aedan's hands stopped fussing, her head rolled to one side, before she continued. Deuc let it drop.

The next hours passed with each of them hard at work. Deuc had the ion stabilizers connected and working by the time the sun slinked behind the Landscaper. It pitched the *Arion* into an eerie half-light with grey shadows painted every surface in a pasty twilight. The air cooled and heated at odd intervals as the climate control continued to malfunction.

Deuc joined Hunter on finishing the thrusters.

"How long do you reckon?"

"Clock says 26."

"Fuck." The Human ran a nano-conductor over the loose wires, "How could the Lestas tear this apart in less than two and it's taking us so long?" He rubbed dirty grey fingers across his brow.

"Exactly, they tore into her," Even Deuc yawned, "You take a few hours on the bunk. I'll wake you in what – four hours and I'll rest after that."

"We don't have time," Hunter dropped the spanner.

"You're hopeless right now. Tell Aedan too."

"Tell me what?" The sting was missing from her tone, grey eyes circled by even darker lines. She collected more copper, winding it around her fingers.

"Sleep."

"Yeah right." Aedan reached for the nano-conductor, fumbling until it rattled on the floor.

"Trust me."

"After I get the AI registering the systems properly."

Deuc raised his eyebrows.

"I'll help her, then rest." Hunter climbed up to the main cockpit leaving Deuc to dwell in the darkness. His eyesight was better than most. He mused over Aedan's hatred for the Osirians, even after she had learned of their primitive origins. Take away all the propaganda, all the half-truths and the false histories of their worlds, Deuc and Aedan were just as Etarian as Hunter. To Deuc their voices drifted down to his workspace like breadcrumbs. Aedan trusted Hunter. What did she see in him, that she didn't see in Deuc? If only he could get Aedan to trust him, Deuc brooded as he worked.

"So what part makes you human?"

"To be direct, I am the Human-Etarian Hybrid."

Aedan paused over his choice of words, as the Human continued. "My mother was human, my father Etarian-Human, spliced together and then implanted back, would have been easier if I incubated in an accelerator, at least my mother would have survived."

"And your sister?"

Deuc heard Hunter's voice sharpen, "Juliette was pure Human. Recent advancements made it possible to cross-breed what remained of my mother's sample with another male human. She was the only one – "

"It's okay," Aedan said. The darkness thickened around Deuc as he imagined the physical comfort her voice inferred. Aedan spoke again, "You called us instinctive......What do they tell Etarian's about ... Oddworlders." A thread of something hot and dark caught in Deuc's chest.

"Only that you are a more primitive species, born of half-breeds and lesser lifeforms. It makes your race more instinctively reactive, like animals."

Deuc nodded in the shadows. Loyalties formed in an instant, some lasted centuries, others blistered like lightening, a flash across the surface of a society already seething. Deuc waited for Hunter's attempt to soften his last statement.

"I mean they completely disown any Etarian connection, wiped it from the histories."

"How do you know all this? I've heard whispers of Buried Histories, but nothing like this. Where did you -" Aedan's last words concealed by her rebooting and testing the AI.

"It was part of my training."

Something about Aedan's voice made Deuc pause, "Why train you with all this knowledge, give you access to Jump Codes, if you were too valuable to let escape?" She'd stumbled across a doubt not unlike Deuc's own. Hunter had secrets.

"My existence was conditional."

"You said, you are the Hybrid, surely -"

"I am the current Hybrid. Once I'm no longer of use, I will be terminated, hence the dead or alive bounty. Is it working?"

Deuc exhaled unaware that he had been holding his breath.

"So far so good."

"Well I'm done. See you in a couple of hours."

"For now, I'll let you sleep, but I'm not done with my questions."

The Human laughed. "Okay, later then."

"Hey Hunter...?" Aedan asked.

"Yeah,"

"What about these other two, what are they?"

"They're a new batch from Juliette's father's sample. Pure human. Twin girls."

"Twin girls?"

"Fraternal twins, extremely rare. Ten years old."

Deuc heard the bounty hunter tinker away for a few more minutes as Hunter settled down on the bunk. Suddenly silence descended the *Arion* and Deuc went back to work. Twin pure-blood girls? Deuc grinned.

CHAPTER 9

The Lestas clicked through half-light shadows to a pair of shaking girls. Aedan turned to her other side. *The clicking grew louder and someone sobbed.* Aedan pulled the blanket up to her chin, and squeezed her lids shut. She could hear the thunderous roar of her heart and Aedan inhaled deeply through a constricted throat. The citrus and wooded sylvan scents of Deuc's bedclothes eased her breathing, and her shoulders dipped. The darkness clawed at her nerves, and a man's nasal voice whispered her name from the past. Great, now her nightmares had nightmares! Aedan's eyes targeted any item to focus on. The picture frames, a notebook, the silver glint of her knife, the medal for valor. Aedan thought of Hunter, the slightest tinge of oil that spread over his iris when questioned. His plight to rescue a pair of girls doomed either way by the nature of their species. Elusive jumps codes that could make or break the dual systems. Could she spare two girls their torturous future and let the rest of their Worlds go to hell?

The image of a thin moustache that disgraced even thinner lips appeared in her mind. Aedan's ribs ached and she released a long slow breath. She would help Hunter, not one molecule in her body told her otherwise. She tossed again. A weight surged on the bed as warm breath tickled Aedan's neck. Her eyes focused on the dark wall in front. The citrus and cinnamon exploded in her senses.

"What are you doing?"

"Getting some rest."

"Here?" She gasped.

"It's my bed."

"You've got to be kidding. Get out." Like an asp coiling for a rodent, Aedan hand darted towards her knife, before she realized the impotence of her weapon.

"Trust me Aedan; I'm too tired to sleep on the deck again." His bulk rolled over, until his shoulders loomed above. Aedan stared at his broad back, pitch black against the sandy grey. The familiar odors of Inox and grease tickled her nose. From this distance Aedan could see Deuc's shield was down, "Trust me…." Deuc yawned.

Aedan rolled over as Deuc's chuckles vibrated through the thin mattress. If Aedan wanted to climb out she'd have to do it over him. Warmth seeped through the mattress, the cabin temperature a blizzard against her weary frame. She'd have to look at the climate control again later. Eventually Aedan slunk down to the covers. It took several slow breaths and Deuc's continued stillness before the knot in her stomach unraveled. Aedan closed her eyes.

"Do you trust him?"

Aedan waited for the revolving nightmares to start again, "For now." Tension ruffled the linen.

"Why?"

Sleep haze coated Aedan's answer, "Don't get me wrong, he is hiding something, but not about the girls. He's telling the truth about that." She yawned and the sting of male cinnamon licked at her taste buds.

"How can you tell?"

Silence hung in the air, and Aedan scoffed as her knuckles relaxed, "Trust me. What was that thing in the water; you called it a skyo or cento something?"

Deuc's deep chuckle, softened by his bulk reached her ears, "A Skyphosian or a Ctenophore."

"Yeah."

"Gelatinous salt-water organisms."

"Fish?"

"No that would be Piscean – these ones use combs or cilia to swim."

Aedan tried to shake the grogginess from her voice, "How do you know all this?"

"It's a hobby. Why do you care?"

Aedan managed a weak scoff as her heavy lids closed against the softened cabin lights, the nightmares muted by warm cinnamon.

The sky shone pale blue, two suns drifted lazily across the horizon and dandelions danced in the daintiest of breezes that caressed Aedan's cheek. To Aedan the landscape seemed drenched in a pale riot of color, as if splashed by water, the shades faded and merged with one another. Aedan trailed her fingers across river stones as hot as lava and the color of burnt honey. Hadn't it been snowing?

Aedan's lashes flickered. Pupils focused. Fuzzy shapes became outlines that slumbered beside her. As if the lava had been real, Aedan flinched, tucking her hands under her chin. Deuc's jaw sagged against the pillow. Several dark strands of hair fell forward like spider webs and graced the bow of his slightly parted lips. A spike of irritation heated her chest, as she realized the comfort his presence had brought. Aedan leant back to find an icy needle pressing between her shoulders and a relaxed grip on her waist.

"Morning."

Aedan palmed Deuc's chest in panic, her head thunked on the wall behind. Bronzed mahogany tumbled onto the floor, as Aedan grimaced through the tolling in her skull.

"Fuck Aedan!"

Aedan inhaled through her teeth, and rubbed at the brewing lump.

"Chaos can't come soon enough." Deuc cursed.

"That was your fault!"

"Like hell it was!"

A vice tightened on Aedan's ankle and her back scrapped against the metal lip of the bunk, landing empty handed. Ridges of steel poked into her shoulder blades. Aedan's instincts kicked in as she sent elbows and knees into Deuc's bulk. He scrambled to keep up with her speed, his legs tangled around her thighs and she stiffened; his skin still furnace hot from their combined slumber.

Tendrils of jet black clawed at her face, pits of polished obsidian bore into her soul, Deuc paused as he registered her lack of movement, his grip retreated, "Next time you can share the bunk with Hunter."

Aedan choked back what would have been her next curse, when she realized Deuc had risen from the floor. "You fucking can!"

"It's either that or the floor." Deuc added.

After the door zipped closed, Aedan threw her hands to her face. She swallowed the lurking scream and channeled it, clenching her jaw. The shakes subsided after her familiar hatred had been satisfactorily refueled. Her survival depended on the infinite hunger of her fears.

Aedan doubted Deuc's coiled violence could be restrained eternally, so eventually she'd have to stop picking fights. Osirians lived by the hard and fast rule, that any person object or craft was fair game. Osirian's writhed in an ever shrinking pool of filth. Deuc had spawned from that pool. Technically so had she. Aedan waited until she heard voices in the main cockpit before she crept to the utility room. Her familiarity with Deuc had crossed a line. She'd become complacent; almost complicit. Splashing cold water onto her face, she stared at her shimmering silver irises. What to do about the Human and his lies? What to do with Deuc? The prospect of a safe and prosperous future hung on a five trillion Ketos pay-check, she'd have to split with a barbarian. Then they would part ways. Until then, she could be civil. She doubled checked her appearance. Civil not enticing.

Hunter handed more Teetas to Aedan when she finally entered the cockpit, and she bit down on the thin carbohydrate. The cheap and flaky food source sucked all the moisture from her tongue. She ran her gaze around the remainder of the console and then quickly down the stairs. She heard more curses from below and sighed before addressing her bounty, "How do you see this panning out for you once we get those girls? Are you really going to let me hand you in?"

White bloomed with orange across his blue eyes, "If that's what you want? Yes. The girls' lives mean more to me than my own."

Oil free. So far so good, "And the Jump codes? How many do you have?"

He sent a callused hand threw sun-bleached hair; eyebrows knitted and rose, "All the dual systems, well that's really only ten Jump Gateways in Etaria. Then sixty-five gateways in the Gaia Galaxy, and over two-hundred Universal codes."

Aedan whimpered, "How many gateways are there?"

"Thousands." Hopeful white collided in his gaze, minutely tinged with blue. All shades, oil free again.

"Thousands?" Deuc said.

Aedan jumped and tore her gaze away from Hunter's curious pink and orange ringed irises as the bronzed warrior climbed into the cockpit. The air suddenly heated in Aedan's lungs. Civil not flirtatious.

"Is he lying?"

Aedan bit the inside of her cheek before answering, "How should I know?"

Deuc wiped the carbon build up from his shielded fingers, and then resumed recalibrating the timing chip, "You tell me." His brows raised but his eyes didn't move from the greased dice.

"I don't know what you mean?" Aedan mused.

"You know all my secrets Aedan." Deuc said.

Civil, Aedan thought. If she followed her intended path then it might save her some time explaining all her decisions and why. They could plan with Deuc's shield, his blood and his strength. They already knew about Kegan. Aedan exhaled, "No he's not."

"How can you tell?" Hunter's dimpled chin edged her direction, his eyes pink as a baby Rhotadon.

"Your eyes give you away," She said. "I can tell when someone lies, a layer of oil crosses your irises. There's an emotional content to it as well, an aura of red mixed with black means violence is imminent. Panic, fear, amusement, sometimes I see yellow I think that means happiness or joy. It's what makes Kegan so successful."

"I knew it. Only when I had my back to you did I feel like I could hide something from you. Can you do it for everyone?" Hunter said.

Aedan regarded her silver buckled footwear, "Almost."

"Emotional aura detection, shapeshifting, shielded skin and healing blood…" Hunter mused.

"Genetic defects my ass," Deuc grunted, his eyes tracked to Aedan, "Well what's the plan Dios?"

"Wait, are you saying you'll help me?"

"I'm in." Deuc retrieved the knife from Aedan's belt. "I'll help you get those girls off Haigon."

Aedan paused, the snow drifted to the windshield silencing her doubts, "You want the codes in exchange for your help. I want that reward. But I have another term for the agreement. Both of you need to swear on your lives that you'll repeat not one word of this, of Kegan to anyone. Understand. It's my survival."

"First, I want to know if you can morph into anyone or anything," Hunter asked.

Honestly Aedan had never tried. "No."

"Sure?" Deuc questioned.

"Kegan is it." Aedan added.

Deuc's hard planes softened around the edges, and he dragged the knife across the palm of his hand and then spat in the center. "On my oath and my life, I swear." He handed the knife to Hunter who did the same.

Aedan sighed before repeating the movement, "I'm in. Get the girls off Haigon." Aedan grimaced as they shook hands and the spittle and blood squished into her palm, "On my oath and my life."

Aedan switched on the scanner, the bright green lights distorted and fractured by the signal of the mighty Landscaper.

"Okay spill it Hunter," Deuc demanded.

Hunter pushed his fringe leaving a pink smudge across his brow, "Well Kegan can get us through the Sandes Belt to Haigon."

"Will they let Kegan bring you in alive?" Deuc said.

"Maybe, I don't know."

Aedan squinted at the red and black storm that brewed under his sandy brows. Instead she focused on the bridge of his nose, the colors dimmed.

"The girls are held at the Medical University. We should be able to sneak into the R & D compound."

Aedan opened up the communication cables and turned the volume to low, "And what about Deuc?"

"Well, I hadn't planned on that. The Eagle was procuring weapons but I guess…." Hunter trailed off.

"Sounds like a splendid plan, what else did the Eagle promise you?" Deuc grinned.

"An end game. They said they had a place of safety for me and the girls."

Aedan's ears, half focused on the nattering cables, pricked up, "A safe haven?"

Hunter shrugged his shoulders, "Yeah, I didn't get much more after that, get to Hades, change transports and get to INNA."

Like the scanner, the mega-machine distorted the communication channels, clipping words and breaking sentences, static bored through the rest. "That's how you got through the Sandes Belt, the Eagle had it plotted."

"Yeah, there's no way I could have…"

The scanner array suddenly squealed in ear piercing decibels as the Landscaper rumbled to life. All three stared at the windscreen as the blanket of snow slid off in one crisp sheet of white. The sky bleached of color now stained by three stripes of silver, each contrail on a different trajectory as the Etarian scouts breached the atmosphere.

"Did you finish the defense system?" Deuc's flat words sliced through the fog in Aedan's mind. The scouts redirected mid descent.

Aedan slid into Second chair, the weapons system now back online.

"We can't kill them!" Aedan snapped.

"They're going to kill us!" Hunter shouted as he followed Deuc down to the *Arion*'s belly. Within moments the ship shuddered to life. Aedan watched the slow and steady blinking of the Gatling lasers.

"Or worse," Deuc spat.

Aedan gritted her teeth. The scouts closed in as the Landscaper pealed back. Aedan ran the pad of her thumb over the activation switch.

"Remind me next time we stop to fix the ignition." Deuc winked at Aedan as he strapped into the pilot's seat, "Hunter you get up here and get ready with another code."

"Trajectory mapping is online." Aedan tapped the console.

"Jump to where? They can follow us through if they're close enough."

Aedan craned her neck and followed the scalene shaped scouts as they circled the *Arion*, the black birds' thrusters still warming up; the undercarriage of each Etarian ship, partially obscured by the cloud cover. Was that a Plasma 30-4? "That's a lot of artillery for just scouts."

The pressure waves penetrated the *Arion*'s hull, the contents rattled and instruments clanged.

"Militia?" Hunter asked.

"Activate automatic targeting!" Deuc ordered.

A knot tightened in Aedan's stomach as her hands tentatively tapped the console, the switch still untouched. Deuc nudged the throttle forward. Hunter spun the Jump drive dials. The tiny red switch grew hot under Aedan's thumb. A bead of sweat ran between Aedan's breasts, as she watched the scanner. Behind their position, the dart-like ships banked right, the 3D imaging shimmered into solid outlines of three

Etarian Militant fighters. A swirl of panic mixed with hope erupted in Hunter's eyes as he strapped himself in. Aedan tore her gaze away from Deuc's soulless brown eyes, the tiny hairs of her forearms stood to attention. The lip of the button scored her flesh, and Aedan licked her now parched lips.

"Ready," She said.

Dual engines increased in pitch. Aedan said a silent prayer to Ea. Deuc strummed restless fingers on the edge of the control panel as each blue increment solidified on the Jump drive dial. Two slices out from full capacity and the roar of fighters burst overhead.

"Hunter shields. Lasers Aedan!"

She watched the ashen surface recede as the *Arion* chased the fighters into the atmosphere, "Just get us to the Jump field and I'll manage the rest."

"Will you?"

"Deuc you need to be quick when we're through the gateway. We'll Jump again," Hunter said.

Sleek blue lines graced the sides of brilliant militant hardware. The glacial clouds concealed the pilot's sharp pirouettes that Aedan watched on the hologram, "Behind us!"

Deuc slammed the joysticks, and pitched the *Arion* into a somersault all on its own, "Jump again Dios?"

"We've got to stop them somehow."

Aedan didn't lift her eyes from the scanner. The three pursuers had decreased in speed; Deuc levelled the *Arion* out for a brief moment before a second Landscaper filled the windshield.

"Aedan!"

"Get us off planet first." She bit back. None of the fighters had fired a shot. They were Etarian after all.

"Fine."

Her stomach leapt into her chest as the *Arion* followed a plume of steam to the stratosphere. Tendrils of fluffy cloud blistered to crisp familiar black, decorated with the magnificent glitter of a thousand suns. Aedan sighed, her hands rested in her lap.

"That's a welcoming party!" Hunter reached the Jump drive as the scanner screamed to catch up with each shape that populated the hologram, "Ready."

A single plasma round careered their direction, fired from any one of the twenty or more Etarian fighters that littered the orbital plane.

"Aedan, damn it!" Deuc spat.

The perspiration dripped from her brow to the corner of her nose and she wiped it back before switching on the communication cables.

A sharp snarl barked, *"Surrender Dios or face the full force of the Etarian Militia, Kegan Capare."*

"What?" Flat Teetas climbed Aedan's throat, "Kegan?"

A second purple fireball of plasma crossed the *Arion*'s nose cone with millimeters to spare, "The Lestas are not above selling info, even if it's the wrong info." Deuc hissed.

Aedan didn't have time to ponder Lestas' bargaining with Etarians as Deuc booted the thrusters to full throttle and zipped between the orbiting fighters. A hailstorm of shots skirted their ship. Deuc contorted the controls and the horizon of their temporary haven, rapidly peaked above, then below.

A sound like burnt leaves being crushed underfoot slithered across the airwaves, *"Have it your way Capare."*

The militia's arsenal opened up and spears of light rained down the *Arion*'s flanks. Aedan's head snapped forward and she tasted blood. Warning squeals and flashing lights demanded her attention.

"Shields?" Deuc asked.

A wisp of olive miasma glided around their boots, and Hunter coughed, "Holding steady, environmental system took a hit."

"Venting!" Aedan said as the *Arion*'s on-board computer struggled to catch up. The irritant gas withdrew like a feline pulled by its tail.

"Deuc the gateway!"

The sweat glistened on Deuc's forearms his face as hard as stone, "Any time now!"

Hunter thumbed keys with heavy fingers and the Jump beacons glowed, "Hold on."

Deuc directed the *Arion* directly across the Etarian's front line, the majority of volleys silenced. It didn't last long and another shot sent Aedan slamming into her seat. Hunter groaned.

"There's too many!" Deuc spat.

The blackness beckoned, the scenery Aedan had of her own life, plummeted into an empty expanse edged with gold. The trinkets spewed forth violet shards of death towards the *Arion*. Hunter groaned, Deuc roared and Aedan cursed as her thumbs found the tiny red switch. The laser targeting system purred into action and she aimed the grid towards their pursuers. Pulsing heat illuminated the field of combat, the joysticks thundered in her palms. Light spun end over end and collided with three Cyan lines. One shape blinked off the scanner. Another spread apart in compressed flames and crashed into two more. The glowing beacons beckoned them forward.

Deuc smacked his fist down on the circular dial. The Jump gateway opened. The gravitational waves from their unknown destination snared the *Arion* in its jaws, and the cabin filled with hot white light.

CHAPTER 10

Deuc inhaled easily as the venting system, untouched by the Lestas' reaping, withdrew the lasting molecules of the noxious gas. He tapped the shields display, holding steady at 85 percent. Dios used the dash to pull himself to his feet and Deuc watched droplets of blood splash on the Human's creased collar.

"Almost ready." Hunter said, eyes squinting at the tiny dials.

The twin anchors positioned kilometers apart blinked twice before two arrow headed ships broke through the gateway, molten silver gleaming like water across a mirror.

"Ready?" Deuc said, "Aedan?"

Aedan sat motionless, her pale lips rigid in sallow cheeks. She refocused the targeting grid.

Etarian-traitor-scum a redundant insult now, Deuc thought. He eased the bow to face the threat, her lashes heavy with dew but unmoving as the lasers spewed forth their destructive power.

The blue increments on the Jump-drive, glowed one after another. Hunter stared at the keyboard, his head in his hands.

"What now?" Deuc asked.

"We can't keep doing this. I'll lose my teeth." The fugitive spat a wad of blood onto the floor.

Deuc let a slow breath whistle through his teeth, he needed to tread lightly, "Go to planet and hide?"

"Maybe. Our plan to sneak in with Kegan sounds screwed." Hunter said, flicking his fringe towards their silent gunner.

Asar. It's the only option, Deuc thought, but he couldn't press it. "The Osirian system?" Deuc said, his tone measured and mild. Could he get Hunter and Aedan to Asar? Moreover, should he? He needed freedom, and Hunter held all the tickets.

"They'll just follow us. Ready?"

The dial peaked and Deuc struck the button, light encapsulated the cabin sound tearing backwards into total darkness.

Hunter's stomach twisted, spreading a heated sensation through his extremities. He'd failed to adjust to the sensation of melting bones trying to escape through his navel. Humans, he decided were not designed to Jump leagues through space.

"Chaos end me!" The warrior shouted, his palms jammed into eye sockets.

Lights melded into one, the scent of singed hair reached his nostrils and his throat worked in slow motion to ease the flavor of burnt paper from his tongue.

"Where are we now?" Deuc said.

"The Forag System, there's multiple satellites to choose from, take some cover."

Sharp edges of the seat drove into the rear of Hunter's knees as the *Arion* answered Deuc's ministrations. Hunter blinked away the lingering black spots before his vision brightened with natural solar light.

"Ready?"

"Give me a minute." Like a comet's trail, a thought dragged through Hunter's mushed up brain.

"We need to run for cover and I mean to surface – we should -"

Hunter cut the Osirian off, "If they can follow us here, they will follow us to your Worlds, do you want Etarian Militia on Osirian doorsteps? I just need a minute to think!"

Aedan's fingers stroked the joysticks, her voice disembodied from the statue that sat in Second Chair, "We don't have a minute."

"Deuc have the computer re-route your emergency signal."

"So the whole fleet knows where we are?"

"They already do! Just re-route it to signal Haigon."

Deuc accessed the emergency application and uttered the demands through gritted teeth.

Haigon, the monitor flashed.

"What are you planning Hunter?"

The Jump codes were no use if the Etarian's made it through. The gateways required an input, a destination code that allowed the waves to target their ship and drag it through. But after the Jump, they had no control over how quickly the gateway closed or how to wipe the slate clean.

"Is it ready?"

"Done. Where to now?"

"Does it matter?" Aedan droned, the resonant retort of the Gatling lasers spurred Hunter on.

"Activate it!"

Deuc initiated the *Arion*'s emergency signal as Hunter reset the Jump dial. This time, the gateway responded with cautious orange hazards.

"What are you doing? Is it broken?" Deuc said.

"Almost!" Hunter couldn't restrain his grin. "Shut down your emergency signal!"

Deuc complied as they watched shimmering pressure waves break the surface between the jump beacons.

"Last one for now, I promise." Hunter said, as the silver surface evolved to golden rays and began spiraling anti-clock-wise, between the jump beacons, "You have ten seconds before it shuts down entirely."

The hinges on the seat creaked and Hunter's ribs compressed.

"On the left" Deuc snapped and the retorts commenced again. As the *Arion* peaked through the gateway, a shroud of gilded essence descended, bursting through Hunter's skin and stealing the light.

The *Arion* glided to a halt behind a sandy gas giant looped by a rocky ochre satellite, both orb's lower hemispheres were shrouded in darkness. The larger planet's cloudy cover swirled across the surface. Aedan watched the wavelike formations as liquid pooled in her lids. She blinked as her breathing slowed. The smaller orb circled its companion, its surface sparkled with bursts of energy, the silent lightshow raised the hair on Aedan's arms. Between the orbs, a strand of dust spawned, as clusters of matter sporadically tore from the dwarfs mass. Aedan could imagine the hushed sounds of the matter withdrawing from one to land on the other like oceans waves against the foreshore. The illumination of the energy transfer between the planets warmed her skin within the chill of the cockpit, the methodical pulses sporadic yet oddly calming. The debris drifted into the maelstrom of the giant's churning weather patterns, like miniscule rubies, the dust disappeared into the butter-colored clouds.

Aedan stretched, expelling the stale air from sore lungs, causing a metallic sting to sizzle her taste buds. She'd opened fire on the Etarian Militia. They had called Kegan Capare over the comms. Aedan eyed Hunter from her peripherals. Could she abandon his plan? Could she abandon these girls? What if Leta had abandoned Aedan?

"They're beautiful," She sighed.

Hunter pulled his hands back from his temples.

Together they watched the spheres in their eternal gravitational dance, the miniscule particles of debris ebbing and surging on the invisible stellar wind.

"Dos Menium and Caelumina minor." He answered, "Or together Dos Caelumina".

"Yeah brilliant, what did you do Hunter?" Fine violet cracks tarnished the whites of Deuc's eyes and Aedan focused waiting to see if the aura altered. It didn't.

"I changed the locks. It's a defense mechanism for a default encryption algorithm. Oddworlder prevention."

"So if an Osirian made it through,-"

"The gateway shuts down, any followers are denied, or if they hit the gateway, disintegrated."

Aedan shivered.

Deuc just nodded, "We need to move to safety, to a planet."

"Possibly, except we've got three giant punches to the face

coming our way, each one worse than the last." The click of Hunter's belt brought Aedan out of her chair.

"We'll go to ground, wait it out." Deuc continued.

Hunter raised his fist and must have thought better of it. Clenched fingers evolved into a single pointed jab, "When the testing is complete, the girls will be terminated. There isn't time to wait it out. The cost of every delay will be felt by those girls and me. Not you."

As if each step solidified splashes of guilt inside Aedan she paced between the warrior and the fugitive. Deuc could probably beat the codes out of the Human and end him. Aedan would have no reward, no Ketos for Leta, no life, and those girls without help. Something must be preventing Deuc from acting and it can't be loyalty. Everyone knew Osirians had none. They needed to remain calm and focused. First things first, three phases of Jump-lag to prepare for, "Where exactly are we?"

"This system in the Caelum constellation is relatively empty, an eclipsing binary star system, orbited by two planets, each with one satellite. I suggest we pull up between CC768 and its satellite to shelter from the rays. This system is very unstable. No-one's coming here." Hunter turned away, stabbing his fingers through his fringe.

Deuc's shoulders dipped and he took a step back, "Unstable? Is it safe?"

"Terminal matter transfer between Dos Caelumina will happen one day, but not today."

The Etarian Commander returned to his plush leather chair, the pneumatic hiss short and sharp from behind the oval-shaped desk, the dark ebony rich under his fingertips. The Captain, all sandy-blonde bravery and breeding stood to attention waiting for his command. The Commander's office sparse, the low lying furniture adjusted to the Commanders height, all visitors slightly uncomfortable, their knees too high, the chairs too deep. The Commander ran his fingers across the gleaming desktop, the resulting fingerprints symbolizing the mar Hunter Dios had left across his plans. Him and the Oddworlders, he'd send all savages to Erebus if he had his way. During the Borders War, as an optimistic recruit, he'd encountered a small Rebel patrol. Engaging in the fight had left the Commanders voice box permanently disfigured. All amount of biomechanics, stem-cell implants and cohesive therapy had failed to change the scraping torture of his throat. Every name he uttered caused him pain and thus earned his revenge.

"At ease Varmil," He croaked.

The only thing relaxed about Captain Varmil's posture was his broad shoulders, everything else had been filled, starched and ironed to perfection.

"Sir, the Gateway is not responding."

The Commander called his fingers into a fist and punched the silver transmitter on his desk. In two tight buzzes, Chief Director Hogan, the Archon, Superior, Presider over the entire Etarian Government and hence the Etarian Militia answered with his holographic image from the shoulders up, his uniform collar ajar, eyes sagging with dark circles, the background curtains drawn tight to hide the twilight hours of Haigon. The Commander hadn't drawn his shades, like the Chief Director, something about the constant brilliance of Etaria's dual suns gracing their manicured civilization, crystalized the Commander's focus. Hogan wiped his aged hand down his brow to his chin, "The Ex-O already gave me the numbers, fourteen down. You better tell me something good."

The Commander didn't mince his words, "The Oddworlder ship Jumped from the Forag system at 59 hours on the Second rising."

Director Hogan's silver brows crinkled, the heat of his dark eyes evident through the shimmering half-light representation, "Damn Ea to Chaos and back. Follow him!"

Varmil stepped forward, his hands still firmly clasped behind his back, "Chief Director, the Gateway is inoperable, and is not responding to our commands, we can try and reset the beacons, but – " The Captain paused.

"The destination code will be lost, the source code may be lost and you'll be stranded." Hogan finished, he ran manicured nails through his silver bouffant. He pressed a button of dark amber into his mouth and swallowed "What's your wager on their return Commander?"

Hogan had been there when the Militia had pulled the Commander in from his miasma laden ship, Hogan knew what each word cost, "Better than a Venus throw in Tali."

The Chief Director snorted and shook his head, the plaque of malted liquor, dissolved by now on his tongue, the ethanol firing his blood. How many centuries did Hogan have left? How many had he squandered postulating instead of acting, "What do you need from me?"

"Issue a warrant for the Mercenary Kegan Capare."

"Capare? Are you sure?" When he didn't answer, Hogan conceded, "Fine, consider it done. I trust you'll contain this situation."

He nodded, "The Troek-tiks will return to their warren of hovels and when they do, I'll have my rats waiting." Commander Braccass struck the console, the silver communication dissolved, leaving himself and Varmil alone, "Go catch me some rats."

Aedan flexed her fingers in anticipation for Jump-lag. She had skulled two glasses of the mineral water to avoid a long recovery. Deuc and Hunter had destroyed a third of the Teetas and protein supply, but Aedan refused. The voice that called her name across the cables, still echoed in her mind. Baubles of cream and cyan popped in front of her closed eyelids. A voice that seemed to drive through darkness with ominous purpose. It had called Kegan's name. Anxiety clawed at elusive thoughts that fled Aedan's grasp. The *Venator* gone, her transponder to Leta destroyed and now her name. Aedan inhaled slowly through her nose, clenching her fists and trapping her cheek between her teeth.

Perhaps it wasn't as bad as she thought. She needed the communication cables but at this distance the *Arion*'s receiver bubbled with white noise. She watched the captive rub his orange tinged blue eyes. Panic. Aedan turned to Deuc. His jaw tight, purple cracks already healed staring at the small solar system landscape. Aedan's tongue began to swell. The narrow corridor afforded little room to maneuver on jellied legs. She collapsed into soft cinnamon linen.

Smooth, solid river stones heated under her touch, soaking her cheek with blissful peace. The ridged honey colored surface leaked strength into her fatigued hands, and Aedan stifled a yawn. She needed to resist the feelings that Deuc's presence unearthed, no matter how tempting. She'd happily avoided this type of closeness, the connection to intimacy severed by fear and loathing. The tactile potency that radiated from Deuc both comforted and unsettled her.

With tentative leg stretches, Aedan crawled from the bunk, without disturbing the bronzed giant that slumbered. She concentrated on her boots, instead of the biceps and taunt flanks barely concealed in black fabric. Asleep with his arms behind his head and shield down, Deuc almost looked harmless. Almost. Aedan wandered to the main cabin.

Hunter's fingers trailed the steel foot plates, his arm dangled askew from the bunk behind the pilot's chairs. His chest rose and fell with the gentle rhythm of relaxed sleep. Aedan helped herself to Teetas and water, resting her boots on the dash and watched the gaseous surface of their shelter. Luminous with cherry and gold wraiths that sprinkled through the thin atmosphere, it sparkled like a feast-time bauble. Would Aedan live to see another feast-time? And if she did, could she ever find Leta again? Finding those girls had given Aedan hope. Leta would reach out and Aedan had to be there when it did.

"It's beautiful isn't it?"

Aedan blinked sore lids over dry eyes, "I thought you were asleep."

Deuc plonked into the pilot's chair, Teeta flakes flying in all directions, "I was."

Aedan continued her reverie. When she found the time she'd make another star-scape, add this system to its data-bank. The cabin's silence was broken intermittently by crunches and gulps. Aedan watched the yellow mineral water sloop in her cup.

Deuc sat back down, "If the Etarian's have burned Kegan, what will you do?"

Aedan sighed, "I don't know." If only she had that damn transponder!

"Have you ever considered…" Deuc took his boots from the console, " – a companion. A side kick…someone to keep you safe, have your back and so on."

A flash of heat tarnished Aedan's cheeks and boiled in her abdomen, "A side kick?"

"Yeah," A pneumatic valve on Deuc's chair hissed, "Don't give me that look, it could be mutually beneficial."

Aedan's chair suddenly swiveled, Deuc ceased when Aedan's knees pivoted between his thighs.

Aedan's eyes rushed over his cavernous chest, roped arms outstretched, hands steady on Aedan's armrests and back to the sharp masculine lines of his face, "Never, not ever." She heard the rustling of bed clothes. A brawny finger shot out, trapping Aedan's jaw as black ringed russet lashed her skin. Jolts of electricity hummed through her veins whilst Deuc continued his languid study.

"Not even a little bit curious?"

Aedan's eyes darted to his mouth, "No," she cleared her throat and retreated.

A curl kicked the corner of his lips, "Let me know when you change your mind."

"If…" Aedan corrected him.

"That almost sounds like a challenge."

Feet made contact with steel. Aedan focused on the glittering gold and ruby beyond the windscreen to blink away images of polished copper and ebony.

A yawn broke, "How long have I been out?" Hunter said, followed by, "What did I miss?"

"An hour and you only missed Aedan contemplating her new future." Deuc rose from his chair.

Aedan clicked her tongue, "We might need another plan. The *Arion* won't make it through to reach Haigon now."

"Nor will Kegan." Hunter scoffed.

"Kegan just opened fire on the Etarian Militia for you, Dios."

Aedan ignored Deuc's praise, her thoughts drifting to the instability of this tiny system, not unlike the atmosphere inside the cabin.

"Do you really think the Lestas sold information to the Etarians?" Hunter asked.

"Someone did." Deuc mumbled. "Good luck to the Lestas, you know what they say about Etarian Bargains."

"Someone else always pays," Aedan answered.

She pushed thoughts of Deuc's offer aside. She had betrayed her Etaria. According to Hunter and Deuc, the Etarians had abandoned their kith and kin, millennia's before. The supreme nobility of a peaceful regulated and intelligent society had let their creations squander in filth, starve in darkness and stew in their sins. The Etarian controlled gravitational jump-gates had created a highway for new frontiers to be discovered, harvested and conquered. Here the *Arion* sat amongst potential life supporting planets, out of reach for those who failed to make the grade.

She'd applied once to the Etarians for a Jump-code, well technically Kegan Capare's name was on the document. Denied, the justification had been security reasons. It didn't seem right. The Etarians had it all. She could understand security reasons against unknown civilizations. But it seemed the security risk was for Etarians to have self-reliant Osirians. Who would mine their poisonous minerals if they could find their own, who would buy their inflated resources, if Osirians could simply Jump to a new pantry. And yet Etarian thirst for domination was still not sated, they continued to exploit others, this time Humans for their own gain.

Deep within, Aedan knew her path was set. A burst of energy erupted in Aedan's chest, "We need to get back to civilization."

Deuc nodded, "The Osirian System is our only option."

"How is that going to help Deuc?" Hunter said.

"He might be right Hunter. What choice do we have? We can't jump to the Haigon field and risk falling into their hands because we've crashed with Jump-lag." Aedan legs felt fluffy. "We're here now and like you said, the last one is going to hurt. When we jump back, we need to go to planet until we recover." Aedan moistened her lips, trying to reduce the stinging in her gums, "We need supplies, weapons,-"

"Asar."

"No!" Aedan said.

"The South." Metal struck metal.

Black spots clouded Aedan's view, "Deuc, no!"

"Trust me."

Dual suns peaked at noon and a shadow clawed across rocky outcrops. The leaves whistled a nasally tune as the wind whipped Aedan's hair into her face and down her back. Scaly Lestas snatched at her wrists, locking metal cuffs onto chains. From the encroaching darkness, a plump shape emerged. Aedan squeezed her eyes, "I can't go back."

"Aedan?"

Citrus infused cinnamon overwhelmed her taste buds, and Aedan rolled backwards from the wall. A slab of muscle prevented her from continuing, "Damn it Deuc! Why?" she said.

Deuc rested on his back, his hands busy scrawling in a brown notebook decorated with black curls, "This is my bed, you could always sleep with Hunter."

"Why don't you?" Aedan's voice had lost its heat.

Syrupy chuckles subsided and Aedan dipped into the mattress when his weight shifted. She heard the clunk of his boots on the steel floor, "Why can't you go back to Asar?"

"Why the South Reaches?"

"The Rebels control the Northern Front."

Aedan sighed, "Zern. Now there's another shining example of Osirian upbringing," Aedan clawed at the shelves, the mini-digi frame tumbled.

Deuc threw his arm behind and caught the notebook he'd just stored, and prevented the collective fall, "More like uprising wouldn't you say?"

"How does he retain power?" Aedan said. Focusing her anger helped subside the anxiety that infected her body. Her fingers tightened each boot strap in turn until the final clasp beside her knee.

"Electricity. Ketos. Resources. Hope. He gains more support than he loses. He is a necessary evil to Osiria, for the checks and balances to the Administration." Deuc slid his possessions back into alignment and rose from the bed, stopping at the doorway to stretch.

Aedan rolled her eyes, her words rambled without pause, "I thought Zern and his Rebels were the opposition. Either way, I call that corruption. Oddworlders need to be controlled and regulated, the contaminated need to be torn down and punished."

Bronzed arms crossed as Deuc rested one boot flat against the wall, "Perhaps the strongest of the species will always survive. The mightiest, most resilient and adaptable will flourish. Your punishment and control sounds like the Etarian Charter verbatim."

Aedan could feel the heat rising in her veins, her argument increased the distance she needed between herself and this man, "Well the Etarian's had something right then. Tell me this, what does Zern do to protect the vulnerable? Give me one example."

Deuc wasn't biting, in fact his calmness irked her even more, "Easy, take a look at you. You've survived."

Aedan snorted and crossed the room, "No. What I've done. What I've had to do has nothing to do with that savage. I survived on my own skills and instincts."

"Because you trust no-one?" Deuc asked. His low words, strummed a chord within Aedan's chest.

She paused at the doorway, breaths shallow and sharp, she needed to end this, Aedan narrowed her eyes, "Trust? I trust myself."

Deuc's palm splayed across Aedan's hip, sending a swarm of wasps into flight, "Sounds lonely."

She'd spent so long, seemingly cartwheeling to stay upright, to keep the breath pumping in her lungs, and to abate the horrors that clogged her pores; the constant fight to prevent the waves that threatened to overcome her. Because alone I float, she thought, "It's better than drowning in the refuse that exists in Osiria."

She sent her forearm down on Deuc's and aimed her palm at his unshielded gut, but Deuc caught it and trapped her wrist.

Dimples rent burnished copper, "You're getting slower, *Laelaps*."

Aedan groaned, "What does that even mean?" She brought her fist down to strike at Deuc's grip, but he tugged her gently forward and slightly off balance.

Taunt rows of muscles trapped her arms against Deuc's chest, whilst thick thighs held her fast, "It's a compliment."

The menace of Asar, the Southern Reaches and her past darkened her thoughts, and tainted her words, "More like another Oddworlder insult." Aedan tried to shift backwards, bring a knee up or just wriggle to freedom. Every square inch of her front connected with raw tension. She sucked in a deep breath, a mistake that accentuated tight ridges and ruthless swelling. Squirming only increased the feather light flames that unfurled in her abdomen. Hot cinnamon caressed her cheek and she squeezed her eyes tight.

Suddenly Deuc's grip released, and for a moment Aedan's

legs refused to move. She rested against his frame. Deuc's chest rose and fell, his arms hung by his side, hands hesitated to cradle her hips. She felt her throat tighten, the urge to rest her head filled her tendons. A noise from the flight deck, stirred Aedan and she lengthened her arms. She couldn't meet Deuc's gaze as she exited.

CHAPTER 11

"We're going to need a few things." Hunter stood at the console, concentrating on the seconds, minutes, and hours that ticked by on the *Arion*'s traditional time dial. Mikro and Zoe. Zoe and Mikro. Suddenly the bounty hunter stormed from the rear room. The warrior didn't surface, "You alright?"

"Fine." She stomped her boot on the dash and re-buckled already tight buckles.

"Would you let me know if you weren't?"

Molten silver captivated his gaze, he exhaled slowly and concentrated at the braided tassel that loitered near her hips. Osirians. Lethal, temperamental, fatally loyal at times, ritualistically sly at other times; their naturally higher percentage of muscular tissue giving them tone, increased strength, speed and sharpened instincts that unnerved Hunter. Yet, they were on the whole, naïve to a common thread that Hunter perceived to run through them all; a wild kindship, almost like savage empathy, that simultaneously held them together and tore them apart. That, and an unrelenting hatred of Etarians. Hunter turned away before his eyes betrayed him.

"Probably not." Aedan murmured as frenzied fingers picked at the seam along her knee.

"I'll say something to him –"

"No it's not hi–" Aedan caught her own words. "Never mind, what's the plan?"

"We need a few things to get through to the compound."

"I don't like surprises Dios." The warrior entered the cabin, hips and shoulders swayed in perfect cadence to his somber tones.

Hunter retreated to neutral space, knees collecting the edge of the bunk, "With the Etarians preferring to exterminate me, we're going to need a way to get to Haigon undetected."

"And land," Aedan stopped fussing, "Give us the details Hunter."

"We need to get to the compound. It's located within the R & D multiplex at the Medical University, which is probably guarded by Etarian militia now. There's a disused helipad on the northern wing we could land on undisturbed, if we get through the atmosphere security." Hunter said.

"Wait, how sure are you its unused?" Deuc said.

"It's too far away from the complex to be of any use that's why." Hunter sighed. His plan was falling apart. Kegan could have marched him to the front gate. "It's over a mile. There's covered walkways for some of the way, at half-dark we could get at least half way. Then there's an open field with a garden escarpment. Above that is the compound."

"Wait. That sounds like an elevated position. We'd be exposed from the moment we set foot on that field." Deuc said.

"We need Etarian ID to go covert." Aedan said, as she rose from the chair. She paced back and forth, delicate white teeth clicked and clacked her thumb nail. Her sweet jasmine perfume filled the air.

"Yes. Potentially." Hunter resisted the urge to swallow. The girls depended on his return. Zoe. Mikro. If he'd met the Eagle, maybe his chances would have been better. Maybe not.

"Great, maybe find some Etarian ID we can use to land. Got any of that lying around?" Deuc quipped.

"Maybe not Etarian. Maybe just Merc ID." Aedan said.

"Yours?" Hunter straightened his back. The legendary bounty hunter was the best in the dual systems. She or more appropriately Kegan might be completely burned by the Etarian's by now, but at least Aedan wasn't giving up.

"Not mine. Another Merc ID, Deuc if we have to go to Asar we could find another Merc ship. I have an ideal candidate. We'll steal, borrow, beg whatever to get his Merc ID to land on Haigon."

"You're forgetting Aedan, that intersystem mercenaries are rare. Even Kegan had privileges that most weren't afforded." Deuc said, nodding to Aedan.

"Why is that?" Hunter asked.

Aedan sighed and for a moment a flash of highlighter yellow peeked under her brows, "They believed I was Etarian."

"You know, Osirian's claimed you as one of their own," Deuc mumbled.

Did Aedan's cheeks just redden? Hunter broke the silence, "Why?"

"He was too dogged to be Etarian, too fast, too ruthless." Deuc added.

Aedan's cheeks brightened and Hunter made a mental note that calling Osirian women ruthless was possibly a compliment.

Aedan cleared her throat, "If we can't get Merc ID, we'll snatch a Transport or a Mining Rig, something."

Deuc rubbed the edge of his jaw, "Next problem?"

"Accessing the compound. I had an ID tag that I left in the *Icarus III.*"

"Shit." Aedan said, "We could go back and get it."

Deuc walked towards the windshield, hands on his hips, "Maybe. But that ship will be on its way to junking. Maybe we attack an Etarian fighter."

The warrior's image quivered and Hunter sighed loudly, "We can work this out later. The big one is coming" He looked down to his forearms and flexed his fingers and wrists, hot liquid writhed under his skin.

"How long?" Aedan rolled her neck, heavy lids lowered over soft slate.

Deuc yawned, "I'll set a timer." He didn't get to, Aedan slid off the pilot's chair and into the warrior's arms.

"Last one, I promise." Hunters eyes closed as his head nestled into the softness of the bunk.

Aedan opened her eyes to the bright sunlight that warmed her cheek. Another delightful dream, the emerald field replaced with soft linen and bronzed skin. The light so vivid it burned her eyes, and cast the room into blue hues with white shadows. Deuc laid motionless beside her, fingers melted river stones into muscles concealed by dark fabric. Such a sweet dream that Aedan found herself not wanting to wake. Strange lulling movements made Aedan think of the tiny boats she saw docked at the edge of Lurland Lake. Is that where she dreamed of? Five trillion Ketos could buy her land in Lur-Kia?

Brown eyes held her gaze. It was another dream and for some reason she had imagined Deuc next to her. A breeze fluttered the sheets and a palm suddenly cupped her face. It was a dream. Safe and secret. Curiosity drove her limbs to seek tender caresses.

Like a leaf drifting to the lake's surface, Aedan pressed her lips to Deuc's. Trembling fingers snagged his hair. Cinnamon and citrus permeated her senses as Deuc's tongue breached her defenses.

Aedan broke away, her lips grazed Deuc's jaw, "See you can be gentle." Darkness lowered an unrelenting pressure over her body and severed the dream.

Deuc let Aedan slip back to wherever she had awoken from. The innocence of her kiss had felt like an invisible fist inside his chest. Then Aedan spoke, and the fist had closed and tugged. He sighed, watching his breath shift tiny autumn wisps across her forehead. Deuc's eyes started to burn as he traced the outline of her scar. Aedan seemed perfect in almost every way, capable, resilient and savagely exquisite. She didn't need his complications. He needed to get to Asar. He needed those codes. He tried to pretend the reason he wanted to 'collect' Aedan was for Osiria and not for himself. Calculations of risk and reward lulled him to a dreamless sleep.

Aedan woke to a muscular sash across her ribs, parting her

breasts and ending on her collar bone. The belt held her tight against a mountain that breathed and groaned. Aedan wriggled her hips resulting in more groans, "Move Deuc!"

"How quickly you forget." Deuc's silky breath sent flames to heat Aedan's cheeks.

"What?" Worms burrowed into Aedan's stomach.

Deuc's grip tightened, "You know it was Kegan's choice of targets that I found endearing, like a collector's edition of the worst of the worst; almost a personal crusade."

Aedan shifted in the linen, hoping to release the tension that ratcheted her muscles.

"You know I can take this away from you?" Deuc's fingers strummed the hardened skin at the hollow of her neck.

Aedan didn't answer. She tried to unravel whether she wanted him to move or stay and whether either outcome would be what she wanted.

Deuc slowly dragged his hand between valleys that made Aedan jump, "Regretting that kiss already?"

Aedan gasped, "That was just another dream."

"You've been dreaming about me?" The mattress dipped and bowed. She heard Deuc release a yawn.

She focused on the silver edge of the digi-frame. He hadn't left the bed, "You're lying."

Aedan spun so fast, she thought Deuc had dragged her off the bed again. Instead, his upper body levelled over hers, his russet eyes bored into her face, "Am I lying? You tell me."

Of course no trace of oil could be seen, but his iris remained devoid of color as well.

Aedan's thumb fell short of touching his cheek. She snatched her fingers back, "I can't tell."

The corner of Deuc's lips kicked up, "Interesting." His thumb tugged on her chin. Deuc's citrus and cinnamon flavor exploded in her mouth as his tongue lashed hers. Despite Aedan's intentions of resistance, the blossoming flames, prevented much argument. Tension rolled from Deuc causing shivers to burst and multiply through Aedan's veins. His lips slanted and his breathing intensified. A grey shadow loomed. Bricks of ice solidified in Aedan's stomach. Strings of muscles winched tight. A scream built in her throat and Aedan exhaled. It didn't work, shakes erupted in her chest. Deuc's fingers scored a tail of fire past the swollen edge of her breast and puckered the fabric at her hip. A single droplet broke free, rolling to disappear into Aedan's hairline as shards of black surrounded her.

Aedan tucked her leg under Deuc's ribcage, which sparked a deep rumble from the warrior. Deuc slid backwards, Aedan's knee rested between his pectorals. Her senses clawed at the air, wanting to taste, smell, or touch anything to dilute the aura of Deuc.

The bronzed soldier hovered, a bead of moisture lingered on his curling lip. He placed his palms upright in a move of surrender and sat on his haunches.

Aedan watched his shield shimmer. Aedan sat up, her head spinning, "I don't need a sidekick, Deuc." The shadows thinned, the walls to the bottomless pit receded.

"Whether you like it or not, Aedan, we're not so different, you and I." Deuc sat on the end of the bed, his palms either side of his head. He blinked one eyelid at a time.

A rush of moisture scaled Aedan's throat, as slashes of hot and cold ravaged her insides, "You're such a fucking … wait … I'm going to vomit."

"Never in all my –"

"No." Aedan flung her legs over the edge. Her knees thumped into the floor and her fingernails snagged in the cold steel. Curses flew from her thinning lips.

"Aedan?"

"I'm fine." Aedan said. The doorway beckoned as Aedan's internal temperature spiked, her skin shivered as if frozen. She wanted to cry out but frothy bile threatened to erupt.

On hands and knees Aedan reached the hall, Jump-lag sickness engulfed her. The hallway widened and elongated, Aedan closed her eyes as the dizziness returned. Somewhere behind,

Deuc roared, before a crash of metal on metal reverberated through Aedan's abdomen. Her plumped up fingers snagged in the steel grate.

"Aedan," A fuzzy voice sung, "Help me."

Hunter lay on his back as his liquid insides swelled to insane proportions, swallowing his lungs and immobilizing his limbs. He had reached the count of 60. He arched his neck, "Help me." He managed before his strength evaporated and his chin slammed into his chest. Suffocation by paralysis, is not what Hunter had factored in this latest bout of Jump-lag.

Aedan slithered into sight and her puffy eyes regarded his motionless condition. Her nostrils flared and lips cemented shut. For forty five minutes Hunter had battled the quicksand of his own body, begging, and pleading with Ea for something or someone to save him.

A roar bounded down the hallway. Aedan didn't move.

Hunter pushed his skull into the pillow, "I can't breathe."

With scrape after scrape Aedan lumbered to the side of the bunk. Coal circles rimmed her eyes above cheeks sucked into her teeth. The air around Hunter glittered with lilac tremors as cold fingers closed around his throat and lifted his chin.

"Thank you," he gasped.

He inhaled the delicate scent that tickled his nose. The amber flavors of vanilla and jasmine cut through the sinister slosh of his organs.

A bellow tore through the cabin and Hunter opened his eyes. The warrior squirmed on the floor, shredded skin, seeped a flurry of red from his brows to his cheeks.

"Deuc!" Hunter called.

A whimper squeaked from Aedan and her fingers left his neck, his chin lolled to one side, "No, Deuc, over here!"

With the squealing intensity of a hog on the run, Deuc's shielded metal frame moved forward.

"Deuc?" Aedan said, her voice quavered, "Come to me, Deuc." Hunter heard the woman's stomach contents roll.

Aedan turned away from the fleshy disaster of Deuc's self-inflicted torture. The pain that Deuc suffered from Jump-lag, appeared to be directed at his eyes. Aedan turned away from the mess. A burp rose in her stomach and her tongue clawed at the roof of her mouth. If she let it all go, would she choke? Would she be able to breathe? Hunter was paralyzed and slowly suffocating him, what the hell could she do? She couldn't even lift herself from the floor.

She tugged on her belt as Deuc closed in. Within a fraction of a second, the skin healed before his fingernails dug deep again. She doubted he could regrow back his eyes.

"Aedan?" Hunter called.

Her jaw ached, but she managed to swallow and looped her belt around Deuc's hands, "Wait."

Aedan stretched her leg until, she thought Deuc's neck would crack. Hunter gurgled above and her fingers found his chin.

"Thank you."

White foam bubbled from Aedan's lips, and the frigid steel floor cooled her fiery skin.

Deuc moaned once more, incapacitated by her boot on his throat and the belt loops on his hands. Aedan tightened the synthetic leather until it cut into her thigh. Her numb fingers rose and fell with the steady breaths of Hunter. If she fell asleep could she stop her hand from slipping? If she could get off the floor, maybe she could turn the Human onto his side. She barely had the strength to keep tension on her belt. Aedan dragged her cheek across the metal ridges to stay awake. Hunter could have warned them this final Jump-lag would have been so brutal. Maybe he didn't know. Maybe he'd never Jumped three times in a row. She blinked slowly as sleep threatened. Fuck. She started counting. A yawn cracked her jaw and she decided to count out loud. She would count to five trillion if she had to.

CHAPTER 12

Aedan watched Asar as it loomed in the windshield. From afar, the over-populated, polluted, and poverty stricken planet looked almost pretty. Tufts of white and grey concealed the slate stone surface, scarred with settlements, ash and clogged rivers.

"Identify," The comms chirped.

"Admin Beta one – twenty-one."

"Is that your ID tag?"

Casually Deuc answered, "No."

The silence reinforced Aedan's hatred of the bare-faced corruption that infected the Oddworlder system.

The Gauntlet, the planet's largest river ran from North to South bringing with it empty promises of food and cleanliness. Like all good liars, the river splintered into a multitude of small creeks and tributaries that flowed steadily past isolated settlements to reach the Great Lakes. Deuc coasted the *Arion* over the wide plain. Centuries of progress mining and manufacturing had reduced the Great Lakes to a marsh land of sandy bogs. If your family could afford it, you'd be cremated in Kepll's Furnace and scattered on Harper's Current. If not, your carcass would be rolled down the banks of the Great Lakes for anyone or anything to finish you. Aedan shivered. The South Reaches had already taken her soul and more.

She caught Deuc watching her from the pilot's chair and Hunter from the weapon's console. Not a word of what had happened passed their lips. Deuc had stopped clawing at his eye sockets before Hunter regained movement of his limbs. Aedan could taste the tension. Deuc pulled back on the throttle.

Neon signs in every imaginable color flickered between the scrap yard structures, the filament cracked or dissolved so the neon ended in a jumble of nonsense, that only the locals would understand. The colors of the city life sparkled in the barrage of rain that emptied onto the narrow streets, the life of Asar squished into the city for hope of sustenance or success. Asar's acidic rain stained already dirty clothes, rusted shanty rooves and widened puddles of slush that Asarians trekked through. In the distance, the isolated settlements glowed, the residents wise to avoid the Southern Reaches.

The storms on Asar could bring down five city blocks, when they struck. The wires strung up between shanties and skyscrapers alike, became death traps for the unwary. Food and women were a premium on Asar, followed closely by electricity. As they neared, the differences in old world and new became more apparent. Ancient stone buildings were separated by modern concrete towers, both types of structures, modified with a mishmash of corrugated iron, steel balustrading, canvas, any reusable resource to make the living spaces functional and weatherproof. Aedan spied another three craft landing on the roofs of skyscrapers, one passenger freighter lifted from somewhere between the buildings and headed to the stratosphere. A rail system crisscrossed from North to South and Aedan's eyes followed the track as it elevated over barricaded bridges before it dipped out of sight into one of the many sub-continental tunnels. A shiver ran down her spine.

Hunter inhaled, "I've never seen anything like it."

"There have always been plenty of hiding spots in the South Reaches." Deuc steered the *Arion* through pollutant heavy clouds.

Aedan's head ached, and she yawned. Pits of ebony burned under raised brows, but Deuc said nothing.

She had been tired, dead tired.

Hunter wiped beads of sweat from his forehead, the blonde hair at odds to his calm features. Hunter should have explained. Why did she care what Deuc thought anyway? The sooner she was rid of them the better, "I hate this place."

"Welcome home."

"Asar is not my home," Aedan said.

Five trillion Ketos could buy her safety and reliable income for Leta. A fleet of ships to call her own. The Etarians couldn't refuse her a code then. She could even buy a plot of land, real green pasture outside of Lur-Kia, semi-detached. No wait, she didn't want Lur-Kia! Heat flushed to her cheeks, Aedan ran her fingers across the graze. So tired, that not one dream crept through her defenses.

"Well it's mine." His top lip curled back to show bright white teeth.

"Keep it." Aedan tuned in the cables and listened for any news on Kegan. She didn't have long to wait.

The tall pretty blonde synth was back on the hologram, "Kegan Capare, infamous intersystem mercenary has failed to hand over Hunter Dios to authorities. Etarian commanders are puzzled at this latest development which cost the lives of 14 Etarian Militia. In a move that has stunned the public and drawn criticism from the Opposition Officials, the Etarian Government has released a bounty for Capare, starting at One Trillion Ketos, dead or alive."

"Rethinking your Oddworlder comments? How many allies does Kegan have right now?" Deuc looped a stray strand behind one ear.

In a fruitless effort, Aedan leaned forward to catch his irises, "You wouldn't?" Was it a smirk or a sneer that made his lip curl?

"Wouldn't I? I'm looking at six Trillion Ketos right now. More fool me."

Hunter's wide blue eyes darted between the nape of Deuc's neck and Aedan. The warrior's skin hadn't shimmered, his hands didn't move from the joysticks. Aedan shook her head.

"On your oath and your life, Deuc?"

Deuc sighed, "Relax Dios. Etarian blood money is not what I want."

Aedan released her shoulders. She had the feeling that if Hunter had explained why she had sprawled across his bunk, this conversation might never had happened. Why it should bother the bronzed soldier at all, escaped Aedan. For now her world had gotten infinitely smaller, she'd have to get used to living in Tuwa as Aedan, could Hunter's bounty buy her a new Etarian identity. Aedan watched Hunter from the corner of her eye, Kegan had a bounty, perhaps Hunter could hand her in for a reprieve. The consequences of risk versus reward collided in her brain. Somehow Deuc was right, she had to trust someone. Why did it have to be him? She regarded the Human and the warrior again. Something tiny slithered under her rib cage and refused to shift.

The Under Currents shunted the *Arion* upwards, crashes and pops chimed behind them. Deuc circled his black bird amongst derelict high rises. Grime scarred tarpaulins flapped violently from the places where glass should have been. Some tarps were decorated with crude markings to claim territory, advertise product or issue warnings.

Deuc manipulated the thrusters and the *Arion* descended vertically. A black calico wall bordered by red fringes called to the soldier and without a word to either passenger, Deuc punched the *Arion* through the flap. Aedan's palms smacked onto the dash, as the ship abruptly came to a halt. The nose cone dimpled the fabric at the other end of the level.

"Amazing. How high are we up?" Hunter already had his belt off as Deuc powered down his ship. The *Arion*'s ramp scraped the bare concrete floor of the structure. Aedan followed the pair as they exited. She squinted against the steam that rose from the ship's exterior panels and billowed under the tarps.

"The twenty third level, there's another seven floors above us. It's a safe house of sorts." Deuc said as he climbed the exposed steel rungs to the residential space above, the underside of the concrete area sullied by engine and grease residue.

"Well the Administration must have wondrous effects being up here. No wonder – "

Deuc cut her off, "Food there, latrine there, and one bed

there." he gestured to the far corner, "one there," the lounge.

Aedan rolled her eyes.

"Shower is behind that wall,"

The only wall, Aedan noticed, on the scant living space. As large as a regular Etarian office block, the open floor setting appeared to be divided into specific areas. The *Arion* parked below, on the left of its haphazard runway that bordered the longest side. In the raised habitable space, a cooking element, kept company with a wobbly table and mix-matched chairs. On the other side, a wire bed frame with skinny mattress loitered. The centerpiece of the room stood a fold out lounge in front of a weird metal structure. As if Deuc had stolen a chain wire fence and hung it from the ceiling. A vision of hovering Lestas and a lone chair leered from the shadows.

Deuc tugged a long hook from behind one calico blind, the returning cord slick with rain. With a few twists, the place hummed with electricity. "Use the pump to get your water. There's stairs, but I wouldn't recommend it. How long this time Hunter?"

Aedan swallowed, her tongue thankfully normal size.

Hunter opened the small fridge and rattled jars of warm Buzz, "Same, maybe three or four hours. Shouldn't be as bad, muted by gravity. The humidity should help." Hunter eased off his brown jacket, the sweat circles stained his blue t-shirt.

Deuc stopped at the wire structure, grey light shades swung in the syrupy breeze and splashed pale spotlights across the bare concrete floor. He swiped his hand across the lowest link and the chain wire fence evolved into a wall of monitors that buzzed and flashed. Communication channels, news feed, security footage and rolling coverage of most of Osiria flooded the screens. Deuc even had the entertainment and news channels from Etaria.

Deuc undid the braid that held his dark strands back as he stepped past Aedan, "First call on the shower."

Aedan held her tongue, and refused to inhale his scent as it fanned over her stickiness.

Kegan's Merc ID tag glared at her from the monitors. One trillion Ketos. How much money had Kegan cashed in bounties? Not even half that. She had killed Etarians. Fourteen of them. How many had Hunter killed?

"Nope, we'll have to wait." Hunter capped his open jar of Buzz and put it into the refrigerator door.

"Is four hours enough time?" Aedan heard the pump plunge into overdrive. The water came from somewhere. It couldn't be on the roof.

Aedan edged to the black tourniquet at the far end, as she pulled, it snagged on the *Arion*'s nose cone parked under her position. Twenty-two floors below the street line disintegrated into mush. People blurred with the edges of the structures

"Too much time."

"Is there any way to check, any contact on the inside?"

Hunter paused, a thick ocean of oil slid across azure, he shook his head, "No."

"I'd rather not cross the Sandes Belt if it's all too …" she stopped herself, "Not even for them?"

Hunter's lashes fanned his cheeks,

"Run it through the Shadow comms via a tracer block."

Hunter ran his palms down his thighs, "It's not that. If they hadn't raised the alarm – "

Aedan focused on the skyscrapers that towered around their high rise, tarps of all colors and creeds flapped against the storm. Electro-funk with heavy base beats travelled on the whirlpool that whipped Aedan's stray strands across her cheek. Her eyes darted from tarp to tarp. She withdrew from the edge.

"Try."

"I don't think her opinion on my escape would have changed."

"Her? Was she another…is she part of the program too?" Aedan asked.

"Nataly? Yeah she is in her own way." Hunter said.

Aedan stood in front of the monitors and activated the lime green hologram keyboard "What happened?"

"I made contact with the Eagle through Nataly, and we started our escape, she had a change of heart. I don't know why. The militia came when she called the guards."

"They didn't name them on the broadcast." Aedan said.

"There were three militia," his lips pealed back and he clicked his tongue, a flash of red and black under furrowed brows, "That metallic smell."

"I know how to count Hunter, they said seven."

"So do I Aedan. I don't know who is in those other four tubes."

"What do you mean?" Aedan said.

"Beats me, maybe they're empty. Unlikely. I hope the med-ico tech that authorized Juliette's termination wound up in one. It could be members of the opposition party, ex-officials. The Etarians like to keep a clean house."

Aedan let the political undercurrents wash over her al-ready exhausted mind. Did Hunter hold more secrets the Etar-ians wanted buried? She punched in the command line for the Shadow comms, recalling the same metallic flavors of her first kill, "The scent never goes away," Aedan tapped the key board and gestured to Hunter. Five trillion Ketos for Hunter returned dead or alive, one trillion for Kegan. Hunter was Human, Kegan was not, "Dial."

A three pronged grey symbol revolved on the black screen, as the Tracer Block commenced. The symbol halted, now white and pulsating on the black monitor.

Hunter entered the protocol address and waited.

Nothing.

"What time is it on Haigon? She might be – "

An asterix followed by a question mark blipped onto the screen.

"She's there." Hunter's fingers flew amongst the iridescent green. "STATUS - 1877 & 1878"

Aedan found her thumb in her mouth and worked her

teeth around the edge of her nail.

ACTIVE.

Hunter wiped the sweat drenched fringe off his forehead,
EDD?

"What's that?" Suddenly Aedan wondered whether she'd
just given Hunter the means to organize his own rescue party.

"Estimated date of disposal. On my oath or my life, Aedan."
He said, eyes concealed by pretty pink and blue hues.

"Sure."

NEGATIVE EDD. PHASE 2 RESULTS PENDING

Hunter released a sharp breath, "Still testing".

"They're still alive, that's the main thing," Aedan navigated to close the screen when another line appeared.

ETA?

Aedan's eyes trapped Hunter's wide stare. The shower
pump grinded to a halt. The monitor flashed back to CCTV and
the newscaster channels, Hunter shoved his hands back in his
pockets.

"You can tell him." Aedan spun on her heels when nasal
pitched words tore the breath from her lungs. The sucking
abyss wound snares of ice up her knees and into her gut. Her
head snapped back to the screen to face the plump faced, thin
moustached villain of her childhood.

Hunter watched Aedan's pearlescent cheeks become
hollow limestone. Mercury eyes burned at the ruddy faced Osirian that appeared on the screen. The caption read "Salacias
Gurt. Fabric merchant and Shire Warden of the Rouge Alleys."

Hunter's ears pricked at the wet footfalls that approached.

Shaking fingers ghosted across the jagged puckers at
Aedan's throat. The Warden kept talking, something about an
election, but Hunter didn't listen. A low growl emitted from
the warrior, but Hunter focused on the bounty hunter. The
broadcast ended and Aedan stalked down the stairs to the
Arion. A bar of pale light suddenly danced across the floor as
the bounty hunter watched silently through the tarp.

"Flesh merchant." Deuc said.

Heat surged through Hunter's limbs and he unclenched his fists, step by step he descended in a stampede of boots. Deuc had taken the elevator, run on a manual dummy weight system. The numbers 12 flashed in red as he leaped over huddled mounds on the slime covered stairs. People, animals, corpses, he couldn't tell under the weight of litter, trinkets and feces. Intermittent movement reminded him of Haigon Hella-roaches when you turned the lights on.

Between level 10 and 11, blackened fingers caught the hood of his jacket, his elbow collided with something malleable and moist.

Hunter had woken to the sounds of Deuc riffling through his kitchen cupboards, drinking Buzz and dressing for a mission. Hunter had hastily rummaged through Deuc's pile of clothing and found a hooded black jacket, and grabbed a length of fabric, red slashed through black, to use as a bandana.

Between level 6 and 7 the smell reached maximum intensity, and Hunter paused, lifting his mask, to retch over the handrail. It splashed into an unknown quantity of fluid instead of concrete. An image of Aedan's rigid jaw, cheeks pale, body racked with tremors during her comatose Jump-lag, forced Hunter's sodden boots forward.

At level 2, the sparse halogens allowed Hunter enough light to see a pool of waste that prevented any further decent. A steel fire-door, lead into an expansive room with poly-ply hallways and walls that jutted in all directions like rotten teeth. Across the distance, steel gates reached the ceiling but between the slats, beams of color from the streets outside, pierced the shadows. Something growled and Hunter's boots dashed to the far side.

Shuffles and moans worked their way to his ears as he passed and a thousand unseen eyes bored into his back. Rust crumbled in his palm, the steel clanged against its' hinges, as rain suddenly danced across his forehead.

A mass of Osirians pressed down the darkened street, the neon back lighting merchants who called their wares over the din of the crowd. The mass hurried to unknown destinations accompanied by a soundtrack of competing techno-funk. Broad shoulders covered by black, slipped through the crowd like an eel through reeds.

Deuc had witnessed Aedan's reaction to Gurt's political announcement and it took seconds for Deuc to make the connection and a single second more to make his decision. Gurt had multiple allies that intersected the South Reaches, he had built himself a nest of blood oaths, his allies turning a blind eye to his abhorrent practices, in turn they received safety and protection from his alliances. Deuc wasn't the only one who sought to bring Gurt down, keeping those in power like Gurt, reinforced all that was wrong with Osirian politics. But fear was an easy motivator; revenge even more so. Ending Gurt was an easy task, he hoped it would offer Aedan some peace. Maybe after all the lies were said and done, she'd find a way to forgive him. Deuc eyed the restless crowd on either side of the street as he walked. A voice sent ice slamming into his gut.

"Deuc, wait."

"Fuck! Dios." Deuc whispered as he grabbed Hunter's collar and dragged him into a side alley as the warrior regarded Hunter's appearance.

Hunter had drawn his hood over his features, the woolen cap from Anpu tugged low over his unruly hair, the bandana high on the bridge of his nose.

"Where's Aedan?"

"Jump-lag. I left her a note." Hunter mumbled.

"You should make sure she stays put." Deuc said, his voice sour, as he released his grip.

"You're not going alone." Hunter tugged down the fabric.

Deuc's lips contorted, "Touching, but I'll be fine and I'm not taking a walking wanted poster with me."

"There's a million people here."

The Osirian regarded the crowded streets, the neon lights that penetrated the downpour and left rainbows in puddles, the crush of Asarians pressed ahead as Tik Tok drivers beeped their dual wheeled transports through the rain.

"Is it worth the risk Dios? If you get tagged, I might not be able to save you?"

Hunter nodded, "I am just trying to even the ledger."

Deuc turned back to the main thoroughfare.

Shards of florescent light danced through the crowd and sparkled on the mist, now the rain had stopped, "Like you said, she toasted 14 Militia for me."

"You and five trillion Ketos..."

Hunter's fists clenched, "I've taken away her ship, her identity and her livelihood and we're not done yet. I owe her this."

Deuc sighed, confident in his own authority and ability that he could prevent a major disaster, "Come on, then."

The human brought up Deuc's Talis and secured the bandana across his nose.

Together, they re-entered the main thoroughfare, as their shoulders connected, the crowd suddenly parted around them.

"It's working so far," Hunter mumbled.

"They're not exactly ignoring us."

Hunter watched the wake of people as they walked, "I don't understand."

"They mistake us for Rebels."

"Better that than easy targets."

Deuc laughed, "I'd rather be invisible. Rebels walk around with pretty big targets on their shoulders down here. Be prepared for anything."

Hunter stared into the faces of the passers-by, impassive and uninterested evolved into fear and loathing.

Deuc lowered his voice, "There will be personal security, highly trained. Perhaps Ordian or Myrmidons..."

The air heated as soon as the rain disappeared now the press of warm bodies and the humidity forced Hunter to sweat in his damp clothes. Aedan had saved his life in Jump-lag, the terrors real or imagined it didn't matter. She'd agreed to help the girls, how could he help humans and not Osirians?

Deuc stopped scanning the passing crowd, the boy had honor. Who was Deuc to deny Hunter a chance for reparation? Deuc threw his gaze wide to the darkened laneways that pocketed his peripherals. Likely real Rebels were watching their passage through Eight Ball Gully. Somehow he had to get Dios to Rouge Alley and back again without alerting the Rebel Leader Zern.

CHAPTER 13

"Cut down here," Deuc ordered.

Three Rebels had shadowed their footsteps as soon as they entered the low lying manufacturing district of Harry's Quays. The small scrap aluminum bridges crisscrossed open sewers of slurry waste and slag. Deuc rolled his collar up to his nose and gestured Hunter to do the same. Damn fugitive attracted Rebels like Tezis to honey. Imagine what would happen if they found Aedan. He cursed himself for not being more – direct. A vision of Aedan's slinky form sprawled across Hunter, fingers on the humans tanned throat, haunted Deuc's thoughts. He forced the bounty hunter from his mind. Deuc threw up his shield.

The streets emptied by the thickening ever-present pollution that slithered between the stacks and factories after dusk. Deuc trotted down one passageway overlooked by shuttered windows and exhaust pipes. Hunter trailed his heels. Deuc turned again, booted footfalls dogged their own.

The corrugated iron drove into Deuc's back, as Hunter sucked in deep breaths. Deuc peered through the moss poison cloud. Suddenly whirlpools stirred around black boots that paced at the entrance to the passageway. Deuc froze. A silhouette dashed to the side of another, and together the figures turned away.

Deuc sprinted left and right and back again, Hunter lagged behind.

"We need weapons." Hunter said, the words muffled behind the bandana.

"Trust me." Deuc answered and put his finger to his nose. Ahead, he listened to the seemingly innocent clicking and humming sounds that carried through the steamy air as Rebel sentries stopped just beyond the corner. Shadows provided just enough hiding spots for Deuc's approach.

He punched his arm forward and squeezed, until the Rebel sagged. Hunter reached for the man's belt, but Deuc twisted his cargo to the ground. Deuc scooped up the treasures and crossed the thoroughfare to another alleyway, Hunter's ragged breaths choked the air.

Someone clicked to his right. Deuc threw his arm backwards and caught Hunter's shoulder. If they spotted him, all would be lost.

Deuc stowed the long blade and arc gun in his belt, "Stay," he whispered before he stepped into the light.

"Hey!" The Rebel called and Deuc launched. The man clutched his abdomen, before Deuc's knee collided with the delicate bones of the Rebel's jaw. He reached into the fallen Rebel's pockets and found what he was looking for. Hunter grabbed ankles and together, they lifted their victim into the shadows. Frantic catcalls echoed off the tin. Deuc stalked on.

The third was down for the count before Hunter caught up. Another bounty of long blades, a cross-bow and Markers.

"You were saying."

"What this?" Eight inches of curved silver gleamed in Hunter's hand.

"They call it Ide-an-kai"

"One two three?"

Deuc laughed and trapped Hunters wrist, "No, one into three" Deuc squeezed the handle and the single blade sprung into three prongs.

"Ah right."

"We need to move, others will come." Deuc let his guard slip.

They trotted down tight passages and shadowy corridors as Deuc lead Hunter to the border of Rouge Alley. The air shimmered red, and the Tank lined streets hemorrhaged people. Men. All men.

Beside him, Hunter reclined into the hood of his jacket, as he rechecked the fabric high on his nose. Deuc didn't bother with his.

"The broadcaster said something about elections. This Fabric Merchant is an official of some kind."

"Self-appointed. Hard to root out, like a wart. Extortion, thieving, murder, slave-trading."

"Don't all Oddworlders –"

Deuc exhaled sharply through his nostrils which forced Hunter's eyes back to the streets. The dark sky barely visible past the crimson halogens, that glittered. A layer of scum coated the cherry tarps that covered each Tank's entrance. Serpentine music, heavy with sultry kitar notes beckoned from every direction.

"How do we find him?"

"He is the only vendor of that kind."

"Aedan's kind?"

Luminous pearl skin, eyes like polished hematite, lips that pouted and bowed with the slightest annoyance and hips that drove him to distraction. What in the world of Chaos was she? A mix, Deuc was certain. Feline, Canine, or Piscean? Perhaps Oviparous like the now extinct silver salmon? The ability to morph, was that a biological chemical reaction like his own? It didn't matter. Her value had multiplied considerably since the day he laid eyes on her and even with her protests and against his best intentions, there was no way, Deuc was letting Aedan go, "Not quite."

As they strolled through the honeycomb web of flesh traders and Tanks that lined the Rouge, a tarpaulin lifted, spilling a patron into their path. Hunter bent forward, for a second time Deuc threw his arm across the human's chest. A pool of dark liquid quickly blossomed on the muddy pavers. Deuc stepped over and continued down Main Street.

The crowd grew so thick, scooters and Tik Toks were abandoned, then Deuc spotted the usual and distinct customer profile of Gurt's Tank. They passed under the elevated cargo train and followed the man, until Green Acres became visible. All the other pleasure houses, advertised their wares in the windows, turning and smiling, while a Hawker stood and called to customers. Gurt's Tank sat isolated, a few men walked past the pale yellow door, before seeming to drip in past the entrance. When they did, the quietest piano lullaby could be heard. A single Asarian male stood on the stoop and whispered promises of the "Freshest" and "Sweetest" of products. Instead of red flags with purple and electric blue, Gurt's flags were trimmed with lace ribbons of white, baby pink and blue.

"You can wait outside if you like." Deuc said.

A tiny vein twitched between Hunter's brows, "Will he be here?"

"Upstairs most likely."

Hunter paused, "No. I need to – "

"Let it fuel the rage for what will follow." Deuc opened the door and drew on his shield.

Aedan sat in front of the *Arion*'s bathroom mirror, the only polished surface she could find. She closed her yellow eyes and thought of the color purple. Opening her lids, a tinge of mauve ringed Kegan's saffron iris.

"Shit." How had she perfected Kegan's appearance? Hunter and Deuc had woken early and left to get supplies. Who knew where from and how long they would be. She had a small window to accomplish what she needed. Aedan had considered asking Deuc, would he have refused? He was an Administrator and yet Gurt remained in power. Damn Deuc to Chaos. Aedan took a deep breath and focused on her reflection, suddenly surprised by the solid black that appeared in her eyes, before it melted to butter. Aedan took a deep breath.

"Your boss, is gonna wanna talk to us. He'll want what we've got. Trust me." Deuc examined the dirt under his fingernails, and wished they ran red with blood, while the Asarian guard, named Chomper regarded Deuc's offer. Hunter stood to the rear, face still covered. Although the human's eyes stared at the floor, Deuc could feel the fiery tension that emitted from his solid frame.

"Whose he?"

"Star-wife. Keeps his mouth shut till I tell him." Deuc smirked and nudged the guard with his elbow, "Know what I mean."

The sentry's silver edged lips remained still.

"Tell Gurt, we've gotten an offer he canna refuse. Best produce this sidda the dual system. We wanna trade."

The guard shifted his heavy boots from side to side. His teeth a mix of aqua and olive slime, biting down on silver. The usefulness of Aedan right now, reading the true emotions of the skinhead that towered over him, did not go unnoticed on Deuc. Scars, either burns or marks of the trade covered his arms from shoulder to wrist. His chest, wider than Deuc's and Hunters together, wore a leather jerkin. Medallions of copper and aluminum shingles decorated the tan, and a Sikth that could circle Deuc's waist had been tucked into the Sentry's beltline.

"Illa getta Herd." The guard trudged down the dimly lit hallway.

"What was that?" Hunter asked.

Deuc sniggered, "Even some Myrmidon won't stand guard over this loot, no matter the price, but others will do anything for Ketos."

"That was a Myrmidon?" Hunter's eyes lifted for the briefest moments before returning to his boots. Deuc couldn't help but scan the clientele, etching their features, clothing, names if they uttered them, into his memory. No one raised an issue with Hunter's covered face, the regular clientele of this Tank always concealed their identities.

"No that was a half-wit Asarian. Here comes the Myrmidon now."

From the far side of the foyer, a door slid open. Deuc took in the cameras positioned above and focused on the hired thug who stalked their way. As tall and broad as Chomper, Herd swayed on thick thighs, with black and white splotched pants tucked into militant boots. His chin, twice as chunky as a normal man's pointed Deuc's direction.

"Deuc Alion!"

Hunter gasped.

"Herd Tinujani."

"How long has it been, oh wait not since –" Herds' slab of a fist spat forward.

"It's been years." Deuc captured his opponent's fingers and squeezed with only half of Deuc's strength until Herd pulled back.

Herd, the Traitor, crossed bruised fingers under his armpits, his black tank-top billowing with pillows of juiced muscles "Whose this?"

"New meat, exactly what I'm here to see Gurt about."

"Yeah right, I know you."

"Then you'll know what authority I carry."

"That's what I'm worried about." Herd's neck swiveled to either side behind Deuc. Hunter held the green eyed gaze of the man-mountain that blocked their path.

"No-one's here to cause trouble. It's a business opportunity." Deuc watched Herd's skull tilt on rolls of muscles. What joy it would bring to end this traitor's life as well. Deuc smiled. "Everyone needs to keep their head above water."

Herd consented and led them in through one door, where they were forced to surrender weapons in front of two more guards, one of them Chomper. Chunky palms pawed Deuc's thighs, and riffled through his clothing. He kept his arms up, and watched Chomper squeeze and shake Hunter's pants, sausage like fingers groped his groin.

"He only needs a couple. Like a hair trigger. That one better be on the house." Deuc said.

Blue eyes flayed Deuc where he stood, but Chomper retracted his hands.

As the Myrmidon closed the imitation gilded doors he

pressed faded buttons to Level 2.

"Didn't fancy seeing you here, what happened?" Herd's acrid breath wafted over Deuc's shoulder.

"Same shit as always."

"It must have been more than that to let you go."

Deuc had to end this lovely reunion before it got too far. Deuc sized up the second guard Herd had brought along, another moronic Asarian, like Chomper. Hunter would have to put his Ketos where his mouth was. As the elevator passed the bordello suites on the first floor, Deuc slid a length of silver from his sleeve.

"Oh you know, found an offer too good to refuse."

"Now that, I don't doubt."

Deuc spun on his heels. The Exile coughed and sausage fingers clawed at Deuc's wrists. The human plunged his Ide-an-kai deep into the flank of the Asarian. Hot stickiness gushed over Deuc's wrist and down to his elbow. He heard the tell-tale flick and crunch of the Ide-an-Kai's springs and watched the Asarian's mouth empty claret down his shirt.

Herd, the Traitor, the Exile slumped to the floor with moans and sucks. A bell tinged as the elevator jolted to a stop at Level 2. The copper and aluminum shingles jangled as Hunter cleaned his blade. The metallic heat barely penetrated Deuc's senses while the shield remained in place. Hunter's cheeks drained of color, but he nodded.

At the far end of the corridor, double felted pink doors were bordered by two more sentries. Each one an odd-shaped mimic of the primary corpse that still gurgled behind.

"Ready?"

Hunter didn't answer, the Ide-an-kai gleamed between white knuckles, single blade forward. Deuc flicked his wrist spraying blood across, cornflower blue wallpaper and plush peach carpet.

Behind the shield, each swing felt feather-light as it cut through pliable flesh and striking chalk bone. Curdles and screams muffled, intestinal fluid splashed on pink velvet and

Deuc only smelt the heavy cloy odor of insidious pleasure that rested behind the door.

Scuffles and gasps answered Deuc's triple knock.

"Herd, I told you not to -" A nasal pitched voice squawked.

"He sent me up here, I've got some new stock for you to – inspect." Deuc twirled the sabre in his palm.

The doors flew open to the tubby frame of Salacias Gurt wrapped in a satin robe and bejeweled with imitation gems. A thin moustache bridged sweaty cheeks, while Deuc took in the pale pudgy skin decorated intermittently with moles.

Gurt's dark piglet eyes stared at Deuc's bloodied face with his wild toothed grin.

By the time the modified version of Kegan reached the street, exhaustion clouded his mind. Kegan's yellow hooded eyes on high cheek bones, were replaced with wide obsidian on a circular face. His pale skin remained and so had his black bob. He didn't have the energy to change anymore. Still Kegan didn't look like Kegan anymore. He had managed to add the light blue slime to his teeth like all the local Iridone addicts. He'd even thought about a beard. Maybe next time.

Deuc hit the internal alarm system. Doors flew open, men evacuated, guards came running. He left Gurt unconscious in the level 1 stairwell.

Time and time again, his sword met flesh and Deuc's skin hummed. His blade caught in the shoulder of one Asarian, as another client dashed past. He couldn't resist and reached out, fingers separating bones, and shredding meat. A spine came free from one. He glanced at Hunter to his left. The human had one guard stuck on the three prong death-dealer when another sentry dashed to his comrade's aide. Deuc retracted his shoulder and unleashed his long-blade which pierced rib cages and organs, driving the man to the floor.

Deuc grabbed another guard and twisted till his neck popped. Another rush of four clients headed for the exits and

Deuc fired the arc gun into their backs. Suddenly the gurgles and gushes overtook the screaming. The silence that only dying can bring settled upon the level. Deuc checked Hunter, the Human's boots squelched in the pulp that flooded the carpet, but on the whole he was unharmed.

Both men dashed from room to room and freed captives before they reached the ground floor. Deserted by fleeing customers, a crowd milled around the entrance way. Deuc locked the front doors. Some of the captives trickled down the stairs their tiny feet shuffled on well-worn carpet.

"Are there more?" Deuc asked one girl, her eyes ringed in grey.

"The basement." She whispered through gapped blue gums.

Deuc lifted Gurt upright, one hand around the merchant's throat.

"He's got bio-sec." said a pubescent male.

"What?" Hunter asked.

"Biometric security measures." The boy answered.

"Right, show me the way." Deuc said.

The boy nodded, shiny blonde curls bounced about as he hurried down the corridor stairs.

"Deuc, what are you going to do?"

"Administrate," Deuc said.

Modified Kegan mingled within the crowd and focused on the façade. He tripped up one gutter and rolled his ankle on another. Rebels stormed through the crowd on either side, heading in the same direction. Kegan kept his head down, the eyes of the masses, bled grey and orange at every turn. He stopped at a food vendor and bought skewers of some kind or another. He pumped his fist and waited for the image to solidify. He'd had Jump-lag, hadn't he?

CHAPTER 14

Kegan dragged his feet clear of the muck that floated passed; the skewer of miscellaneous meat hadn't improved the rolling turmoil that brewed in his belly. He squared his shoulders. Kegan's reflection shimmered in the red paneled window, and Aedan took a moment to round out the mimic's eyes again. The concentration to walk and hold onto the abridged version of Kegan proved too difficult for the little energy he had left. And he only had a single knife.

The air shimmered of body glitter and sex as modified-Kegan winded through Tanks, food vendors, and Iridone sellers. The tart herbal hallucinogen permeated the air, and if Kegan didn't notice the pearly shine in the client's eyes, he certainly noticed the olive slime on their teeth. Kegan ignored the Hawkers that called their wares, stolen from INNA or raided from some other source. How could Deuc defend his Oddworlder way of life, where decency rapidly corroded into cesspools of exploitation, debauchery and murder?

Kegan reached out hesitantly and caught a neon sign. Maybe the predators would think he had too much Buzz or too much Iridone? Maybe he should turn back? The familiar screech of rail wheels on steel tracks above his position drew imaginary fingernails down his stiffened spine. He was close. Black shadows snatched at his ankles and his hands covered his ears. The ground sped under Kegan's boots as he ran. Behind the modified Kegan, a pair of boots soundlessly did the same.

Hunter followed Deuc as he dragged Gurt onwards. The bronzed soldier had raided the merchant's safe and found a bunch of "goodies" he had called them. Thousands of Ketos, fresh fruit, Francium, numerous ID tags and data devices that held who knew what.

The ages of the captives startled Hunter, but most of all,

the pure number they had found in the basement, that and how advanced Gurt's biometric security system had been to hold them all.

A splash of stagnant fluid landed in Gurt's face, a twitch of his eyelashes unmasked his false unconsciousness. Deuc grabbed the Ida-en-Kai and pricked the flabby skin under his chin.

"What's the meaning of all this! The Merchants Tenants have been agreed upon!"

"No, they've expired." Deuc grabbed Gurt by the jaw and dragged him across the front of each row of cages, his thumb imprinted, iris scanned and security phrase spoken.

As the captives ran, Deuc slid his knife between vertebrae, a primal scream rent the air and Gurt sucked in deep breaths. Deuc picked up a pear from Gurt's stash and began enjoying the fruit.

Hunter didn't know where to look, a crowd of captives had accumulated on the stairs, Gurt aimlessly floundered on the floor, dirty food bowls and grimy blankets littered the cages.

"Deuc?"

"Fine." Deuc finished his pear and tossed the core toward Gurt. The warrior, pulled out a Marker and placed it's red crystal upwards on the steel strung stairs. "This is a Marker," he spoke to the crowd of youthful faces, "When I press it, you have a choice. You can take all this – " he gestured to the pile of Ketos, "And make a run for it. Try and make it on your own, some of you may have safe houses, people you can go to, some of you may not. If you choose to stay, the Rebels will come. They will rehouse you, clothe you, feed you. But they will take all of this and then some."

"Deuc No!"

"Despite what Aedan says about the Rebels, they are the best and only option right now."

Hunter pocketed his hands.

The same blonde haired boy from before, the youngest of the crowd being about 13 or 14 years old, approached Deuc,

"How long till they come?"

"Maybe 15 or 20 minutes. If I were you, I'd stay. Keep the little ones with you. You will grow old repaying your debt to the Rebels. But not like this. Not at the hands of men like Gurt."

The boy nodded and directed the older participants upstairs to where the smallest of the captives waited. He lingered on the stairs, "What's your names?"

Deuc wiped his hands on his pants, "Does it matter?"

The boy paused, bare feet caking in dried blood, "No s'pose not,"

Deuc laughed, "You will do well. My name is Deuc Alion and this is – "

"Hunter Dios."

"Sure, whatever," the boy snorted, "Then where's the famous bounty hunter Kegan Capare?"

Hunter pulled down his bandana and chuckled, "Sleeping."

The boy's mouth gaped, Deuc shook his head.

"Well my name is Maethan, but I hate it and I don't know my other name."

"Pick a new one." Hunter replied.

"I think I will," The youth put his fist to his chest, "In all under the light of Ea and in the shadow of Erebus, I thank you."

Hunter and Deuc repeated the gesture, "Until the Dawn of Chaos."

The boy scaled the steel rungs which left Deuc and Hunter with the flesh merchant.

"You will not find rest with Erebus. Chaos comes for you." the soldier said as he crouched down to the flailing body. He dug the blade of his knife under Gurt's chin and ended it.

Hunter sighed, tendons and muscles he didn't know he had, finally relaxed. The overripe smell of digested food acid, feces and blood had reached maximum saturation and Hunter felt confident that walking down the stairs in Deuc's building would appeal more than remaining in this basement one moment longer.

"We need to get out of here."

Deuc nodded and activated the Marker.

Hunter headed to the stairs. He turned to regard the empty cages, doors hung open, grubby contents, food bowls and stained blankets discarded for hopefully a better life.

Back on the street, Hunter rejoiced in the sensation of fresh air that flowed freely through the bandana to his lungs. The humidity has passed with the cooling of the night, and a breeze gently eased away the lingering odor of torture. He followed Deuc down the footpath, ten steps apart, as directed by the Osirian, so as to avoid any more Rebels.

They hurried in numbers towards Gurt's tank, decorated head to toe in black fabric and armor. Silver blades at their backs, crossbows and arc guns at their belts. Hunter heard snippets of their conversations as they passed. Most genuinely excited at the prospect of Gurt's treasure. It took Hunter a while to believe they discussed Ketos and not the captives.

"Bound to happen eventually,"

"What took Zern so long?"

"He's head so full of prophecy that's what!"

"Did Zern give the order?"

"Of course, it's Rebel Markers pinging at the scene?"

"Why didn't he order us then?"

The crowd thickened and Hunter pushed his way through the throng that stampeded to see the fallout. A waft of jasmine drifted through the haze of sweaty bodies. Hunter turned to follow the source, but collided with the solid chest of a Rebel. Long brown curls swayed as the warriors elbow slammed backwards. Hunter clutched his stomach and melted into the throng.

Modified-Kegan stood outside the rear fire door to Gurt's Tank, the alarm system barely audible. Why set off an alarm? He crouched down to the narrow window that lined the footpath. Basement windows barely wide enough for a slender waist to crawl through. A fog of shadows descended the bounty hunter and he sat on his haunches, clutching the knife's handle, he sent glass shards inwards.

Kegan precariously balanced on wire cages as the smell of entrails seared his nostrils. The eerie silence pierced the thick thumps of his heart. Something was wrong, very wrong. His boots scrapped the chain wire as he landed neatly on the concrete. A single lamp hung over a pile of mess and blood in the center of the room.

Duplicate Kegan vanished and Aedan stood facing her tormentor. Suddenly the treasure hatch opened and a pale faced boy appeared on the ladder rungs. Aedan had time to call for Kegan but not the modified version.

The boy's mouth gaped as wide as his eyes.

Kegan lifted a single finger to his lips. The boy's blonde curls bounced in agreement.

Pale slender legs and rusted feet tiptoed over to stand by Kegan's side. The boy's soft cheeks hollow, green eyes fierce as he stared at Gurt's corpse.

"I thought you were sleeping."

"Sleeping?"

"Yeah, I didn't believe them, but you are him aren't you, you're Kegan Capare?"

"Believe who?"

"The others, Alion and Dios? Did he escape? I've ne'er heard of anyone escaping you?"

Kegan blinked with moistened lids. Hunter was here? Alion? Who the fuck was Alion?

"No, he didn't escape." Kegan grimaced. Every night, Aedan, the girl hidden in the façade, had dreamed of this moment and damn Deuc and Hunter had beaten her to it!

"Did he have a bounty? Wish I had of known!"

"No, no bounty."

The boy gaped again and then as if seeing Kegan for the first time, regarded their current predicament. His soft hand, wrist scarred with years of bondage reached for Kegan's. A swirl of constellations halted in front of Kegan's eyes; a binary star system on the furthest reaches of a registered constellation, "Phoenix."

"I like it," the boy smiled, "I came for this. But you can do it if you like." He pushed a flint and steel into Kegan's fingers.

The bounty hunter choked and Kegan almost slipped.

"Thank you."

Thumps and bumps sounded upstairs, layered with hushed orders.

"A couple of grey skirts came already and took the babes. They're back for the girls."

It was Kegan's turn to gasp. How did the Sisters of Leta get here so fast? They must have agents across dual systems. Aedan could climb those stairs and end all this. Run to Leta and hide; let Deuc and Hunter find their own way? Aedan's life as ruined as it stood, would never get back on track without that five trillion dollars.

Kegan shifted his boots, they wouldn't take this boy; in his early teenage years, hormones and all. What of the others his age and older? He'd be left behind.

"What about you?"

"Few of us are staying for the others."

Others? Perhaps Leta had a secondary haven, a place for this boy? Kegan took in the stack of Ketos in the corner. The Sisters of Leta would need that to fund their new adopted. All Kegan had to do, was climb that ladder. What of Hunter's girls? On her oath and her life.

"You bett'r be quick. Rebels are coming – "

Aedan crawled on top of the cages, the sizzles and pops pushed dark shadows from her mind. She willed her legs forward, as fraudulent Kegan climbed safely back in place. He reached for the shattered window and shimmied out. Two sets of hands grabbed Kegan's forearms and dragged him clear.

Kegan let them, while he chewed over the tirade he would launch on Deuc for taking the bounty on a midnight stroll. Instead, the figures spun Kegan around, shoulder pressed upwards, boots scuffed the ground. Kegan's cheeks met iron as the weight forced him backwards into the exterior wall.

"Who are you?"

Shit! Aedan scrambled to hold onto the façade, and took a deep breath, low and gruff he answered, "Rold. First names not important."

"Never heard of you?"

"Transferred from Anpu. Amber-Laor Tank."

Kegan's boot heels toppled underneath and suddenly green eyes that simmered ruby and sunset stared back. The Rebel stood a foot taller, square jaw and tanned skin. His shoulder length brown hair tussled around the leather collar of his black armor, "What are you doing here?"

"Heard a commotion, and thought there might be an opportunity." The modified Kegan tried to slur his words, how did Iridone smokers sound?

"Check him."

His companion, shorter and wiry holstered his arc gun. The same tangerine and crimson waves tainted his blue eyes. His fair hair braided at the rear, clean shaven, Kegan guessed both were around 20 or 25 years old.

Calloused hands penetrated and plucked at the bounty hunter's pockets, a single clang of metal on the footpath.

"Should we take him?" The blonde Rebel asked.

Kegan watched the green eyes evolve, orange replaced with ebony and Kegan instinctively fell to the ground. As he rolled, his heel collected soft groin. The second Rebel pulled his arc gun and Kegan slashed out. He clutched the faintest scratch up his forearm.

Aedan's boot struck something hard this time and her nails dug into the crumbling bitumen, her strength vanished and with it Kegan. All her remaining energy pumped her thighs in time with the echo of her heart. A crowd milled about the side of Gurt's tank and Aedan plummeted into it. The mass expanded and she tore at shoulders like a swimmer through wet cement. Her lungs burned and her lips cracked. Stopping at one corner, she closed her eyes and called on the façade. It slipped twice before she could settle it comfortably over her feminine form.

Fraudulent Kegan licked his lips and swallowed hard. A mob of Rebels passed his shadow. The bounty hunter tugged at the black bob and then sped out onto the street.

Deuc released his shield, the worn springs of the couch pressed into his thighs, his hands still sticky plucked at his laces.

Further into the level, Hunter cursed, "She's gone."

"Well you only have yourself to blame Dios."

"What!"

"I fucking told you – " Deuc trotted to the elevator ready to descend when it suddenly moved. Hunter paused at the monitors, palms under arm pits. He hung his head and sighed. Deuc watched the slinky shape appear from the bulk of Kegan as she entered the elevator. The black and white pixels, failed to effectively replicate, Aedan's lush peaches and cream complexion. What in all of Chaos was she doing walking around like that! Too much adrenaline still coursed through Deuc's veins to be too close to her. He sat back down and continued with his laces.

The cage swung back and Deuc peered into the darkest corners of his ceiling. The shower door slammed then the pump wound up to maximum. He closed his eyes again.

Visions of Aedan in the shower swirled through his mind until he sat up. Hunter had washed in the kitchen sink and he might as well too. There had been so many Rebels. He let the monitors buzz and hum around as he dried and changed. He had spare clothes and fetched the best fit for Aedan.

Her delicate fingers reached past the concrete pillar and snatched at the towel Deuc offered. She emerged, plait unwound, hair pulled back in wet strands. Deuc rolled his back against the pillar and let his imagination take over while he watched Hunter suck down a jar of Buzz.

"I suppose you want my gratitude."

"It wouldn't hurt."

Soft rustles of micro fiber drinking dew from the hidden suppleness of Aedan set Deuc's blood pumping. He stretched his legs and momentarily threw up his guard. It muffled the sounds of zips and straps but sweet jasmine and vanilla seeped through. He cracked his jaw as he inhaled, and released his shield, beads of forbidden flavor peaked more than just his taste buds.

"His life was mine to take away. It was mine, not yours." Her hand shot out, and he handed over the singlet. "Why?"

"Because you're right Aedan. There is no room in my Osiria for men like Gurt."

Aedan rounded the corner and pulled the hem away from her waist, silver eyes glared under wet brows as she sized up the obviously feminine garment. One eyebrow raised and her head tilted to one side.

Deuc winked and pointed to her scar, "You know I can take that away from you."

"No thanks."

"Why not?"

"Does it offend you that much?"

"No. Why hold onto it? He is gone." Deuc expected a storm, instead the blaze in her eyes dimmed.

"It is so much a part of me."

"No, it's not. Do you think his last thoughts were of you? Why hold onto it, onto him." Deuc's skin at flash point, the moment her waist connected with his palm. Despite her savage exterior the fragility of her soul made his chest tighten. "He may have given it to you, but it does not make you. Take it back, take it away from him. Reclaim as much of yourself as you can."

Deuc shoved his hands in his pockets and took a step back.

Aedan considered his offer. Deuc being tender again, confused her. She wished she had seen the life extinguish from Gurt's eyes, seen his last breath and heard his desperate pleas for mercy.

"Tell me you weren't gentle with him."

Deuc laughed and sauntered to the kitchen, "Only with you."

CHAPTER 15

Aedan sat around the littered kitchen table and sipped her fifth jar of Buzz. Whether Deuc had made it himself, she didn't care. Someone had made a clean brew. She'd felt sure she would have been able to plunge the knife in and watch the stone cascade over Gurt's eyes. Would his spilled blood ease the weight that labored her breaths and fueled her night-mares? Could she wash her hands in Gurt's blood and suddenly be redeemed? No. She didn't need cleansing or redemption, she needed to rebuild.

If anything she should be thankful her foundations would be clean and not tainted. Now, how much of her pride would she have to swallow? How much praise could she offer?

A rawness existed inside her, to acknowledge her past, the deplorable circumstances had twisted her thoughts and her emotions, the anger and fear that had fortified her inner walls. Deuc and Hunter sat watching her. No wait, they were sitting with her. No judgment, no false sympathy, no explanation demanded, no justification explored. Was it acceptance? Understanding? Fuck! Aedan blinked back tears uncertain the warmth that had crawled in under her ribs would ever shift.

She listened intently as Deuc and Hunter recalled the events of their night, with each passing drink, they grew louder and more obscene.

"He's eating a fucking pear!" Hunter slammed the jar onto the table, shoulders slumped forward, "It was horrible." He hiccupped.

Aedan reached up and grabbed the lamp that rested on the melamine table top. She tugged, highlighting Hunter's weary frame, "You told the boy your real name?"

"I know." He laughed, "And I told him Kegan was sleeping!"

They all laughed together and the sound lightened Aedan's

heart. The shock of Gurt's massacre had passed, the Universe had been relieved of one less villain.

Deuc balanced a mobile monitor on his lap, "Lucky no-one spotted you." He tossed another data device into an empty jar.

"Or him." Aedan turned the light. The fizzy ethanol and caffeine popped and sizzled on her tongue, "Is Deuc Alion you're real name?"

He plugged a stolen ID tag into the monitor, "Yes." He tugged it free and flicked, it bounced off the rim before it landed.

Aedan let all her bubbling questions rise to the surface, "Is this where you live?"

"Sometimes,"

"Sometimes, what kind of an answer is that!" Hunter gulped down the last few dregs, and plonked another round from the fridge.

"When I'm not in the *Arion*."

"Where were you born?" Aedan asked. She remembered the Alpha-Centurion constellation she saw when she shook his hand.

"I don't know,"

Between hiccups Hunter asked, "What else can you do beside rip out men's spines?"

Aedan's boots smacked the floor, "Whose spine did you rip out?"

Deuc smiled, "I don't know, some clients." He tossed another ID tag.

Aedan laughed and sipped again. Was this her fifth or sixth? "How long have you lived on Asar?" She tilted her head, the buzz warmed her belly and loosened tensed limbs. Her eyes ran over the hard lines of Deuc's face. His clean shaven skin pierced with dark eyes under dark brows.

"Almost all my life."

"And how long is that?"

"In Etarian years or Osirian?"

"Etarian," Aedan didn't like the softness of her voice and

cleared her throat.

"Twenty six."

Burnt copper shimmered under her watchful gaze. Did he just roll his shield? Aedan eyes targeted his lips, the top marginally thinner than the bottom. Why did it kick up at the corner?

Aedan halted her surprise inquisition and she reminded herself that she was not inspecting stock. Another ID tag flew into the waste, "Any clean?"

"None, if they aren't already in Kronos they're dead."

"Well fuck it. We'll march into another Tank tomorrow, kill everyone and take their tags. No problem right Alion." Hunter belched.

"Sure, sounds good." A grin too toothy to be genuine slid into place.

Aedan rolled her eyes. The darkened corners of the room blurred and she skulled the remainder, "Whatever I'm off to bed."

"So am I." Hunter added.

Aedan propped her knuckles on the sticky table top, "I never said thank you for tonight, for what you did and what risks you took to do it." Aedan focused on the spills and stains the Buzz made under her fingers.

Deuc held an ID tag in his hand, paused in mid throw, his eyes flicked from Hunter to Aedan and back again.

"To both of you. Thanks."

Hunter hiccupped, and stood, his hand on his heart, "Well if Deuc isn't going to say it I will, thank you Aedan for the Etarians, for pledging to help save the girls, for… for …saving my drowning Jump-lagged ass. Three torturous hours I never thought I'd live through."

Deuc just winked.

With a wallop of cushions Hunter spread out on the couch.

Aedan climbed down the stairs and entered the *Arion*, and removed her boots. The wooded cinnamon pillow billowed around her head and rubbed the citrus tang softly across her nose.

Deuc sat at the table and finished his drink until Hunter's snores ripped through the air. The horrendous last leg of Jump-lag had almost made him tear his own eyes from his skull. He'd woken with Aedan's boot on his chin, and her belt around his hands. How she'd managed to hold on, in her state had amazed him. Why did she save him? He poked his head into the *Arion* expecting to see Aedan on Hunter's bunk. Deuc rested against the doorway to his bedroom. What in the name of Chaos was he going to do about Aedan? He wanted to pretend it was only Osiria that needed her. In the end, it wouldn't matter, he thought. He closed the door as he exited.

Aedan writhed in sheets that tangled her legs. The sunshine of green pastures faded into the ashen slopes. The empty bed swelled and dipped as her bare feet seared across freezing steel. The shower pump groaned around Hunter, and Aedan dragged the sheets and pillows up to the living quarters, and plopped onto the couch. Deuc stood at the single cooker, an odor of herbs and something else reached Aedan and her mouth salivated.

"What is that?"

"Eggs."

"Where did you get eggs from?"

"People like to keep their secrets."

Aedan scanned the room. Data devices gone. She flicked on the monitors and a hard lined synthetic appeared,

"For reasons unknown, Salacias Gurt was assassinated last night in what is being called an unauthorized raid. Administrators are unwilling to comment and Rebels were observed fleeing the scene".

"Not for reasons unknown, this Government -" She threw her hands up and let them slap in her lap.

"Give them time. An act as large as this will filter through the proper channels. It will be reinforced."

"And in the meantime, bodies will still be exchanged for Ketos."

Cautiously Deuc slid the eggs onto three chipped plates, "The bonds of fealty are necessary for some,"

"What?" Aedan thought back to the boy. The others? "What did you do?"

"What we had to do. The Rebels will take care of them – "

Aedan's pitch increased, "You mean they'll take their pound of flesh too – "

"Not like Gurt."

"Bullshit! You all need to be exterminated." Aedan folded her legs underneath her. And what did you do? Leta wouldn't take them, but you didn't even wait around. Aedan pulled the sheets tighter around her shoulders.

A pan clattered in the sink, "Have a look at Dios and those girls. The Etarians are no different. With all their legislation and governing, they will take their pound of flesh too. What does that Etarian Charter stand for? The provision and protection of their own kind to the exclusion and destruction of all others. They stole our resources and shut the door. They left us to rot because we didn't make the grade."

Hunter wandered into the firing line, a towel rubbing his renegade hair. Purple, blue and pink sung to Aedan circled by yellow. Amused? Aedan couldn't tell either of them about Leta. Somewhere in the middle of both worlds, Leta flourished and no one had to compromise their soul in order to do it.

"I've been thinking about that. If the Etarian's knew about you, and your talents, they would never have let your DNA go? What do you know about your lineage?"

Empty jars banged in the sink, and Aedan shut her mouth. What did she know? Nothing. Not a single thing. "I know I was ten when I was sold to Gurt. Before that, the old man, Yuri, looked after me, until he died. I think he knew my parents."

"Who sold you?" Hunter asked, there was no malice in his voice.

"Yuri's son, Jurk." Aedan's throat burned, "The first man I ever killed." She'd tried and failed to end Gurt. Her failure,

Gurt's revenge had shredded the skin at her collar.

"Your eggs are ready." Deuc interrupted.

The table rocked on one leg as cutlery dug into the fresh scrambled eggs on flat Teetas. It took the men seconds to devour but Aedan let the yellow fluffiness sit on her tongue.

"My Father was the Etarian hybrid mix and my mother is Human, that's what I was told anyway. It's the best, for want of a better word, recipe. But I don't get either of you. Etarian's let their inferior products waste away over here and millennia later, they start producing Specials."

"No," Deuc wiped the back of his hand across his mouth. "You said it yourself, Hunter. The Etarians took a while to find the correct 'recipe'. Before, that Strands of DNA were taken from all over the universe, assisted by Jump gateways, those that showed signs of prosperity were mixed with the base product."

"Yes when they found Humans…."

"No Dios. They started with a different species, one that's older, wilder, and right next door."

"No!" Hunter leaned back in his chair.

"Yes. Pure blooded Osirian's hunted like vermin. The Etarians experimented, splicing them with their own DNA first, then Human DNA, the resulting HEO Hybrid, Human Etarian Osirian hybrid was unstable."

"Where's all this information coming from, the Buried Histories?" Aedan asked.

"So they say. Take the Lestas for example, they're a mix of the Osirian Etarian hybrid and something else. Sharp teeth, beak shaped nose, suction cup feet, reptilian features."

Aedan shivered, "I don't believe there's anything Human in a Lestas."

"Well, they breed like roaches." Deuc picked up the plates and took them to the sink, "You're right though, the Lestas are an ancient hybrid mix, before the addition of Human DNA. However, the HEO Hybrid was superior in strength, speed, intelligence and fertility; yet highly volatile. They were uncontrollable and dangerous. The Etarians cancelled the program and tried to destroy the HEO hybrid and all the spliced results. The true Osirian species had been decimated, too many splices. Some new species were naturally barren, the others, Etarians sterilized. When they tried to destroy the miscellaneous hybrids, some escaped. Since neither of us have tails or horns, Aedan's, mine and most of Osiria's ancestors, have more of the HEO Hybrid than anything else. Still unstable I guess." Deuc scoffed. "The Osirian DNA was no longer spliced, the Etarian Human Hybrid, more reliable, stable and compliant."

"What batch are you?" Hunter asked.

"Don't know, I think we can safely say the best." Deuc laughed at his own joke.

"You're definitely more Human than Lestas." Aedan added.

"Thank fuck!"

Hunter laughed as well but Aedan focused on the table, picking at crumbs with her fingers. Then what was she? All in all, a part of her was still Etarian. Another Human and another part unknown. It didn't matter. Etarian guards, held those girls for that exact purpose. The bounty still sat on Hunter's head. Aedan was still homeless and Kegan a marked target. Maybe Leta would make contact with her? They had found her once.

"Now we only need to find some workable ID tags. I like your plan Hunter, but I think it'll draw too much attention." Deuc fingers splayed across the back of the chair.

"Do you have any safe houses on Anpu or Hades? Lots of mercs -" Aedan turned to the monitors. A flash of light caught her eye.

"We'll have to change the *Arion*'s appearance. Plus I need a separate Merc tag for her."

The elevator cords swayed in the breeze and Aedan rose from her chair.

"Then weapons -"

"We have the Rebel weapons from last night – " Deuc's head tilted to one side and his gaze targeted the stairwell door.

Metal echoing across concrete split the air, before their ears popped and smoked billowed from three separate canisters. Aedan's knees smacked the floor, she threw the sheets over her head. Sour powder clogged her throat and peppery flames stole the moisture from her eyes. The edges of the bed wear flapped and tangled as boots stomped into her view. Mercenary brown. A weight collided with her back. She twisted and the attacker overbalanced. Aedan coiled the fabric around his neck. Shouts and cries gradually returned to her bruised ear drums as life slipped between the sheets.

"Deuc!"

"Get Dios!" He shouted back.

Tendrils of white powder pocketed by grunts and arc blasts swirled around Hunter's frame as he surrendered to a mountain of figures that straddled him. Aedan scrambled upright, and her bare feet slid as she ran.

Deuc launched forward, a blaze that tore through attackers. Tarps on the far side of the *Arion* split. A rush of bodies climbed the staircase. Aedan watched the seconds dawdle as Deuc turned to meet the threat. A plasma round, purple pulsating ball of death, caught the bronzed soldier in the middle of his chest.

A trickle of blood dripped behind his ear as Aedan's scream split her throat. Chips of concrete became missiles as ammunition rounds missed their targets. Dark strands swept past closed eyes as Deuc's spine met the floor. The crack of his skull on concrete reverberated through Aedan's chest.

Invisible tethers seemed to snap through Aedan's resolve. A wall of bodies poured through the slashed tarps and meaty fingers snatched to capture her.

Mercenaries fired at Myrmidons and Aedan dug her heels in. She reached the table, potassium nitrate hacked her lungs. She bumped her shoulders on the underside. Deuc's form supine, the charred remnants of his shirt smoldered in the fog. His chest didn't move. Aedan blinked and wiped the salty grime from her lids. Two burly Mercs held Hunter, each one punched, kicked and bit at three others who wrestled for the prize. One Merc unloaded his arc gun into the face of a Myrmidon only to be fired upon by another Merc. Aedan brushed broken glass from her thighs as she made her way to Deuc's side.

Her fingers trembled as she prodded his pliant skin. Slabs of bronzed muscle remained unmarked across his chest, edged with singed fabric.

"Deuc," she croaked, his head heavy in her hands, "Deuc." Slippery heat moistened Aedan's palm.

The last two Myrmidons had fallen, the legs still twitching on one. Aedan put her ear to Deuc's chest. An icy fog enveloped Aedan over the silence that lingered. The mist of her disbelief sliced by a voice she'd heard many times before.

"There she is, my black beauty, all sleek and pretty, and a Jump-drive that's been tearing up the galaxy, just waiting for me." Calder Vien's chuckle cut short, "Whose the girl?"

She hadn't called for Kegan, or his weak duplicate. She crouched over Deuc bare foot, singlet and small clothes, all female.

"Deuc," she whispered, her eyes obscured by moisture. Every chord, tendon and muscle ached, her arms fatigued. His chest remained still, no pulse, no response.

Calder Vien, Oddworld's second best Merc called a halt, "Five trillion can be split between one, two,...." Aedan wiped the blood that pooled around Deuc's ear, "All seven of us, but that – that is mine - first."

Aedan's insides heated slowly as her heart assaulted her rib cage. Calder must have had the plasma rifle. A dark malice blistered inside Aedan. Rifle? Long arm. Her hand crawled down Deuc's bicep, passing his elbow and clutched at the soldier's hand. She closed her eyes.

Behind her, Hunter groaned and Aedan caught Calder's eye, well the working one. The surface of his right iris had been long shattered from incendiary rounds he'd made himself. An insult about his competence brewed and she let it slide. Instead, she counted steps, seconds and breaths.

The other iris glowed iridescent purple so bright, she could barely see the red rings.

Aedan swallowed. Hunter's eyes targeted hers, orange, grey, black and red swirled so fast her lids fluttered. She held his gaze and tilted her head slightly. Still the same sunset riot tainted Hunter's iris.

Calder handed his webbing to another, and stepped forward. The crisp clicks of unfastening buckles sent shivers down Aedan's spine. She shifted one foot back. Hunter wriggled against his bonds, perfect white teeth dug into rope.

"Boys you might have to hold her." The Oddworlder's bottom lip protruded past his chin on a slant, which cascaded into a shaggy beard, his tough grimace more of a comical pout. Aedan's breaths came ragged and hard. She looked to Hunter, and ground her jaw.

Finally a burst of white shot through the storm and Aedan smiled. Hunter threw himself forward. Two Mercs went down. The commotion made Calder pause and Aedan ran. Her palms clanged on the railing as she swung onto the stairs, she tumbled down the last two, the momentum bringing her to her feet. With her thumb frozen in its impression, she clutched the *Arion*'s hatch.

"Hey!"

The roller shut in place as Calder's shout rung out, "You can't hide in there forever. Boys!"

Aedan didn't listen to the rest. She pressed her thumb impression onto the fingerprint panel around the long arm trigger. The lock popped.

She'd considered the lasers, but the targeting would be limited in these close quarters. With Hunter captive, timing was paramount.

Scrapes and bangs echoed from the hull. Aedan loaded the cartridges and found the panel that led out onto the wing. Too narrow for the long arm, she dashed to the cargo door. The roller squealed its surrender and Aedan hit the hatch. The first round struck skull and it split like a ripe persimmon. The second one knelt down for cover and lost his head all the same. Above her, Hunter rolled out of sight and Aedan ducked under the *Arion* to the tarp side. Calder's boots scrambled one direction while another pair went the other. She levelled the long arm at kneecaps. When the third Merc landed on his back, she ended him. Hunter scrambled down the stairs, his feet crunched someone's groin. Aedan didn't understand at first why his shoulders poked at odd angles until she saw the blue hues of magnetic cuffs.

He crossed the floor towards her and turned.

Aedan spied the magna cuffs and lifted the rifle, "Hold still."

The pulse round struck the cuffs, severing them in half. Hunter lunged behind Aedan and collected an advancing Merc, the splintered edges of his cuffs sunk deep into the attacker's cheek bones.

"You bitch!" Calder's backhand sent Aedan's shoulders ricocheting off the floor, trickles of warmth splashed her top lip. The long arm scraped across the ground and Aedan watched its trajectory under the *Arion* to the window ledge. On hands and feet, she raced to recover the rifle. With Calder by her side, she dove under the *Arion*'s wing, concrete imperfections scored her abdomen. Suddenly her speed increased, as Calder's hand shot out. The tarp flashed in front of Aedan's eyes as the lip of the window passed her ribs. Her fingernails snagged the torn tarp, fibers bit into her skin and the material roared as it took her weight. The rifle butt skidded to a halt and Calder stumbled on wind milling limbs. Aedan grabbed Calder's sweat stained collar and kept his momentum. The tarp sagged, as both pendants swung in the hazy blue morning sun.

"Fucking bitch!"

The fabric screeched its protest, and Aedan's fists burned as her feet scrambled for purchase. Below her, Calder cursed. Below him, twenty two floors down, the bustling street loomed.

"Fuck you,"

Calder adjusted his grip and flicked the tarp, Aedan's feet slipped, her fingers opened.

A screamed clawed at her dry throat, Calder pulled hand over hand upwards.

Aedan's shoulders burned, her strength drained and muscles fatigued. Calder kept coming and Aedan's feet scraped the exterior wall. The slippery tarp caused her chest to slam into the pillars, the breath rushed out of her lungs. She looked above to the lip of the window a full arm's length out of reach. A flash of brown caught her eye. To one side, the electricity cable snaked into the level, behind it, repulsion ropes lead to the roof. Aedan put soles to the wall and heaved.

A thick weight clamped onto her ankle, the rough and calloused skin tugged. Aedan gasped for air and licked her lips. She kicked back, momentary weightlessness allowed her to clamber forward. The butt of the rifle dragged back from the edge. Aedan's breath stalled.

A figure made of mahogany colored glass stood on the lip of the window.

CHAPTER 16

Aedan's chest tightened just as the long arm's pulse round struck a fixture that burst the worn render into ash. Calder shouted something and Aedan cricked her neck as the unshaven Merc retrieved a knife from his belt. He gave Aedan a milky wink before his hand released. The brute skimmed the surface of the building, arms and legs flailing wildly, until his blade bit into tarp. He lurched forward onto a level, ten or more stories below. His legs scrambled for purchase before he disappeared entirely.

The material dragged upwards and Aedan clawed the narrow distance until Deuc clasped her forearm. Aedan's palm shot forward and she relished the strong rhythm she sensed. Deuc's chest heaved and Aedan shuffled back from the ominous edge. For a brief moment, Deuc's chin skimmed her hair. Aedan made sure her voice wouldn't break, "I thought you were dead."

"Me? Never."

Aedan felt both irritated and relieved at the kick of his lips and dimples that mocked. She rested his frame against the *Arion*'s flank. Deuc rotated the long arm in his grip. His brows furrowed and lips thinned.

Hunter sprinted to their side, "Fuck Deuc, I thought you were dead. I honestly – " Hunter's palm fastened onto Deuc's and the human pulled the soldier into a brief shoulder embrace.

"Not my style."

"Vien Status." A voice like a paper torch burst from the upstairs quarters. Deuc's skin shuddered under Aedan's touch, but remained hot and pliant.

"You need to rest."

He clicked his tongue and stumbled under the black tail,

"I'm fine."

Together they moved upstairs, stopping at the fallen bodies, Hunter's Ide-an-Kai tight in his fist.

"Vien Status" Again the voice crackled like Teetas turning to dust. Aedan shivered. Hunter retrieved Calder's webbing, where he'd discarded it near the couch. A single black transponder flashed red, "Vien? Vien?"

"I recognize that voice," Hunter said.

"Me too," Aedan said.

Deuc stood at the monitors, the keyboard clicked in a flurry.

"The Etarian commander from the Theia System."

"That's right," Aedan said, the words echoed in her brain as she repeated, "Have it your way."

"We need to leave," Deuc mumbled, his shoulders hunched in front of the chain structure.

Aedan walked to his side. How had this man survived a plasma round to the chest? His skin broke out in a sweat. "What are you doing?"

"Wiping everything."

"At least we know who they were working for?" Hunter picked through the weapons and wiped his triple blade on shirt sleeves.

"And how they found us!" Deuc spat.

Aedan faced the monitors, a single black screen remained. The white asterix blinked followed by a thousand question marks.

The blood drained from Aedan's cheeks in competition with the bile that rushed upwards, "It was Shadow comms, with a tracer block!"

Deuc's lips thinned, white teeth cracked on his jaw, "Get in the fucking bird."

Deuc squinted at the dials as he entered the *Arion*'s cockpit, "Hunter you're going to have to fly this after I get us out."

"Deuc it was my fault."

The pain at the base of Deuc's skull remained. He'd called for his shield and it shimmered momentarily into place before it glided away like wet hands on glass. The moment it peeled away the pain returned. Loud and fuzzy in both ear drums, the bones fused together. Why did his chest hurt? The purple harbinger of hellfire! Calder-Fucking-Vien, scourge of the underbelly, in his loft with a plasma rifle! Sent by Etarians to capture the Human and Kegan, or did Aedan orchestrate this attack? She'd direct-dialed Etaria. The so-called-covert shadow communications channels and flimsy tracer-blocks meant nothing to the Etarian Militia. Didn't Aedan know that? Did she intend on cashing Hunter in without Deuc? And his throat? Why did Deuc's throat constrict? Why did his eyes burn when he looked at her? Deuc shook his head and the landscape warped. "Just fly the *Arion*."

The joysticks trembled in his palms, as a skyscraper blocked their path. Upwards they spun, until the *Arion* topped the building.

"The roof's a little cluttered." Deuc croaked and Hunter aimed the lasers, Calder's brown and rusted single engine jet exploded into sparks and flames.

The *Arion*'s thrusters surged, the curtain of slate and dust parted. Deuc sighed as the final thread of Asarian gravity snapped and the black bird disappeared.

Deuc felt the shift as the false gravity regulator activated, and wandered down to his cabin. He rested the long arm in the crook of his elbow, the edges of the hallway swelled and dipped. He needed sleep desperately. His shoulder snagged on the doorway. Deuc paused as he surveyed his room. Expecting to see the rifle cage busted and lock demolished, Deuc retrieved the fingerprint guard from the bed covers. He rolled the security panel between thumb and forefinger.

Black boots with excessive buckles peeked into view.

"How did you do it?" He called for his shield and it lingered for a moment longer before fleeing like a coward. He didn't want her vanilla jasmine scent, anywhere near him in this state. Thunderclouds roared through his skull, his forehead rested against chocolate silk.

Deuc heard Aedan's sigh before she stood in front of him. She pressed her thumb to his and a shimmering heat tickled his skin. The swirls and whorls warped and flourished, a mimic of Deuc's thumb impression now duplicated on Aedan's skin. A weight sunk through his chest. Thief, liar, traitor! She was going to leave him for dead! His words of accusation fell silent as the pillows caught his head.

Aedan wet her hands under the facet and scrubbed the flaking blood from her cheek, the tender welt morphed black and purple as she cleaned. Damn Deuc! Damn him to the end of Chaos and back again! What was she supposed to do? Let them die? And then the coded message, Hunter's plea to Nataly! Aedan had given them an open coded source to track. Shit!

The mirror's surface cooled her forehead as Aedan closed her eyes. Nobody had ever recovered from a plasma round to the chest. The vision of Deuc's limp body replayed in her mind. Life extinct. Gone. The moment stole something from Aedan. Something tiny and fragile that lurked inside. And then, to see Deuc rise; the tiny something had sung. She buried it.

Aedan straightened her shoulders. Pale grey challenged her to right her wrongs. Hunter had risked his life to avenge Aedan's past. If Hunter's retelling was correct, Deuc had left first to seek out Gurt. He'd given Aedan peace. They both had. And she'd brought Etarian hired Mercs to their doorstep. She had to move, those girls needed their freedom, the girls would lead to Leta and Aedan's freedom from Kegan. Aedan took a step back from the mirror as her last thought ricocheted. What would her life be like, free from Kegan? Aedan paused outside Deuc's room, as she listened to Deuc's slow steady breaths. A sliver of an alternative future began to blossom, and Aedan didn't like the image or the occupants.

Hunter rested in the pilot's chair, his leather jacket hung over the back as he picked and prodded cuts and bruises. The dark blanket of space sparkled with gemstones and cooled Aedan's temper.

"I tried to tell him."

"Don't worry about it, I made you do it. Forget about it."

"Where to now?"

"Faros."

"Where?"

Aedan clicked the monitors, and tuned the communication cables to a low hum. A quaint little planet, three out from Kenina spun on the 3D hologram.

"Faros – next one over. We'll take the AK jump station."

"What's there?"

"Rubbish."

Hunter flicked his fringe over furrowed brows, "Rubbish?"

Aedan's boots rested on the dash and she reset each buckle, "The *Icarus III* should be there by now, we're going to get your tags."

"Do you think that's wise?"

"We just blew up the *Nifitsa*, Calder's ship," Aedan went on, "We might have been able to salvage her tag, but that won't change a thing. We need Etarian ID. So we go to Faros." Aedan mused over the fireball that had erupted on the roof. Calder. Serve him right to have his incendiaries, the unstable HMX crystal, brewing in the *Nifitsa's* belly.

"Do you know him well?"

Aedan scoffed, "Calder? Yeah, he's been trying to sabotage Kegan for a long time. I've almost brokered him twice. He takes huge risks with his crew's life. He's been lucky a few times and it's paid off."

"The Etarians took a bet on him."

"Exactly and look what he did. Rushed in, in broad daylight, multiple weapons, a plasma gun of all things – " Aedan paused. Something leaked from the corner of her eye and she caught it on the back of her hand.

"I thought – "

"Same." Aedan nodded, not trusting her voice to remain level.

Asar grew faint in the distance, INNA the orbiting trade center reduced to a tiny white speck as the Ante Kenina jump station blossomed into view. Aedan reset the jump drive dials and plugged in the Osirian's code. "Ready?"

"Yep."

The *Arion*'s lights dimmed, the outer panels quaked as the ship skated over acres of space. Slowly strands of pearls became individual stars, the inky blackness still and quiet.

"What's a Myrmidon?" Hunter broached when his stomach had settled.

Aedan sighed, "Have you heard of Fletch?"

"Isn't that a disease?"

"Yeah – the infectious strain, there's rumors you cure it, if you have enough Ketos. The genetic strain, passed from mother to son, effects the body's growth from birth, larger muscles, stronger bones, smaller brain. Myrmidon are those selected from the pool of those children, trained in hand to hand combat, weaponry and then juiced with all and any kind of synthetic drug they can find. The lumps they develop later in life, is all part of the rapid declination of the disease. They have an expiry date, 80 years at best. Employers will pay a mighty price for a fighter with nothing to live for."

"Really – 80 years?"

"I know, nothing but a blink in the eye of an Etarian," Aedan paused, what was her expiry date? Etarians had been documented to live well past 1000. Visions of DNA strands collided with ribboned pony tails and brought Aedan back to the present, "Some Myrmidons work for themselves, like Mercenaries, the profit and loss is on them. At some stage Myr's were used for the Administration but the Rebels kept poaching them for laser fodder."

"I've never seen anything like it, the Osirian system at full tilt."

"Changed your mind about those codes?"

Hunter paused and Aedan honed in on his irises, "No. I gave my word." Peaches bled into whites, all oil free.

Aedan studied her fingernails. He didn't even ask if she'd changed her mind about his reward. A herd of flutterflies burst in her stomach. Where in the name of Ea had she landed herself? Maybe Hunter had an escape plan when they got the girls, maybe it was a suicide mission. The thick rattles of Deuc's slumber reached Aedan's ears, and she focused on the field ahead.

"Back in the safe house, you waited for something? What was it?"

"Huh?"

"My eyes, you waited for something, a sign."

Aedan smiled, "They finally colored over into white. Hope. I took it as a good sign."

"I thought you had a plan."

"I did."

"Throw yourself out the window?"

Aedan laughed out loud and the sound caught her by surprise, she turned to Hunter and watched a new swirl of turquoise drip through yellows and pinks, followed by a flash of lilac. Purple. Calder's eyes had practically ignited with violent hues of violet.

"You hungry?"

"Sure."

Aedan scavenged Deuc's reserve stores without finding much else other than flavored Teetas and protein paste. She caught a shiny surface and paused. Kegan had never drawn the color purple. Aedan shook her head. Humans. Endearing. Loyal. Naïve. The Etarians had burned the bounty hunter. If she couldn't have Kegan, she would need that five trillion dollars. Well, sixty-five percent anyway. The twin girls had to go to Leta. She pondered her end game.

"Let's hope Faros has better," Hunter bit in, flakes floating down to his lap, "Any Buzz?"

"Sorry, just this – " Aedan took a big gulp of the mineral water and squinted, "Should have restocked before I decided to broadcast our location to the dual systems."

"How were we supposed to know?"

Aedan picked the threads near her knee, "I should have known."

Hunter shrugged his shoulders, "Don't. It's over, we're all still alive."

Only just, Aedan thought.

Calder Vien stared into the flames that engulfed his *Nifitsa*, the acid laden rain insufficient to extinguish the fire on his single drive cruiser. Calder tilted his head, his one good eye struggling with the distance between his present position, atop the skyscraper's roof and his melting possessions. His boots struck refuse, Calder's footsteps inaudible against the crepitation of his spaceship.

His grizzled cheeks rasped against his thick fingers. Well you decided to smuggle your latest batch of HMX crystals in her belly, you stupid bastard! Still, the risk had been worth it. He'd banked on cashing in a bounty of six Trillion Ketos if he'd successfully cornered the pretentious Kegan Capare and the bounty hunter's latest mark. Calder blinked amidst the torrent of rain that coursed through his hair, the *Nifitsa's* heatwave entwined with the infuriation that unfurled in his chest.

"Damn Osirian Rebels!" Calder spat.

He'd chased Capare and the Human to this Rebel Safe House, on advice from the Etarian Commander, only to have his reward snatched out from under his fingers. Was it a set up? Did Commander Braccass know what awaited Calder's ambush? Everyone knew an Etarian bargain was as good as a vulture throw in Tarli, and Calder should know, he'd thrown his fair share of vultures and lost more than his share in Ketos.

The radio chirped, "Calder, report!"

"Yes Commander Brac-ass." Calder snorted.

"Insolence is unwise in your predicament Calder." The words

crackled across the radio waves, like a thousand Hella-roaches on parchment.

Calder cleared his throat and said, "They've escaped. Capare and the Human."

"Follow them." Braccass snapped.

Calder laughed as he brought the transponder to his thick lips, his back teeth ground down, "I can't. They destroyed the *Nifitsa*. You want them, come and get them."

White noise erupted from Calder's communicator. Let the Etarian Commander chew on that for a while. Calder had already hopped in bed with the Etarians more than he liked, although not a loyalist, or a Rebel sympathizer, making deals with the enemy crawled under Calder's skin like fish fighting for air.

"You heard me Commander. I'm done."

"Perhaps you need reminding of what is at stake."

Calder inhaled, the acrid odor of scorched electrics ghosted across his palette, he closed his eyes against the late afternoon hues pocketed by rain clouds. What little remained of Calder's family, his last living son, his elder sister and her offspring, depended on Calder's success. Etarians enforced swift punishment for non-compliance. He shivered into his jacket, the aged imitation leather fraying at the edges.

"Unless you're going to negotiate me a new ship, Braccass I don't see how I can follow." Calder's voice broke as his thumb slipped from the receiver.

Calder shook his head. If the Osirian Rebels discovered Calder had been dealing with Etarians, he'd swing like yesterday's linen. If Calder failed the Etarian Militia his whole family would perish.

The radio sizzled, *"There's always room for negotiation, Calder."*

Faros expanded in the windshield, eddies of Verdigris and teal churned the surface of the tiny bauble, the midday hurricane in full force. Amber halogen lights lurked through the gaseous atmosphere as the pump plants and refuse stations bore down in the storm.

"Ready?" Aedan nudged Hunter out of the chair and he willingly obeyed. Aedan had set the *Arion* into orbit until the eye tracked over her mark. Under Aedan's fingers, the *Arion* danced through turbulence and washed off sheets of rain as it banked low over the compounds. The speed and agility was second to none. Where had Deuc procured such a magnificent piece of hardware?

"What is this place?"

"Oddworlder trash. Everything from everywhere ends up here to be recycled in parts or melted down."

Hunter tilted as far forward as his belt allowed, "They haven't called us over the comms?"

"Midday hurricane, natural weather disaster whips the frequency, and allows a quick drop in zone."

"Fascinating! How did you work that out?" Hunter's knuckles tightened on the arm rests.

"Followed a mark here, Julion Thiuu – Fraud. 34 days and ten thousand Ketos." Aedan walked through that afternoon again. The barge-hut door swung inwards to the blackened interior and Thiuu's pendulum-like corpse.

The black bird skimmed the white peaks of Viridian waves, teased to maximum height. Splashes and sprays licked the undercarriage.

Growls and gurgles emitted from Hunter's stomach. Out of the corner of Aedan's eye, she saw the human lick his lips, "What will you do now that Kegan is burned?"

"I'll work it out." While they'd orbited, Aedan had solidified her plans. She'd follow the girls to Leta and hide. Only until she managed a new identity; one that didn't drain all her energy, "You know, you two could go on without me?"

"That's true. But what type of person would I be. I'm trying to prevent two girls succumbing to their fate, how could I do that, and leave one behind?"

"I'm no girl, Hunter."

His rainbow highlights muted to cherry-lilac, before they melted to blue, "Oh, I know. You can take care of yourself. But how? Helping me took away your livelihood, your ship, your name. All that kept you from falling into the hazards of these worlds."

"You're not responsible. I chose to help you and those girls."

Hunter turned his fringe over his ear, "Why?"

Aedan took a moment to gather her thoughts, Hunter's inquisition tugged at her essence, the drive that kept her going and here she sat discussing it with her latest mark. "Salacias Gurt. I know it's not the same, but for me it's too close to distinguish. And you took him for me. I owe you. I owe them."

Hunter's forearms tensed against the wind shear that rocked the *Arion* from side to side and managed a weak smile, "Well it was worth it then. You're not thinking about landing in the ocean?"

Aedan laughed again, "No." Humans are not designed to travel by sea, it would seem, Aedan thought.

The blustering gusts decreased, and the *Arion* levelled out. Aedan pulled back on the thrusters and let the ship flutter and dip over the currents. Crests upon crest beat a whirlpool of waste across the broadest ocean in the dual systems. The compound and residual plants and factories rested on giant steel structures pierced into the bedrock.

Hunter's palms braced against the windshield, "It's refuse, all of it."

"Most of it, yes."

Hunter's forehead rolled across the glass, "How do they survive?"

"The ocean was fished out centuries ago, the water useless except to support the flotsam. They trade Ketos for junk and turn it into more Ketos to trade for supplies."

"And the *Icarus III* will be here?"

"What else would they do with it? The Etarians aren't coming to get it." Hades wealth-obsessed officials wouldn't let an opportunity like that slide by, Aedan thought. The *Arion* glided away from the hurricane locked settlements. She punched in a set of coordinates and let the computer do the rest. Within minutes, the *Arion* plotted a course south of their current trajectory, "It'll just be a matter of where."

Aedan curled Deuc's ship around a single point plotted amongst the vast rubbish tipped swell that rolled across Faros' surface. Amongst the immense array of plastics, foams and miscellaneous objects, a charcoal colored barge loitered, its thatched hut barely visible from this height. "It's not the Etarian Governor's office but I don't know anyone else who knows about it. I never did enough reconnaissance to use it permanently as a base. The daily hurricane puts me off."

Hunter nodded, "It didn't do Julion any favors. Could he have told anyone about this place?"

Aedan paused. One of only two bounties she'd handed in dead. Validating his warped features had been one problem, cleaning the syrupy rancid smell from the *Venator* had been the worst. "No. He took his own life."

"But you said – "

"Look it's not one of my proudest moments,"

Hunter harrumphed and gripped the chair supports again.

"Hold tight." Aedan put the *Arion* into a spin, the wheels tiptoed across the worn surface.

CHAPTER 17

A mixture of salt water and debris sprayed over Aedan as a breaker squeezed between the barge and surrounding wreckage. The cold water soaked her boots, "Tie her down, I'll get the cover." Aedan dashed across the rusted planks to the hut at the far end, plastic of all kinds and shapes swarmed around her ankles before gravity stripped it over the side and back on its journey. The door swung inwards, the hut just as dark and empty like it should be.

By the time Aedan retrieved the tarpaulin, Hunter had done his job and the *Arion* had been safely anchored with a high tensile wire at the front and two at the back. Together they hitched the tarp over the *Arion*, slightly bigger than the *Venator*, which left a 2 foot gap to crawl in and out of.

"I'm sure he'd kill me if I let it rust. We'll wait out the storm, then go hunting."

Aedan ignored the rolling swell that dipped and peaked, she enjoyed the drum roll of intermittent sprays and splatter of rain the cyclone whipped up. Mixed with Deuc's snores she could easily drift off to sleep on Hunter's bunk. She sat up. Complacency was dangerous.

"Everything alright?" Hunter asked.

"Yeah, fine."

First, Aedan did a stock take of the weapons, recharging the arc guns stolen from Asar. Then, she decided to root out a re-action vessel. She found it and a length of hose with valves on it to use as an airlock. By the time the storm passed and the waves lulled, the mixture of Teetas and proteins had finished boiling on the cooker.

"What's this?" Hunter asked.

"A new batch of Buzz," Aedan tossed the gelatinous mixture into the fermentation container.

"Tell me about Nataly."

The Human rested his back against the shelves, and crossed ropey arms over his abdomen. "She's complicated." Hunter's irises brewed a trio of candy.

Aedan washed her hands and glared at the human, "Tell me. Look what happened last time."

He blew out a long breath between his teeth which shifted his fringe.

"She's Etarian. She's 19. She's blonde. She's five foot ten -" Blue shot through with purple in a heartbeat.

"Alright!" Aedan laughed, "I get what she is to you, what is she to the Etarian genetics program?"

Hunter worked fingers across his brow, "She's a tester."

Aedan's mouth gaped.

"Not like that!" Hunter caught a laugh into his fist, "She's also the Chief Director's daughter!"

"Oh okay," Aedan walked outside and reveled in the sunshine that painted the dirty ocean turquoise. The barge itself had been enveloped by bulkier items of flotsam providing a nest of rubbish. Half sunk containers, machinery, and housing items secured a buffer around the barge from the majority of rough swell. Aedan unclicked the tarpaulin and stared out to the horizon where millions of tawdry plastic diamonds glittered in the afternoon sun. So Etarian politics played a closer part in Hunter's world. What role did the Chief's daughter play in all this? She betrayed Hunter in the end, did one of the seven crematorium tubes contain her body. If so, who did they message in Etaria? She licked the salt spray from her lips and returned inside. She waited for the clicks from the other chair before dusting off. They'd search the south first.

Hunter watched the white caps minimize in the windscreen, musing over Nataly. She'd sold him out again. The thought rested uneasy over his heart. Had she? His tagline had been the hash tag and yet lines and lines of Nataly's tag, the asterix and brackets had appeared on Deuc's monitor. The Chief Director's daughter had been an unhealthy distraction of Hunters for a long time. She'd returned in kind, flirtatious smiles and subtle innuendos had set his nerves on edge. Then one night, Nataly arrived at his containment unit, eyes ablaze and moist. Nataly had unloaded, her words jumbled with hic-cups and sobs. His nearing expiry date, the twins, his sister's death. Then the Etarian princess had vanished. Those tortur-ous days in the middle, the rage he had to simmer, the pretense he had to maintain. Ten days later Nataly had returned with a rescue plan. Too late for Juliette, Hunter mused. Hunter's fore-arms ached, glancing down he released the arm rests.

Deuc dreamed. He never dreamed. The bones at the rear of his skull had finally fused together and his platelets must have reached optimum levels. So now his mind dreamed.

He stood on the mountain of ash, bleached bones jutting through the rubble. In his hands he held a silver ribbon that snaked through his fingers to the ground. He tried to stop it touching the dust, stop the ribbon soiling itself in the muck, but the tighter he held on, the slipperier it got until it unraveled. The tiniest fragment connecting.

Deuc's eyelids flashed open. A dark blue haze coated the inside of his room, sending white shadows over the knick-knacks. His long arm stowed but not locked. He sighed. She'd fucking lied. She'd taken a part of him. His chest compressed and he stared at his thumb. How long had she waited over his *dead* body to steal a part of his identity? And the infamous bounty hunter had led Etarian paid Mercs straight to his door. Why? Had Aedan and Hunter hatched an escape plan? He'd worked so hard to gain her trust and she'd destroyed his.

From his bunk, Deuc could hear the purr of the *Ar-ion*'s engines through atmosphere. The reverberations rippled through his mattress. The *Arion* was in flight on-planet. What the fuck had they done now?

He called for his shield, it drove the air from his lungs as it slammed into place. Nothing hurt. Deuc repeated as he strode to the main cabin.

Aedan sat in the cockpit, one boot folded under the other knee, her observation interrupted with laughs and grins to Dios who did the same.

"Where are we?"

The girl jumped and Hunter's cheek split into a wide grin, "You look like shit!"

"Missed you too Dios. Where are we?" Deuc checked himself before he approached the chairs, standing in Aedan's peripherals. She'd see the shield, but something told Deuc, it was necessary.

"Faros." The human answered.

"Why?"

"The *Icarus III*," Hunter gestured for Deuc to sit.

Deuc waved his hand and stepped back, "What's that smell?"

"Aedan's making Buzz."

He let the silence stretch with the tight muscles that bunched behind his shoulders.

Aedan didn't move.

"It's getting dark, my bird doesn't touch the ocean."

Aedan finally spoke, a tiny fractured thing with poisoned barbs, "Trust me."

The sun set on Faros, turning the oceans to silken ebony. If Aedan let the image drift, she could envision the peaceful all-encompassing curtain of space. Deuc hadn't even addressed her. He had looked like shit. Dark marks circling his eyes, cheeks drawn and lips tight. He'd held onto his shield.

Aedan inhaled the pitchy salt air as her fingers brushed caked residue from the barge handrails. The tiny trash-can planet, had no moon, so the glistening Charoen, glowed violet in the night sky. Appearances could be deceiving. The delicate lilac surface looked enticing from afar. Even though Aedan had never been to Charoen she had been warned about its' brutal and inhospitable climate. The sparsely populated sphere sizzled during the day and at night the air could steal limbs with frost bite. Settlements had begun underground sometime around the Eon of Nesoi. Unprepared travelers had moments within dusk and dawn to reach the inner settlements before perishing in the elements. If they deemed you suitable to enter that is. Aedan mused over the savage isolation of Charoen, did it envy those orbs with satellites?

The hut door squeaked on its hinges, Deuc appeared, seemingly satisfied with the safety and remoteness of the barge. He stalked into the *Arion* without saying a word. From under the tarp, the glow of the ships low lights shimmered across the rusted ferry floor and Aedan hesitated.

First she checked the buzz, which bubbled away nicely, as she listened to Deuc and Hunter.

"I freaked out about the girls and the time we'd spent in Jump-lag. I needed to know."

"She should have known better."

Hunter sighed, "She said the same."

Aedan entered the main cabin and Deuc's jaw closed. A tiny vein twitched. Aedan stalked past the back of his chair.

"Tomorrow we'll have about five hours to search until the hurricane covers this area." Aedan said.

"Okay and if we don't find it?" Hunter asked.

"The currents sweep the debris in only one direction. We'll find it."

"While you're wasting my fuel cells?" Deuc finally spoke.

Aedan sighed. Confrontation itched her neck, like a noose. "You got a better option?"

"Not since you burned Asar." Deuc spat.

"Ease up Deuc." Hunter tried.

"Hunter, don't. I don't have time to wrestle your ego Deuc, I'm going to bed."

Deuc didn't move, "Go on, jump right in. I bet it's still warm."

194

Aedan wanted to tear the sheets from the bed and drive her knife into the pillow, but a tantrum of that magnitude would solve nothing. Charoen watched over her as she slept.

Deuc relaxed on his bunk, traces of vanilla jasmine irritating his skin. He ignored Aedan this morning and decided not to participate in the pointless search party. Even if they found the *Icarus III*, there was a high probability that the Etarians had worked out which ones Hunter had pilfered and simply revoked the permissions. They needed more and attacking Etarian's seemed a fine option for plan B. Was Aedan buying time for an Etarian rescue mission? He'd checked and re-checked the comms every chance he got. Not a single transmission had been sent from the *Arion* since they landed. He'd let them waste this time while he worked out his next move.

Damn Mercs and Myrmidons crawling all over his Asarian hideout. He had to get the girls, but what to do about Aedan? The conclusion he tried to avoid seemed to be drawing closer despite his efforts. Yet if her loyalty remained with the Etarians, maybe it was for the best.

Aedan and Hunter's conversation stirred him from his cabin, the topic luring him to loiter just out of sight. Deuc watched the interaction between Human and Osirian, with a mix of jealousy and curiosity.

"Why did you come with me on Hades?" Aedan asked the Human.

"I thought you were the Eagle remember."

"But why? What's an Eagle?"

Hunter clasped Aedan's forearm, "Go on."

Aedan's brows knitted before she flushed Kegan's tattoo into existence. Black ink swirled through until broad feathered wings shone on her skin.

"That's an Eagle." Hunter said. His blue eyes connected with Aedan's silvery gaze.

"And the Eagle, a Rebel sent you to INNA?" Aedan took her arm back.

"Yeah, perhaps I should have made contact, but judging by what I've heard of their leader Zern, and the ones I saw in the Alley's they'd probably hand me over just the same."

"Well someone sold the information about Kegan picking you up on Hades to the Lestas."

"Zern's Rebels working with Etarians?" Hunter pondered.

"Sounds just as corrupt as I'd expect,"

Deuc's entered the cabin and Aedan gulped.

"Do you know whose minerals we process on Hades?" Deuc interrupted. Hunter sighed, his brows dipped. "The ones that clog the atmosphere and poison the inhabitants?"

Aedan's silver iris stayed glued to Hunter.

"Etarians. I know." The human said.

"Do you know who sets the commodities, exchange rates and quality of supplies that reaches INNA?"

"Etarians," Hunter answered again.

"You know nothing about Osirian history Aedan; blood feuds run deep on our side of the Sandes, forgiveness does not. There are only a handful of Osirians who would consider bargaining with Etarians. Calder Vien is one."

"Why should I believe you?"

"Common hatred makes the best bedfellows."

"So by your assessment, Calder hates Osirians as much as they hate Etarians."

"No Calder is an entrepreneur whose earnt himself an injection of Francium."

Aedan swiveled back to the dash, "Storms closing in, we'd better return."

Aedan's voice drove under Deuc's skin. So she was loyal to Etaria, even after they'd put a bounty on her head? Was she trying to defend Calder, him of all people?

"If it's not here, then where is it?" Hunter said and moved back to the overcast windshield.

Deuc's lips curled around barred teeth, "The compound."

"We can wait for –" Aedan started.

Bubbles of heat stirred within Deuc's blood. The deceiver,

the thief, if she had a plan he'd force her hand.

"No. No more waiting. Use the cover of the storm to fly low enough over the compound. If it's there we'll return at night." Deuc pulled on his shield even though instinct told him to release it. He pumped his fists.

Her poisonous tone spat, "Fine."

Deuc's skin itched, "Does that not suit your timeline *Laelaps*."

"Let it go Deuc," Hunter warned.

Deuc cracked his jaw, finding the mattress on Hunter's bunk too rigid to ease his temper, "That's exactly what I'm doing, Dios."

Aedan rerouted the *Arion* back to the north. Hunter strapped himself into the chair and gripped the arm rests. Deuc's back slammed into the bulkhead. So she might have tried to run with Dios after all?

The compound rested on a massive steel structure embedded into the sea floor. From one end, the debris entered the dual hatchways for processing, separating to one side for recycling and the other side for smelting at the foundry. The compound narrowed and both sides converged on two landing pads, their giant white H's vacant, the transports hidden. The whole compounds' storm shutters had been sealed against the salt water onslaught, leaving halogens flicking on half glow. Rusted solar panels pocketed, every other surface as massive wind turbines sat silent. Hunter rested his head against the *Arion*'s windshield.

Aedan's neck craned, questions upon questions burst in her brain like bubbles from Buzz. She had to focus, "See it yet?"

"There. There it is!" Hunter said.

Aedan leaned forward, banking the black bird to the left. Sure enough the yellow and grey stickers of the *Icarus III* bobbed in the swell.

"There's a lot of debris penning it in." Aedan ventured. The haphazard pontoons clung together buffered by the rusting buoys and torn nets that guided debris into the entryway.

"Perfect." Deuc said and stalked down the hallway.

Hunter's iris exploded in white, "What's the plan?"

The storm whipped a furry of white peaks under the nose cone as Aedan followed the beacon back to the barge. For the next few hours, Aedan formulated plans and countermeasures with Hunter. Her eyes drifted back to her forearm. She'd spied the Eagle markings somewhere and copied them, but where? Where had she been before Asar? Eventually as Kenina's sapphire disc sunk into the sea, Deuc returned to the main cabin. The prospect of an apology crossed Aedan's mind, but the words refused to surface. Instead she let Deuc's anger seethe, he still needed her, moreover he needed Kegan.

"The workshops shut down at night, the outer stock-ponds shouldn't be under surveillance. And even so -"

"Where are you going to land?" Deuc jibbed.

"Huh?"

"Where are you going to land? You're not putting my bird in that water."

Aedan gripped her knees, "The landing pads are – "

Deuc cut her off, "At the other end. You saw them."

Aedan inhaled sharply, her cheeks blistered as hands rested on hips. She glowered at Deuc's hostility, "I know what I'm – "

"So it's not another trap?"

"What Deuc? Just fucking say it!"

"You led Etarian-paid Calder and his Myrs straight to us! And Now, we're just supposed to trust you?" Deuc spat.

"This isn't about trust, Deuc" Hunter warned.

"Sure it is, she lead them directly to us. Were you going to turn Hunter in without getting those girls? Such a shame your friend Calder hadn't done a proper job."

"Fuck you Deuc!" Aedan snapped.

"Deuc...." Hunter started.

"The Human here trusts you, but did you tell him how you got my rifle?"

"I didn't know, … I did what I had to." Hadn't you always? She thought and gritted her teeth.

"She stole my fingerprint."

"What?" Hunter's eyes glistened pearl.

A spike of heat rushed Aedan's veins, and she spun to the windshield. She was losing ground, "I didn't know I could do it until I had to."

"That's great – we can change the permissions on the tags – we can -" Hunter mumbled to no-one.

"Well who knows what other secrets you have? Any more plans we should know about? Here I am risking it all and even after Green Acres. So much for loyalty, Aedan, now you're going to do – "

Aedan smacked the dash and faced her accuser "Risk, you want to talk about risk? I lost everything!" She could hear the screams barely restrained. She'd never tell him about duplicate Kegan. About dark eyes that cut through the yellow. She sucked down sharp breaths and tried to focus the anger. "I never asked you to end Gurt. I could have handled that on my own. And what would have happened if I'd been holding onto Kegan – we'd both be dead, you know that! What was I supposed to do? Hunter would have been captured, you'd be…" She'd saved their lives, and now Deuc turned her actions against her. Fucking instinctive Osirian, his rage had multiplied her own. Aedan's anger drove her from the chair and she paced her steps to the stairs. She reached the cargo hold, the frigid air a balm to her emotions as she paced in the shadows.

Deuc's shield shimmered, while his blood heated, the resulting adrenaline rush colliding with his frayed nerves. Trust! He exhaled slowly releasing his shield and took a step to the rear.

"Deuc!" Hunter hollered.

Deuc paused. The human's hand snared his shoulder, his words soft, but threatening, "Deuc you didn't see her."

Deuc eyed Hunter, the man stood almost chest to the chest

with him, preventing his movement, his brows raised, blue eyes sparkled with furious intent, "They had me cuffed and trussed like a feast-time hog. She ran to you. Crouching over you where you'd fallen!" Hunter drove a finger in Deuc's chest, he kept his shield dormant. "She's wearing that singlet, hair all a mess and Calder said, Calder said, he would go first. First! He's telling his boy's to hold her and she's not moving. She's begging, pleading for you to wake up. She wasn't running, Deuc."

What the hell? Aedan played a wild game. Pretending to give a damn, while stabbing him in the back. He'd had enough, he'd shake the truth out of her one way or another. "Only one way to find out." He pushed Hunter to the side, the booted echoes from steel rungs, concealing the Human's plea.

Fuck! Aedan paced back and forth in the cargo hold, managing her thoughts with deep even breaths.

"I want the truth Aedan. Had you figured on snatching Dios and escaping?"

Aedan's knees started to twist but she focused on the Buzz bubbling away instead. The knuckle she wiped under her eyes, grazed Calder's bruise.

"Were you going to leave me to the wolves and run? Had you and Calder planned this together?" Deuc's breath fanned the nape of her neck, lethal heat coiled inches behind her.

Aedan shook her head, "You tell us to trust you, Deuc but look where's it's gotten me, look at what I'm left with and yet you doubt me." Aedan gritted her teeth.

"Is it about the Ketos? Fine, have my share, I'll take the Jump Codes and go."

Aedan's own doubts about the bounty crept into her mind as Deuc continued through her silence.

"Are you with us or the Etarian's, *Laelaps*?" Deuc's words slammed into her chest as his fingers drove into her shoulders. Aedan's heels tripped over each other, until she faced him.

"I gave my word Deuc." She snapped, her forearms smacked his wrists.

"And what is your word worth?" He snarled, "Trading Kegan's bounty for Hunters?"

Aedan palmed Deuc's chest, his bulk stepped back, black eyes wild, "I thought you were dead!" her voice cracked. Aedan turned her back on Deuc and inhaled sharp, exhaling slowly. Deuc remained silent somewhere behind, as Aedan's temper cooled.

"Look at me," Deuc's whisper teased Aedan's ears, she squeezed her lids tighter, "Please Aedan."

The gentle plea eroded the last of her anger, as Aedan turned to face him. Her hand shot up between them as Deuc stepped forward. Her palm came to rest on his unshielded chest.

Deuc leaned in, one hand cupped her cheek, his thumb scored her cheek, collecting the moisture that fell, "Are these for me?" his husky tones slithered through her ribcage.

Aedan knew the answer, but instead she asked, "Why Green Acres, Deuc?"

"I told you Aedan, you and I are not so different, we both want change, the Administration – "

"No Deuc, why now?"

Deuc forehead came to rest against hers, "You know why," he said as his fingers wandered across the scar at the bottom of her throat.

Aedan's chin lifted as Deuc's lips clamped down on hers, steel chilled her back. Fingers locked behind Aedan's neck while Deuc tilted her to fulfil his thirst. Hard flesh pressed against silky softness. Citrus cinnamon penetrated her senses and slithered to a halt when Deuc pressed merciless swelling to hidden suppleness. Aedan wanted to resist, but her body deceived her. Flames uncoiled in her abdomen so swift it set nerve endings to ignite. She clenched her fingers around the fabric stretched across his chest and relished the ache of desire, before the shadows returned. Her stomach clenched, and her skin turned clammy, she finally relented. Aedan's palms met unyielding granite, until skin cells knitted and shimmered.

Aedan gazed into black satin, wondering if they'd ever glow purple.

"Are you with us?" Deuc asked as his lips savored the streaks of betrayal that coursed down her cheek.

"On my oath or my life, Deuc, I wasn't running. I have no loyalty to Calder, and I'm not about to hand in," She stumbled over the commitment of her words, "...not until we get those girls." Aedan thought back to the grey skirts at Gurt, "I thought you were dead."

Long fingers stroked the nape of her neck, "Aren't you lucky I'm not." He returned to nip and sup the moisture from her lips. Aedan held fast to his imposing bulk, tension ripped through his shoulders, coiled power restrained in her arms.

An all too feminine whimper escaped and Aedan cleared her throat, "Stop doubting me, I made an oath."

His breath tickled her collarbone, "I will. I told you I like to know friend from foe, so you can never mimic any part of me again. It's too danger- please, I'm begging you." Deuc's vulnerable tones compounded his kisses.

Aedan frowned, never again to use his fingerprint? What if he'd known about duplicate Kegan? "I promise."

His rigid forearms trapped Aedan against his inflexible arousal, the tip of his tongue flickered across the sensitive hollow of her throat. She wriggled calling forth a resigned groan from Deuc.

"Enough."

His shield shimmered, as he complied.

"The *Icarus III* is waiting," She added, "And this time, try to stay alive."

Deuc's lip kicked up at the corner, "I'll do my best."

"Worked it out?" Hunter asked as Aedan topped the stairs. A burst of rainbow scored her frame. She nodded, and his irises settled to cherry amusement. Aedan suddenly regarded the fine detail of the steel floor.

Deuc raised a single eyebrow "Yeah."

"Good because that wasn't awkward at all." Hunter snorted.

CHAPTER 18

Deuc strummed his fingers on the rear of the pilot's chair, the dark synthetic material moistening under his grip. She'd have to acknowledge the risks. Right?

"How's your swimming?" Hunter ventured.

"My swimming's just fine, but you're not coming."

"Coming where?" Aedan entered the main cabin and tucked her single knife into its resting place at her hip.

Deuc inhaled and regretted it instantly. The sweet jasmine and salivating vanilla tangled his thoughts. He called for his shield. It shimmered into place and Aedan's brows raised.

"I'm going to retrieve Hunter's tags. You're not landing my bird in that pile of shit."

Aedan stalked to the pilot's chair, "You're joking? It makes more sense – "

"You keep our ride safe for a fast exit," He opened drawers and pulled out a small transmitter. "Pick me up when I'm done."

Aedan shook her head but Hunter interjected, "Got a spare."

"This is madness, – "

Deuc shook his head. The barge with its obscure, isolation would shelter Aedan until he radioed for collection. "I'll be in and out. Choose the most sheltered spot to hover, and lower the ramp."

"Sounds easy," Hunter said.

Deuc's fist itched when the Human's toothy grin appeared, "No."

"We don't want you to have another dizzy spell now do we?" Hunter riffled through the drawers.

"I hit my head pretty hard, Dios, but not that hard -"

"It's safer than going alone." Aedan murmured.

Deuc registered the softness in her tone. Fuck, what had he done to her? No-one had agonized over his mortality. He was the eternal warrior, the constant soldier, at all times an instrument, a tool, a weapon. The weapon that was to be used for other's destruction until it was broken and then discarded. He shouldn't expect anything different.

He was using Hunter and his codes to buy his freedom. When would the weapon be rested, put back on the shelf, display only? But it was something small and warm and fragile that had weevilled its way under his ribs and made him want Aedan to see more. And now she had. It seemed pointless. There was no safe resolution. Any links to Aedan only weakened him. Maybe she'd kill him eventually, or him her. Together they were as fatally flawed as Dos Caelumina or whatever Hunter had said. If he was wrong about her, if her ruse of concern was just a delay tactic for more Etarian interference, then at least he had the bounty with him. She wouldn't leave without Hunter.

He cleared his throat. "Fine."

Aedan twisted to the windshield, working her thumb. When she caught Deuc watching, she stopped. His shield wavered. What had Aedan done to him and how quickly could it unravel?

"Right." He holstered some Merc's arc gun. Was it Calder's gun? Deuc regarded the purple bruise under Aedan's eye. He'd make time to find Calder later.

Aedan tried to ignore Deuc's gaze, disturbed how his eyes never changed color.

"It's gone!" Hunter said.

"No!" Aedan snapped out of it. The Plant didn't work that fast. Between midday cyclones, employee strikes and blackouts the *Icarus III* had to be in one piece.

"Inside, it's inside." Deuc said.

Aedan nodded "Yes, you're right. That mining rig had been behind the Icarus and now it's at the gate."

Deuc tapped the back of her chair twice.

The *Arion* spiraled behind a flock of shipping containers that jostled and groaned with the black bird's prop thrust. Deuc opened the ramp.

"Call me," Aedan sniggered. Deuc's expression lost in the shadows as he jumped from the edge.

"He made it." Hunter said, "I bet less than an hour. Red box, blue box." His knees dipped and suddenly the emptiness of the *Arion* echoed through Aedan's chest.

"Red box, blue box." She repeated the collection point. She navigated back to the barge, leaving the cool night air to whip around the cabin and temper her nerves.

Aedan had dreamed of safety and security and here she stood, tiptoeing on that unknown precipice. Faros and Charoen weathered the hazards of the Osirian system in solitude. So could she, and five trillion Ketos could buy her that sanctuary. Leta would be in constant supply and she'd be free. An image of Hunter's naivety, his plea for assistance echoed in her brain. Could she trade one man to avoid all the others?

The *Arion*'s landing gear scraped across the rusted deck and Aedan relished the salty gusts that buffeted her cheek. Aedan leaned across the barge railings, deep within the *Arion*'s shadow as she watched the passing waves, Charoen reflected in the dim turquoise of the single sun, Kenina. The hut door squeaked behind, and Aedan sighed. Clearly living with tarps for doors and windows had left Deuc complacent. Aedan watched Charoen's surface shimmer with each passing ripple. I guess Charon had Faros and vice versa, she thought. Boot's scraped the deck.

Knees bent, fingers splayed, and Aedan turned when Kegan settled into place.

"I knew I'd find you here."

Rubber soled shoes snagged across the uneven surface.

"Vance?"

"I knew it, I just knew it!" He stifled a chuckle as his rotund shape evolved from within the tiny hut.

Kegan thumbed the handle protruding from his belt.

A smile crinkled across Vance's weathered face, his belly wobbled, "No need to panic. This damn incessant listing! How can you stand it?"

"What are you doing here?" Kegan stepped forward, trying to catch any colors under his shadowed brow. Nil. He'd have to get closer.

The Kronos prison guard waddled forward, palms flat and outstretched, "I figured you didn't have too many hiding spots left. You forgot you told me when you handed old Thiuu in, didn't you?"

Kegan could kick himself. But why did Vance come here? A quick scan of his body showed no weapons. What in the name of Ea was he wearing? Vance encroached further, his form stuffed in a shirt too small. Had he come to help? His crinkled brown eyes appeared highlighted by the soft mauve and azure glimmer of Charoen. Pink and yellow broke forth sliced with grey and white. No sunset reds, or midnight blacks.

"How can you stand all this movement?"

"Vance, what are you doing here?"

If Vance could get them to Kronos, he might be able to get them to Haigon, or give them cover until they got close enough. Without the slightest slick of oil, Vance answered, "I've come to cash you in, kid."

The barge railing dipped, water splashed at Kegan's boots and solid steel crashed into Kegan's skull. Flaked rust stabbed into his skin as Aedan clung desperately to the Kegan facade. Suddenly Kegan's wrists felt the cool chill of magnetic cuffs. Kegan bit the deck. No, Vance! No!

"Got him boys!"

Cheers carried through the throbbing in her ears, Kegan barely within grasp.

"Kegan?"

"Get him up!" A tremor broke over Vance's jowls as Kegan yanked backwards, the metallic cuffs sliced fresh skin, "Where's Dios"

Kegan's stomach rolled as his vision cleared.

"Where's the Oddworlder?" Vance's bushy silver eyebrows raised, his hand absentmindedly rubbed his bulging waistline.

"Fuck you Vance!" hot liquid pooled at the rear of Kegan's teeth.

His eyes dropped to his boots and he visibly checked himself, "What are you doing mixed up with an Oddworlder, Kegan?" A splash of disappointment colored Vance's tone.

It certainly wasn't loyalty, Kegan thought, "They're long gone."

"Get him on the transport. Search this and then we'll leave. They have to be here somewhere." Another Kronos guard said.

Kegan's boots scuffed the edge of the deck, the other Kronos guard held her upright.

Vance leaned in eyes, "Where's the girl? I don't want any surprises."

Kegan paused to realize that Vance's posse must have been in surveillance on Faros for some time. "If she's with you, call her out to hand herself in. We'll let her go peacefully."

It came out more of a spray than Kegan had intended, but it landed on its mark all the same, as Vance wiped crimson spittle from his face. Lips peeled back over yellowing teeth, "It said Dead or Alive, Kegan." The aging sentry's eyes covered in a mesh of slick olive oil and he checked himself.

Kegan was safe for now. But he had to think fast. Why had he thought Vance would be any different?

Kegan's buttocks slammed onto the hollow plastic bench of the prison transport. Brief dampness spread across his lower back before it stemmed.

"Be careful!" Vance shouted. Confirming the concern Kegan had read earlier in the man's irises.

"What happened to Dead or Alive, old man?" A guard barked back, his hands stroking spiky remnants on a balding head.

"Kegan's mine. Hunter's yours do what you want with him." A splice of orange and grey spread through Vance's iris.

Kegan's curiosity peaked. Deuc's rage would not be contained this time, when he discovered how Kronos prison guards had tracked Kegan to Faros. Purely cause you couldn't keep your mouth shut! Fuck! Twice Kegan had messed up. Twice!

"Years ago, you told me about this place. And you didn't think I'd remember did you?" Vance knelt down beside Kegan, the last three fingers on each hand bent at odd angles. He ran them down the pale strands of his bushy chin.

"Why?" Kegan concentrated on the façade of Kegan, the pain from the guards blow to his skull dissipating. Kegan isolated his wrists. The cuffs had locked onto Kegan's bulked out frame, not Aedan's feminine build.

"Ketos."

The bald headed guard sniggered, "And you owe me twenty thousand and Braccass fifty or is it more like a hundred now after that last game?"

The Haigon v Tuwa game? "Gambling?" Kegan asked. A hundred thousand Ketos debt?

Vance's eyes sought out his boots.

"But you fought in the Borders War, you have a veteran's pension, you could have – "

"Yes I do, it's coming. But do you know how long I've got till I can cash it in? Have you ever met Braccass?" Vance threaded the rear shaft through the cuffs.

Kegan's shoulders almost popped. All war veterans had a healthy settlement pension when they retired from Etarian Civil employment. Whoever Braccass was, Vance was suitably terrified.

"You said it yourself when you cashed in Skeeter. A year on Kronos is 996 days. I have at least another ten before my pension is accessible and Braccass can't wait that long." Vance visibly shivered as he tugged on his silver beard.

"And you promised these guys Hunter Dios if they helped you?"

Vance nodded binding ankle cuffs to the secondary shaft.

The year old smell of oil and piss reminded Kegan of where he was. When full, the transport corralled at least twenty prisoners in one spot, high tensile wire threaded through cuffs that secured prisoner's with their backs flat to the bench. Vance drew Kegan's only weapon from his belt and pocketed it.

The other Kronos guard scoffed, "And he better deliver or we go straight to Braccass."

Kegan concentrated on thinning the structure of Kegan's ankles and wrists that were pinned by the cuffs. The prisoner transport banked to the right and verified his assumptions. If Deuc and Hunter had been successful they'd be on their way to the containers by now. If not, they'd be trapped inside when Vance and his thugs landed. Kegan eyed up each sentry in turn. Only four of them, one young, the rest pushing six maybe six and a half centuries, armed with blue bars and arc guns. Together attacking with stealth, the guards might have stood a chance. If Kegan could get free, this could end right here before they landed. If not, Deuc would destroy them. Vance passed stacked supply boxes as he tracked back to the primary sentry station. Above him, the pilot's boots swiveled in and out of view. Kegan exhaled slowly. One magnetic bracelet slipped.

Hunter swallowed his fear and dipped under the dark waves to come up surrounded by more floating debris in the Plants holding pond. Creaks and groans echoed off red rusted steel walls, the alloy hand rails dusted in white, even the pockets of copper had turned green as each piece of flotsam transformed from ordinary machinery to the foreboding unknown. Deuc glided through the oily water, arm over arm, without leaving so much as a bubble let alone a wake. The Osirian dragged Hunter clear by the forearm and water rushed down Hunters legs to pool in his boots. Droplets of diesel or some other fuel slimed over his neck and between his shirt, but the yellow and grey stickers called to him from the other side. In the center, the items ready for scraping, released an eerily squeal as they rubbed against each other. On the edges, walkways and gangplanks crisscrossed the warehouse, low light casting fuzzy orange shadows. Dated cameras buzzed in each direction.

Together they clambered over and between the debris, swallowed into shadows and flattened against barricades. Hunter released the *Icarus III* hatch, the pneumatic hiss, squealed through the chemical laden air.

Bright lights burst around them, Hunter ducked inside, followed by Deuc, who clicked the door closed.

"Do you think they saw us?"

Deuc shook his head and peered through the grimy windshield, "Sensor lights." He whispered.

From one end of the *Icarus III* to the other, they searched through torn wires and scattered components. Hunter had hidden the tags in an AI Drone. Gone.

The exterior lights dimmed on a timer until the holding pond, returned to thick tangerine shadows over murky water.

"They've junked the interior." Deuc stood at the emergency hatch.

Hunter pointed to a raised production line that lay behind thick Perspex, enabling a view of the watery graveyard. There, rows and rows of spare parts had been set out and sorted on a silent conveyor belt. "In there."

Scaling mountains of ordered debris, Hunter paused at a row of single hulled transports moored at the pontoon. "Wonder what they use these for?" Hunter ran his hand down the safety orange and lime green single seat, water craft.

"It's a Tug-jet. Rescue deployment. Focus Hunter – tags."

The door creaked under the pressure of Deuc's shoulder and he crumbled the red ochre flakes that fell to the rubber matted floor.

Hunter ran his palm down the seat of another Tug-jet that sat eviscerated on a center bench, "Up for repairs."

"You made a wager of under an hour Hunter, and don't think I'm going to let you wilt on that bet." Deuc said.

Hunter let the taunt wash over him and concentrated on

the task at hand. Creeping between enormous columns of junk, they read dated labels and contents lists.

"Over here, looks like these are from the ships in the bay."

Deuc eased one box to the center, and tipped, parts and springs, wires and devices tumbled in every direction. Hunter snatched at a dismantled piece of Icarus paneling, the AI Drone miserably clung to the underside, legs askew, power silent.

"What's that?"

"An autonomous explorer. Deploy, search, collect and return." Hunter ran his fingerprint over the rear panel, the housing sprung apart. Wings stretched and fin-like metallic legs recalibrated. "Whether rain, hail, snow, extreme pressure, low gravity or no gravity. The drone can even detect and repair faults without instructions." The bot blinked and crawled towards Hunter. The lenses whirled and zipped, until the two front mandibles opened, the tags spat into Hunter's hand, "Designed it myself."

"Nice piece of tech."

"Built in plasma cutter, poly welder, UPS and totally programmable. Just set and release."

"I'd want a thousand of them, in a swarm thanks."

Hunter ran his thumb over the carbon alloy thorax and pondered Deuc's idea. They could be weaponized. Did the warrior ever stop wondering about how to destroy Etarian's? He paused over his creation, toying with the idea of destroying it there and then. He would rouse Deuc's suspicions, if he left it for junking, likely Osirians would destroy it and save him the trouble. Judging by what he saw on Asar, the Osirians didn't have the technology anyway.

"Call Aedan," Deuc's husky tones replaced with smooth velvet.

Hunter kinked his eyebrow, "She said you call her."

Deuc's cheeks stayed flat, and his eyes narrowed until thin slits of darkness bored into Hunter.

Hunter smirked. Hopefully Deuc's allegiance could work

in Hunter's favor.

Deuc raised the transmitter and spat out her name. Hunter chuckled and disconnected the Drone's power. No need to send a signal to the Etarians again. He strolled to the Perspex window, beyond the smaller conveyor belt lay more workshops. A surveillance monitor clicked through grey and white images of the exterior structure. First the pond, then the room where Deuc stood, the furnaces, the mess hall, a large set of corridors, and finally the landing pads. The images circulated again while he waited for Deuc. The Etarians had managed to reduce Osirian's advancement in technology and economy, but they still survived. The Jump Codes would shift the balance and Hunter didn't mind at all.

Boots thundered on the rubber matting, "Nothing."

"What do you mean?"

Deuc's fist squeezed the transmitter until it matched his expression, "No response."

Hunter faced the monitors, the empty corridors flicked to the landing pad, lights increased, salt blasted in each direction as a shuttle touched down. A thick coat of paint had been haphazardly thrown over the top of what Hunter recognized as Etarian stock. The three would-be cyan stripes, encircled and stamped with a hidden "K". The Kronos emblem bleached through the white snow of the monitors. The image shifted to recycle with the other feeds.

Hunter entered the monitoring station, his eyes stung as he peered at each screen. The landing pad image recycled. One man, with a light colored beard, had exited and spoke to what could only be a Faros employee. He pointed to his ship the cargo door. There another man turned the bruised cheek of a captive, stocky, black bob, and a pair of heavily buckled boots before the image cycled.

"Get out of here Dios!"

Hunter spun on his heels but Deuc had already gone.

CHAPTER 19

The Kronos shuttle's ramp closed as Kegan slipped another cuff. Lopsided figures blocked Aedan's view. Did they think all Osirians dressed this way? The guard's clothing consisted of an Erebus's assortment of mismatched rags as if the guards had raided the lost and found box of prisoners' belongings. "How many have you put away? How happy they'll be to see you."

"Ebin stay alert." The call came from the front.

Ebin drew forward the sweat from his forehead with gnarled fingers.

"Kronos Mist give you that?" Kegan asked.

The sentry turned his cramped digits under his nose, the arc gun painfully tight, "Five trillion Ketos will get me off that cesspool, but one trillion all the same." He winked at his captive, "Goonty, wait till Vance and Hooka are inside and then dust off."

Kegan's eyes flew wide. No honesty amongst the desperate. If they made it off Faros, who knew how far they'd get? Ebin's boot hovered on the lowest rung when shackles clinked against steel, but Kegan had already rolled, coming up short with a fist in Ebin's solar plexus. He went down, but not out. Kegan clawed the arc gun from failing fingers; his boot slipped off the ladder when the drives increased in pitch.

Goonty, a spotty faced youth shrieked when the arc gun connected with the bony tissue at the side of his face. He bounced off the chair, the smell of scorched skin sticking to Kegan's nostrils. He leapt back down to the cargo hold and opened the side access.

There'd have to be an emergency hatch somewhere. Kegan had limited time to reach Deuc and Hunter. Either by Osirian hands or Etarian hands, Vance's expiry was imminent. Kegan slid across the landing pad to the Transport's tail, finding the edge a lot closer than he thought. Bits of gravel snagged his clothing and he limped to the ventilation hatch. Kegan disappeared. Aedan's energy returned, as she tucked the arc gun into her belt.

Hunter spun around the last corner that he'd seen Deuc. His legs throbbed and his lungs arched. The damn Osirian had sped off to Aedan's rescue and Hunter had lost him! The heat of the idling furnace had assaulted Hunter's unshielded frame and made his eyes water so he frustratingly chose a secondary corridor that lay shrouded in darkness. He tried to recall the structure from the fly-by, two arms of the structure met at the manufacturing hub and then speared off to separate landing pads. Which one had the Kronos ship landed on?

Hunter trailed his fingers on either side to mark any unusual textures, writings or doorways. Every two meters, a hatch to somewhere arose, the entrance sealed shut, and then every twenty meters a new corridor opened up in alternating directions. Sparse ruby lights glowed intermittently along the ceiling and marked Hunter's doom.

Hunter's boots echoed his ragged breathing. Suddenly camera's whizzed and sparked, multiple electronics awoke from their slumber. One by one, the hallway lights reached maximum luminosity, and Hunter used his forearm as a shield when bright white and yellow stained walls came into focus. The corridors stretched left and right, Hunter's chest rose and fell, ears pricked at the sound of camera lens zooming. He scanned his surroundings, military style numbers marked each hatch.

Pure white energy surged through Deuc's veins as the floodlights chased his heels. He stormed across the foundry floor, muscles and limbs moved effortlessly under his shielded frame. It muted the pain in his chest and the wheels spinning in his brain. Each lunge brought him closer. He hadn't done enough reconnaissance to recall the layout of the compound, only that there were two landing pads at the far end. Who and how didn't matter, so long as he got her back. He rippled his shield, each cell winched tight over already strained muscles, until his throat eased.

Deuc clipped his shoulder on the foundry doors and he stumbled into a row of low stainless steel benches. Heaving upwards, his boots slid on the steel, tools and clipboards clanged from shiny surfaces. His hands grazed the ceiling as Deuc stomped over vices, and drawers alike.

As he landed on the far side a loud speaker boomed, the last strands of sleep dripped from the panicked voice that called, "Hunter Dios."

"Fuck." Deuc froze at the swinging doors. Dios or Aedan? Fuck the reward, he'd told Dios to run. The man could handle himself. The Ida-en-Kai had become an extension of the human's body that sliced and pierced with brutal efficiency. Then again, Aedan had vicious speed and superior instincts. They hadn't found Hunter yet, but they already held Aedan. The invisible fist returned to haunt Deuc's chest. It pulled him onwards not back.

"You are ordered to surrender, by order of the – "

A muted commotion scratched the speakers before a second voice crossed the airwaves, "Etarian Government."

The muffling increased, a squeal scorched the metallic structure. The last words of an argument barely audible, "Etarians hold no authority here!"

A thick laugh roared from within Deuc as he tore forward.

The steel groaned and creaked under Aedan's knees as the ventilation shaft, dipped and rebounded with her every move. Below sleeping Farosians woke to loud speakers that howled a mini-rebellion. Halogens turned to full power. Aedan's knuckles grazed the intermittent grates and grills that lined the shaft. The roof buffered her head and shoulders. The confines of the shaft narrowed, the walls too close for comfort. It wasn't a cage, just a ventilation shaft. Not a cage!

She shut her eyes before the dizziness took hold. She gasped and exhaled slowly, repeating it until she could open her eyes. Aedan peered down into the darkness of the vent, as the sound system continued to relay the barrage of grunts and strikes. She wriggled forward, choosing paths and turns that would hopefully lead over the main corridors and fresh air.

Hunter had been seen, somewhere in the compound. But where in all-of-Ea was Deuc? The shaft descended over a lip of sharp steel and Aedan calculated her next move. Light dripped down the column at odd angles, obscuring the depth. The tremors in her legs eased slightly as the salted breeze clawed at her hair. She stretched to the other side, heel sliding for purchase and her belt dipped. A scraping sound tore her gaze downwards as the butt of the arc gun floated out of sight.

A string of curses flew from her lips, as her knees bounced off steel.

"Did you hear that?" a muted voice reached Aedan's position. She scrambled onwards.

Hunter's fingers snagged the final corner only to face the same dark green cross on faded white. Hunter kicked the wall and sprinted back again. He'd take a left instead next time. The clang of his boots along the gangway soon joined a chorus of boots that stampeded his direction. He took the left turn and faced more white corridors with military numbers. A maze of storage units and supply docks branched out in every direction and Hunter recalled watching rodents in the same predicament, not knowing at one end, a serpent had been loosened into the labyrinth.

Hunter followed the corridor, and his pursuers' footsteps dimmed. He passed an archway that emitted a briny odor so strong it stung Hunter's nostrils. He concentrated on muted scrapes and bangs up ahead. More pursuers?

A hatch opened, dark creases and sleep laden eyes adjusted to the brightness, "Hey Boy!"

Hunter's boot squealed and slid until his shoulder collected the archway. He groaned into the thickened darkness. Cross-hatched steps lead downwards guided by a chalky white hand rail. The brine stench peaked and Hunter held his breath.

Deuc rammed his shoulder into the hatch, which groaned under the pressure. The speakers had stayed silent, the winner so far unannounced. Up ahead he spied a long hallway with halogens at waist height on one side and a long Perspex wall on another. He'd felt his steps dip and rise at weird intervals to the layout of the compound. Deuc paused. From this angle it appeared a bridge of some sorts, above which rested a long tower with signal lights and radar antennas. The main control center, beyond which had to be the landing pads. The whole compound drifted upwards, moving product up a giant conveyor belt for transportation. He'd already passed the foundry with its pitchy tar and smelting odors.

A tiny thought snagged in the back of Deuc's mind as he passed the power plant, electricity humming from wind turbines and solar panels, the battery acid so strong he tasted the bitter scent through the shield. Where were the residences? The employees?

He stepped onto the bridge, long strides between long shadows. His eyes scanned across the Perspex to the secondary arm. The plumbing and hardware stained by the waves across which he spied the compound's desalination plant. Another Perspex window split the shutters, salt crusted and seals perished. The white bearded Etarian from the footage, strode down the walkway with another guard. From this distance Deuc could see his brows furrowed and shoulder's broad. Osiria had lost. Poisonous flames engulfed Deuc so fast, his shield quivered. Thank Ea you are on the other side otherwise Chaos couldn't come soon enough for you! Suddenly the stodgy Etarian raised a transponder to his lips. The fat man threw an arm to his companion's coat. The other guard, paused mining for dust in his nose, a blue bar rested on his slim shoulders. Suddenly the two Etarians retraced their steps to the North.

Aedan froze mid stride. The radio crackled through the grate. The scratchy words of someone, Ebin or Goonty pierced Aedan's ears.

"Escaped, are you sure." Vance said. Aedan heard the transmitter click and fizzle. "Damn that Ebin!" Vance snapped.

"What about Goonty? We can't get back through the Sandes without him."

Aedan smiled, Goonty would have a giant headache if she hadn't fried his mind already.

The radio sparked again, "No stay there. Where are you?" Ebin ordered.

The cogs spun in Aedan's mind. Had Vance's expiry date arrived? She let her breath stagnate in her lungs until it burned. The portly Kronos guard had come to chase her down and cash her in. But did that earn him a death sentence? Aedan had killed enough Etarians already and she had to find Hunter and Deuc. The loud speaker remained silent, what had Vance done to the Faros workers?

"We're outside the desalination plant, two clicks south of you."

"On my way,"

"Dios is AWOL, now Kegan. We haven't even found the damn Oddworlder. Braccass is going to tan my hide even if I pay up."

"And Ebin won't let you forget it." The taller man's words mumbled.

"Don't I know it, Hooka! Wait till he finds out what you did to that poor fellow,"

"What's another Oddworlder to him? Ebin won't mind."

Aedan's eyes watered and she craned forward and back. Her elbows and ankles began to shudder and she delicately twisted onto her belly. The slats allowed minimal vision. Suddenly Vance appeared, behind him, Hooka's boots barely visible. She watched the black leather twist and pace and a blue bar sizzled into view. If she could see Hooka's eyes, see the murderous red and black swirls that always occurred before violence, Aedan could confirm Hooka's intentions.

"Six trillion is a lot of Ketos," Hooka added. Aedan held her breath.

Hunter's sole slipped from the last step and splashed in slimy brine. The warm air coated his skin in a slight sheen of sweat in contrast to the cool water at his feet. With his clothes still damp from his first swim, he reluctantly entered the lower level.

Waves crept an inch up his calves and retracted to the right as a ledge appeared on Hunter's left, orange and lime green stickers loomed through the darkness. Four Tugjet's stood moored to the pontoon. A giant red lever, medical kits and a stretcher pod had been secured to the wall. Hunter splashed his sodden boots onto the fiberglass and yanked the lever. From the source of the waves, a roller hatch raised, salted gusts stung Hunter's cheeks.

Hunter clasped onto the single seat that now reverberated with power.

By the time Hunter reached the landing pads, his fringe stood upright, his lips and clothing coated with salt. He tied the Tugjet to a set of rungs that had been cut into the compounds exterior hull. His knuckles scraped the hand-holds; the night air cramped his fingers. The Etarian transport rested on the Heli-pad, cargo door open and engines silent. The gravel grazed Hunter's stomach until he reached the outer door. Inside his eyes adjusted to the darkness, the cargo hold empty.

Metal glanced off metal and Hunter's face bit the floor.

"Gotcha!"

Hunter dragged his shoulders through darkness that shifted and waivered. Dual images of a spotty faced youth appeared before the blackness became total.

From across the divide, Deuc followed the Etarian's trail, the shadows slipped and glided over Deuc's blackened frame. The two sentries headed north, their steps now unhurried. They paused outside an archway, no other employees in sight.

A third guard, balding in ill-fitted clothes met the first two and pointed south. Together the Etarian's marched further into the compound. Again the group halted.

"What? Are you sure?"

Aedan had wriggled forward with the group, Ebin now in view. She concentrated on their eyes but the narrow slats blanketed her vision. The radio crackled to life.

"Dios?"

Fuck!

"Goonty caught Dios in the cargo hold!" Vance exclaimed.

What in all the name of Erebus was Hunter doing? Shit, he'd come to Aedan's aide.

"He's sure?" Ebin drawled. The prickly scalp turned south where Aedan knew Hooka lingered. She caught the tiniest flicker of black and red. "Better head back then."

"What about Kegan?" Vance asked.

"Fuck Kegan," Hooka stepped into view, ebony and crimson bored into Vance's back like poisonous barbs.

Aedan's skin became clammy and she sucked in a deep breath. Could she let Vance be executed by those that pretended to be his ally? If she took a few out now, perhaps she could turn Vance to help Hunter escape. The grate flew backwards from her boot. Kegan's fist collected Hooka, who doubled over. Weight collided with Kegan's shoulder and she rolled forward. Someone held Kegan's wrist and dragged, the bounty hunter went with it, sending his boot high and wide. It met Vance's chin, his buttocks thundered the metal floor.

Kegan spun to meet Ebin, as his fist connected to Kegan's chin. His vision waivered, a boot landed in Kegan's ribs and something cracked. The air rushed out in a burning torrent.

Kegan spun to his feet, only to have Vance's hefty weight bear him down to the ground. Kegan rolled again, and collected groin. A Kronos heel found Kegan's temple and the façade shimmered. The injury cost Kegan precious time to resettle the alter-ego, his eyelids closing in a haze. Fuck he had to hold on.

"Wait!" Vance shouted.

Bile rose in Kegan's throat so fast, he couldn't swallow. Blood trickled into his eyes. The odor of unwashed male swamped by briny air.

"That's the Oddworlder!" Ebin dragged Kegan to his feet in time to see Deuc across the waves his fists raised, the Perspex cracked.

"Back to the ship!" Hooka ordered.

Aedan reinforced Kegan as the ground wavered beneath his slack boots. Kegan. Deuc. Kegan. Deuc. Kegan's capture afforded him another chance to free Hunter. Kegan blinked away bloodied tears, nerves shredded like raw skin in acid. Kegan. Kegan. Kegan.

The moment Deuc saw Kegan land amidst the three Etarians, the invisible fist ripped through his chest. Aedan had launched from the ceiling but why? Hunter? The call over the radio? Deuc's shield healed his split fists and kept the fatigue absent from limbs that pumped. The guards dragged Kegan towards the landing docks. At least Aedan, moreover Kegan held onto consciousness. For now. The reinforced door terminated the corridor and Deuc's advancement. Instead, Deuc clawed over edges and crevices until the wind lashed his frame. He leapt over turrets and exhaust pipes, until a gust battered Deuc sideways. A spike of guttering snagged his leg, and the black waves closed around him.

Deuc spat out the acrid water and let the ocean current rip tendrils of debris around his sinking frame. Aedan had warned them and now Deuc banked on the currents all leading in one direction. Arm over arm he battled the swell, and clutched at the flotsam as the compound slid by. Kegan. Just hold onto Kegan.

The walls of the structure ascended, leaving no handholds or footholds to grasp, the Heli-pads loomed above. Deuc kicked straining muscles, and heavy boots through concealed obstacles. The structure neared, an orange and lime Tug-jet like a beacon amidst the grey.

The whine of engines roared overhead as hand over hand Deuc climbed the ladder. His grip slackened on a rung. His lungs heaved and his heart thundered in his throat. The jet wash blasted his face and he slammed his eyes closed. The force drove all air from within and peeled back already tired fingers from the frozen ladder. His back slapped the waves, as Deuc watched the single drive transport, rise into the atmosphere.

CHAPTER 20

Inside the Kronos transport, Aedan's eyes targeted any shiny surface she could find, Kegan's yellow iris bored back. Hunter slumped to the left, his head lolled from shoulder to shoulder. The silver arc of Faros floated crisp against the pale blue edge of Kenina. The planet Chareon's purple surface leered like a child poking out its tongue. Asar would be next and then how long until they reached the Sandes Belt? Five hours? Could Kegan stay awake that long?

"What luck!" Vance chimed.

"They were going to kill you." Kegan's disembodied voice strained his fuzzy ears.

Vance's lips narrowed.

"They we're going to cash me in and leave you here."

The aging sentry's eyes darted from Goonty's boots swinging from the raised pilots' chair, to Hooka and Ebin who rested against the supply stacks. How long had they camped on Faros? Across each of their knees an arc gun and blue bar rested.

"Extremely lucky for me then, hey?" Vance's iris revolved from lemon cherry to slated ginger. Kegan's words had struck a nerve.

Kegan's blood soaked lashes didn't screen his view to Ebin's and Hooka's gaze, "They're still going to kill you."

Hooka chucked as he admired the single prong of silver, he'd stolen from Hunter, Ebin whispering in his ear. Vance twisted gnarled fingers together.

An ache grew behind Kegan's eyes. Concussion? He exhaled when violent yellow reflected back. He tapped Hunter's thigh with his knee. The Human's head lifted briefly until it slammed onto his chest. Deuc. If they got out of this he'd never let her forget it.

Kegan lifted his weary eyelids and focused on the black stands that bobbed with the turbulence. Time ghosted through his options. He needed to heal, to shake the lingering confusion that slowed his reflexes and dimmed his senses. The view warped with Kegan's headache, distant stars pin-pricked the darkness. The temperature dropped and ice coated the narrow windshield. Ebin crossed a leg over the other, the muzzle pointed at Kegan's chest.

A wave of reckless delirium ricocheted through the bounty hunter, "I tried to save you from him. Why did I bother?"

Silver brows raised, "Them or the Oddworlder?" Vance answered.

"Both."

Vance regarded his boots, "Kegan, you've got to understand -"

"Yeah yeah debts have to be paid," Kegan croaked.

"Think we need a gag?" Hooka hovered over Vance's shoulders, the Ida-en-Kai rapping on one knee, the blue bar tapping the hollow flooring.

Kegan squeezed his eyes shut for a moment and rolled his neck, the headache had eased and he flexed his fingers, "I thought of you as a friend." Kegan chuckled, the blue bar caught his forearm, Hunter's shoulder buffeted Kegan's head. Strands of brown curved within sight and Kegan snapped his eyes open, the masculine image clawed back into place.

"Gag him."

Vance's eyes met Kegan's. Pale tangerine, muddied pools of steel, as the aging sentry fumbled with Kegan's gag, the smell of talc and pine wafted from Vance's crooked fingers that lingered on Kegan's square jaw.

"As a father," Kegan tried.

Vance stalled, a pool of liquid curled across his eye lids, his snowy brows furrowed. With elbows tucked into his ribs, he thumbed the inside seam of his weathered cloak and cold steel suddenly pressed into Kegan's boots, "Shut it." Vance said.

Kegan swallowed and twisted his wrists from side to side, thinning the fleshy structure to Aedan's feminine wrists. Ebin and Hooka chatted. The air stretched out, thick and hot as the dark looks were tossed around the narrow cabin. The color across the Kronos guard's irises intensified, any minute now and Ebin's ambush would be enacted. Kegan had to be ready. He tipped his tongue to the gag material and blinked.

Yellow eyes snapped open to the engagement of autopilot, followed by the clink chink of Goonty's belt buckle. Kegan's wrist slipped from the cuff, his boots slick from sweat and blood.

"Vance!" Kegan mumbled.

Vance's belly collided with Ebin, as Goonty stepped down to the hold. Kegan tackled Hooka into the supply stacks as his arm retracted and he stabbed forward. His knife slid to its hilt, Hooka's lips slack, the blade buried in Hooka's chin.

"Get him!" Ebin snapped.

Slender hands snaked around Kegan's throat, but failed to close on bloodied skin. The bounty hunter lashed out, and Goonty shrieked. The youthful guard scrambled upwards to the pilots chair. Kegan snatched at his boot. The pilot tumbled, and kicked out. The ladder rungs caught some of Goonty as the youth squealed again. Goonty's boot swung back. Kegan dodged the blow, but Ebin's ankle struck Kegan's knee. Vance stumbled behind, blood coated one side of his face. Kegan landed an elbow in Ebin's gut, just as he heard the comms click with urgency. Fuck! Kegan lefty the winded Ebin, and hastily climbed the ladder to the cockpit. Goonty squeaked, as Kegan's fingers wound through the youths' shirt front. Fist into abdomen followed fist into face. Goonty fell backwards, his arms wide to the console. Kegan tried to follow, but his feet fell out from beneath, as Goonty's clumsy palms had deactivated the autopilot. The pilot's chair thundered into Kegan's abdomen. Ebin and Vance howled below, as Hunter cried out, his shoulders would be hyperextended in their cuffs. The drives roared and gravity vanished as the transport spun out of control. As Kegan's fingers reached for the controls, he hollered numerous commands at the transport's computer to no avail.

"Hard Reset, Emergency protocol, K21245 Authorized!" Ebin called.

The drive gurgled and spurted before silence. Kegan's stomach landed in his boots, vaguely glad he'd skipped a decent meal. The thrusters sparked, the drive hummed back to life. Kegan plummeted from the cockpit to the level below as gravity returned; his fingers hyperextended as he tried to stop his decent. Shit he'd have to remember Ebin's authorization code if Vance didn't make it.

Vance's arthritic hands struggled to climb the cockpit ladder. Kegan's ribs ached as he stumbled to his feet. He spied Hunter barely conscious, still alive. He searched for an arc gun, the Ide-an-Kai, anything to use, as he saw Ebin clawing up Vance's hefty frame to reach the cockpit.

"Hooka!" Ebin called.

Kegan snatched the gag from his face, Hooka's blood slick across his cheeks, "That's where I left it," Kegan chirped. He scrambled to the dead guard, and withdrew the blade. Kegan's strength ebbed and instead of the blade landing in Ebin's flank, it razed his ribs and tore his cloak. He fell backwards all the same. Kegan spied the moment and climbed again. If he got them under control, he could turn the ship around. A weight closed over Kegan's ankle, his forehead slammed into the rungs. The sole of his boot collected mushy bone and Ebin yelped. He kicked again. Something cracked.

The whole cabin shook. White light burst across the windshield. The pressure on Kegan's ankle released, his fingernails snapped on any edge as he tried to gain purchase. Like a brick landed on his back, Kegan fell forward.

Kegan brought the blade up and again found fabric instead of flesh.

"Kegan!" Vance shouted.

Kegan blinked through a shower of red to see Ebin's boot above his head. The balding guard's eyes black pits slashed with ruby.

Another burst of white struck the windshield. Olive green miasma spilled forth from the electrical components and Kegan scrambled for the vent.

Forearm over forearm he hauled himself upwards and threw the switches. A tiny arrow shaped hologram dominated the transports scanner. Kegan laughed, as a sleek Osirian craft chased them down.

Deuc flogged the Tugjet to an inch of its life. Deuc had headed south in a blind rage, the little watercraft whining and struggling against the current. The *Arion* bobbed up and down in its rusted prison. Deuc launched his black bird as fast as he could. Estimating a delay of at least an hour, he hurtled himself full throttle through the AK Jump Station towards Asar. The invisible fist clutched tight and sticky against his ribs.

Just past INNA he found them. The tarted up prison shuttle travelled at a reasonable pace, unable to utilize the AK and PK Osirian stations. Then the ship took an unexpected nose dive. Deuc let a round go to gain their attention but the ship began to float aimless and instead drove them into it. Another long round meant to straighten the ship but the pilot regained control and it clipped their tail. Fuck!

Deuc's fist slammed into the console as another coil wound its way through his heart. He kept the *Arion* at speed with a plan to overtake them, his comms channels chirping and buzzing with news of the Etarian raid on Faros. The radio sparked with a rapid brittle cry, "Voita, Voita, Voita. Etarian Prison Transport *180B* under attack. Request intercept. Seek coordinates on Emergency Protocol beacon."

"Chaos can't come soon enough!" Deuc picked up his receiver to call but another ship answered.

"Transport *180B* what's your location of departure?"

Deuc held his breath,

"Source Faros, Kronos Bound. Captives on board."

Deuc dropped the receiver like a hot stone, "Wave a fucking red flag why don't you."

The comms channels ignited with sound, and he turned the volume down. The dual systems all knew who'd they'd been chasing on Faros.

The dusty transport's thruster illuminated and the distance increased, the *Arion* slipped. Whichever pilot navigated the ship now thrusted wildly from side to side and Deuc followed. The *Arion*'s drives faulted. Icy liquid poured down Deuc's spine. The *Arion*'s lights dimmed. The thrusters faded. Power winked out and the generators hummed. The *Arion*'s fuel cells gone, as *180B* continued out of sight.

"No!" Kegan screamed at Vance, he'd hit the thrusters, hands and fist flew from guard to guard as he wrestled with Goonty, Vance's distress call unable to be recalled.

Kegan kicked at Ebin who rolled to the rear and landed beside Hunter. The human's blonde fringe fell forward across half closed eyes. Kegan tried the ladder again. Goonty's knee shunted Vance's belly to no avail. His jagged teeth bit down on the veteran's forearm.

"Acknowledge *180B* on our way."

Kegan would recognize Calder's voice anywhere. Hunter moaned. Priorities, Kegan told himself, he needed to cut the thrusters and Ebin still breathed.

Deuc picked up the receiver, his fingers shaking, thumb ready to press the button. Ready to make the call. His hologram scanner squealed. The rotund shape of a large cruiser sped into view, his proximity alarm struggling to keep up with it's speed.

Calder Vien twisted his head to gain a better view. Just over an hour ago, Captain Petyr-fucking-Varmil had sprinted into the cockpit claiming something called an AI Bot had registered Dios's face on Faros of all places. Shortly afterwards, one of Calder's own Crows had radioed a garbled message about Etarian's hunting Dios through the Faros desalination plant. And now as they sprinted to answer the Kronos distress call, the sleekest black bird he'd ever seen floated helplessly within his reach.

"Is that my beauty?" His good eye squinted through the windshield of his new cruiser.

"You cannot delay –"

"Relax Huul," Calder faced the Etarian Lieutenant who sat shotgun, thin lines sunk thin lips, "It's not as pretty as your little princess down stairs, but I bet it's faster."

Huul's sandy hair as starched as his attitude, and even stiffer than his collar. "You've bungled this already –" his voice a nasal whine.

Calder cocked his head. If the whore's rust-cutters hadn't fired on his ship, he wouldn't have to hold hands with the scum-bag Etarians. But not for long, Kegan Capare, that superior welp of a bitch would pay for that. Dios was the real investment. Spinning cogs fell into place, this little black jewel had been firing on the Etarians! Well he'd answered their distress call and he'd help himself to the treasure.

"It has a working jump drive Huul, Braccass won't like all the tech floating about in the Osirian system, now would he?" The Etarians had sent over the sharp little man in his own private Etarian jet, white, petite and precious like it's owner, to watch Calder. Huul had even brought himself a Captain and four second class assholes to boot.

"Oddworlder's couldn't — "

"Oddworlders? Do you remember what side of the Sandes your ass is currently on, Huul? My ship my rules." Calder winked his one good eye at the Lieutenant.

Huul's lips contorted and his pale eyes narrowed, "So destroy it."

"Too close for lasers and plasma."

Huul clicked his tongue, "Braccass will not – "

"He can wait. Boy's rein it in."

"Calder – "

"And be prepared. Blue bars, arc guns and I don't know how that primates' scrotum survived the plasma round, but warm it up again."

Deuc found Hunter's cozy hiding spot and disregarded it. His bulk might fit past the excrement tanks and plumbing but fighting his way out would be impossible. Instead he'd pulled apart the wing paneling and slid in.

He let the cruiser haul in the *Arion*. Each second they delayed him, the muscles coiled tighter under his already overwrought shield. His head grazed the roof, the air momentarily chilled until the massive cruiser's doors closed. He watched as the crowd thickened with Osirian Mercs and cyan striped uniforms. Calder had made his bed and would have to lie in. It gave Deuc a handy excuse.

Vien ran a narrow eye over the *Arion*, his hand rubbed his stomach, "Used the carbon scanner yet?"

Deuc held his breath. A carbon scanner? How many minutes until they closed in on the Kronos transport? Would his shield keep his position concealed? Aedan! She'd thought he was dead.

Boots thundered up the ramps and fists tore open hatches. His skin knitted and shimmered. His heart roared in his ears, his throat tight. Aedan had found no heartbeat. Something jagged in the back of Deuc's mind.

"A still of Buzz." A thick Tuwa accent called.

A thin steady stream of beeps made it to Deuc's hiding spot. He closed his eyes and focused on the moment the plasma round had struck him. The faintest shroud of tingles caressed his skin. His lids flew open and it disappeared. Shit! He'd been close. Something about that moment, roused a sense of awareness. He'd driven his shield internal. Either by luck or chance, it had saved his internal organs, his fractured skull. It had awoken his ability to dream.

"Weapons still intact." The voice echoed loudly off steel.

Deuc closed his eyes again and inhaled slowly through his nose. The shroud returned, his heart thunked solidly, until the rhythm altered, blood swirled instead of pumped, his lungs shallow, muscles relaxed. His heart hummed and quivered, the vibrations reducing to flutters and flurries. Bubbles adhered to the underside of his ribs.

"There's organic residue all over the place."

Deuc's mind clouded over, grey fog rolled from either side, the Etarian's disembodied voice floated through the mist. The paneling at his back disappeared, the sweat taste in the air evaporated and Deuc sunk, further into the abyss.

"Nothing,"

Calder's voice dawdled through space and time, "Strap her down and stand guard. Let's go get our bounty."

Deuc succumbed.

Kegan crawled towards Goonty in small increments. His ankle swished passed Kegan's head, and he ducked. Goonty squealed as Kegan drove the knife into his foot.

"Kegan!" Ebin cried.

With Goonty finally incapacitated. Kegan struck the thrusters before he climbed down to the level below. Blood dripped over Ebin's tightened jaw and onto Hunter's cheeks. Hunter's consciousness sparked as the tip of Ebin's blade scored the human's neck. "You want him to live?"

"Ebin, he's worth five – "

"Dead or Alive, you said traitor."

The ship lilted, as the loss of gravity lifted the occupants into the air. Hooka's body ascended, the Ida-en-Kai released from under his body. The spotty faced youth howled through the misty air as his foot fought knife-hilt.

Kegan wedged feet and elbows between the supply stacks, his fingers closed over the Ide-an-Kai. Gravity returned, Kegan stumbled, Ide-an-Kai in his grasp.

Clangs and scraps chattered to the rear of the ship, Kegan

glanced over Ebin's shoulder to see the lowering ramp door.

Kegan's grip ratchetted closed and the prongs sprung to life.

"Capare – weapons down!" Vien boomed.

The Ida-en-Kai gleamed bars of light across Kegan's line of sight as Etarian uniforms filled the gaps between Calder's men. Kegan's shoulders sagged under a weight of a thousand suns and Hunter moaned.

Kegan twisted the handle and three became one. The silver clinked on to a supply shelf as Kegan discarded the instrument.

"Wise choice, my friend." Vance waddled down the ladder.

Calder snorted, his one good eye writhed in oceans of yellow, aqua and pink "You too old man!"

Magnetic cuffs adorned each Kronos guard as they marched from the belly of the *180B* onto Calder's newest acquisition. Goonty limped and whimpered in front of Kegan who wrestled to size up as many of the guards and Merc's as he could. His teeth cracked his jaw as he watched Hunter being dragged by his cuffs, his shoulders bulged to dislocation point. The Etarians sneered as the human fought to silence his screams. The combined crew dragged the train of captives further into the hold, the fatigued metal and bubbles of deterioration rapidly painted over. In one corner, a dainty white twin hulled craft had been strapped down – Etarian lines on either side. In the other corner, a dark shadow loitered, panels discolored by salt-air. Aedan inhaled slowly, Mercs and Militia stood at the open ramp into the *Arion*, their shoulders relaxed.

A blue bar swung low and caught the human on his flank, Kegan turned and caught the second on his ankle. The muscles instantly swelled upwards to his knee. If he could see the skin, Kegan knew it would blush purple, red and black. His eyes narrowed on the *Arion*, would Deuc attack against these numbers? His heart skipped and he willed it to stillness.

"You traitorous pie-eater."

Could anything Kegan say or do save Hunter? "He's my

bounty asshole!" Kegan growled.

"Ha!" Calder stepped forward, a thin pale man loitered behind, two pips on each shoulder. "Not any more Capare,"

"This is the infamous bounty hunter? I can honestly say, I'm underwhelmed." The Etarian Lieutenant top lip slithered over grey gapped teeth.

"Judging by your bed-fellows I'm sure that's nothing new," Kegan rolled his yellow eyes over Calder's swagger.

Vien's spittle splashed over silver buckles, "You've got a smart mouth for a captive, Capare."

"Bit of pie stuck in your beard there Vien," Kegan added as the Etarians shuffled him into a two by two cell. The Perspex and electro-plasma bars hummed into place.

"Lieutenant Huul, Capare killed one of our own. We're Etarians! And you're throwing us in here?" Ebin whined.

"Who gave Kronos guards permission to abandon their post?" Huul's shiny heels squeaked in his pivot.

"What?" Ebin's reply from the cell adjacent to Kegan.

"Section 5696(b) sub paragraph (i) states Kronos staff are to apply for and have approved – "

Kegan stopped listening and focused on Hunter. His body landed on the floor with a thunk, legs askew, skin at his wrists raw. Kegan did a head count, Calder had eight and the Lieutenant, seven. The Mercs wandered up the corridor and out of sight. Three of the Etarian guards lingered at Hunter's cell, spittle sizzling as it struck the electro-plasma bars.

"Come on, later." One said.

"And what says you?"

"Huh?" Kegan grunted.

The Lieutenant's lips twitched and his eye's burned ruby and violet of all things. He stood before Kegan's cell, "You stand accused of unlawful homicide – "

Kegan clicked his tongue and tossed his black bob over one eye, "Under section 8917.5(e) subparagraph (a) states an entity with covenants over another entity on warrant of their apprehension or death, may use bodily force including lethal force to secure and defend such covenant from other entities with the exception of the Etarian Militia – " Kegan croaked the last words as across the void. Hunter's eyes violently flashed black.

"And there is your downfall – " Lieutenant Huul sneered.

"No, Lieutenant Huul – I opened fire on the Militia, Capare had nothing to do with it."

Huul's eyes flew wide, heels squeaked as he approached Hunter's cell. His frame hid Hunter from Kegan's desperate silent pleas.

"Capare was down for the count and I fired on the fleet."

Kegan rocked from side to side, the blue bars searing his knuckles. Fuck Hunter! Why? He'd mouthed off again, hoping to give this Lieutenant a piece of his own rhetoric bullshit. Pale beige shoulders prevented Kegan from undoing his stupidity.

"That's a few more to add to your body count, the troops won't like this at all," Huul laughed. A shallow dry husk followed him up the stairs and out of sight.

"Hunter!" Kegan called.

The human's eyes muted to maroon as he lifted cuffed forearms. Vance leaned forward and grabbed his own ankles. Out of sight but not ear shot, Ebin chuckled.

Kegan peered between the electric blue bars as far as he dared before the sparking singed his stray hairs. Huul's laughter set a nest of wasps to flight in his stomach. Deuc. Where the Hell was Deuc?

CHAPTER 21

The silver ribbon tangled between Deuc's fingers, the atomic pollution fogging the horizon, only the ash clouds at his boots stirred. The ribbon sizzled and squirmed before he pushed the image away. Tiny vibrations snuck through his veins as another bubble freed itself from his rib cage. The silver ribbon tangled...

Hunter dozed, his mind spun wildly. Aedan had taken the first chance to cash him in! He'd stared down Deuc, slaughtered Gurt and his Merc's and now at the appearance of Aedan's beloved and holy Etarians, she'd rolled faster than a canine. Had Deuc been right all along? Aedan had egged him to call Nataly and she chosen to land on Faros? Was this the only way she could finally be rid of Deuc by calling Etarians to her aid? Did her oath mean nothing?

Hunter's chest burned, Deuc. Where the fuck was Deuc? For all his bravado, the Osirian disappeared as soon as the Etarians had the upper hand. The girls would surely die, now. Like Juliette. Molten rage poured through his system. He knew the risks, but at each turn, he'd improved his chances of success. At each step he'd had hope. His magnetic bracelets dug into already open wounds as Kegan hissed across the hall. Hunter squeezed his eyes tighter.

Kegan rolled his head to the other forearm and resettled the shift. He tried to signal Hunter again and again but the human had rolled over and refused to roll back. The halogens had dimmed, the air warm and sticky. Kegan yawned for the fifth time and shuffled. The guards had long abandoned the *Arion* and yet nothing stirred in the holding dock. Kegan stretched his neck and counted the blue bars for the fifth time that hour. The *Arion* was here, so where was Deuc?

Footsteps brought Kegan back into focus. The boots strode

through the corridor, four, no five militia appeared before Hunter's cell.

Lieutenant Huul stood before Kegan's cell obscuring his view of the human, "Warrant's been recalled."

"Huh?" Kegan grunted.

Across the hall, one Etarian militant with collar length sandy curls called to Hunter, "Dios!"

Kegan could see to the portly Kronos guard's cells, and Vance mimicked Kegan's moves coming to stand as close as the bars would allow.

Hunter's shoulders shifted as he answered the pale Captain, "What took you so long?"

Huul returned to fill Kegan's vision and smirked, his flat ears listening to the exchange between his Captain and the Human, "Not his, Oddworlder. Your warrant, Capare."

Kegan froze.

Huul continued, "You're still under apprehension for aiding and abetting until a Hearing, but an injection of Francium is off the table for now."

Kegan had to swallow his heart when he saw Hunter's eyes.

Huul nodded to his Captain, a single stripe on the pristine Etarian uniform, "Captain Varmil." Huul strode out of sight.

Captain Varmil smirked at Kegan. He struck the power release with his meaty palm and the electro-plasma dissolved with a snap, taking with it, the Perspex panels of reinforcing.

"You can't!" Kegan screeched, drawing Vance's eyes. He didn't care, "Hunter!"

"Fuck you Capare, you had your chance – " Another Militia, answered, shorter and stockier than the first, his forearms covered in dark fuzz.

Damn Deuc in all under the Light, the Shadow and everything in between, may Chaos rip his soul asunder preventing salvation even from Erebus! "Stop!" the words tore from Kegan's throat as two guards lifted Hunter's cuffs, shoulders popped until he stood upright. Kegan had to think fast, the warrant stated dead or alive. Even if Hunter burned an infernal hatred, he had to fight. Kegan started to voice an insult about striking a man in cuffs, when the tallest militia, Captain Varmil, demanded their removal. Hunter's fists curled.

"No!"

"You can weep at his funeral." Said Varmil as the first fist landed in Hunter's abdomen.

The wind rushed out in force. Hunter pitched forward, but militia either side held him up for the second fist and then the third and so on. Kegan's heart thundered, the meat drenched air stung his lungs and brought bile to the back of his throat. Each strike ended in a bone mashing thud and Kegan covered his ears. Long shadows drew curtains over the scene, a cage reminiscent of childhood nightmares. Kegan sunk to the ground. What could he do? Blow by blow they destroyed Hunter. Memories of an illuminous rainbow exploded before Kegan's eyes and awoke a sensation that suspended reality. Something splashed onto the floor, somewhere a blade unsheathed.

What would you give to let him live? Something snapped in Kegan. His thighs shuddered and hands trembled. Kegan faced the divide. The militia had traded places, the stocky guard and the fair haired Captain held Hunter whose face resembled bloodied porridge. A gust of claret splashed down from his blonde fringe, both eyes swollen, one completely shut, lips split and puffed. Another militia tore Hunter's shirt from his bruised frame, silver glinted in the dull diodes.

Hunter's leg dipped and bowed, his body suddenly weightless, and numb. Dark spots spun in front of his eye, the other no longer working. Fitting that he would face another traitor on the moment his life extinguished from this universe. Kegan's eyes alighted. His mouth worked furiously to Hunter's dulled ears, then he stepped forward. Hunter must have reached the End, because he saw Aedan.

Vance blinked and blinked again. Kegan had uttered "On

my oath and my life" and stepped forward, out of the olive skinned young man Vance had grown to accept as the bounty hunter, the shimmering beauty he'd spied on Faros, appeared. He blinked again, expecting Kegan to be standing behind, a shell left open like a cupboard, but the image vanished.

Aedan stood at the bars, their surging power, raised the hair on her forearms.

"Boys." She called, her voice as feminine and steady as she could manage. The air cooled around her and for a moment, she expected to see snow drifts and sleet under her boots. As in her nitrogen induced hallucination, one by one the Etarian Militia turned to face her cell.

"What the fuck are you?" The stocky guard spat.

"Just another filthy Oddworlder, how about you open up this cage, and we make it an even fight."

"Like fuck, Capare!" Varmil said.

"You're Etarian militia? Don't tell me you're scared?"

Aedan's fingers twitched at her thigh, knee's bent.

Why weren't they biting?

"You know, it was a real light show, watching those pretty little ships disintegrate on the scanner, but I kept counting. One, two, fourteen," Aedan's voice caught. "All that Etarian training gone to waste; I suppose what does it matter, when there's five trillion Ketos at stake?"

The stock guard dropped Hunter and marched forward, "I owed Rinton my life!"

Another Etarian stepped out of the cage, and Varmil caught his shoulder, "Shut your mouth Capare!"

"It wasn't hard, pulling the trigger." Aedan continued.

"I'll see to that Francium injection Kegan." Varmil said.

"Why wait?" Kegan baited. The five Etarians converged on her cell. Hunter's cage now empty except for the Human who still hadn't moved.

The stocky Etarian spat against the blue bars of her cell, "Fucking traitor."

"Ketos is Ketos," Aedan hissed as she stepped backwards into her cell. The Etarians irises glowed ruby but not black. She'd have to be quick as her last words formed on her lips. "And their lives weren't worth a single chip."

"Fucking Oddworlder trash!" The stocky guard slammed the access panel, and the blue bars disappeared.

Real quick.

Another bubble peeled away from Deuc's lungs. *The silver ribbon tangled between his fingers…*

Aedan's first kick landed in the groin of the stocky Etarian, her second kick glanced his inner thigh and he went to one knee. Another Etarian took his place, but her palm collected his nose, he slumped to the floor. The stocky Etarian snatched her arm. Aedan pulled the soldier forward, meeting his nose with her forehead. Sticky heat splashed over her cheek. Aedan squeezed her eyes tight against a waterfall of red and clutched at the Etarian's belt.

Aedan found her prize and rather than retrieve it, she swung the blue bar until it struck the soldier's groin. He squealed and fell forwards. Captain Varmil threw his weight forward and trapped Aedan's arms. She rained elbows down as his shoulder slammed into her chest. She twisted and clawed at the wall. Varmil's weight against her back, and he kicked her ankles apart.

"Now bitch, you will feel the full force of the Etarian Militia!"

Dark curtains drew inwards and Aedan swallowed, Hunter sagged in his cell, the doors left ajar in Etarian haste, the human's chest rose and fell, but only just. Aedan used the image to push the shadows back.

"Charming," Aedan said as she flicked her neck but missed and the Captain clenched her braid the resounding crack sent a shaft of white hot light upwards through her cheek. She blinked until sight returned.

Aedan squirmed underneath his weight, her elbows and heel flying back with speed, but no accuracy.

"Keep pushing like that and I won't have to do a thing," The Captain chuckled, his elbow drove between her shoulder blades and she sent her head sideways colliding with the thin flesh of his ear. He swung his head and Aedan seized her advantage. She dropped her weight and slipped to the side, her palm grabbed his neck. His forehead clanged with the cell wall. Captain Varmil slithered to a heap on the floor. She faced another Etarian soldier and sucked down sharp breaths. The soldier eyed the arc gun on his fallen compatriot. He launched, Aedan's boot trapped his hand, her knee caught his temple. The final Etarian retreated into the corridor. Aedan followed and slapped the access panel behind her, the bars slid into place. She'd managed to trap four Etarian's in her cell.

Aedan pivoted to chase the fifth, when he suddenly wilted to the floor. Aedan's breath caught behind her teeth as she faced Calder's wicked one eyed smile.

"These boys keep forgetting what side of the Sandes they're on."

Aedan bent one knee and shifted one boot behind the other. Five Mercs with violet gemstones silently coveted what the Captain had failed to complete. "Tuck him in for the night will ya?" Calder ordered and two mercs dragged the final Etarian into an empty cell.

One Merc, with dark dreadlocks to his waist smacked the switch, sealing the bars in place before he returned to Calder's side. The Merc's braids decorated with silver clips and trinkets.

"Imagine my surprise when I hear a bunch of Etarians have got themselves a female, and then to my utter delight, the monitors reveal you." Calder's oily chemical laden scent washed over Aedan.

"Calder... what about Lieutenant Huul?" The Merc's braids clinked as his gaze swiveled from left to right up the corridor.

"He can eat my pie, Owin. Until his pilot gets us through

the Sande's she is our property, Finders Keepers."

Aedan scanned the room, other than Calder and Owin, three more Mercs filled the cell door. One with blonde spiky hair and rows and rows of tiny teeth, a fresh Myrmidon, and another Merc with a lilac scar running from receding hair line to rigid jaw line. The last hired thug covered to his neck in dark winding tattoos that crisscrossed immense pectorals and a cleavage any night-walker would be jealous of. All four of Calder's crew overshadowed their leader's height by a full foot. Why hadn't she snatched a weapon from the Etarian's before she'd locked them away!

"Besides, Tuck and Flake have Huul handled for now."

All of Calder's men had more shoulders than brains, and grinned wildly Aedan's direction, cherry violet danced across their eyes. Calder undid his belt buckle and pulled the full length out of the loops.

Vance stared at Aedan. There's no going back, Aedan thought. Vance had witnessed her transformation, Ebin if he hadn't seen it had definitely heard the result. Aedan focused on Calder's nose, "Thanks for your help Calder but this isn't going to work," She pulled on Kegan and waited.

Calder's eye bulged, his stubble covered lips dropped open. Owin, the braided Merc, crossed his chest and kissed his fingers in some silent prayer to a faraway God, while the baby-teethed grunt fell backwards over his own feet.

Scarface thumped his chest twice and hissed, "Shape-shifter."

Calder's good eye blinked furtively "Even I can see that, but what does that mean?"

"Cursed by Arae, one who may walk between light and shadow but answers to none." The grunt answered.

Kegan lifted his chin, "Superstitious bunch this time Calder?"

Vien rolled his belt between his hands. His wandering eye suddenly ringed with circles of grey and orange.

Braver, Kegan stepped forward. "Don't risk your salvation

by messing with curses Calder, especially you of all people, your last ship destroyed, your crew slaughtered, one would think you're already cursed."

"By you none the less," Calder stepped forward, two thugs at either shoulder, "I'm willing to take a gamble."

Kegan shook his head, "Is that the same logic that has you dealing with Etarians?"

Calder grimaced, "Ketos is Ketos."

Kegan's back struck the wall as he caught Calder's first strike on his forearm and circled under his flank, Kegan's image drained energy but he managed to plunge a knee into Calder's abdomen. Calder's arms trapped around Kegan's legs and they went down together. The edge of the wall caught Kegan's skull. Fuck! The scene in front shifted and shimmered, echoing the vision of Calder and his men. Kegan fluttered. She needed strength now, not camouflage. Aedan wriggled underneath Calder's bulk, his onion breath searing her cheek. She struck out, but baby teeth had already grabbed her wrist, and Owin and someone else had an ankle each.

With her free hand, Aedan dragged her fingers down Calder's face, sinking her nails into his one good eye. Calder roared and her ears rung. The corridor afforded little room for movement. The blue-bars of nearby cells hissing threats to singe their skin. Calder swung another fist and caught her chin.

The silver ribbon...

The last bubble burst. Deuc's eyes snapped open. His clothes felt damp across his limbs. He could feel artificial gravity, the scents of the *Arion* roused his mind. Aedan. Hunter. Calder. Deuc's fingers snagged across steel, his legs wobbling under him as he stumbled down the ramp. Aedan. Hunter. Calder. His eyes focused on the electro-plasma blue that fuzzed his vision. A scream cut through the air.

Aedan levered her legs upwards, hoping to push Calder into the electro fields, but his knuckles collided with her cheek bone. Suddenly, the pressure on one ankle released. She kicked out with full force and struck metal. Another ankle free and she squirmed away from Calder's hands that dug under clothing. Suddenly Calder howled, his body lifted free and dangled over Aedan. Her fists and feet clashed with body and bone until all energy had expired.

Solid copper arms enveloped Aedan and pulled her upwards. She lengthened her arms across Deuc's chest, as fingers pushed back bloodied strands.

"Hunter," She barked, her throat a nest of dry leaves. Aedan plucked weapons from Calder's men before she turned to Deuc. Unshielded, eyes deep brown and ringed in black, his hands trembled as he stared at Hunter. The human lay on the floor in a pool of liquid, eyes closed, and breaths shallow.

Aedan's boots slid as she dashed into the cell, gently she rested Hunter's head in her lap, "Can you do anything?" Aedan wiped back his sticky fringe. But Deuc had already slashed more cuts into Hunter's chest and abdomen. Deuc dragged the knife across his own palms and painted every cut, slice and bruise on the human. Deuc's lips paled to match the color of his cheeks. He opened his palms again and again, until finally Hunter's skin knitted together.

Deuc sunk back on his haunches, his bronzed complexion gaunt, the veins visible through his skin, like faded golden lace. Hunter sighed and his eyes rolled in their sockets, focusing first on Aedan and then to Deuc. She'd have to explain later. Aedan regarded the fatigued soldier, guessing she felt better than Deuc looked.

One of Calder's thugs groaned.

Her words rushed out, as she dragged the dreadlocked Merc by his ankles into an empty cell, "There's at least two more Militia and three more Mercs."

Deuc stood over Calder with a sword in one hand, and blue bar in the other.

Aedan placed a sticky hand on his shoulder, "Enough blood has been shed for today."

Deuc helped Aedan drag another thug next before Hunter

was able to sit upright. From within his cell, Ebin chuckled as Aedan crossed his cell, her dark braid swung over slender hips.

Deuc's black eyes slowly addressed every inch of the Kronos guards' frame. Ebin shivered, his boot clipped his heel, and he cascaded to the cell floor.

"I'm fine," Hunter snapped when Aedan shuffled under his arm.

"She saved your life boy!" Vance spat.

"You can hate me later, right now that Lieutenant and his pilot are about to cross the Sandes Belt."

CHAPTER 22

"We could take the *Arion* and run?" Deuc rested Hunter against the metal balustrade. If Aedan was right, some Lieutenant, a pilot and three Merc's maybe more would want a piece of them as soon as they opened the main cabin door. Deuc's shield hung precariously in the balance, between active and functional, to sending him into a coma. He recalled every minute spent in the *Arion* wall cavity, unable to wake until the last bubble peeled from under his ribs, his heart slowly returned to a healthy pump rate, his mind like stepping through a sandy bog. A scream brought him to full consciousness. He'd sliced meat and tendons to gain his freedom. Deuc had healed by the time he'd found her. White rage poured through every limb but his shield remained intermittent.

"No." Hunter snapped.

The invisible fist had closed over his chest when he spied Hunter's condition. His shallow breaths and clunky blood filled gurgles. "I'm not turning back." Empty, exhausted, confused Deuc rested with the human as Aedan handed them both an arc gun and blue bar each. Hunter's glare never moved from Aedan's back. You can hate me later? She had said. What had Aedan done now?

"I agree, we're on an Etarian ship with Etarian ID, we go forward."

She'd chosen to keep Calder and two of his men alive. Had it been a ploy of some sort? Deuc took in every injury that laced her ivory skin, from cuts and grazes, blackened eyes, and finger marks on her arms. He clenched his fists to his side. Deuc had found her. That's all that mattered for now.

Aedan shifted into Kegan, the corner of masculine split lips kicked upwards, "Maybe I should bring them to you?"

"No, I'm ready," Hunter's knuckles paled over the arc gun

cartridge.

Deuc tested his shield, like pulling on a jacket made of razor blades, it slammed into place. He felt the sweat beads increase, "Ready." How long could he hold it?

Tuck and Flake sat behind Huul in the co-pilots chair, the Lieutenant's bony fingers clutched over each arm rest. Beside Huul, the Etarian pilot struck buttons and switches in response to multiple lights that demanded his attention. The pilot's hair line ran a feathered ring around his scalp and deft hands tiptoed the clunky ship forward. Ahead the field littered with asteroids.

Huul picked up the comms receiver, "The *Minos* is commencing to cross now Commander Braccass." The voice reminiscent of snapping scorched bones crossed the airwaves. Hunter's jaw tensed, Aedan's shoulders squared. Braccass!

Tuck pulled out a fob-timer from his blue and grey camo jacket and then glanced at Flake. The Merc's thick arm stretched to a monitor, tuning back in to see, Kegan's cell full and Hunter's empty.

Boots echoed off the steel and Kegan smiled at Deuc when the knife slid under Huul's clean shaven chin and levered the Lieutenant upright. The smile faded when Hunter fired the arc gun into the ear of Tuck and then the face of Flake.

"Sir! Sir." The pilot squawked until Deuc reefed him backwards from the Human's aim, the arc round narrowly missing Deuc's belt line.

"Fuck Dios, I was only joking with all those star wife comments."

Hunter didn't laugh.

The *Minos* started to bank right and Deuc pulled the Etarian pilot to face him. "I'd set this bird to orbit if I were you."

The weathered pilot with his rounded middle settled the *Minos*. Thrusters spurted sporadically when an asteroid closed in.

"What in the name of Ea are you doing?" The Lieutenant

barked, and Kegan added more pressure, "The warrant's been revoked."

Deuc's shield wavered and he relented. It fled. Kegan's warrant revoked? What the hell had happened? Hunter slid between the dead mercenaries and Deuc.

"Didn't tell you that did she?" Hunter's brow dipped, his chest widened.

"Yet here she is Dios, with a knife to an Etarian throat." Deuc let his hand fall on Hunter's shoulder and eased forward. Huul twitched, his lips worked silent to keep up with the cogs in his brain.

Hunter's shoulder quivered under Deuc's touch.

A boom resounded inside the cabin as an arc round ricocheted and fried electrics. Hunter twisted the arc gun from shocked fingers, Deuc slammed his blue bar into the back of the last Mercenary's skull.

"I told you there were three." Kegan sighed.

Deuc let his smile fade when he had to peel the arc gun from Hunter's vice grip. Deuc riffled through the Osirian's pockets and came up empty handed. As he rose, the vision shifted and he caught the seat behind. Kegan caught his arm.

The *Minos* sat idle in a sea of asteroids, each one as individual in size, shape and trajectory as the last.

Hunter let Deuc rest after they'd imprisoned the rest of their captives. He'd bit down a comment that Aedan deserved a cell on her own. His ribs hurt, in a chest already numb. Deuc. He'd eventually come to his aid. He'd promised Deuc the jump codes to change his system's future. You had his loyalty until then, Hunter mused.

The *Minos*'s size reminded Hunter of the Lestas' seize-machine. Sleeker and faster, and even when carrying an outdated Etarian weapons system, the *Minos*, was a definite improvement on Calder's last transport. But the *Minos* was a Junker all the same. Etarians weighted every bargain. Calder?

The Osirian Merc had been there, in the cells. Why? Hunter

closed his eyes and yawned. The healing effect of Deuc's blood must have ebbed. How'd the blonde Captain end up in a cell as well?

Hunter accessed the *Minos* security footage.

Aedan sat on a bed in one of the many cabins, this one might have been the tattooed giant or the balding hulk she guessed by the trinkets and statutes of multiple gods and deities. She unbuckled the last clasp and sloshed off her boots, she stuffed them with the cabin's bed sheets and hung them upside down on the second bunk. Aedan winced as the shower found every cut and graze on her body. The adrenalin had worked its way through her system and now Aedan's ribs came back to haunt her. Dried and dressed she wiped a trembling hand across the fogged mirror. Red veins crisscrossed both whites of her blackened eyes, bottom lip swollen, teeth marks in the flesh. Her left cheek enflamed to twice its size a bruise so deep the edges glowed purple, the pale white slashed in two. Her eyes tracked down and counted finger bruises on her arms, nail gouges on her collarbone and one purple jagged scar to boot.

Hunter appeared over Aedan's shoulder, he'd scavenged an Oddworlder shirt, mesh and fabric sewn together at the shoulders and hemline, "I need to apologize."

She met his gaze, his eyes solid blue, the absence of his emotional aura in the reflection, somewhat calming, "There's nothing to apologize for."

He ran damaged knuckles through his ruby fringe, "I saw the footage – I don't know what to say."

"It's okay, seriously Hunter."

The rainstorm of Hunter's eyes settled to steady greys and whites. "I'm sorry. The words are not enough I doubted you, but – "

"I'm fine, Hunter." The adrenalin totally gone, her head spun.

The Human followed her to the bunks, eyes downcast to

the steel, as Aedan fussed with her precious boots. "I thought that..."

"You took the blame for the Etarians, I'll straighten that out."

"Aedan!" Hunter snapped and plopped on the bunk opposite, knees touched hers, "Fuck all that. I need to thank you for saving my life."

Aedan paused her buckling as a fresh outbreak of red, black and blue glistened in Hunter's eyes.

"We're both alive."

"Barely." Hunter caught his face in his palms.

Aedan tugged his hands down. A vision of a constellation with six suns slowly revolved into position. It was a system of multiple planets with miscellaneous satellites including a huge orange globe trailed by even more satellites. She didn't recognize the system or the primary star of the constellation.

"I doubted you and I hated you." Hunter continued.

Aedan returned to the present, "I know. On my oath and my life, Hunter I meant it. But you need to know, to hear it from me, I'm done with your bounty."

Aedan continued through Hunter's silence.

"I'm done. I was done before we left Asar. What I've seen, what happened –I can't be a part of that. We get to Haigon, we get the girls and we run."

Hunter dragged fingernails through his stubbly growth and sighed. "This is not what I intended. I... " No slick of oil covered his eyes. He told the truth. Only hopeful white and blue. Something akin to loyalty Aedan had worked out.

Aedan squeezed his forearm, "Agreed?"

"Agreed."

She tugged on her boots and rose from the bunk, as she did, warmth enveloped her. She inhaled the sweet leather and pine fragrance of Hunter, a bitter after scent of metal clung to his frame. "You need a shower though!" she said and Hunter's chest reverberated through hers and he peeled back.

"Interrupting something am I?" Deuc leaned against the

doorway, miniscule flutters stirred across burnt sienna.

Deuc dreamed in natural sleep.

A silver ribbon had curled around his fingers, it writhed and wriggled pouring out of his grasp as it delicately lowered to an ash cloud of sun bleached skulls. The ribbon cascaded despite his best efforts, threading loops through his knuckles and swirling it around his wrists and neck. But still the ribbon descended, until Deuc stood on tiptoes with arms outstretched, the hem touched ash. A carpet of green blossomed outwards from his feet.

His eyes snapped open.

Deuc showered and tentatively tested his shield. It slid carefully into place and he released it, Deuc's confidence returned with each successful effort. He needed to be cautious and detached. Deuc wandered through sleeping cabins, his fingers traced over uniforms, memorabilia, and weapons, each cabin a small measure of its occupier.

He wandered from Calder's double cabin with charred trinkets and salvaged memories to the Lieutenant's smaller but tidier room. The bare necessities graced the Etarian's bedchamber. Where Calder's crew had hoarded an Erebus's assortment; the Etarian's bunked rooms were perfectly regimented, segregated and sparse. Albeit not totally empty.

Deuc eavesdropped outside the room where Aedan and Hunter mended erroneous judgements, until the voices went silent. As he rounded the corner, the couple broke apart and Aedan's appearance squeezed every drop of control from his muscles. He stepped into the room, instead of down to the cells.

Hunter clasped palm to palm with Deuc, "Thanks Deuc, I know what those codes mean to you and I'll transfer them before -."

"No Hunter, It wasn't about the codes." Deuc embraced Hunter shoulder to shoulder, fists between chests, "*Mao Adelfos*" he said.

Surprised, Hunter retreated before replying, "*Mao Adelfos.*"

Deuc nodded to the human, whose eyes flew wide. "I mean it, Dios." Of course he did, the moment Deuc had seen Hunter's tortured bulk drowning in his own fluids.

"I've never had a Brother before." smirked the Human.

"I've only said that to one other and he's dead. It's not an honor to be taken lightly."

Aedan's brows peaked. For an Osirian, she knew so little about their Osirian society it astounded Deuc.

Hunter smirked, "What sweet words Deuc, you've almost made this awkward. So I guess this means that…"

Deuc smiled, "No, Dios. The bet still holds."

Aedan's brows notched even higher, the swollen left cheek twitched to catch up.

"Aedan's had a change of heart so there's no way – "

Deuc laughed, "That should make it interesting then."

"Where were you?" Aedan's voice cracked.

"Dreaming."

Aedan stepped out from the narrow gap between the bunks, "No seriously."

"That plasma round on Asar."

"You're still affected?" Aedan snapped "You should have said something earlier, rested longer – "

Deuc tore his gaze from her tortured expression, any doubts he held about her concern evaporated. Deuc shifted his shoulders until the strange feeling dissipated. "No, Aedan it changed something, brought something out I didn't know was there." This was hard enough explaining it to Aedan let alone with Hunter as well, but they deserved to know. "I warned you about the *Arion*'s fuel cells, just as I closed in on that Kronos piece of shit, they died. When Calder scooped me up, his crew used an organic scanner to search the *Arion*. I had to stay hidden, until they finished. It worked a little too well."

Hunter narrowed his eyes, "What worked too well?"

Deuc regarded his fingernails, the blood and muck scrubbed clean in the shower, "I'd call it a hibernation of sorts."

Aedan whispered, "Hibernation?"

Hunter ran his gaze over Deuc's physique, "Hybrids" He mused.

"I don't know what ingredients are in my recipe Hunter and I don't really care," Deuc couldn't handle it anymore. Aedan's jasmine and vanilla scent soaked through even his standard defenses. There she stood, wet un-braided hair more black than brown, bruised brows knitted, eyes accusatory. "Let me look at those injuries."

CHAPTER 23

To Aedan it seemed Hunter vanished, the human muttering about finding the showers. Deuc encroached further into the room. Tiny tremors flushed the burnt copper that blinded her. His palms ignited the skin at her hips. Aedan caught the bunk with her thighs. Droplets of water trickled from Deuc's hair, some falling on his singlet, others chaotically rolled over polished amber. Russet gemstones assessed every inch of her frame and she exhaled slowly, hoping her breath would take the color from her cheeks.

"Hibernation? That's new." Suddenly Deuc's aura-less eyes made sense to Aedan: an internal shield.

"I didn't think it would have been so all encompassing. If I had of known, I would never had – "

"It's fine. Hunter's fine. I'm fine."

"Far from it, you risked a lot for Hunter." Deuc cleared his throat, why did his Brother's name twist across his tongue?

"I told you Deuc I'm not running. I forgot Vance, the Kronos guard, knew about Faros. I tried to find you in the plant, but by then they'd caught Hunter. When the Etarians attacked him in his cell, I figured I could fight my way out of it, and then Calder ...." Aedan licked her lips.

"I believe you," Deuc's hand retreated behind his back and he handed Aedan a dark handled silver blade, "I found it on one of Calder's men." Deuc moved to the opposite bunk, his thighs trapped hers. An artery pulsed under the cinnamon surface of his clenched jaw. His nicked thumb spread over Aedan's left cheek, "He will die."

Aedan closed her fingers over Deuc's wrist, "Not now."

The corner of Deuc's mouth kicked up, "Not now," he ran the pad over the blade again, the salty warmth begged to be licked.

Aedan focused on the water droplets, instead of the palm that cupped her jaw or the fingertips that ghosted across her skin. Deuc's healing sent warmth southward, his caresses spiraled into desire. She broke away to the utility room and glanced at her reflection, charcoal rings evaporated to cream, cheeks reduced to feverish peach. In a single touch, Deuc had removed any remnant of those perilous moments, "Thanks."

Over her shoulder, Deuc pulled her braid back behind her shoulder. Her skin flushed with goosebumps.

Aedan tugged the strap of her singlet to one side, the purple jagged scar leered at them both. "Take it. I want it gone."

"Sure?" Deuc's gentle tug on her wet locks sent shivers down her spine.

Aedan's throat bobbed, before she whispered, "Yes."

Deuc directed Aedan to one end of the bunk. He rested on his haunches, thighs between Aedan's. Eyes like polished steel stole his concentration. "Trust me."

The hint of a smile kinked her mouth. The simple act tore tendrils of desire through his veins. Deuc pushed his body upwards so their eyes met, "Whatever pain I cause you, take it out on me." He raised the blade to her neck, the apex pressed into the rough skin at the base, "Bite down."

"Wait, what?"

Deuc seized Aedan, his bottom lip snagged between hers as the knife sliced across her body.

Aedan tasted a burst of silky salt as her teeth dug into his flesh and Deuc withdrew. A tremor stole through her body as, his tongue pooled the blood from her damage. She watched as Deuc dipped his head and scalded her with his healing kiss.

The air around Aedan sizzled, her breath stolen as Deuc licked, nipped and kissed his way across her scar. A chill cooled her skin, yet inside, Aedan melted as if facing a furnace. His arm wrapped around her hips and Deuc dragged, nestling Aedan over his arousal, the hardness of his flesh seeking her silky warmth.

Aedan's fingers wound his satin strands through her knuckles. Trapped between dark shadows and intense heat, Aedan chose the light that scorched up her forearms and spread across her chest, his shelter from her internal tempest.

"Again," Deuc demanded.

Aedan absorbed the cinnamon citrus sting that released a fiery coil in her abdomen.

Deuc withdrew, "Aedan?"

"I can't," She said and dragged her fingernails across the base of his neck. This time she sought out his sweet heat, her tongue streaking across his. The hem of her singlet curled between Deuc's fingers.

A low rumble reverberated from Deuc's throat, the edge of his restraint rapidly approached when his cool fingertips graced the soft velvet at Aedan's ribs. His lips slanted, arm tight on her hips, strained flesh begging for release. Each point that Aedan collided with his body rocketed feverish spikes through his veins.

His thumb traced the tender groove, above which endless suppleness waited. Aedan gasped and she arched backwards, her lips closed in retreat. With a gentle caress Deuc found his petite treasure already puckered and tight in the center of her plush breast.

Aedan's teeth tore at his delicate flesh, and Deuc smiled, droplets of red swelled on his bottom lip. "That's my girl."

Aedan drifted on a sea of trepidation, flames of desire breached tender boundaries, the tide rose, until it peaked and she succumbed. She tumbled below the waves into delicious golden temptation with only Deuc to anchor her. Valleys and cliffs trembled beneath her roaming hands as she peeled back the fabric that denied her access. Taunt muscles crushed her already yielded flesh. The sweet citrus scent intensified and she inhaled drawing it deep within, hot river stones quaked, a grown man growled.

Deuc pulled Aedan toward the hard ridges of his body that begged for release. He stole the whimper from her lips, and sought the nourishment and pleasure Aedan's hot wet kisses promised. She met him in kind and the soft comfort of the strange mattress should have strummed a warning in Deuc's mind. He held his shield, at the edge of his limit. The shield would dim the carnal electricity that coursed through his body. Limbs tangled together and Deuc's lips tracked down throbbing veins, to soft creases and taunt centers. Aedan whispered garbled pleas of resistance and encouragement that drove Deuc forward. His deft fingers made short work of Aedan's buttons to discover the soft plateau below her belly. He felt the slightest rigidity sneak into her suppleness. He tested his shield, fainter, but still within reach, until he reached the secret velvet core of Aedan. Aedan writhed to meet his palm, her silky heat called him forward, and Deuc's shield fled. Only sheathing himself hilt deep into this woman would bring him sanctuary. He lavished the soft corners of her mouth with his tongue as he drew forward a torrid of sensual satin. He released his belt buckle, and Aedan tore her lips from his. He fumbled with the buttons on his fly as she drove her fingernails into his chest. Vanilla and jasmine scalded his senses, as Deuc snatched at Aedan's hips. She wriggled underneath his grasp.

"No. Enough. No, Deuc. Please."

Her words blasted him like broken glass, he drew back on his haunches, empty hands rested on pulsating thighs. With nerves shredded he hauled on his shield. Aedan's eyes flew wide and she scrambled to the far end of the bed. His heart thundered under ragged breaths and Deuc looked at himself, flesh strained against flimsy fabric, hard as a rock and denied entry; his quarry afraid and livid.

"Aedan, I'm sorry…"

But Aedan had already straightened her clothes and fled.

He let the shield cool his fervor.

Aedan ran to the utility room and slammed the shutter. She tucked the knife into the handle. Deuc had overwhelmed her and breached her inner walls. Worse she had let him. His kisses and deft ministrations had sung to the weaker side of her sex and left her reckless and unprotected. She activated the faucet. Deuc had managed to keep the long shadows at bay, piercing the fabric of her nightmares like water on oil. But only temporarily. Eventually the corners pulled down and seized her in the familiar darkness that threatened to destroy her. She yearned for the closeness, yet terrorized by her past. She let the water drip from cheeks onto chest. Aedan regarded her fresh pale skin, a tiny sliver of red remained. Deuc had repaired the surface damage only she'd have to do the rest.

Aedan opened the utility room door to reveal Deuc sitting frozen on the edge of the bunk. His head in his hands, eyes on his boots. Suddenly his gaze targeted Aedan, brows furrowed, his lips parted as if to speak, instead he rose from the bunk.

An objection formed, but Deuc strode away before it passed Aedan's lips.

Deuc returned to the main cabin, his mind ticked over on Aedan. Serenity, sanctuary; his salvation. He had her trust but lost it. He was running out of time.

Hunter had re-emerged to the main cabin freshly pressed and dressed in time to watch Deuc pull his singlet over still twitching skin.

"Feeling better?" Hunter smirked.

"Never."

Hunter scoffed and flicked between monitors. Most captives awake, the numbers of the dead stood at two a side, "We've got a population problem."

The Kronos guards separated in three different cells, Lieutenant Huul and his pilot in another, the blonde Captain Varmil had come to his senses and with him the other Militia argued across the void to Calder and his two remaining Merc's.

"We keep Lieutenant Huul. Rank counts for a lot in the Militia." Hunter directed.

"We keep the pilot, I've got the Sandes mapped but I don't want Captain Petyr Varmil left with any assets." Aedan's hair finally braided, clothes demure.

"You're going to let Varmil live?" Hunter's irises ablaze, Deuc's jaw tensed.

Aedan's silver eyes reflected the monochrome images, "It doesn't matter what side of the Sandes we're on, a man like that needs punishment and to be taught humility, but it needs to be official not vigilante."

"What?" Hunter barked.

Deuc sighed. He could see Aedan's point, had the Captain not just tried to filch her for himself and his men, as well as trying to propel Hunter to Erebus with his fists.

"It's not just my decision Hunter. It's yours but like you said, the Etarian's value discipline, intelligence and civility and he showed us none. To do the same to Varmil makes our weaknesses as brutal and as vast as his own. I will not sacrifice my humanity because of his deficiencies." Aedan faced Hunter, "Revenge is quick and easy but mercy is a long lasting torture that we are forever his superior."

Deuc suddenly felt small, he looked at his boots instead of Hunter, whose hands twitched at his side. If Hunter agreed, Deuc would concur.

"And what of Calder?" Hunter asked.

Aedan turned shimmering eyes his direction, "You are an Osirian Administrator are you not? If there was an Osirian Charter – what would it say for Calder Vien?"

Fuck. After Aedan's benevolent lecture to Hunter, how could he get his hands around that traitor's throat? "He conspired with Etarians to the detriment and persecution of Osirians. He attempted to cross the Sandes without Sanction,"

"Sanction?" Hunter parroted, eyes narrow.

"And he attempted to liquidate an Osirian official."

Aedan scoffed, and Hunter snorted.

Deuc paused, he found a loop hole, "I am an Official Administrator for the Osirian Government and we have a clearly defined policy for Traitors, Aedan and it's not pretty. Do I send Calder to face the atrocities of the System or deliver the punishment myself?"

"Nice try Deuc," Aedan stared him down.

"Over played it – atrocities?" Hunter shook his head.

"Fine, send him into the system." Confident of the result either way, disappointment still stung that it would not be Deuc's hands that crushed Calder's throat.

"What of the Kronos guards?" Aedan asked, her gaze tracked back to the monitors.

"They broke whatever section of the Etarian Charter you quoted let the Etarian's decide." Hunter turned away.

"Yeah, I guess." Aedan's eyes slid around him and back to the monitors.

Hunter stopped at the stairs, Deuc lifted his arms from the back of the chair and waited for Aedan, "Next question – do we have enough cuffs?"

Aedan's buckles jangled as she descended into the cargo hold, the electronic blue haze coated her ankles and she paused. Aedan turned over her forearm as dark feathers materialized. From where Aedan stood, she could see Hunter's sandy hair at the bottom, and Deuc halfway between them. He leaned one arm across the railing. Aedan drew in a deep breath but courage deserted her.

Kegan Capare entered the cell block, his yellow eyes sized up the captives.

Hunter stopped in front of the Lieutenant's cell, "Time to shine."

"How so Dios?" He asked his long fingers gripped sharp angled knees.

Calder hollered a whistle meant to embarrass and Varmil scoffed.

Lieutenant Huul's eyes narrowed and his puckered mouth parted as Aedan reinforced Kegan. They knew Kegan was a fraud, and here he was about to let them live.

CHAPTER 24

Lieutenant Huul knelt stoically as Kegan's heel pinned his calves, metallic bracelets looped, knife at his throat. Deuc and Hunter had already removed the fuel cells and disconnected the comms from the Kronos *180B*, ready for its cargo. Huul's graceful space craft received the same treatment.

"Found this," Deuc spun the Ide-an-Kai through his fingers, Hunter plucked it from the air. "And this." Deuc gently opened his fist to a palm full of HMX crystals.

Kegan sighed "Well it is Calder's ship. Did I ever tell you how he wrecked that eye?"

Hunter stopped outside the Etarian cage, Captain Varmil rested one boot against the wall, arms crossed. The remaining two militants mimicked his arrogance. Kegan recognized the stocky Etarian, who tried to leer through blackened eyes. The other Etarian, fresh shaven and dark skinned, wheezed when he breathed. Calder's men had done alright. The air became flooded with masculinity, meaty, warm and tense. The blue bars low hum sparked into a sizzle as Varmil spat at the electro-magna edges.

"Traitor," Varmil said.

Hunter's fists clenched and the silver multiplied before their eyes, Kegan tightened his grip.

"Degenerate," answered the Human.

Varmil snorted, clearing a bloodied nostril. "I'm not done with you."

Deuc wandered behind Hunter, his ebony stare trapped Captain Petyr Varmil's hazel gaze.

"Who the fuck are you?"

"He is my – " Hunter started.

" - *Mao Adelfos*." Deuc answered, Hunter's spine straightened.

The Captain with only a few years on Deuc, measured his new opponent, "Brother?" Their shoulders squared as both drew parallels between the possibilities on either side of the Sandes Belt. Deuc's dark exterior with burnt copper skin, fiery instinctive temperament: an unflappable patriotic renegade. Inside the cell Varmil answered Deuc's heated glare with cool detachment and institutionalized prejudice: programmed, preened and proud.

His eyes targeted Kegan, "If I'd known she was a cross-breed." Varmil's impassive and well-disciplined expression never altered the hard lines of his face.

Hunter's forearms twisted, but Deuc took a step closer to the cage and Varmil did the same. Deuc's face twisted into a menacing grin.

"She's an Oddworlder whore," The blue bars cast jagged lines over Varmil's smirk.

Deuc's grin widened, "It's a measure of a man how he treats the weak, so I'm going to let you live."

A deep chuckle burst from Varmil's throat, "When I find you and I will, I'm going to – "

Deuc interrupted again, "You're going to what – write my name on a list of all the people who did you wrong in your life and one day when you're brave enough you'll come find me? Well at the top of that list you should write everyone who never explained to you that in my Worlds, no-one gives a fuck. Write my name down in your little revenge ledger – I'll even spell it for you, Deuc Alion,"

Across the gap, Calder's breath caught in his throat.

"You got it?" Deuc lowered his voice, his words even and flat, "So when you come and find me, when your balls are big enough, I'll shove my name and everything else down your fucking throat until you choke." Not a single hair or muscle twitched on Deuc's surface.

Varmil didn't respond.

"Glad we agree." Deuc hit the switch and sent the electro-plasma bars into the ether, "These two have enough decency and humanity to show you mercy -," He shackled each militant in turn and retrieved items from his pocket. Deuc twisted the items in his hand long enough for the militants to recognize, "- despite your spineless and deplorable actions."

Kegan watched the bizarre exchange just at Deuc stopped at Varmil. He ran his finger across the power pad of a mini-digi frame, a single portrait of a young woman pixelated, sunshine spilled through the background, blonde strands silver in overexposure. "Nataly Millicent Hogan must be very proud of her – what are you?" Deuc tucked it into Varmil's top breast pocket, only to have Hunter's fingers retrieve it.

"Nataly?" Hunter paused over the tiny frame, Kegan led Huul back to his cell, pausing at Hunter's shoulder. Blonde, blue eyes, pale skinned beauty smiled back.

"Betrothed." Varmil let the words roll off his tongue, his hazel eyes glowed towards Hunter.

Kegan's chest constricted at Hunter's hoarse whisper, "I guess I know why she sounded the alarm," Hunter tucked the digi-frame into Varmil's pocket.

Deuc continued unfazed, "Now I'd take that with two hands, and run. All the way back to where you come from, and know that your life has been returned to you by a Traitor and a cross-breed."

Kegan shook his head. Deuc tossed another item into the cargo hold of the *180B* and closed the hatch. Kegan's hand square in the Lieutenant's back. Kegan shoved Huul into the cell and activated the bars as she addressed the Etarian pilot who quivered, "You've got a cell all to yourself now," he said. His eyes never left the floor.

"You're superstitious too?"

No answer.

"Hey, Kegan?"

One of the grunts hissed between the bars, Calder's one good eye tracked Kegan's every move. Another grunt stood at the rear, dreadlocks and trinkets silent. Kegan tried to ignore the oily sweat scent that wafted through the plasma, and concentrated on Calder's grizzled and bruised jawline.

"What Calder?"

Calder twisted his head, his one eye fluttered between panic and fear. The remaining prisoners a captive audience, "I hope for your sake sweetheart, you know what you're doing."

"Flattery will get you no-where with me Calder," Deuc interrupted, "Lieutenant Huul, your Kronos guards here broke some charter of yours. They're Etarians so eek out whatever punishment they deserve."

Safely behind bars, Huul's lips thinned into a smile, his high cheekbones blushed with color, "They killed an Odd-worlder, a Faros employee."

"Lieutenant!" Ebin snapped, his bald head sweat-bound and dirty, "We are Etarians, you can't just hand us to this bunch of savages. We were chasing the bounty – we did – you can't!"

"You killed an – Osirian?" Kegan's forearm hairs stood to attention.

Deuc's chest rose and fell in time with his clenched fists, Hunter watched silently from the side.

"Lieutenant!" Ebin called, his hands temptingly close to the plasma bars.

"Do what you want with them, but kid...Kegan...." Vance boomed from across the gap, "I didn't kill that Faros fellow. You want to send me out then do so, but I'm not going back to Kronos and if Huul says I am, we both know I won't make it. I'll throw my lot in with you, if you'll let me." A blue haze from the cell bars painted the white of his beard an eye water-ing aqua.

"What are you talking about Vance?" Kegan crossed the distance.

"Something happened here, right now at this moment, I don't have the words for it -" Vance's eyes completely oil free, spun like a summer sky, "It's new and it feels right. I want a part of that."

Kegan felt Deuc at his shoulder, rather than seeing him.

The air stiffened as Deuc drew on his shield. Kegan turned to Ebin and spot-faced Goonty his foot wrapped in shirt scraps.

"He's lying – he stabbed him in the kidneys – I saw it," Ebin sneered.

Kegan smiled as a thick sheen of oil appeared, snippets of the Faros conversation floated back to Kegan, "You're lying Ebin. Hooka killed him while Goonty and you were in the *180B*"

Deuc faced Huul, "You would sacrifice three of your own?"

Huul lifted his chin, "You wouldn't?"

"No, but after all this" Deuc gestured to the Kronos guards, "The outcome is becoming unavoidable, wouldn't you say?"

Huul laughed, "I look forward to it."

Kegan approached as Deuc stepped back. "You can keep that one if you like, but he stays here. The rest can go with Calder, to be judged in the Osirian system. In the good Lieutenant's ship."

Lieutenant Huul's lips pursed, "That's stealing -" his eyes sparkled with enjoyment.

"Let's call it Profit. And besides, there is no way that tech is going back to Etaria!" Deuc's mouth kicked up at one corner.

Huul placed his back against one wall and stretched to the ground, "So be it."

"So Deuc – "

"Yes sweetheart?"

Calder shuffled his feet, "If I make some plea, some oath, you going to spare me from my fate too?"

"I won't dice with curses Calder." One thug snapped.

"Nor will I," said the other.

Calder's' mercs retreated further into the tiny cell.

"Save it Calder, your crimes are by far the worst and it's not me you need to make an oath to." Deuc said.

Deuc and Hunter frog marched each prisoner to the Lieutenant's pristine transport. The Etarian's ride smelt like fresh plastic and lavender, each surface sparkling and scratch free. Kegan settled Ebin and Goonty in the rear while Hunter tied

Calder and his two thugs at the front, their rag tag Merc clothing at odds with the stark environment.

Kegan sighed, he needed a new ship. Why couldn't he keep this one? "What's her name?" Kegan called back to the cells.

Hull's shrill voice called from within his cage, "*Katharita,*"

Deuc scoffed, "Of course it is."

Hunter's shoulders peaked.

"It means *Purity*," Kegan answered.

"Ha!" Calder laughed, the metallic cuffs provided enough room to wipe his boots on the cream colored carpet.

Deuc shuffled between the seats and tucked his hand between the cushion "You have a safe trip now boys."

"Chaos can't come soon enough," Calder answered.

Kegan closed the *Katharita's* hatch and retreated to the interior hold. Hunter ratcheted the inner doors closed, as the exterior doors flashed in warning. A whoosh of metal on metal returned Kegan's breathing to normal.

"Purity?" Hunter queried.

"Believe me, today I'm one of the converted." Huul sneered, his iris churned crimson amusement.

A shiver ran down Kegan's spine and after double checking the remaining three cells, he took the stairs two at a time.

"What's Huul talking about?" Hunter said.

Aedan released Kegan and threw her braid over one shoulder and strapped herself into the pilot's seat, "I don't know, but something tells me, it's not good."

"Can you get us through here?" Deuc ducked his head upon entry into the cock pit.

"Are you joking? This is my sandpit." Aedan pushed the thrusters forward.

Deuc strummed his fingers on the arm rests, his knuckles and wrists sore. Aedan hadn't lied, she knew this asteroid field like her own personal rock garden, however the *Minos's* size had caused some close calls.

Each asteroid, most similar in size and composition, but

not trajectory, pirouetted on its own axis whilst hurtling in hap hazardous directions. And that didn't include the magma-mines, hidden gemstones of death. Hunter's face glistened as Aedan decided to follow one asteroid chunk, as it tumbled end over end.

When the *Minos* safely emerged on the Etarian side, Deuc cracked his knuckles.

"I think that's a record!" Aedan exclaimed, silver eyes wide, peach cheeks flushed. The wide, three paneled wind-screen had offered Deuc and Hunter a 200 degree view of their journey.

Hunter's pale face swiveled to Deuc, "Great."

Deuc smiled, she could navigate the *Arion* through at twice that speed. Which reminded Deuc, he was running out of time.

He riffled through the cupboards, finding no Buzz – of course with Etarian's on board – but on the second level he found a fully stocked galley of military rations that echoed his growling stomach.

"Looking for this," Hunter slid the make-shift still onto a bench.

"Perfect!" Deuc poured himself a glass and one for Dios, he had made this man his Brother. Would his loyalty be ce-mented? "So how many hours till Haigon?"

"We're just passing Kronos now, so three and half maybe four hours."

"Braccass is going to want an update after we've crossed the Belt, we need to get Huul ready for that. I take it we're aim-ing for stealth now?"

"Unless otherwise,"

Deuc chinked his glass with Hunter and skulled the con-tents. He poured another for Aedan. "And in retreat, we hit the Sandes at speed."

"Are you going to explain this *Mao Adelfos* and what I'm in for?"

Deuc laughed away the sentiment, his feet leading him

back to the bridge, "It's an Osirian custom, and you didn't get much of a choice."

Aedan's head turned as they entered the cock pit and Deuc focused on the tender skin behind her ear.

"Does that matter?" Hunter continued.

"Only that I have no promise of loyalty from you. You've got enough of my blood in you now that you're probably entitled to the name, without any oaths or ceremonies."

"This will wear off..." Hunter turned his palms over in the stark sunlight of dual suns.

"Maybe."

Aedan's lips made contact with the edge of her cup and Deuc's chest constricted. Time poured through the galaxy, rushing on a collision course he couldn't alter.

"And what happened to the other *Mao Adelfos*?" Hunter asked.

Deuc's lips curled back from his teeth, "He betrayed me." He measured out the HMX crystals into each canister, "Don't worry Dios, he died at another's hands."

Aedan faced the windshield, the *Minos* lumbered, through space. Besides the weapons, Calder had been given a lemon, a giant shiny lemon and he didn't even know it. We've probably done him a favor, Aedan thought. The *Minos*'s heavy hulled figure stole most of the power from the four drives that pushed her forward. Although the weapons had been installed within the last decade or so, the *Minos* must have been a cargo ship or freighter in her past life. The mustard brown upholstery screamed cheap and versatile, the sensors, tech and comms all last century. Calder hadn't been trusted with a jump drive, Aedan kicked the vacant casing, specifically removed before the Etarians handed over the keys. The comms didn't have 3D projectors and only three portals prevented any hacker cable access. Her mind returned to Deuc's statement. She hadn't bothered to learn much about Osirian customs and beliefs. A ceremony of Brotherhood, Calder's mercenary's fear of curses and whatever else they'd called her. The notion of loyalty hadn't evaded Aedan, she'd never had to give it, or rely on it. Deuc sealed up the third canister and began on a fourth.

She'd promised Hunter she was done with his bounty. She'd get the girls to Leta and take time to re-group. Maybe the Sisters would loan her enough money for another ship. She'd repaid the cost of the *Venator* at least ten times already.

Behind her someone yawned.

"Looks like this piece of shit is incapable of rushing, so I'm going to grab an hour unless you need me," Hunter said.

"Do what you need, Dios." Deuc said as he programmed the tiny detonator on top.

"You should get some rest too," Aedan said.

Deuc gently laid down each canister under the rear seats, "I've slept enough." Deuc replied. The co-pilot's chair swiveled to catch his bulky frame. Out of her peripheral vision, Deuc leaned forward as the *Minos* approached Lur, the green and blue bulb of beauty suspended in space.

"What's that?"

"That's Lur – The cliffs are steep in the northern hemisphere, they have several districts designated to terrace farming, their survival is dependent on the altitude. Only a few of the valleys are able to support areas for settlement. The southern hemisphere is more undulating, the settled parts are primarily residential. The first metropolis, Pinot, is renowned for rejuvenation treatment centers, and other modification processes. Lots of tourism near Lurland Lake."

"Tourism?"

Aedan smiled, "Yeah, when someone pays to visit and stay at another place, other than where they live. A holiday."

"Like staying at a Tank?"

Aedan's eyes traced the arch of her eyebrows, "Yeah, kinda."

"And people pay for this experience – the holiday?"

"Yes -" Aedan's heart pumped warmth through her veins.

"Where do people stay – at the farms?" Deuc's brown eyes devoured the engorged bulb of prosperity.

Aedan nodded, and without thinking more words fell from her lips, "There's a lake, in the middle of Lurland. They have cabins for rent, and little boats -"

Deuc's throat erupted in a chuckle so deep and thick, Aedan jumped, "What?"

"Osirian Tourism – imagine, boats on the Great Lakes, their paddles stuck in the dust and corpses -" He threw his head back and laughed.

Aedan had to give it to him. More than just a foreign concept, it was implausible and unobtainable for his kind. Your kind, she thought. "The Etarian's already sneak in to visit Tanks and the Rouge Alley's, I wouldn't be surprised if money exchanged hands for a safe trip over and back."

Deuc's laughter died, his voice small, "Ketos is Ketos."

Aedan squirmed in her seat, "That's why you have Sanctioned travel– you're running Etarian flesh-tours." Her exasperated voice strained in her throat.

"Not me directly, but it's been known to happen."

"And what does the Administration do about this? Nothing I bet." Aedan continued.

"The Administration does what it can."

Aedan's hands flew to her cheeks, "I can't believe it, one minute I feel sorry for Osirian's and the next I discover a whole other reason to hate them."

Deuc spun her chair to face him, "We're trying to change it, believe me. But -"

"Whatever," She withdrew her knees from his grasp and returned to face the console. She tried to focus on the plotted trajectory as it updated; the lime green hologram doing nothing to ease her anger.

"Aedan, I need to talk to you -"

"I'm not listening."

"Not about Osirians or slavers or any of that."

She activated the ships diagnostics and scrolled through the systems status as a distraction.

Deuc's tones softened, "Listen, Aedan, I'm serious -" He

tapped the console, the scrolling diagnostics vanished. "I'm serious about my offer."

Aedan watched Deuc's throat bob under the glorious burnt copper, his lips slightly parted, black ringed umber eyes framed by long lashes. He licked his lips, "I haven't got lakes and cabins and boats, but…"

Aedan's stomach somersaulted.

"I feel a need to stay off-planet for as long as I can. Away from Asar. My work carries me far away, and with the rest of Hunter's jump codes I don't expect to be this side of the Gaia Galaxy for a long time."

Aedan eyed the dark planes of his face. He leaned forward in the chair, the distance between them narrowed and their forehead's met, "I will keep you safe, I promise." Deuc withdrew, russet targeted silver, "Aedan, I'm asking you to come with me."

CHAPTER 25

Aedan pulled back, and wished upon Aodhfin and Fintan, that any color or shade would cross Deuc's irises. Nothing changed, she'd have to take him on his word.

"Lieutenant Huul," a voice like a thousand insects scuttling across paper, punctured the silence.

"Perfect," Deuc scoffed, and Aedan withdrew. Thank Ea the Etarians never gave Calder a 3D image transponder.

"Lieutenant Huul!" The speaker crackled again.

Deuc picked up the receiver and clicked the button twice, his boots rested on the dash, "Whose this? Is this thing on?" Deuc's voice squeaked, "Hello?"

"This is Commander Braccass, who are you?"

"It's Owin – um sir do I call you sir, Calder ne'er said to call no-one sir. Whose it you looking for?"

Aedan stifled a giggle.

"Listen, Oddworlder – you're in Etarian territory now. I want to talk to Lieutenant Huul, now!" Braccass' crackled voice slithered around the cabin.

"You's soundabit upset there, sir I'm gonna find him for ya," Deuc tossed the receiver onto the dash which sent another squeak down the microphone. Braccass cursed.

Aedan remained in the cockpit, the air dropped a few degrees and thinned with Deuc's absence. With the warrant removed Kegan was back on the table. Could she continue trading bodies for Ketos or could she take Hunter's jump codes and disappear? Aedan flicked her thumbnail between her teeth. Could she disappear with Deuc? Leta. Leta needed Kegan's income. That dampened the flock of flutterflies that stirred. Maybe Deuc could help? He was an Osirian Administrator after all. Could his offer of a side kick be genuine? Aedan watched the shimmering lights ebb and flow. Boots echoed off the steel. Could she imagine a life with Deuc? Safe? Not likely with Lestas and Jump-lag and Skyol-whatevers. Would it be freedom or another cage, just more appealing and coated in sienna?

Lieutenant Huul sat in the pilot's chair, his chin edged upwards, skin pink and puckered with Kegan's knife. "Lieutenant –" Deuc paused, "Kegan is going to tell me if you lie."

Kegan's heart quickened but he refocused on Huul's sandy eyes and even paler hair. The rubbery texture of Etarian mans' ethereal skin caulky and pliant under his fingers.

"You lie and – is this a Sam or a Samantha -" Deuc held up the tiny digi-frame of a hairless babe, asleep in his mother's arms.

"Oddworlder -"

Kegan angled his wrist, "Concentrate Huul – I can tell if you lie, I can tell if your hiding something and I can tell when you're about to do something really, really stupid. Now tell this Braccass exactly what you would have told him, had everything gone to plan."

The Lieutenant's lips quivered and thinned, "Commander."

"*Lieutenant Hull, status update.*"

Aedan's eyes watered, Huul's sandy iris began to curdle, "We've had some difficulty with the passengers I'm afraid to report."

"*Huul.*" The receiver burped.

A thick shine of murky oil slicked into view as Huul began his lie. Kegan raised an eyebrow, silver apex drew a single bead of claret from the elastic skin under Huul's chin.

"Dios is dead I'm afraid. Some of the men, couldn't help themselves. They were overcome with grief and rage -"

"*That is unfortunate.*"

Kegan glanced at Deuc at the measured response from Braccass.

"*And the others?*"

Lieutenant Huul's tongue furtively flicked over his top lip, "Calder's men suspect nothing." He whispered.

The knife blazoned in Kegan's fist.

Deuc shook his head.

"Good. Everything is in place for your arrival."

"Excellent Commander."

Deuc slapped the receiver out of Huul's slender fingers. The thin man came to eye level with Deuc, his frame slipped down into his uniform. "What's the plan Huul?"

Kegan's fingers snatched at Huul's wrists and the pale man winced, his buttocks slapped the seat, "Well I can't see from up there, Deuc." Kegan snapped. Calder? Huul had counter-measures. Braccass had countermeasures. Layers of oil collided with levels of scum as Kegan tried to sort through Huul's lies.

Huul ran his hands down his chest and brought his collar down from his ears. He used his palm to smooth back corn silk strands from his damp brow, "Upon returning to Haigon, we were to land at Notian Keep."

Kegan twirled the black handle between thumb and forefinger as he recognized the lie, "Try again."

Huul's eyes flew wild, "My mistake, Huttington Plains."

The oil slick across his eyes vanished.

"Truth – the Etarian Military base," Kegan tapped his toe on the floor, "Go on."

Huul licked his lip, "After declaring Hunter dead, Calder would be ambushed."

"Cleaning house?" Deuc snorted.

"Exactly and then they would fly to New Populas for a broadcast, and – " Huul dug his fingers into his collar, and tugged. Kegan's nose cringed at the sudden moist almond odor that resulted.

Kegan dragged the Lieutenants elbow down, "And ?"

"Myself and Captain Varmil would claim the reward." He squeaked.

Deuc nostrils flared, "You wouldn't let an Osirian cash in a bounty like that, so you'd stage an ambush, Calder would push back and more militia would lose their lives at the hands of Oddworlders. Am I right?"

"Yes that's a brief summary. And besides imagine all that money in the hands of an Oddworlder, Ha!"

Kegan's mind jangled like an insect caught in a web, "Who are the four others you've added to Hunter's tally?"

Huul's eyes betrayed his statement, "It's Etarian politics, I'm not privy to all the directives."

"Try again," Kegan added, Huul's oily gaze churned again.

Huul folded his hands, one over the other in his lap, "Members of the United Etarian Command."

"That's your own party! You're in power." Hunter said.

"They're loyalty had become questionable." Huul's lips pressed shut.

A slick coating of corruption tainted the back of Kegan's throat. The Etarians were prepared to deliberately sacrifice the lives of their own. Even when discussing the fate of Ebin and Goonty, Huul had attributed guilt to an Osirian death.

"There are factions and splinter cells – Democrats undermining – oh why am I even bothering to justify this to you savages." Huul crossed his arms.

With the promise of Hunter's reward, before the twin girls' fate had been known, at some point, Aedan had hoped she'd have enough Ketos to feed Leta and buy her freedom, eventually retire safely in Etaria, without the need for Kegan.

It all seemed like a bad Buzz hangover, none of it real, none of it different from the corruption and exploitation Kegan ran from in Osiria, "And what about me?" Kegan said.

Huul's brows arched, without a lie, he said, "You'd have suffered the same fate as Calder."

A weight lifted from Kegan's shoulders. He'd sent lasers end over end into Etarian Militia ships, blasted them to meet their Maker. Kegan's thoughts finally settled, Huul still wasn't making sense, "Then why remove my bounty, why bother?" Kegan stuttered.

Huul babbled, the heat climbed from his neck to his cheeks, "That was not Braccass' decision or mine. Probably budget related. Do you honestly think Varmil and I could keep the reward? In-all under-Ea, No! We'd get a portion of it, the rest would go back into the Budget for next year's elections. No-one could revoke Dios's reward, so revoking yours saved Ketos and paperwork."

"Good to know." Hunter lowered his shoulders into his jacket. Kegan stirred from his loathing, as Dios, hair mussed, red lines still imprinted on his cheek, entered the cockpit.

Deuc retrieved Huul's collar and together they disappeared from the room.

As if the gravitational regulator had been switched off, Kegan revolved into Aedan and her legs became jelly. Removing Kegan's bounty was just hitting pause. "I should have guessed with their attack on you," Hunter's hand came to rest on Aedan's shoulder, "It wouldn't have mattered who handed you in." Deuc returned to the cabin, and Aedan recalled his first steps in the hold of the *Venator*, appearing from the shadows to ruin all her plans, "If he'd never fucked it all up," she pointed at Deuc and tried to laugh it off. The rest of her words came out in a hoarse whisper, "I'd be dead."

Deuc crossed his arms over one another.

"Don't you fucking say I told you so." Aedan's words fell off into a whisper as she returned to the windshield, the stars of a million suns flickered between the liquid. You're just tired, that's all, she told herself. Tired of running, tired of being afraid, tired of picking sides! The dual sons of the Etarian solar system cast stark shadows across the console. Aedan focused on the brilliance and the shade. Ea and Erebus. It didn't matter what side of the Sandes she was on. Snow or ash, polished or pitched. What had she spat at Deuc? *The darkest malice survives in the most prosperous of places*. Aedan's laugh stirred a rush of adrenaline and clarity. When her last breath reduced to a manageable level the last beads of moisture had dried, she turned around, "So what's the plan?"

"Arc guns drawn, ripping spines and snapping necks?" Deuc said.

Hunter added, "Fucking instinctive Osirians."

Aedan laughed. Amidst the tiers of filth, Aedan had found gold. "No, I think a quiet plan is best. We have Etarian ID, we have the *Minos* and we have Huul." Aedan answered.

"Let's get that pilot up here then."

Cameruin Thou shrunk into the pilot's chair, his mousey brown strands, departed in large numbers from the band that ringed his skull.

"Cameruin, remember what I told you."

Thou's head bobbed up and down like a sparrow-fly on the hunt.

Kegan held the receiver up to his lips, "*Minos* to Tower 5."

"*Minos this is Tower 5 go ahead with ID.*"

The Pilots voice quivered, "5667E, *Minos* – 40955 Poppa, Alpha, Echo. Haigon bound."

"*Please wait while we verify.*"

Hunter cleaned his Ida-en-Kai waiting for the Etarian Militia comms to reply.

"*Go ahead Minos – what's your relay,*" The radio crackled.

"Tower 5, Relay message to Commander Braccass – unexpected delay has affected our port-side drives. ETA 1 hours and 25 minutes, via orbit station 12."

"*Received. Emergency response required?*"

Thou stammered on the radio, his green eyes searched from Kegan to Hunter.

"Negative stand by for update upon landing," Hunter whispered. Thou reiterated the instructions word for word. "Well done." Hunter patted Thou on the back.

"Can I go now?" The pilot stammered.

"Not just yet – "

The covert shadow communications channel chirped, "*Huul!*" a crackle like dry leaves suddenly aflame.

Hunter held the receiver forward, "Second Class Thou

here, sir" the pilot whimpered.

"*I want Huul!*"

"He's injured Sir. There was an uprising, with the Odd-worlder," Thou's voice cracked, "The others are taking care of it now, but Huul was struck."

"*Varmil?*"

"He's seeing to Huul. The Lieutenant said you needed to know."

Silence stretched until Aedan's ear's burned.

"*Station 12 you said?*"

"Yes Sir. It's the closest, and we're heavily damaged on our port side drives."

"*What about the others?*"

Thou's shoulders shrugged, and Kegan whispered in the pilot's ear.

"Kegan is still alive sir."

"*That'll have to do.*"

Deuc's eyes popped but he'd have to wait till he secured the pilot before getting an explanation. He re-entered the cock-pit, ready to change Aedan's mind on whatever she'd decided. An itch nagged between his shoulders. He still waited for his first answer.

"Huul told us their grand Etarian plan, I'm just sticking to it." Aedan rested in the pilot's seat, hands between her knees. She shivered and Deuc knew it had nothing to do with the climate control.

Splendid prosperity glistened through the glass, the rose-colored tint finally removed. The white's suddenly painfully bright, revealing the stark bones of truth. Every fault line, every teeth mark bared for Aedan to see. Inside, Deuc knew she searched for the crushing solace only the dark could bring.

Hunter interrupted Deuc's revere, "Orbit station 12 is on the southern hemisphere, Braccass should assemble his forces there, while we land at the R & D complex. You shouldn't have to use Kegan at all."

Aedan's voice quavered at first, until she cleared her

throat, "I know but Braccass seems to be, the type of man who'd have countermeasures on top of countermeasures."

Deuc sighed, "He loads the deck to win every hand."

"Exactly," Silver targeted Deuc's gaze, "It was either Kegan or Calder and we no longer have Calder."

Aedan took quick stock of the weapons she could hide, two in her boots, two up her sleeves and one in the small of her back. Hunter did the same, his Ide-an-Kai strapped between his shoulder blades.

"Whatever happens, Aedan, I want you to know you have my gratitude for...for everything."

Aedan snorted, "Same Hunter."

"The words are just inadequate, you've saved my life, twice, and it probably won't be the last, I owe you." He dipped his head for a second, "When I left Haigon, I never imagined where I would end up. I want you to know Aedan, I'll always have your back."

"Mine or Kegan's?" She joked.

"Both,"

"Thanks," Aedan passed him a blood soaked sheet, "But the same goes for you too. I will always have your back. Yours and those girls." For a laugh she tagged on, "Trust me!"

Hunter's lips split into a grin, "Of all Erebus's sins you cannot take that one!" he laughed.

"He is your Brother now."

Hunter opened the medic store and activated a stretcher, "And what does that make you?"

Aedan sighed. Would Deuc compromise? "Only one way to find out."

She found Deuc in a single bunk room, as he stretched Etarian fabric over Osirian bulk. Aedan laughed, the gaps warped and popped, "My offer still stands."

"If we make it out alive, you mean." She tucked her hands behind her back and leaned against the wall.

"I said I'd protect you and keep you safe,"

Aedan couldn't help herself, "You've been doing such a great job so far."

Deuc's boots moved as if to take a step, but he reclined against the wall mirroring Aedan's stance, offering the largest gap between them, "If you stopped throwing yourself head first into things, or jumping out of air vents it might be easier."

She didn't trust her voice so kept it short, "You found me."

Deuc slowly crossed the room, "I said I would."

Aedan didn't move, "I don't need you to protect me."

"Then what do you need?"

Aedan dipped under his arm and stood in the middle of the room, "Kegan may be gone, but he had expenses. I don't want charity and I don't want – leverage. I need an income." The words caught in her chest, she crossed her arms to simmer the flame.

"You want to keep trading bodies for Ketos? Aedan I'm not a Mercenary."

Aedan suddenly studied her boots, he'd managed to make her feel small, "That's not what I meant."

The corner of Deuc's lips curled, "With Hunter's jump codes, Ketos will not be an issue."

"Not smuggling. I know with Calder gone, there's now a vacancy but -." Aedan liked being close to the right side of the law, if not on it all the time.

"My father was a smuggler, but no, my loyalty is to a greater Osiria. You keep what you earn. You can pay me mileage on the *Arion* if you like, and we can sort out the minor details later."

Aedan's vision filled with Deuc, his sweet tang soothed her nerves, as his hands came to rest in the small of her back. He's loyalty to Osiria, his hopes to affect change struck a chord within Aedan. The Jump Codes like a lightning rod to that end. Like a splinter in her thumb, Aedan couldn't avoid the question anymore, "I won't be someone's sidekick." The sentence bounced off Deuc's chest in the narrowing space between them. Aedan's ears cringed at the tone of her voice, the fragility of the words that stripped bare her fear. She pushed Deuc back further, "Even more so because -" Why did her chest hurt, the back of her throat raw and swollen. Internal and external scars thundered with treacherous self-pity. Aedan straightened her spine. Reclaim, her mind screamed.

Deuc's thumb streaked across her bottom lip, his fingers tangled in her hair, "Not a sidekick." He drew her eyes upwards, "Partners."

"Why?" Aedan whispered.

"For all that is dark within me, is marked by the light from you, Aedan."

He pressed a delicate kiss to her lips and withdrew.

"Yes," the word escaped before she could take it back.

"I will work on self-control." Deuc said, his hands retracted, Aedan's feet back on solid ground, "I promise."

"Good idea," Aedan bundled her fists behind her back, "Maybe you should try one of Varmil's shirts?"

Deuc laughed, "This is one."

Hunter double checked Lieutenant Huul. The straps cut into his shoulders, the belt dug into his thighs. The magnetic cuffs hummed with life, sturdy and latched.

"Nice and snug?" Hunter jested.

"I don't know what you're thinking? When you land at Huttington Plains, Notian Keep or even New Populas you'll be instantly recognized and executed."

Hunter rubbed the gravel that sprouted from his chin and cheeks, "You reckon?"

Huul nodded, "And they won't have any mercy for your friends. None, you're better off turning yourself in Dios. Calling Braccass – "

"It's good we're not landing at any of those sites then," Hunter smirked.

Huul's lips pursed.

"Don't worry, Lieutenant – it's nothing personal, oh wait yes it is." An itch ached in his chest, his palm's sweaty and hot.

In less than twenty minutes he'd find the girls. Alive or dead?

"Hunter," Aedan warned. Black bob covered one cheek.

"So help me Ea," Hunter murmured. "It's on the eastern front, northern hemisphere."

The Lieutenant's lips puckered and twitched, "North East?"

"Everyone dressed?" Deuc asked.

Hunter nodded his acknowledgment. The Osirian had saved Hunter's life, made him his honorary Brother and was about to risk his life. Again. Despite Deuc's weakened state after hibernation, Deuc had to be his weapon, his ammunition and his backup. He wondered about Deuc's talents, immense strength, healing blood, shielded skin, and his newest ability, sending his body into a comatose state at will. The Etarian's experiments and subsequent neglect had inadvertently created a super soldier. Hunter sighed. Deuc was now a tool for Hunter's purpose. Aedan's cheeks blushed as Deuc winked. Similar, with the bounty hunter's increased speed, morphing capabilities, emotional aura and deception indicator, she had to be the ruse, the silent assassin.

"Ready Dios," Deuc said.

Aedan smiled, molten silver glowed against the blackness of space. The blue and green arc of Haigon beckoned the *Minos* forward. Now Aedan fought for no reward, Deuc would fight as his Brother. He owed them.

"I'm ready," Hunter answered. Ea – hear me now – let them live.

CHAPTER 26

Kegan honed in on the Lieutenant's irises "This is *Minos* 40955 Poppa, Alpha, Echo. Etarian code 5667." Huul spoke softly through the receiver.

"Reading you loud and clear Minos – expecting you at Orbit station 12."

"Roger that, on our way."

The *Minos* bubbled and hiccupped her way through the crystal atmosphere of the planetary jewel in the Etarian crown. Deuc's eyes popped when long slender towers, wide harbors, and rolling blue oceans sprung into view. The leafy green plateaus sprouted white and cream settlements, Haigon flags flew from every turret. A wide river system covered portions of the green, with either side, graced by multiple green-energy industrial sites. Immense windmills and solar panels covered every roof, vehicles and trains moving from site to site that heralded prosperity and wealth. The *Minos* closed in on the small sliver of shadow that crept across the surface, a narrow slice of shade between day and night.

"It's never really dark, only twilight." Hunter mused.

"Impeccable isn't she," Huul sighed.

"Only on the surface," Kegan answered.

"Isn't everything," Huul said, his eyes flickered between all three of them.

"It looks – tedious" Deuc mumbled, yet his gaze returned to the splendor of symmetrical mono-cart system, landing pads and sports stadiums. Kegan banked the *Minos* to the north, as directed by Hunter, to the Meddleholm District. Spires and domes blossomed between wash pools, and residential cubes.

Kegan worked his bottom lip. Kegan's warrant had been revoked but not his imprisonment, Hunter was supposedly dead, and they should have been landing with a full crew of Etarian Militia.

The landing gear touched down on the main Heli-pad of the medical complex, the *Minos* whizzed and snuffed her way to idle. Hunter re-checked Huul's magnetic cuffs, before he snapped the belt release.

Kegan lowered his voice, even though the Lieutenant and his pilot were on the other side of the hold, "The Heli-pad is two clicks south, instead of a red X it's faded green on white." Kegan reiterated Hunter's directions to the abandoned Heli-pad. "Shut the hatches and wait." He handed Vance a transmitter and tapped him on the shoulder, his chubby bulk wobbled under the blow.

"No rewards only glory," he answered, eyes bright blue.

Lieutenant Huul let the magnetic cuffs dictate his movement.

Once in the holding bay, Hunter snapped one cuff to the rail and set the proximity limit before he climbed aboard. On the other side, Etarian uniforms stretched to their limits. Deuc's hand rested on the pilot's shoulder, long strands slicked back, and despite the heat, a bizarre Etarian cardigan pulled tight and tucked in at the waist. Vance poured into another uniform and chased up the rear, his crooked fingers fidgeted with his hefty waist line. Kegan regarded the pair of disabled magnetic cuffs that adorned his wrists and ankles.

"You think this will work?" Vance asked Kegan.

"Undoubtedly no."

Hunter yanked Huul's twin cuff and the Lieutenant yelped, "Do you want to keep that hand? Then keep close."

Kegan's stomach rolled to the rhythm of Huul's iris that churned in panic and anger. "Enough," Kegan snapped, the ramp doors opened.

The late afternoon heat of Aodhfin and Fintan had basked the walkway in a sultry auburn glow as they strolled hastily towards the compound. So far, Huul only greeted shift personnel from afar. A wave of his free hand had resulted in strange nods and chin wags, but nobody approached.

For a moment, Hunter lifted his head from the hover-stretcher, enough to recognize the escarpment with crimson peaches and dusky mauves. He tugged on the Lieutenant's cuff and indicated to turn.

Dual white arches traversed the entry to the research and development section, the hallway beyond would lead to a web of clinics, laboratories and nurseries. The stretcher haltered. Hunter tightened his grip on the twin cuff.

"Good evening, is it First Class – "

"Tenko,"

"First Class Tenko it is, well Commander Braccass wants this one cleaned up and this one -,"

Kegan's boot shuffled, the anklets and bracelets, usually heavy and pulsating, rested hollow and empty against his skin. Huul's lowered his voice, "Suitably sedated for tonight."

Hunter counted slowly, the Ida-en-Kai grew hot, steel edges prickled his itchy flesh.

"The infirmary is over at D block Lieutenant."

Hunter schooled his lungs to measured breaths, his stomach liquefied.

"Tenko – Commander Braccass is well aware of where the infirmary is, however he has specifically requested these two be held here."

"Lieutenant?"

Huul huffed, "Are you questioning Commander Braccass' orders?"

"No sir."

A techno-blip squealed and the doors hissed open, "Go on through, Lieutenant."

"Thank you Tenko."

The multi-colored clouds replaced with stagnant ivory and bright white diodes streamed through the sheet. The hover-stretcher wheezed to a stop. The bloodied sheet retreated and Hunter lifted his head. Deuc's oily hair, and knitted cardigan, made Hunter's ribs convulse, he'd make him pay for it, later.

"Level three."

Deuc's hand tapped Hunter's shoulder. Huul's brows raised, his mouth puckered.

Hunter ignored him, "Second corridor on the left."

Kegan's fingers wrapped around his forearm and squeezed.

Ea-hear-me-now, Hunter thought. He pulled the sheet up to his chin as the elevator doors swooshed open.

"Next one. This one's full." Deuc snapped. Hunter heard a gasp, before the doors closed again.

He resumed his counting, a mixture of blood and sweat wiped from the floors of the *Minos* cells had been smeared across his flimsy shield and now, bile rose to the back of his throat.

"She was very pretty and very blonde," Kegan's voice low and deadly, reached Hunter's ears. He swallowed hard. Nataly? He pushed thoughts of Varmil and Nataly from his mind, yet they collided with stabs of ice in his stomach. She was betrothed to Varmil? Had she ever meant to help the girls? The discovery of the truth behind Juliette's death had started the thunderstorm of heartache for Hunter. After that Nataly had kept her distance until she told him the escape plan. Had it all been a trap? What bargain had Nataly made with the Eagle for their rescue?

Hunter sighed and the sheet billowed, "Easy there," Deuc warned.

Hunter heard the familiar scrape and bang of the surgery's grey double doors before their small crowd halted again.

"Lieutenant Huul." A voice boomed from the far end of the bleak hallway.

"Thonson, isn't it. What a pleasure."

"Aren't you supposed to be over at –"

"Yes yes Thonson, Braccass allowed us a short delay to fix these two up for the broadcast."

Hunter heard boots scuff just as the sheet retracted. Red

light poured through Hunter's closed lids.

"Dios!" The Militant spat. "Fine – go on through. I'll let them know you're coming."

"No thank you, that won't be necessary." Huul tried to dismiss the Militia.

"Have it your way Lieutenant, but you might be facing a large delay if I don't. Both medi-labs and operating theaters are at full capacity."

Hunter willed his body to stillness, both operating theatres! Was he too late! With Hunter's capture, had the girls' termination been brought forward?

"I'm sure my authority will suffice," Huul made a move forward, the unattached cuff hummed and clinked against the stretcher. Huul had breached the proximity distance and it sent bolts of electricity through his wrist. He crumpled to the floor as a shrill scream echoed off the stark medical walls.

Hunter rose from the stretcher in time to see Kegan's boot fly into the nearest jaw. The guard went down, hard. The Idean-Kai slithered across his skin and into the neck of another militia. Deuc wiped his palms; two bodies slumped at his feet.

The pilot retched.

The Lieutenant managed to crawl within safe distance of the stretcher and wiped his lips with the back of insipid hands, "Impressive."

Deuc snatched at Huul's collar and dragged his toes across the melamine floors, "Satisfied?"

"Deuc" Kegan said and the Lieutenant tumbled onto the stretcher.

Hunter's fingers fumbled through the dead militant's uniforms. Ea please, damn it! The pass-card folded into his hands. His boots slipped across the hard plastic floor, the smell of antibacterial potions coated his tongue.

"Come on!" he shouted as the doors slid open.

"Hey that's Dios?" came a shout from his left, a nurse decked out in lime overalls stood up from behind an observation hub, his hand pointed at Hunter. An exhausted Militant rose from his reclined position, only to have Deuc fire an arc round into his chin. The nurse reached between the diagnostic screens and Kegan launched over the desk top, boots landed in the nurse's abdomen, he fell backwards, his Etarian skull collecting the edge of a narrow hand basin; the intruder alarm unsounded.

Deuc opened locker doors, to reveal personal items, no weapons, while Kegan secured the unconscious nurse, magna-cuffs now activated. Hunter crept up to the fogged double doors that barred their next entrance. He crouched below the obscured glass and rose slowly. The next corridor bustled with hover stretchers, nurses, medi-techs and orderly droids. Fuck!

"Wait Hunter!" Kegan held a clipboard and scrolled through hologram lines of data, some lines were green, others orange, and two red.

"What's today's date?"

Deuc pulled out Tuck's fob-timer, "76th day of the second rising of Fintan – so is that Ektamer or Oktomer?"

"The 76th? This is dated the 78th!" Kegan said.

"What?" Hunter backed away from the double-doors.

"Are their names Mikro and Zoe?"

Hunter read and re-read the data, injuries, casualties, and surgery details that had been included. "It's scheduled for two days' time."

"Then what's all this?" Deuc observed the bustling corridor ahead.

"Forag system casualties." Hunter answered. The Etarians had finally fixed his broken Jump gateway.

"Kegan!" A shout rang out from the hallway, and Kegan returned through the doors to see rivers of claret snake through the clutched fingers of the Etarian pilot. Huul gone.

"What happened?" Kegan barked, his palm squeezed the abdomen of Pilot Thou, more blood poured onto the ground.

"He said to be brave." The pilot's cheeks turned ashen,

lips waxen. Kegan wanted to turn away from his eyes, but he forced himself to watch. A waterfall of stone cascaded over the pilot's eyes, solidifying as it descended into a frozen wraith beneath his lids.

Kegan's bloody handprints painted the wall, "I don't understand."

"He wants a war." Deuc's neck swiveled to the surveillance junctions that lined the roof.

Kegan shook his head, "What now?"

Hunter dragged Kegan backwards to the observational hub. Surrounded by mint green surgical walls, Hunter directed Kegan to the narrow hand basin, the automatic pump splashed antibacterial solution over Kegan's fingers. He hastily scrubbed them clean, as Hunter handed Kegan the medico clip-board.

"We need Aedan not Kegan right now," Hunter said. He grabbed a long white jacket from the lockers.

"Really?" Kegan fled as Aedan's arms slid into white sleeves. Deuc's fingers wound through her hair.

"You're safer walking around as Aedan rather than Capare." Hunter added, "Remember what side of the Sandes you're on."

Aedan paused and for what felt like the hundredth time, wished on every star, she could read Deuc's eyes. Did his brows dip because of her appearance? Did his head tilt because of where they were, and where they'd come from? How could Huul's actions start a war, an Etarian war? She pushed it from her mind, and focused on her boots, "Even with these?"

"Maybe keep it closed." Hunter said, he scavenged cards and transmitters from the dead guard. "We're running out of time. They're either in the garden or the sleeping quarters, there's no way, we're getting through to the quarters so you'll have to search." He clipped the tiny black dot onto her ear lobe, squawks and chirps exploded.

Deuc's hand slid underneath her coat, to secure the arc gun covertly in the small of her back, "Safety's off," he added.

"Wait, Calder and Varmil saw me, they would have told

Huul. He'll know."

Deuc paused, "It's possible."

"Possible, it's highly likely – I can't -"

"He never laid eyes on you."

Aedan exhaled slowly, she was in Etaria after all. They'd be looking for Kegan, maybe no-one would believe the pale lipped officer if he told them the truth, "Okay."

"Fifth floor, follow the blue corridors, if you reach the green hallways you've gone too far. We'll head to the garden. If you find them call," Hunter pinned a tag on her left breast pocket. Deuc tore off his Etarian costume, bronzed skin strapped down in muted black.

"If we find them, retreat to the *Minos*." Hunter ordered.

Deuc's hands fumbled with Aedan's buttons.

"Deuc," Hunter called as he walked back to where the Osirian refused to move. Hunter's hand came to rest on one bronzed shoulder, the human's other hand found Aedan's wrist.

"My oath, my life." Deuc said, his grip gently trailed down Aedan's fingers, the touch faded only when they'd disappeared around the next corner.

Aedan found her way back to the first hallway. Thoughts of Deuc and Hunter permeated her mind. Neither man had given instructions if she found the girls, and they never made it back. Matter of fact, neither had she. Aedan felt ridiculous, the white coat tangled with her buckles, the hidden weapons grinded across soft skin, hair fluffed and loose, the strands snagged in her mouth, her collar and elbow.

A stampede echoed off the concrete walls, dulled by the melamine as militia suddenly rounded the corner.

Aedan clutched the clipboard to her chest, the arc gun dug into skin slick with sweat, "Sorry ma'am," someone barked as the brigade passed. A fragile and weak smile crept across her cheeks. One militant dipped his head, blue eyes quickly took her measure and winked in reply. Aedan's cheeks played their part.

Aedan selected level 5, her thumb flat against the "close door" illumination until the elevator responded. A shout sped down the hallway, the sound of metal on metal reached Aedan's ears. The door closed.

Hunter retracted the Ida-en-Kai with a sucking slosh, the metallic taint coated the inside of his throat with bile. Aedan was right, he'd never get used to this. Deuc had ended five and himself three.

"Not bad," Hunter added.

"You want to add to your body count?"

"I'm not saying that."

"When you can beat three hundred and thirteen in under 5 minutes, we'll talk." Deuc said.

Hunter's jaw must have hit the floor, because Deuc scoffed, his eyes crinkled slightly at the corners. Perhaps the Osirian never got used to it either. Hunter scooped up the militia's expanding shield, and activated the handle, the electro-plasma buffer sprung to life. He tossed one to Deuc.

A wry smile crossed the Osirian's lips, "Honestly Dios? Why don't you give it a try?"

Hunter paused, "Huh?"

Deuc dropped the baton, "Shoulder's back, breath in from your gut."

Hunter knew what Deuc meant. Since the cells on the *Minos* he'd felt different. A strength in his limbs, a shadow of something almost tangible loitered over the horizon. He squared his shoulders, feet flat, and drew a deep breath in from his abdomen. A breeze fluttered across his skin and the hairs on his neck and forearm stood to attention.

"Now push outwards."

A slab of ice slid into Hunter's stomach and he lost grip of whatever it was.

"Try again."

"We don't have time for this,"

"Fear is a great motivator Dios."

Hunter nodded. Tiny increments intersected and united, miniscule fragments overlapped until the world cleared. The far end of the corridor came forward, edges sharpened, the temperature cooled. Across his surface, cells bonded and muscles tensed, an invisible armor settled like tempered steel. He stared at his hands, fists clenching like vices, "Holy fuck, this is temporary right?"

"Only Ea knows. There's enough of me in you that it might not be." Deuc's throat released a hearty sound, and Hunter clicked his tongue.

"What a way to make it weird."

Deuc chuckled, "Come on."

Hunter dropped the baton and together they tore forward.

CHAPTER 27

Aedan raced along the tunnels until turquoise morphed into mint. She halted and took a left turn. A pale melamine bench manned by two women barred her progress.

"Little early for obs isn't it?"

"Er, yes, I -" cogs in Aedan's brain spun on full tilt, nothing. She knew so little about this World, about this place.

"Did you forget something?"

She blushed, "I did. I'm sorry, don't tell – "

"We won't," the older woman smoothed grey whiskers into a mousy brown bun, sun wrinkles etched the corners of her eyes, "I can't let you through, the Chief is on high alert, the complex is on lock down until things are secure."

"Sounds exciting, but I really need -"

"Do you know how are the Forag injured are tracking?"

Aedan looked down to her ID tag, shit!

"They're still working on a few, but I'm being optimistic," She bumbled.

"I didn't think Dios would turn like this. First his attack, then his escape, and now Forag. It's so sad, he was such a lovely boy." The older woman turned to her companion, a tight red bun tucked in place, sunspots and freckles gracing her elderly face, her upturned lips coated in cherry-red lipstick. They reminded Aedan of the Sisters of Leta.

"If I could just…"

"I can't. If the Director finds out you'll be toast."

Aedan smiled. You have no fucking idea! She screamed internally, "I really need to get through to find my – reports. If they're not on *his* desk by tomorrow, I'm toast anyway."

"Sorry love, but you'll have to wait till the alert is cleared. You should go to your unit and wait it out. I'll have a look when it's over."

Aedan thought of Sister Yulna and Sister Marg, "I promise I'll be five minutes maximum. A quick look and then I'm a ghost." She begged, hands clasped, eyes wide and lips pouted.

The red head's eyebrows raised, her ruby lips smacked together, "Five minutes max or we'll be toast," She hit the door release.

"Thank you so much," Aedan's head bobbed and she dashed forward through the opening Perspex. If they presented a problem on the way out, she'd regrettably have to take action.

"Be quiet – they're asleep."

The older woman continued to natter and Aedan caught a single word, one name.

Bubbles burst in her stomach as she crossed the darkened threshold. Aedan missed a step. Nataly? Hunter's bounty had been ridiculously high and Aedan had thought it related to his Human status? With a five trillion Ketos price tag, the Etarian's had guaranteed anyone chasing his bounty would take the easiest option and kill him. Calder tried and Varmil. Even Commander Braccass had been "relieved" when he learned about Hunter's "death". If being Human had been so important they should want to destroy such a precious resource. No this was very personal indeed.

Aedan crept through the darkened play room, toys littered the floor, gaming consoles lined the walls, teddy bears stacked in one corner, doll houses in the other. A myriad of paintings covered the benches, and despite the shadows, Aedan identified a mural of mythological creatures. A prison all the same, Aedan mused. In the center of the room sat two oversized recliners containing two slumbering figures.

Their boots propped up on miniature rocking horses, a child sized kitchenette, complete with plastic food surrounded them. Aedan sighed and tiptoed backwards. Two arc guns, two blue bars, and four hands stationary on the two sentries. Aedan's eyes caught the edge of two bed frames, one purple the other blue. Both empty.

Aedan's ear piece chirped at the same time of both guards.

"Confirmed sighting Level 5, Garden Enclosure."

Hunter paced across the 15 foot long glass panes that separated him from his quarry. Mikro and Zoe chatted like a pair of baby birds as they circled their well-weathered nurse. Black pony tails restrained by bows bobbed and swirled in the breeze, their oval eyes widened as Hunter approached.

The squeals alerted the two militants who gambled in the far corner, and Hunter buried the girls face into his neck as Deuc dealt the final blows.

"You came back!" Zoe chirped,

"Are you here to stay?" Mikro said, "It's been so sad without Jules?"

Hunter's throat constricted. Juliette. Sister. Angel. Gone. "I've come to take you with me."

"With you?" Zoe, the most assertive twin quizzed. Her nose a little bolder, chin narrower than Mikro, eyes sparkled green instead of Mikro's mahogany brown.

"Yeah, I promised I'd take you to see the stars." Hunter regarded the exits. He'd heard the alarms already sound. He took measured steps to the far end of the escarpment. His mind spun as adrenaline poured through his system. He didn't want to scare them, but time had run out. He pumped his fists and focused.

"Really?" Mikro's smiled blossomed across her heart shaped face and rosy cheeks softly echoed on Zoe's darker complexion.

"Yep," Hunter put the transmitter to his lips and called Vance. Nothing. Hunter turned around to where Deuc had the nurse subdued in the corner, hands fidgeted in her lap. Thick drag marks in the polyfoam grass indicated the militants had exited via escarpment. Hunter clicked the transmitter again, the radio seared Hunter's ear drum and he tugged it clear. Alarms wailing in sector E4? He hoped Aedan was in retreat? He called the Kronos guard over the radio.

"They said you we're bad, that you hurt Nataly." Zoe sent

her chin skyward, one eyebrow raised.

Hunter's veins already infused thick with heat, now pierced with poisonous rage. He buried it, "Well that's not true. I'd never hurt Nataly." The words felt like sand on his tongue.

"That's good." A tiny voice rose on the breeze.

The arc gun hilt collected one militia behind the ear, the chair caught his buttocks. The other turned to shout but the electric blue pulse illuminated his teeth. The radio squealed all sorts of directions and commands, units responded to the call for urgency. Hunter and Deuc had been located in the Garden.

The double doors whisked closed, "Must be somewhere else," Aedan smiled at the two women, their faces reflected the ashen tones of security monitors. Neither woman looked up. Suddenly the red head wailed, "The girls!"

Aedan broke into a run as she turned the corner.

The green painted walls twisted and turned. She passed more clinics and laboratories, complicated medical terminology relating to the latest advancements. Biomechanics merged with genetics, stem-cell production, cohesion and disintegration therapy and finally Storage. Aedan's heels squeaked on the melamine as she marched backwards.

Her knife twanged when the lock popped and sung when it sliced through the guard that attended to investigate. Further inside, Aedan shivered into her lab coat, the violet corners and icy surfaces, reinforced her assumptions. Her ear piece squealed containment and isolation orders; clearly Hunter and Deuc had everyone's attention. Inside the darkened storage freezer, another guard rose from his chair, long enough for Aedan to kick out his feet and land her clipboard on his nose.

Inside the cryonic columns, a single scientist wandered between the tubes, transparent monitor in his arms, his stylus recorded any fluctuations in the cylinder's status. Aedan read the lids of waist height silver tubes and shivered when her fingers trailed over four black letters. "Dios" she said aloud, and the scientist hunched shoulders turned. He scurried out of sight but Aedan caught him before he could sound the alarm. Her clipboard tore the soft flesh behind his ear. After a quick pocket search of the lab coat, Aedan surfaced with his security pass. On the far wall, the control panel beckoned.

By the time the alarm did sound, Aedan had closed the door on a turbulent scene of foaming cylinders rolling in shards of glass. All safety extinguishers emptied, all DNA canisters drenched. As she re-entered the labyrinth of medical corridors, she flattened her back against the wall as a herd of nurses, and staff stampeded south. Aedan headed north.

The northern corner of the complex's penthouse had been designated for the Garden District, a 20 foot escarpment provided a natural barrier to one side, Etarian military posts on the other side of a 15 foot panel of glass. Aedan weaseled through the growing crowd, a wall of cyan and blue with palms on chests, kept the onlookers at bay.

Aedan scanned the area as crystal skylights shuddered and wilted amber light when Etarian convoys flew overhead. She pushed through the mob and stopped one row from the front. Crackles and orders exploded in her ear.

"Atlas 1 has landed."

Aedan swallowed hard.

"Two targets, two hostages. One friendly."

One friendly?

"On route – hold your positions." A voice like a sandblasted inferno burst across the airwaves.

Over the heads of the militia barricade, Aedan glimpsed Deuc and Hunter surrounded by a ring of electro plasma blue. Two smaller shapes stood in front, from shoulders to ankles in calico dresses, bows at the elbows and neck, silken black hair pulled back into sweeping pony tails. Rainbow kaleidoscopes on fast forward.

Zoe. Mikro.

A very pretty, very blonde figure faced Hunter. Aedan had to squint to dilute the red tint that exploded from Hunter's gaze.

Nataly.

Zoe and Mikro swirled around Hunter's wrists, torn between the pale apparition that stood between him and a hundred arc guns. Imitation grass and paper daffodils crunched under Hunter's heels as more soldiers spilled into formation.

"Hunter, please," Nataly pleaded.

"Stay back!" One guard shouted, his fingers snatched at Nataly's trailing white coat.

The Etarian beauty, twisted, her bottom lip quivering around perfect white teeth, the hollow in her throat fluttered with each word, "Stand. Down."

"Dios?" Deuc's boots squeaked on the poly-foam pebbles.

Nataly cleared her throat, "Stand down!"

The Etarian girl reached forward and the twins quivered between the pair.

Hunter tilted his head to one side, "Don't try – "

"Hunter, I'm so glad you're alive, when I heard the AI Bot had registered your face, when I saw you and Kegan in the elevator I just knew -" Words tumbled end over end, pale strands floated free on the breeze.

"Stop!" Hunter shouted and she obeyed. His heart strummed frantic chords, stalked with dark notes.

Nataly's lids heavy with moisture, "Please – I had to tell them. Give them some reason you left. They found me in the control center releasing all the doors. They -"

Hunter's mind wheeled in time with the beats of his heart. "Varmil?"

The Etarian princess's ruby cheeks became translucent, slender fingers twisted on her wrist "My father's idea." A faint blue vein twitched across her jaw. "Hunter, please." Nataly begged. He hadn't cleared the fog in his mind. The trap. Calder on Asar. The guards.

Glass panels shimmered to the stampede of boots as beige uniforms with shiny silver pips graced their presence, the line of Militia now reinforced, as three men stood protected in the middle. The dual suns of the Etarian system spliced pale oranges and creamy beige into the court yard, a serene sunset belied the tension in the air.

"Dios!" The Chief Director shouted, thin lines tore down his hair line, passed his hook nose and into a thick snarl.

Nataly cursed as she spun to face her father.

"I enjoy a great reunion Dios, but we're running out of options," Deuc snapped, his top lip peeled back.

On the right side of Chief Director Hogan, stood Lieutenant Huul, a smirk split his long face. On the left, a dark gaze blazoned across the void. With black hair shot through with silver above the ears and a nose that spread across his hard cheeks, Commander Braccass dominated the arena.

"Aedan?" Hunter whispered.

"Hopefully on her way back to the *Minos*." Deuc said.

"You have a transport?" Nataly's words crept from the corner of her lips.

"Nataly return front and center." Hogan ordered, a crooked finger pointed at his boots.

Nataly's ears reddened, but she stood firm.

Hunter's answer snagged in his throat. She'd betrayed him again. He shuffled the shield, like a thousand elastic bands snapping his skin, it settled into place. "Go back to your father, Nataly."

"You have to take me with you, please it's the only way they'll let you leave."

His blood heated beneath a river of steel. A gasp hummed through the mob and the onlookers parted.

"Oh Fuck!" Deuc cursed. A non-descript male stepped forward, shiny buckles chinking, yellow eyes darted from side to side.

"Braccass!" Kegan called.

"It's Kegan!" Nataly exclaimed.

The sound of tearing tendons echoed as Braccass spoke, a collective shiver whipped around the crowd, "Capare!"

"Kegan Capare is here?" Zoe's innocent voice caused the encircling soldiers to swivel their heads.

The nearest called, "Miss Hogan?"

Nataly spread her arms wide and stepped backwards, but it was too late.

"No!" Hunter shouted as Deuc's fingers closed in on Nataly's throat.

She fell backwards against his frame, a smile cracked her streaked cheeks, "Good!" She sighed, "Tell them to let him through. Capare is not to be touched!"

"Let him pass. Touch him and she dies!" Deuc shouted.

Hunter's heart almost fractured his ribs. The bounty! Nataly had recalled Aedan's bounty. But why?

At the edge of the barricade, Director Hogan's shoulders squared while Braccass furtively whispered in his ear. Huul's grin widened and he tapped a pale finger to his chin.

"My Osirian brother will not hesitate to end her." Hunter shouted, his breath tightened around his ribs.

Hogan's hand raised and Braccass recoiled like a snake, "Let him through. Let my daughter go."

Kegan sauntered past the inner circle, and Deuc issued further orders. The Etarian Militia hierarchy agreed and arc guns bounced over the polyfoam.

"What happened to falling back?" Deuc snapped but Aedan's alter-ego ignored him, yellow eyes only for Nataly.

"What's the plan girl?" Kegan said.

"If you have a transport, call it now. You take me with you." She tried to face Hunter, but Deuc prevented it. "I knew you'd come back. I couldn't risk, the girls or my contact with them if I'd been caught. You have to believe me, please Hunter, please,"

An itch crept under Hunter's shield, he didn't like it. He wanted to shake it off. He turned to the bounty hunter whose eyes had never left Nataly's. Kegan nodded and called the Kronos guard on her transmitter.

"They will not attack, my father will not let it." Nataly's eyes tracked back to the barricade. "It's okay girls, we're leaving now." She smiled, and Deuc's fingers relaxed.

Zoe and Mikro reached out to Nataly, their hands tugged on Deuc's pants. "Can you let Miss Nataly go now?" The eldest twin asked.

"When I'm sure her father isn't going to do something stupid, I will." Deuc replied, his eyes darted between Chief Director, Commander and Lieutenant.

As the *Minos* hovered on the lip of the escarpment, Hunter loaded the twins, the noise of the thrusters cut off shouts from the other side. Nataly stood firm, the prop wash stirred her white coat to whip around Deuc's black trousers. A spike of something, dark and small crawled into Kegan's chest and he pushed it away.

Braccass and Huul stood either side of Chief Director Hogan who held onto the image of his daughter. As Nataly stared at her father, her gaze melted into a somber sunset. Kegan turned to Hogan. The same reclining peach coated his. He did love his daughter.

Kegan focused on Braccass. Something about the man standing still and composed, belayed his inner restlessness. Crimson fused with ebony so tightly in the Commander's eyes, Kegan gasped. Everywhere Braccass looked, the same fatal hatred reflected. His gaze tracked to the Chief Director's stalwart jaw, and a volcanic thunderstorm erupted.

"No!" Kegan cried, as Braccass' fist stabbed forward, the electro plasma burst smothered by Lieutenant Huul.

"The Director!" Huul lamented and dragged the Chief's twitching frame to the floor.

Nataly squealed. Deuc pivoted and his frame became highlighted in electric blue.

The Osirian roared and Kegan's abdomen collided with the

ramp railing, the air exhaled in short sharp bursts. He reached forward, feminine Etarian bones bent under Kegan's grip. The *Minos's* thrusters sparked and spluttered. Braccass turned into the crowd, his arm waved wildly overhead.

Lasers buried into the ship's flank. Kegan pulled with all his strength and Nataly wriggled. Deuc swung on to the railing, his feet dangled over the limestone blocks of the escarpment. The hazardous scene grew smaller, and Vance banked right, which rolled Nataly onto Kegan and both into the cargo hold.

"Deuc!" Kegan shouted, the ramp door closed.

"I'm here." He responded, the air still, muted laser blasts decreased in intensity as the *Minos* stretched to the stratosphere.

The radio squealed, "You are not authorized to disembark."

"Push it through old man!" Deuc's hands wrapped around Kegan's bicep and Nataly's elbow.

"They have air to surface missiles, EMP's, field snares and an entire Etarian fleet, I'm pushing Boy." Vance replied.

"Get them settled in the *Arion*." Deuc ordered to Kegan.

Nataly gathered the twins to the edges of her white coat. Kegan dashed to the *Arion*, double checking all the systems, especially the fuel cells. Deuc had trashed the jackets that held the cells, wires dangled on one side, pulled tight on the other. Kegan tossed spare parts out the way, to reach the indicator panel. A spare rotary manifold rolled around the floor. Kegan picked it up and turned it over in his hands. It must have come from the *Venator*. Kegan spent the next few minutes rushing the ignition protocols and reflected on the Etarian's end game.

Braccass had wanted a war all along. The Commander and Huul would sacrifice any and all Etarians to achieve his vision. Including Chief Director Hogan. Kegan eyed the pale Etarian who dashed up the ramp to the *Arion*, her neck slightly more slender, ears flatter against the skull. Nataly's chin and forehead both narrow and long, behind her the twins followed, tanned skin and porcelain, green eyes and brown, the difference was startling. "Now, stay here, girls." Nataly pointed elegant fingers to Hunter's bunk.

Kegan gave up on the fruitless search and entered the main cabin. Nataly regarded the rough masculine frame of the bounty hunter.

Kegan smiled. He looked at the tiny girls with their heart shaped faces, and long eyelashes, cheeks filled with color. There was something about them, all humans, Kegan decided. He tilted his head from side to side. They were creatures of Ea, they had substance, filled with energy and light.

Mikro's fingers tangled in Nataly's pocket. Zoe's chin tilted.

"Thank you for shielding me as you did at the compound." Kegan said.

Nataly swallowed and turned away, "I should thank you."

"Huh?" Kegan's fingers twitched. Did Nataly have an end game?

"Skeeter."

Kegan's throat constricted. Cogs and wheels began to spin. Nataly had recalled the bounty. Skeeter. Chigslin Skeeter? Kegan's hand reached for Nataly's shoulder and the Etarian recoiled. Zoe and Mikro slid further up the bunk.

Kegan regarded the thick fingers, "Can I show you girls a trick?"

Zoe's face illuminated. Mikro bit down on her fingers.

"I'm sure neither of you two will be scared, but I have a secret." Aedan said as Kegan slipped silently away.

Nataly's skin tones paled lighter than her silver eyebrows, her bottom lip only slightly darker than lilac.

"This is the true me. My name's Aedan, the other is just -"

"An illusion!"

"A trick!"

"A bit of both, I guess." Aedan scoffed, "Once this is all over and we're through the Sandes, I have a place I'd like to visit. Would you come with me?"

Flushes of white and joy swirled in Nataly's irises.

CHAPTER 28

Like silver dartfish, the Etarian fleet commenced pursuit, contrails scarred the perfect Haigon atmosphere. The *Minos* tore into the silent chill of outer space, only to be met by the second fleet.

"Open them up," Deuc snapped, but Hunter had already engaged the weapon's systems.

"Shields activated."

At least the Etarians hadn't skimped on weapons, Aedan thought. But Calder still got ripped. She watched Deuc shake his head at the dials that wound slowly forward, thrusters at full capacity.

"*Arion*'s ready," Aedan said, a smile unable to be restrained.

Deuc recovered from the surprise and winked.

"Is she telling the truth?" Hunter's voice thickened.

Aedan nodded, a hand coming to rest on his shoulder. "They found her unlocking all the security systems and she had to tell them something so they wouldn't get suspicious. She never gave up on you returning. Varmil found your -," Aedan paused, "Our message to her on Asar and..." The chairs swiveled 180 degrees, "Dug a version out of her. She never told him about the girls" Aedan replayed what Nataly had disclosed, without adding the disturbing truth of why the Etarians, including her father, had believed her so called lies.

"She recalled your warrant." Hunter answered.

"I know she told me."

"Why?"

It wasn't Aedan's secret to tell, so she shrugged her shoulders, "You can ask her yourself but I think it was to help you." she added.

Hunter watched the weapon's output, switching the targeting grid from the flanks now to the rear the Etarians still in pursuit, the purple bars of light peppered the radar as each blip extinguished on the screen.

Rounds burst across the starboard side, "Shields are at 73 percent," more lasers found their mark, "No wait 69 percent." Vance said, "How long can we run like this Boy?"

"They're only firing pulse lasers, no plasma rounds. Why?" Deuc asked.

"I contaminated the DNA storage." Aedan said.

Silence descended the cabin, breached intermittently by the laser bursts and miasma purging vents. Even Vance's seat swiveled from the windshield to face Aedan.

Deuc finally spoke, "Well we can keep this up until we hit the Sandes,"

"That's ambitious. You better have a backup plan."

"We do." Deuc added.

"65 percent,"

"Then we'll see Aedan make a personal best!" Deuc exited the cabin, leaving Hunter's knuckles to grip arm rests in his wake.

Hunter rolled his shoulders as the Kronos guard snorted and whooped at the shells, "47 percent, that last one."

"Cargo hold is ready. How much further?" Deuc ducked upon entering the cabin and stood behind Aedan. Blushes danced to the rhythm of Deuc's whispers and the knot in Hunter's stomach loosened. Aedan had taken a moment in the chaos to destroy his stolen legacy. The laser rounds still peppered the *Minos*'s tail, but a tiny wisp of something warm tentatively stretched. They'd survived.

"We're over halfway – wait," Vance maximized the hologram radar, tiny barbs decreased in speed. Vance clicked again, the lime green laser lines exploded around the cabin. Etarian scouts slinked back, as if all the pilots had taken their hands off the thrusters.

Aedan's iridescent silver gaze interrogated the hologram. She reduced the radar's scale. A wall of Etarian ships squealed into position ahead of them, "Countermeasures." She mumbled.

"Fuck," Deuc snapped.

"Game over," A voice like trampled leaves crackled into the cabin.

Vance's shoulders shuddered.

Deuc snatched at the transmitter, "Oh Commander Bracc-ass isn't it? On the contrary, it's only the beginning."

A series of barks that sounded like ice cracking leagues under the sea emitted from the radio, *"You're deluded, Savage. End this, before you force our hand."*

It was Deuc's turn to laugh, "Don't pretend this isn't exactly what you and Princess Huul wanted. I'm playing *into* your hands, Bracc-ass."

"Deuc," Hunter cautioned. The cabin lights dimmed. Aedan's eyes flew wide.

Hunter drew up the diagnostics systems, as one by one the tiny lines of data suddenly read *offline.*

"They're trying to shut us down." Hunter hissed. He navigated through the computer's applications and commands blocking each hacker command.

Deuc turned to Hunter, "How?"

"It's an Etarian Ship!" Hunter said. His fingers scrolled through the list, attempting to salvage the systems. He felt gravity waiver, the regulator indecisive as to who's instructions to follow.

"Venting system gone." Hunter said.

"Weapons?"

"Disabled."

"Shields?"

"I'm trying Aedan!"

The bounty hunter accessed her own screen to watch the Etarian Militia's attempts. She managed to re-route basic systems.

The transmitter sparked again, *"You can prevent the death of thousands, right now."*

Deuc clicked the receiver, "So can you."

"Manual override successful," Aedan shouted as the *Minos*'s lasers returned to full capacity.

"Shit it's been a while." Vance joked as his gnarled fingers clamped onto the control joysticks.

Braccass' laugh started and ended like wildfire, "*Where are you going to go?*"

"Home." Deuc tossed the receiver onto the dash, the squeal caused all passengers to flinch, "Hunter help me with the *Arion*."

In the cargo hold, Deuc briefly evicted Nataly and the twin humans from his black beauty while it spun. He wanted her lasers first. As the nose cone scraped the external doors, he signaled Hunter to strap down the rear wheel only, while he prepped the *Arion* for a fist fight rather than a sprint.

"What's that all about?"

"They want a war. There's never been a treaty with Osiria."

Hunter sighed, "Well there's no need to taunt them even further."

Deuc let the sentence hang heavy on his shoulders. Oh yes there was. Would Hunter ever see it the way he did? What about Aedan? Deuc had offered and she had agreed. He flicked the weapons switch, his eyes drawn to the transmitter. He'd run out of time. Even in the cockpit of the sluggish *Minos*, he'd whispered reinforcements, "You still with me?" and Aedan had answered with a quick nod. Silver bands of satin wound around his chest. He turned the ignition to phase two and exited. He rechecked the digital detonators, activating the final signal on the remote as he returned to the cabin.

Inside the main cabin Vance sat in the pilot's chair, his silver hair stark against the black windscreen. The *Minos* steadily encroached towards the Etarian fighters. Aedan sat the row behind, fingers on triggers, her back straight, her whole body tense.

"Ready." Deuc ordered. Aedan's chair swiveled but her

rump remained in the seat.

"Up you get old man. Aedan you're flying the *Arion*."

Mercury darted over his frame, "And what are you going to do?"

"Just go fly my bird."

Vance didn't argue when Deuc's fingers slid under his collar and dragged him clear, "You're throwing the switch." He handed Vance, the tiny remote he'd just finished programing.

"Where's Hunter?" Aedan asked.

"In the *Arion*, waiting for you."

Deuc leapt into the pilot's chair, the seat uncomfortably warm and hollowed by Vance's stature. Silver buckles and black synthetic landed on his knee, a pneumatic hiss responded to Aedan's pressure.

"And what about you?"

He couldn't prevent the corner of his lips sliding up any more than he could, the path his palm chose to track. He wanted to close his grip and drag her onto his lap. He sighed. "You're not leaving without me, are you?"

"No." Aedan didn't flinch as he passed her knee.

He ran head first into a nest of wasps and yet here he took the time to covet the barest of touches, "Good." Aedan's lips parted and with the deftest trace, pressed her lips to his. Fuck it, it was his last anyway. Aedan's thighs came to rest on his hips, and he lavished satin vanilla threads of moisture from her lips. Her fingers trembled against his neck and she returned in kind.

His forearms reluctantly coiled and he levered Aedan upwards, "When I reverse thrust, start opening the exterior doors."

"And?"

"I'll be there. Trust me."

Aedan turned on her heels and dashed to the *Arion*. She wanted to say, "You better be," But kept it to herself. Suddenly the terror was almost over, the journey at an end. The *Venator* gone, five trillion Ketos with it. That's not fair, you were never going to get that, Aedan corrected. Still, Kegan destroyed and with him, some of Aedan's freedom. More than some. She entered the *Arion* and strapped herself in. It could be worse, she thought, smiling as she claimed the first chair.

Hunter manned the quick release for the tie down. Hunter's bunk modified for Nataly and the girls secured with make shift straps and blankets. Vance stoically filled the hallway.

"Where's Deuc?"

"He's going to be fashionably late as always."

Hunter scoffed, "Ready girls."

"Zoe gets hover car sick," Mikro piped up.

Hunter opened his mouth as his eyes tracked over Aedan's hands on the console. Whatever he was going to say it remained unsaid.

"This isn't a car, so I'll be fine." Zoe's bottom lip quivered.

"Exactly." Nataly cooed.

Aedan remembered Hunter's pale shades. Whether flying, jumping or sailing, Humans were not designed very well at all. Three prisms of rainbow met her gaze. Aedan smiled, no they were designed just perfect.

The anchor chain clinked, and Aedan clutched at the seat. A loud crack echoed and Vance slumped to the floor. Aedan levered her boots on the dash and heaved backwards. Someone squealed behind them.

"Hunter - doors." Aedan shouted.

"On their way." Hunter spat.

"Vance? Vance?" Aedan called with no answer.

"He's on the floor, I can't see him," Nataly squealed.

Suddenly the *Minos* roared forward. The *Arion*'s wheels came free from the metal sheeting. What was Deuc doing? The *Arion* hung from the anchor chain, nose cone pendulum like against the moving exterior doors.

A small voice screeched, "I'm slipping!"

"Hang on, not much longer," Hunter threw an arm behind

Aedan. The exterior doors split. The *Arion* tugged against the restraints. Loose cargo became missiles. Aedan prayed they struck an Etarian target.

Deuc pushed the thrusters into reverse, his forearms stung, and the *Minos* responded. The third brigade of the Etarian Fleet, scattered in formation across the first ring of the Sandes Belt. The G-force slammed Deuc into the rear of his seat, as the *Minos* pirouetted and stretched upright. He pealed forward and jammed the throttle on. With his shield settled into place, Deuc leapt from the chair. His boots collided with the stair well, palms clanging to the railing. He dropped again. The cell wall collected his frame. Next the cargo well. The black pit of space opened underneath him, the *Arion* in between. The single cargo door, the tiniest of landing pads. He swung his legs from one side to the other. Again. The doors widened. The *Arion*'s drives increased, waves of turbine heat penetrated his shield. He leaned back and kicked forward. Deuc's fingers released.

His boots thundered onto the fuselage and slipped sideways, the vacuum of space too great. He crooked his fingers and drove them into the metal. The *Arion*'s ramp only a stretch away. He dug into the vents and heaved. The wind wrenched Deuc downwards. His shield barely concealed the energy that ebbed from his muscles. Through the metallic haze, he felt a vice tighten on his wrist. Hunter. Half the human's body extended over the side of the ramp. Together, Deuc's dragged upwards until the ramp closed around them.

"She'd kill me if I let you fall. Honestly, I thought about it."

"Thanks."

"Hey what are brother's for?" Hunter jibbed as they embraced palm to palm.

"You better remember that." Forgiveness is a hard taskmaster, Deuc thought.

Aedan simultaneously sighed and clicked her tongue as

Deuc clambered into the cabin.

Vance's snores drummed in time to the exterior door's final opening maneuvers, "Concussion," Hunter said.

"Get the Detonator. Aedan punch it!" Deuc ordered.

The pilot's chair caught Deuc's chest. The seat belt cut into Aedan's hips. The *Arion*'s drives increased, the thrusters at maximum.

Hunter kicked out, the release cable squealed metal off metal and the *Arion* plummeted into a thick wave of Etarian hardware.

"Now!"

Aedan heard her laden heart beats and one click. A silent fiery explosion danced across the Etarian windshields. Aedan's forearms burned as the *Arion* levelled out, a field of unpredictable missiles her safe haven. Aedan clutched the manual joysticks, the ship's trajectory mapping unsuitable for the speed and dexterity needed in the asteroid field. Hunter engaged the lasers. She'd brought the fight so close to Leta without realizing it. What if the Etarians found it? What if they destroyed it?

Aedan's fingers cramped, her buttocks glued to the seat, lower back and forearms ached as she maneuvered the heavier than normal ship. The hologram radar blipped and squealed unable to decipher comet from fighter from magna-mine. Aedan angled the *Arion* around the obstacles, beige and cyan wings followed.

"They're fast." Aedan muttered

"We're faster." Deuc answered.

"Only just."

"Just enough is perfect." Deuc mumbled.

The field thickened, no-one fired. One dangerous unpredictable projectile was enough. Maybe it would thin the herd, Aedan thought.

A hulking monster rolled end over end in their path. Etarian fighters hovered like twin wasps on either wing. Icy gas and space dust shredded from the giants surface. Through the striations, the Giant loomed. Aedan calculated size, spin and trajectory as best she could and dove deep.

A bursts of lasers split through the Giant, chunks showered the *Arion*.

Deuc interrogated the shield display, the percentages failing. An exhaust popped, one drive coughed. Deuc cursed and Hunter refocused the lasers, the chamber opened.

The olive green devil circled their ankles.

"Vent Deuc!" Aedan shouted.

"I'm trying," Deuc's seat jerked backwards and he disappeared.

Aedan heard coughing but couldn't look.

Hunter unclicked his belt.

The swirling miasma coiled and licked her silver buckles into rusty clips. Aedan inhaled slowly and blinked. A cluster of boulders rotated together. The Etarian wasps returned, lasers glowing red. A heat wave trickled over her ankles and she pulled her knees into her chest. The Etarian fighter taunted closer and Aedan retreated, yanking on the joysticks to avoid the ship on her port side.

Aedan inhaled shallow. The acrid odor seared her nostrils, and constricted her throat. She filled her lungs once more as a line of sweat rolled down behind her ears. The venomous cloud clung to her clothes, the fabric now crinkled and stained. The asteroids soared past, her forearms burned as much as her eyes. The moisture streamed down her cheeks.

Suddenly she heard a shout and the poisonous serpent retreated as if pulled by its tail. Hunter's hand found purchase on the shelves, before he returned to his seat, "Vance will have some blisters but he's still breathing. The rest are safe."

The co-pilot seat spun, and caught Deuc's unmarred frame.

An asteroid separated the *Arion*'s rounds from striking home.

A sheet of pure black beckoned and a worm of ice slid into Aedan's chest. The hologram radar's distortion cleared, behind them twelve, no thirteen darts solidified. "Hunter get a

Jump Code ready," Aedan ordered.

"No, we're almost there." Deuc answered.

"Exactly and so are they!"

"No more Jumps!"

"Deuc?"

The *Arion* burst clear and sparkled ebony splashed the windscreen. Deuc's forearms collided into Aedan's as the joysticks slipped from her fingers. A crack sounded in Aedan's ears and sent sparks across her eyes. Heavy lids closed as an arm curled under her neck. Like lifting water soaked clothing, her eyelids finally peeled back and focused. Ruby lights streaked through the blackness and ignited silver cyan fishes.

"Sorry Aedan, I had to." Deuc's words drifted through a quagmire of ringing bells.

Aedan's tongue thick and reluctant, "Whose firing?"

"Osirians?"

Deuc helped Aedan to sit up. The *Arion* drifted calmly out of range. Etarian fighters destroyed with every plasma round. Osirians? "Who? Calder?"

Deuc chuckled, faint and short lived, "He wishes."

Hunter's shoulder collided with the hallway.

"Hunter, Hunter is it over?" Mikro's voice sliced through Aedan's ears.

"I wasn't sick not once!" Zoe added.

Etarian fighters poured out of the Sandes. Definitely more than thirteen, maybe fifty ships, chased down by plasma and laser rounds. Aedan watched the deathly splendor with fuzzy thoughts. She clasped the arm rest, her boots rose to the ceiling as the *Arion* lost gravity. Deuc wedged himself between the seats, his chest and arms cradled Aedan. She squeezed her eyes closed and inhaled. Citrus and cinnamon, blood and steel. Aedan withdrew, Deuc's lips moved but the words sounded unfamiliar. She shook her head. What did Kegan have to do with this?

Her back lowered to the grate as rusted and puckered boots dragged underneath. A trickle of crimson flooded her right eye. Deuc's teeth nipped his thumb.

"Kegan, now would be the time to use Kegan."

"Huh?"

"My ship, my rules. Kegan." Deuc's voice cracked.

Light spilled through the *Arion*'s cargo hold, as scrapes and cheers burned Aedan's ears. Ice solidified in her stomach. One boot slid back, knee's bent, she clutched the pilot's chair, "What have you done?"

Deuc's fingers vice like on her upper arm, "What I had to."

CHAPTER 29

Aedan's leaden legs moved forward, her ears filled with heated threats and raised voices. She squinted through the champagne pink tears to Hunter and Deuc with their fists at each other's shirts, nose to nose. Deuc's voice softened, "Trust me Hunter. *Mao Adelfos*. Own it!"

Hunter fell back, his rainbow irises targeted Aedan, "If you're wrong?"

"Take it out on my hide." Deuc answered.

Her boots tracked forward to greet a gun ship of passengers. It had to be a gun ship, Aedan could hear the retorts of exploding plasma cannons above, muffled by the sound of applause from tiers of men and woman.

A man swathed head to toe in black, strolled forward, arms behind his back, mop of thick black curls splashed with flecks of red and silver demanded Aedan's attention.

"Who are you?" She said, only the sound of Deuc's boots softened her tone.

Aedan's eyes flew wide, a young woman, stood behind the man's right shoulder, a ring of burnt gold hemmed her face, woven back to reveal a riot of freckles over her sharp features. Clad in black, strapped, holstered and buckled from chin to wrist and waist to ankle.

"Relax Aedan, trust me." Deuc warned.

Her heart thundered into the back of her throat, another man, flamboyant green eyes, and wavy walnut hair stood at the man's left shoulder. Similar black strapping covered his right shoulder. Aedan knew him! Memories of her boot into his perfectly square jaw outside Gurt's circled in Aedan's mind. Rebels!

Deuc's blood removed the last hint of concussion from her mind, just in time for icy disgust to slide right in.

"Kyran Zernito, this is Aedan Cassio – "

Aedan gasped. A vision of data devices flicking into empty Buzz jars brought her back to reality.

"You mean Kegan Capare?" The older man spoke. His bottom lip moved softly over his teeth as he talked, and Aedan's insides turned to nest of asps. Applause and fever spread around the tiers.

"And Hunter Dios," Another round of applause burst the air.

Zern, Rebel Leader, Harbinger of Doom, breeder of corruption, destroyer of peace treaties, moved forward and clasped Deuc on the shoulder, palm to palm, chest to chest. Bile rose at the back of Aedan's throat. The female's eyes sizzled as Hunter stood beside their traitor.

"Welcome back to the fold." The green eyed warrior stepped forward and repeated the gesture.

"Hold your praise Gato." Deuc whispered before his voice became loud, "Be warned, I have named Hunter Dios, *Mao Adelfos*,"

A collective murmur spread through the crowd, heads turned to whisper to one another. Gato, the green eyed warrior spat at the ground. Aedan squinted at the emerald and red that spewed forth from his irises. Like a hive of bees coming to after a smoke haze, a cheer erupted amongst the onlookers. Deuc's palms raised.

"Be warned," Deuc paused, his dark brown eyes, targeted Aedan, "I have named Aedan Cassio – *asteri-Kardia Mar*."

The crowd erupted. The auburn female's brown eyes narrowed. Was she older than Aedan or younger? Zern's lips pursed, his sun-wrinkled eyes spun with black and white, orange and pink. What did it matter? He betrayed you! He betrayed Hunter and he betrayed those girls.

"The twins?"

"Inside and the Chief Director's daughter."

"First Calder, then Varmil, you bring me a treasure trove Deuc."

Something small and crystalline snapped within Aedan her hands filled with cool silver that suddenly splashed with metallic heat. A solemn weight solidified in her heart and it had nothing to do with the boot in the square of her back, or the floor against her cheek.

Deuc stumbled backwards into Hunter's arms, his palms outstretched, salty crimson spilled onto the deck.

"She's fast." The woman's throaty chuckle filled Aedan's ears.

Aedan closed her eyes, the moisture tore down her cheeks and worse, Aedan's bottom lip quivered.

"*Kardia Mar* indeed Deuc." Zern sneered.

"Don't hurt her," Deuc's last words barely audible over the uproar in the stands.

All Aedan's energy expelled from her lungs, the scream pulled down the final curtains of total darkness.

Hunter paced in what Deuc called the war room, an oak desk, elegantly engraved dominated the center of the room, an assortment of recycle pilots chairs, kitchen stands and bar stools surrounded the primary feature. At one end, an immense chain wire wall, similar to that of Deuc's Asarian hideout, sat silent. Hunter's heels squeaked across the speckled polycarbonate floor. After Aedan had collapsed and only after Deuc had reassured Hunter sufficiently of hers, Nataly's and the twins' safety had Hunter agreed to meet with Zern. Deuc had promised upon his punishment of death that neither girl would be harmed in any way. A vision of flaming red hair, and generous freckles suddenly disturbed his thoughts. Whoever she was, she'd survived. Hunter had spied women in the balconies too, unchained and jubilant at their victory. *Mao Adelfos*. Deuc could have mentioned it earlier, could have shared his end game strategy. Then why did Hunter feel as if he'd leapt from the bear pit to the snakes' nest. What more, other than the jump codes, would Zern want from him? He turned his palms over before his eyes, the skin still bonded. He inhaled and pushed outwards. Nothing changed. How long had he been holding onto this? Hunter exhaled and closed his eyes. As if severing elastic bands, the shield vanished.

The door creaked and Zern entered followed by Deuc. The bronzed soldier albeit repaired from the slashes at his flanks from Aedan.

"Let's talk small." Zern gestured to an empty chair. The dual plasma cannon retort snagged the Rebel Leader's attention. "Not giving up yet."

Hunter's back rested uncomfortably against the plush support, the Ida-en-Kai pressed into his hip. Why hadn't they disarmed him? The velvet caressed his skin, adrenaline leaked into his system.

"The Etarians will make a proclamation of war now," Hunter said. How's that for small talk!

"Yes. Although, we were heading on this trajectory for a long time, you and Deuc just brought it about earlier than expected."

Hunter smiled, at the absence of the shield, a reckless fever spread through his veins, "Premature proclamation?"

Deuc sniggered.

Zern's face remained unmoved.

Excited delirium snaked through Hunter's body, and he ran his fingers over the glossed surface of the oak as tastes, sounds, scents all returned in volume.

"While *Mao Adelfos* offers you Deuc's protection and hence by extension mine and every other Rebel, you're not immune to all threats. You are indebted to me."

"I can't pay you five trillion if that's what you're asking." Hunter twisted a thread between his finger and thumb.

"I never paid your bounty, or more appropriately a ransom."

Hunter focused. The Etarians could pay Zern a ransom to hand Hunter and the girls back? Chief Director Hogan would certainly pay a ransom for Nataly. Something about Zern's callused palms, the etched lines around his eyes, told him, like

Deuc, this man would never accept Etarian Ketos.

"What then?"

Zern turned to the monitors that sprung to life behind him. A pretty little blonde synth reported the night's exploits. Rolling script conversed along the bottom of the screen.

"With confirmation from Deputy Chief Director Braccass, the Etarian Expedition ship known as the Minos has been shot down tonight whilst attempting to cross the Sandes Belt. All occupants, including Chief Director Hogan's daughter, two juveniles and the fugitive Hunter Dios are confirmed expired. The mercenary Kegan Capare has also been pronounced expired.

Reports are sketchy from the front line of defense, which Oddworlders have attempted to cross the Sandes. Etarian forces have engaged with unconfirmed casualties on both sides,"

"Deputy Chief," Deuc mumbled.

"They don't want news of you reaching safely into Osirian hands to filter through to the populace. Imagine the panic, the failure. Take note, they failed to mention Deuc at all."

"He's not that noteworthy," Hunter sneered.

"*Mao Adelfos. Kardia Mar?* You chose well." He rubbed a thick finger across his wide jaw.

"I did." Deuc said.

"I see there's still enough of his essence floating through your system." Zern said.

Silence drifted out of reach for Hunter, the reckless delirium had hold of his tongue and refused to let go, "Essence," Hunter twisted his mouth like he'd tasted lemon, "Is that what you call it?"

"Enough!" The crack popped in Hunter's ears and he focused on Zern's knuckled hand, palm down on the table.

Over his shoulder, Deuc's eyebrows knitted, his jaw jutted forward slightly. The hairs on Hunter's arm stood to attention. Deuc's head flicked from side to side in minuscule increments.

"While you enjoy these last humorous moments remember I hold all your cards."

"And I'm holding some of yours."

Zern nodded, "The jump codes you promised to Deuc. I will take delivery of those as intended."

"And then?"

"Your DNA of course."

"No deal."

"You haven't heard my terms."

"No deal."

"Your current elated state is a side effect of being exposed to the essence at the core of Deuc's abilities. But it's temporary."

Deuc's brows knitted again, his eyes studying Hunter's frame. "Deuc tells me he's already explained some of the Etarian's DNA trials to you?"

"The Etarian Human Osirian Hybrids."

"Yes." Zern leaned back into his chair and retrieved a vapor stick. He chewed the plastic pipe for a moment, "The Etarians might have portrayed their failures as genetic engineering, but I look at their DNA trials as successes. The Etarians created multiple new species, in some cases whole new classes of living things."

"Lestas for example."

Zern nodded, "Problem was,"

"The Etarians were no longer the dominate species."

"Exactly, they decided to eradicate those that didn't align with Grand Etarian Plan. But what did Deuc tell you of the Osirian blood lines?"

"Those hybrids that escaped made it to Osiria, the others were decimated."

"Correct to a point. You know the Osirians were a race all on their own, but he failed to explain to you the most important fact of the Buried Histories." Zern leaned back in his chair, "Tell me what you wondered about the origin of Deuc's abilities or that of Capare or Cassio or whatever she wants to call herself."

Deuc's shoulders tensed briefly.

Hunter racked his brain for the information, "Trial of other Hybrids, other splices assisted by the jump gateways."

"Correct again, mixed with the HEO hybrids. Superior intelligence, strength, speed, increased fertility, yet highly volatile and therefore extinguished."

Hunter ran his thumb nail against the edge of the desk, all very interesting but what did it have to do with his Human DNA.

Zern sighed, "The Etarians muted the Osirian splice, choosing the Human Etarian hybrid as more successful. Eventually, the bunch of Osirian freaks grew in such numbers, that we could no longer be ignored, or enslaved while our worlds were reaped for the Etarian benefit. The first conflicts began. And then..."

Hunter exhaled slowly, the pieces fell into place, "They lost."

Zern's eyes were ablaze with the dim lights of the room, the plasma guns long fallen silent. "Yes! The Etarian's lost and it cost them dearly, and hence we have the first of many false peace treaties. But despite the Etarian's attempts to eradicate their biggest threat, they never realized what success they buried in the DNA. Thanks to the Human DNA addition, those HEO hybrids that made it to the Osirian system had the ability to cross-breed. Not all mind you, as some species had been genetically engineered for infertility." Zern raised his arms upwards as his voice took on a feverous tone, "The wonder of nature and evolution created the strongest and most desirable qualities to be passed on, live off-spring flourished with no Etarian DNA. And more importantly in some individuals, the genes of the Osirian DNA were passed on more often than the others." Zern slid his palms down on the table top and leaned in to Hunter, his words soft, "Individuals emerged with increased abilities, and almost no Etarian DNA. Pillars"

Hunter rested his forearms on the desk. The whole nature of the conversation intrigued him, he'd snagged on this thought with Aedan earlier. If Aedan had been tested, would they have destroyed her or weaponized her abilities? Did Etarians know what their meddling had led to? The Etarians struggled with fertility, struggled to pass on their own genes to the next generation without outside involvement. It made sense that through the generations, the Etarian DNA would be silenced, "Pillars?"

Zern continued, "Pillars indicate the largest percentage of Osirian DNA, they are the foundations of the Osirian species. It enhances the natural abilities of the miscellaneous DNA, hence the extra survival talents." Zern cracked another tube of vapor and inserted it into the inhaler, a waft of tobacco singed the air.

"You mean to build on that Pillar DNA don't you, create more super beings with advanced abilities." Hairs stood to attention on Hunter's neck.

"When you say it like that it sounds ominous," Zern's' chair wheels squeaked on the floor, "I have no intentions of destroying anyone to do it, quite the opposite. And I have ethics."

Hunter snorted, "What you mean is, you don't have the tech."

"Not yet. But take my word on this Dios, Pillars offer the possibility to restore the Osirian Race. If under the grace of Ea, or Erebus whichever you follow, that somewhere, somehow, these evolved species had successful offspring, who am I to stand in the way of evolution? The Osirians existed in their own right before extermination, medical sterilization or other means. The Etarian's stole their legacy. I intend to rectify that."

"And destroy Etarians in the process?"

"There are always casualties. Think of it this way, I'm offering your friends sanctuary, freedom. All I ask is a sample of your DNA."

A yawn cracked Hunter's jaw, his eyes suddenly heavy, "And the Jump Codes"

"They're out there now, advancing their own race while

we starve. I want to stop them eradicating any other species. Deuc has explained to you his role, he collects things. Etarian things for Osiria. These items, substances, people are not to be used as weapons, I'm happy to hold onto them to secure our future. Jump codes further that mission."

Was it possible, Zern was holding him as ransom to the Etarians, "What of the girls, will you expect a sample of their DNA?"

"With yours I don't have to. Etarians used Human DNA for fertility and variety," Zern spread his arms wide, "I have all the variety I need."

Hunter considered his options. Zern didn't have the technology, Ea-only-knew how close he was to it? He could be millennia away. A sample of his blood was all it took for his and the girls' freedom.

"My freedom?"

The Rebel leader shook his head, "*Mao Adelfos* bought you freedom. Same as *Kardia Mar* bought Cassio's freedom. I'm talking about the girls. Three girls, three vials."

Over Zern's shoulder, the bronzed warrior suddenly studied his finger nails.

"What will you do with it, since you don't have the tech?"

Zern leaned in again, his fingers clasped together, his thumb gently rubbed knuckles, "Inoculations my boy! Humans have an impressive immune system, I'll have my scientists start immediately on curing the Myrmidon ailment Fletch. Then I'll store it. I won't lie to you Hunter, knowing I took you from the Etarians is pleasure enough while I wait."

Metallic DNA strands spiraled with political undercurrents and Hunter wondered how long it took Deuc to agree to his bargain. Something about Deuc's flared nostrils drove Hunter forward.

"Wait for what?"

"You can trust that your DNA will be used as directed until the moment of your death."

That sounded even more ominous. What if Zern and his

scientists finally worked it out, would he terminate Hunter to use his DNA. "Or renegotiation of this agreement?"

"Yes, whichever comes first."

Hunter sighed. Mikro. Zoe. "What of the twins?"

"They will be safe. I give you my oath."

"And Nataly?"

"She is old enough to make her own choice."

Hunter regarded his new Osirian Brother, what bargain had he made with Zern, how much had this cost him? He thought of Nataly and the twins, could he let Zern hold them against him. He needed sanctuary from the Etarians and Aedan had destroyed his DNA storage. Safety with the Rebels sounded like a reasonable countermeasure, for now.

The veil of darkness receded as cold steel floors bleached into Aedan's skin. The room supported a double bunk that she couldn't lay on. A bulkhead desk, with stool, that she could not sit on. Everything smelt like treacherous tangy cinnamon. The scent of Deuc's betrayal coated the walls, her clothing, her hair. A digi-frame rested on a ledge. The red headed girl stood on one side of Deuc, the dyed blue Rebel now looking directly at the lenses, Gato's green eyes glared through the pixels. Aedan's shoulder recoiled, the resulting smash immensely satisfying.

Aedan's hands caught her face. Fuck. She'd walked herself and the others into a Rebel trap. They would be destroyed. Aedan was already destroyed. Damn Deuc in the light of Ea, to the pits of Erebus! He handed over Calder and Varmil. He'd handed over the twins. His deceit had begun the moment she'd met him. Visions of Deuc's torn flesh by her own hand, flashed into her mind and the tears started again. She'd slashed and hacked at his flesh. Worse, Deuc hadn't called for his shield. A strangled sound burst from her throat. He knew it was coming, and even worse, he'd asked that she not be harmed. Aedan rested her chin on her forearm, drops splashed onto her clothes.

Aedan had to move. As she rose from the floor, Aedan surveyed her quarters. Everything that wasn't nailed down was useless. The red head had bolted the door; her knife somewhere on the other side. Aedan faced the wash basin, the mirror chipped and scratched. Who gave a fuck what Kardia, fucking whatever! Aedan ground her teeth. Pits of ebony reflected back at her. Seething lava erupted between her ribs and the image convulsed. As if invisible strings tugged from her abdomen, her energy shuddered, the flame snuffed. Aedan watched a duplicate of Deuc disappear as bronze faded to pearl. Aedan's limbs numbed, the moisture evaporated from her throat.

Aedan focused on the dark strands. She closed her eyes to focus, disappointed when they remained chopped and black, not blonde. If she could mimic Hunter, she might be able to walk out alive. Visions of a blood splattered cell, Calder's fists, and her braid wrapped around Varmil's wrist revolved in her mind. The silver surface hummed and quivered with the gun ship's last retorts, the image of the stocky dark-haired Etarian stared back at Aedan. Aedan's forehead ached with the memory of the head butt she delivered, her tongue coated with the ghost of salted metal. She could duplicate the Etarian with relative ease. It must be in the blood.

"Kegan? I mean Aedan," A whisper slid under the doorsill.

"I'm here." Aedan squeaked as the façade fled. She drew deep in through her nose, her toes stretched in disintegrated boots.

"Are you hungry? I brought fruit." A hatch no thicker than the width of Aedan's arm opened, silver curls and green eyes peaked through.

Aedan squatted at the hatch, "Sure."

"Hey, why the tears? Deuc Alion is still alive."

A steel plate of apple slices landed in Aedan's hands.

Something about the boy's curls made Aedan pause. "I know you, what's your name?"

"Phoenix," He answered "Cheer up, you made it out of there. I made it out of there."

Aedan hummed a non-committal response. Gurt's Green Acres. "And you still ended up here."

Rustles and shuffles whispered under the sill. The hatch clanged open again, "Things aren't so bad."

Aedan didn't think they would be for an adolescent boy. Deuc's homicidal tendencies had obviously flourished. What would happen to the twins now? What about Nataly? A victim of Chigslin Skeeter, now surrounded by Oddworlder savages?

"When are you going to take them to the grey skirts?"

The apple slice snapped between Aedan's front teeth.

CHAPTER 30

Aedan followed the youth, as he weaved through half completed hallways. The gun ship had four levels of occupation, and after the current victory, all but a skeleton crew had retired to the Mess for celebrations. Aedan found the Etarian princess furtively pacing across carpeted floors. Nataly had already worked her magic on the twins who complied to temporarily leave Hunter. He'd thrown his lot in with Zern. He could hate Aedan later, right now she hated him.

Zoe and Mikro chatted happily to Phoenix, eager to meet new faces, whether Oddworlder or otherwise.

"I can take you back the way we came, but I cannot leave the residential block. You will find your way unobstructed to the cargo hold."

"Cargo hold? I need to find the dock?"

"Not if you're taking the *Arion*?"

Aedan snorted, steal Deuc's black beauty? What had he called it, profit, "Of course."

Outside the residential barrier, sounds of drunken revelry trickled down to Aedan as she paused, "Thank you again Phoenix."

"If you see Penefopine tell her..." He caught his bottom lip between thumb and forefinger, "Tell her Maethan say's hello and I'm glad she's safe."

Aedan nodded.

"Or make something up that sounds way better."

"I will," Zoe answered and threw her tiny arms around the boy's neck. Mikro mimicked her big sister's gesture.

"Down the stairwell and take the right corridor, it will get you to the junction. Go down again."

The dim lights infected his blonde curls and transformed them into golden rosettes. She wanted to say something, instead Aedan's fingers found his hand and squeezed.

Open panels contradicted the carpet and picture frames. Shadows stained the walls where strange shaped side tables might have rested for years. On the right, hatch doors had been spaced at regular intervals. They dashed passed one half ajar, and Aedan's toe collected her heel. The same disturbing carpet graced the interior, on the far side of the room, a window propped up by an imitation balcony. An arc of the Sandes Belt revolved into view, a necklace on the diamond studded ebony of space. Where had Zern found this ship?

"It's an old cruiser," Nataly answered, "Marvelous, it would almost be an antique by now."

The Etarian continued, "They were used to cruise the Opal Routes."

Aedan couldn't be bothered to work out where Zern had found a ship like this.

"Themis Luxury Liners, I'd guess judging by the size. Classics." Nataly added.

Luxury Liners? Aedan had shared with Deuc the notion of Etarian holidays and his warrior brain had fizzled and popped. Yet the Flagship of the Rebellion was a retired cruise liner? It didn't matter. All that mattered to Aedan lay hidden in the folds of the Sandes.

Deuc's hands pressed to the small of his back as Hunter's fingers combed through blonde strands. Three vials. Three girls. Surely Hunter would see the risks outweighed the benefits. Deuc's forearm pressed inwards. Muscles strengthened, skin healed and invisible silken threads tightened.

"So if I agree what happens to me?"

Zern smiled, and Deuc internalized his relief, "The Etarians have already pronounced you expired, you are a hero in the eyes of Osirian's. Why not capitalize on your success. Enlist in my -"

"*Mao Adelfos* circumnavigates your requirements, Zern." Deuc added.

The Rebel Leader chewed his tongue, "The Administration has crumbled, my Rebels have seized power in all the major ports. I have resources, ships, weapons, Ketos. Stay close to Deuc. Stay close to me. Follow orders and stay out of trouble. I will provide you with food, shelter, equipment and offer you opportunity to strike fire into the heart of every Etarian you meet in order to avenge your sister's and your mother's death."

Hunter's jaw tensed. A shimmer began and ended at Hunter's hair line. Perhaps the Human elements of Hunter reacted differently to Deuc's blood. Only time would tell.

"I offer you a place in history at the dawn of a new Epoch, the halls will be filled with the accolades of those mortal men who, in the face of savage oppression and against the mightiest of adversaries, became heroes."

"Think you over did it a bit with heroes and accolades but my mother was a nice touch."

Deuc held his breath. Zern had extended considerable leeway already. *Mao Adelfos. Asteri Kardia Mar.* Deuc would pay for that later. Every minute Hunter drew out this negotiation, delayed his explanation to Aedan. Silver satin constricted.

"Where will the girls go? How will they get there?"

A rap at the door broke the negotiations.

"Enter."

Deuc sighed. Egil dipped her carrot topped braid into the room. More fucking delays, he thought.

"Yes?" Zern barked.

She didn't answer and Deuc's lips kicked up at the corners. The Eagle, activated the monitors, and cycled through to the cargo bay. The *Arion*'s rear ramp door lowered, which allowed both twins, led by the hand of Nataly to enter. Aedan buzzed and fussed around the wheels. Each ratchet she released tugged on the invisible satin wound around Deuc's ribs.

Zern stood and peered into the monitors, throwing Deuc a side long glare. Deuc tested his shield.

The Rebel leader spun on his heels and addressed Hunter, "I

don't doubt that you're friend Aedan is saving me a trip."

Egil's brown eyes targeted Deuc. He owed her an explanation too.

Damn Aedan! Every inch of trust he gained, she sliced through with irrational instinct and fear. Diving head first into a swarm of ty-ty wasps, a society built on corruption, complex nuances, and a Leader consumed by prophecy, all balanced on a knife point. He'd pay for this dearly. "Let her go." Deuc answered. The silken threads evaporated.

"Sort it out, Egil" The Rebel Leader ordered.

The Eagle nodded to Zern and left the trio to decide Hunter's fate.

"Smart move, Dios" Deuc answered as the Human's hand reached for Zern's.

When Zern had finally left, Hunter landed in his chair and tugged the Ide-an-Kai loose. Hunter rotated the weapon in his palm.

"I understand your hatred. But they will be safe where Aedan is taking them. You heard it yourself, Zern would have had a shuttle take them anyway. And you're alive."

"Don't worry, I trust her. But you? You fucking lied." Hunter flicked his wrist, edges skimmed over edges, "You made an oath."

"I made an oath to get the girls off Haigon. I never made an oath on what happens afterwards."

The singular steel spun into three, "Slippery, just like him. The whole time, Zern was looking for angles and you're just the same. You put it all at risk. For him, for the Rebel cause?"

"For the Osirian cause!" Deuc snapped.

Hunter twisted his wrist again, the trio of blades reduced to one, "I hope she understands."

Deuc's knees buckled slightly, "And what about you?"

"I take it *Mao Adelfos* is irreversible?"

"Only by death."

The Human's eyebrows raised, a bitter smirk split his cheeks. "That bet we made is off, for one." He tucked the Rebel weapon into his belt. "Secondly, no more lies, tricks, half-truths, omission or denials."

Deuc's shoulders relaxed. "Fine. But I want your word on -"Deuc folded his pointed finger back into his fist, "Now you've met Zern, you've seen for yourself his value of commodities is based on their advancement or furthering *his* Osirian cause." He raised a hand to forestall the Human's argument, "And I am guilty of the same, but you touched on it with…"

"Aedan."

"Yes. If the Etarians had known, they wouldn't have let her live. Zern wouldn't have let her go just now."

"I agree. He can't know."

"He can't know about her deception detection or her ability to read their emotions, or my fingerprint, nothing!"

"On my oath and my life."

"And my blood. He thinks he knows everything but he doesn't. Not one word of my hibernation or otherwise should reach him."

"Deal."

Deuc sighed. He'd bent so many regulations and broken enough tenets already, "Good. Now test it."

"Huh?"

"The shield."

Hunter complied, skin cells closing ranks, "Not so temporary."

"I'm guessing, but I'd say, it's the human adaptability potential in your genes. Perhaps, like a disease."

Hunter rolled his eyes, his jaw dropped for a sly comment, but Deuc clasped a hand on Hunter's shoulder. "As *Mao Adelfos*, I can ask all and anything from you and you from me. What is yours is mine to protect and what is mine, is yours to defend. I will never ask more than you can give. And I will never ask you to give me what is yours."

Hunter nodded.

"In all under the Light of Ea and in the Shadow of Erebus, until the Dawn of Chaos I give you my oath, my life, *Mao Adel-*

fos."

Hunter repeated the words. Palm to palm and chest to chest Deuc embraced his brother.

"Now that's over you can let go Hunter."

Hunter threw a fist into Deuc's shoulder.

"Who's the redhead?" Hunter asked, readjusting his Ide-an-Kai for a second time, "And why does she look like she wants to eat me?"

"I think she's mad you stood her up, and trust me you're not her flavor."

Two days into her search for Leta and it took Aedan by surprise, when the *Arion*'s communication cables chirped with greetings from the hidden planet. She'd passed the haven, hours before and with bated breath she entered the coordinates into the ship's computer. When the *Arion* finally touched down, the Sisters had been reluctant to approach.

Aedan's legs leaden to the hip, ran into the arms of Sister Yulna. Zoe and Mikro sparkled as perfect gemstones in the crowd, their words tumbled over each other, interested to find Penefopine and convey the newly edited message to whoever she was.

Aedan walked through the stone arches that marked the inner sanctum.

"How did you know it was me?" Aedan asked.

Sister Yulna smiled warmly, "Leta is far reaching, we have allies across the Dual systems."

"Plus we watched all the newscasts!" Sister Marg added.

Aedan recalled the Sisters hastily rescue of the children from Gurt's. Stunned Aedan could only nod. She walked ahead, the Sisters didn't move.

"We'll send food to your old room."

"I want to be away," Aedan whispered, her words trapped in her throat.

Aedan turned on her heel, the view changed, liquid welled in her lids. She tore fingers through her hair as she made it to an isolated unit on the outskirts of the settlement. She peeled off miasma rotted boots and sunk onto the bunk. The *Arion* would stay secured in one of the many hangers. But Aedan's spine suddenly felt like jelly.

For the first week Aedan complied with her self-imposed isolation. She ate sparingly from the offerings the Sisters brought. Aedan had brought three extra mouths and no extra Ketos. The only visitors she allowed to bother her, Sister Yulna, Sister Marg, the twins and every other day, Nataly.

In the second week, Aedan paced around the lush and murky grounds, the minty humid atmosphere crawled under Aedan's skin and soaked her clothes. She'd braved the control center and watched the vacant radar swish and swirl. Etarians and Osirians departed, leaving the Sandes Belt scarred but Leta safely untouched. Each day Aedan replayed thickly veiled conversations and heavy lidded gazes. At night, her sleep alternated between mourning citrus cinnamon and hands that sought burnt copper, to sweat drenched night terrors.

On the twenty-first day of Aedan's return, another ship landed. Sleek and black with silver tipped wings, it pirouetted to the surface. Aedan watched the Sisters greet the muscular pilot with regular familiarity. Sister Yulna tugged a flamboyant flame colored braid.

Aedan ended her last lap of the tree line and waited until the trio were out of sight before she headed to her room. She rested her back against the timber and exhaled. A three toned knock brought Aedan's eyes open. Nataly snuck inside, ballet flats scurried to the bed, her grey skirt tucked under her knees.

"Did you see her?"

The timber trembled against Aedan's spine, and Nataly gulped. The redheaded Rebel stood at the threshold, fantastic boots silently tapped on the stones. A corset covered her ribs, strapping over both shoulders and slacks that curved and flowed over her hips like water over ice. She carried a box in one arm and tossed it onto the single bunk. Nataly scooted to the far end of the bed. Sister Yulna tugged on the door and hid guilty greys as she left the three women alone.

"That's my singlet." The Rebel said, her fingers tugged at the black hemline. Aedan's cheeks infused with heat, nostrils flared, chin upright.

The warrior's brown eyes sparkled with pink and orange as she unclicked the buckles and straps at her shoulders. She hung the synthetic armor in Aedan's opened cupboard. The material tucked and stretched, a silver feathered shape stamped onto the armor.

Aedan and Nataly gasped in unison as the warrior spun. Inky black feathers streamed down taunt mesh and sleeves that end at her elbows. Exquisite silver embellishments had been added, to exaggerate the wing tips, "You know who I am?"

"The Eagle," Aedan said.

"Yes, some call me that but my real name's Egil." She paused, her head tilted from one side to the next, "You stole my bounty. You stole my survivors and you stole my rewards."

Aedan shifted one ankle back, heel raised, a cloud of dust rose from the bare stone floor.

Amusement exploded across the Eagle's eyes, her freckles danced to the tune of her smile, "I'm not as fast as you." Her ginger crown tilted to the other side and brown eyes pierced Aedan's composure. She had to be older than Aedan but only just, "I've come with an offer."

Aedan clicked her tongue. Zern. "Whatever he has to offer, I refuse." Aedan spun and she stared at the lush green forest beyond her window.

"What says you?" Egil asked.

Aedan listened to a long slow exhale.

"I can't." Nataly's voice scratched her throat, "I can't face Hunter. I don't belong in your Worlds and I can't go back to mine."

Aedan swallowed the lump that thickened as she listened

to Nataly's sobs.

The Rebels' voice dropped an octave, "Why can't you face that Human?"

Nataly hiccupped, "Aedan if you...Ea-save-me, you have to tell him. He has to know." With that, the Etarian princess stole from the room, leaving Egil and Aedan alone.

The Eagle faced Aedan, "Tell me. If it affects this planet, the Osirians or the Rebellion, I must know." The tones of the Osirian brokered no argument and Aedan took pause to register the priorities of this fiery woman.

"She signed the test results on Hunter's sister Juliette, effectively sending her to execution. That's why her father and Captain Varmil believed her when Nataly told them Hunter had found out and sought retribution. She was allowed to stay close to the girls, get them out if you or Hunter ever came back for her."

"Did she tell you why I found her?" Egil fussed and tugged at her wrist bracers.

Aedan nodded, "After telling Hunter only half truths about his sister, Nataly had wandered the streets confused. She hadn't heard Skeeter following her."

"Yes."

Silenced lingered like any unwanted guest, Egil broke the tension first, "That Kronos guard is chewing everyone's ear off asking where you are, it's exhausting."

Aedan watched the movements of Egil's preening, Aedan's mind on fast forward. "Who are you?"

The redhead sat down on the bed, one leg under the other, her elbow on her knee. Despite the girl's muscular frame, she barely ruffled the bed clothes.

"I think a better question is, what am I?"

"Yes."

"Not unlike yourself, Aedan. I'm Osirian and I'm a woman."

Aedan pulled out the tiny stool under the desk and sat, her hands clutched her knees.

"Have you come to drag me back to face Zern and some

corrupt Rebel punishment?"

"No. *Aster Kardia Mar* protects you from that."

Aedan's neck heated, "What does that mean anyway, his property?"

"No."

"Hunter Dios is *Mao Adelfos* and I know there was more than one of those. How many *Kardia*-whatever's does Deuc have? Are you one?"

"No. You seem offended. It is a great honor to be named *Kardia Mar*."

"Is it?"

Egil tilted her head from side to side again as she peered through Aedan, "He has named no other."

Aedan paced to the cupboard, "What does Zern want?"

"What he always wants, Osirian success, Etarian destruction, but Zern has not sent me. It is my offer to make."

Aedan's toe kicked her heel, "What?"

"Firstly, where in this fucked up galaxy did you think "the Eagle", or Zern for that matter could hide two Human girls? Leta had always been the destination for the twins, you just saved me the trip."

Aedan sat back on the edge of the bed, "I don't understand?"

"I gave Leta the *Arion*'s call-sign. Where was Zern born?"

Aedan's shoulders dipped, "I umm -Asar?"

"No."

"Tuwa?" Perhaps Zern hid an Etarian heritage?

Egil shook her head, "You suck at this game. No," She rested callused hands on her hips.

Aedan gasped at the silence of Egil's movements, "You're quiet."

"Oh, that," She rose from the bed and pirouetted, "Takes most a lot longer to figure out."

Aedan edged closer to the redheaded Rebel, and watched as boots spun, imitation leather crinkled, mesh twisted and nothing not even a whisper rose from the Eagle's movements.

"How do you do that?"

"How do you *wear* Kegan?"

Aedan's eyes narrowed, "I don't know."

"Concentrate, Aedan. Leta exists under duplicitous protections, total ignorance from the Etarians and consecrated loyalty from the Osirians. The babes from Gurt's? I was there, I dogged your footsteps all through the Rouge Alleys. The Rebel markers pinging at the scene had been set by Deuc, because he knew I'd be there. Zern is a necessity that enables my protection and assistance to Leta. I also deliver Zern's annual tribute."

Aedan had heard those words before, "Despicable, immoral corruption is a necessity."

"You can lecture me on corruption when your hands actually get dirty."

"What's that supposed to mean?" Aedan snapped and curled her fists.

Egil lowered her voice, her brown eyes challenged, "You know I was there on Hades, you really are quick. But what I mean is, you've skimmed the surface, picking bounties and paying debts. You talk of Osirian corruption, brutality and filth, but what have you done to *change* it?"

Aedan's mouth closed.

Egil continued, "Secondly what can you achieve from here?"

The inside of Aedan's cheek sizzled, her throat tight and sore. She'd turned her back on Osiria the moment Aedan had turned 17 and her feet left Leta. Sure she'd given tribute to the Sisters, helped them feed the needy. She'd caught their despicable criminals and sent them to Kronos. But had she ever really made an impact?

"Where was Zern born?"

Aedan closed her eyes against the inner turmoil, "Leta."

"Correct. His mother took refuge here, like so many do. When he grew too old for Sanctuary he made his own way in the Osirian worlds. He climbed upwards, not out. That's the deal, he pays tribute, he takes the youths. He provides for them, educates them, shelters them from the rampaging savagery that we both know exists."

"And takes his measure at the end."

"He gives them choices and options. It is a means to whatever end they want."

"And what do you want?"

Egil gestured to the box, "Open it." A pair of fabulously buckled boots lay buried beneath a layer of woven calico, a handle peaked from inside. Her knife. "Not unlike myself, you have moved past this place, Aedan. I want you to stop surviving and start fighting."

Aedan's fingers trembled.

"I want you to come with me to Asar, to the Northern Front."

"Why?"

"Deuc needs you."

Aedan pushed the box away as her chest compressed. "He has Hunter."

Egil crossed her legs and unfolded the knee high boots as Aedan's examined the creature. Direct, fierce and beautiful, Egil's brown irises swirled into a majestic tornado of snowy azure and peaches. Now that Aedan focused, she realized the peaches scent gently emanated from the Rebel girl. The browns cascaded into sheets of shadowed plum and orange, "That Dios can't fix this."

Aedan mused over her words. Images of Deuc's claret covered frame tore through Aedan's mind.

"I attacked him, how do I know the Rebels won't kill me on sight?"

"Trust me, they've had to cope with worse, and besides he is healed; more or less." Egil carefully placed the lid on the box. Was that pride Aedan heard in the Rebel's voice?

Aedan sat down on the edge of the bed, "What does *Laelaps* mean?"

"*Laelaps*? Um, strange question...."

"Even so, it's only fair."

Egil rested her dainty chin in cupped hands and peered down the straight edges of her narrow nose, "It's a character in a children's fable. The story is more about a sly Reynard with sharp teeth, and claws. He had an ear-splitting howl and was sent by Erebus to prey on the children. *Laelaps* is the mythical hound who was sent by Ea to catch him."

"And did he?"

Egil paused her narrative hand gestures, "She? Did *Laelaps* catch her prey? Well the enchanted *Laelaps* had been chosen because she caught everything she chased, but the Reynard had also been gifted with special abilities, that of never being caught. Eventually Chaos cast them into the heavens, and there they continue their eternal pursuit known as Canis Major and Canis Minor."

Aedan's mind recalled the sparkling baubles of Dos Caelumina, and the eventual fatal consumption of each other. She wondered about Faros and Charoen, who weathered the galaxy in isolation, no satellites to protect them, only each other. "Why does he need my help?"

Egil fumbled with her fingertips in her lap, "Zern protects Osirian interests, but we have to protect our own against Zern."

"You were just singing his praises!" Aedan's eyebrows climbed her forehead.

"I know." The Egil sighed, "He is punishing Deuc because of you."

The hairs on Aedan's skin all stood to attention and she exhaled slowly. Punishing Deuc for her or for Gurt? Because Aedan fled and kept the *Arion*? Or because of *Kardia Mar*? "I give up, what does *Asteri Kardia Mar* mean?"

"My Heart-Star, Star of my heart, center of my worlds; the gravitational point at which my existence becomes whole or something like that." Egil said.

Aedan's eyes squeezed tight, her throat thickened, Aedan's own words echoed in her mind. What would she give to let him live? When Aedan's eyes finally snapped opened, Egil had already risen and re-strapped her armor to her corset. The Rebel girl smiled when silver buckles ratcheted closed.

The End

EPILOGUE

Commander Braccass strummed his fingers on the ebony desk, a wall of Etarian uniforms surrounded his seated position. Some faces he'd grown to trust, others had failed to earn his disgust. Pale faced Huul stood at his right shoulder. From inside Notian's Keeps largest tower, Braccass watched the twilight shadow crawl across the Haigon surface, turning the sparkling white and gold spires and domes to murky slates and ruddy orange.

"I want every Jump gateway manned, every outpost on high alert." Damn fucking Hunter Dios had taken off with thousands of Jump Codes, worse he had the knowhow to change them, "You see anything but Etarian stock and you blast it to Erebus."

"Your instructions regarding Dios?" Captain Antiq squealed, his shrill voice at odds with his juiced up frame.

"Let them go, for now." He didn't have the resources or the support to go diving into Osiria right now. He had authorized the blockade and trade sanctions, he'd starve them out to buy some time. Reports trickled in from Osiria that the Rebels and the Administration had crippled each other from getting a strong hold in any city. Yet, the gun ship that had met the Third Brigade on the Sandes had been disturbingly organized. If only they could reach Varmil.

"Sir?"

"See how long he lasts with those savages." The question was how far did the Human trust the Oddworlders? Whilst in Etaria, Dios had been unsuccessful on all directives. Chief Director Hogan had voiced to Braccass, his suspicions on Hunter's so-called failures. After the Human's escape, all attempts by Hogan to let the secret die with Dios had also missed their mark. "Tell the blockade to remain at position three, outside the Sandes. If even one ship crosses that line..."

Doctor Polltz stepped forward, "The DNA storage is damaged beyond repair."

Braccass inhaled slowly, the destruction of the DNA storage was a minor hiccup as Braccass saw it. But the population had to be reassured. "Reanimate the others." Braccass stood from his chair, the plush leather back and seat rest still imprinted with his solid frame.

Lieutenant Huul stepped through the crowd of advisors and cleared his throat, "Enough." The pale man seized a white cloth, hemmed with shimmering cyan and draped it over Braccass' shoulders, "None of you will be responsible in delaying the Chief Director's coronation."

ABOUT THE AUTHOR

Louise Crouch loves all genres of fiction mixed with a healthy splash of romance. When she is not writing, Louise spends her time frustrating her wonderful husband and raising their two marvelous children.

"Under the Light" is her first foray into the genre of Space Opera, with book two of the Sandes Chronicles "In the Shadow" to be released soon. The final and third book, "Until the Dawn" will be released later next year. A prelude to the series, titled 'Across the Sandes' is available on Amazon. Find it here: https://www.amazon.com/dp/B07V4FZJPQ

If you wish to read more from the Osirian/Etarian Universe find a collection of short stories here: http://loucrouch.wordpress.com

If you would like to join the Sandes Chronicles Readers Facebook Group find it here:
https://www.facebook.com/groups/458495348233301

Louise has published three Western Historical Romance novels, her first "Even Spinsters Need Company" was released in 2016. The first book of the Belles and Boots collection, "Hammer & Lock; a Texas Romance" was released in 2017 while the sequel "Ruby's Texas Ranger" was published 2019.

Find them here: http://loucrouch.wordpress.com

If you want to follow Louise Crouch on Facebook find her here: http://www.facebook.com/LouiseCCrouch/

If you want to follow Louise Crouch on Twitter find her here: http://twitter.com/LouiseCCrouch

If you have enjoyed this book please leave a review at your

favorite retailer.

IN THE SHADOW

In the Shadow is the second book in the Sandes Chronicles and follows Aedan Cassio's journey from bounty hunter to Osirian Rebel.

Thanks to Aedan Cassio, Deuc Alion and Hunter Dios opening fire on the Etarian Militia, the Administration has fallen and Kyran Zernito the Rebel Leader is now presider over all Osiria. The Jump Codes are in his clutches; but Zern is obsessed with fulfilling a prophecy to find the one true Osiria in the hopes of uniting Osiria.

The Rebels are facing their own threats, political sabotage, a terrorist threat in the name of Venom and a rioting population thanks to the Etarian sanctions. Osiria once seethed with corruption, now the Oddworlder system is on the brink of imploding.

Aedan returns to Asar in the hopes of releasing Deuc from Zern's torturous punishment only to be drawn into the Osirian cause. What is Aedan willing to sacrifice to achieve safety for herself, Deuc and Osiria? Kegan Capare is declared dead. Aedan can't hide within his façade any more. Aedan must adapt if she's going to survive.

Deuc made the mistake of naming Aedan *Kardia-Mar*, heart-star, thinking it could somehow keep her safe. It only tightened the already taunt strings that held him to Zern. The power vacuum they created in the Rouge Alleys has attracted Venom, a malevolent organization driving the riots against Rebel's regaining control. Aedan brought Chaos with her, how could Deuc keep her safe?

Hunter Dios is finding his feet in the political undercurrents that undulate through the Osirian Rebels. But Zern is providing him safe harbor, shielding him from Etarians. Any moment the Rebel Leader could ransom him back to Etaria to lift the sanctions and save his people. Hunter better earn his place.

Egil Luan, the redhead Rebel Brawler, convinced Aedan to return to Asar. As Zern's military commander Egil she's already calculated the likelihood of Osirian success, but Egil has her own take on Zern's prophecy. She promised Deuc Alion she would protect his *Brother* and his *Kardia-Mar,* however she deems necessary, unless that is, they stand in her way.

Releasing 2020.

Follow Louise Crouch to find out more.

A SPECIAL THANKS

Well hello there!

If you have immersed yourself into the Osirian and Etarian Worlds with me and want more, then here is another special Thank You dedicated just to you!

The advice is always to write what you want you and readers will find you, so it's nice to finally meet you and I can't wait to continue this journey together!

There is always more to the Osirian and Etarian Worlds, the minor characters have stories of their own begging to be told. If you haven't checked out the Sandes Short Stories on my Wordpress then please do. There is a link to a free ebook if you haven't already found that and downloaded it and before the next release, I will publish another free ebook of short stories.

I hope you enjoyed reading as much as I enjoy writing about these Worlds, that hopefully show us good and evil are never as clearly defined as we would like them to be.

Take care,

Louise

www.ingramcontent.com/pod-product-compliance
Lightning Source LLC
Chambersburg PA
CBHW020243200626
46816CB00001BA/109